Twins in Contemporary Literature and Culture

Twins in Contemporary Literature and Culture

Look Twice

Juliana de Nooy
University of Queensland

palgrave
macmillan

First published 2005 by
PALGRAVE MACMILLAN
Houndmills, Basingstoke, Hampshire RG21 6XS and
175 Fifth Avenue, New York, N. Y. 10010
Companies and representatives throughout the world

PALGRAVE MACMILLAN is the global academic imprint of the Palgrave
Macmillan division of St. Martin's Press, LLC and of Palgrave Macmillan Ltd.
Macmillan® is a registered trademark in the United States, United Kingdom
and other countries. Palgrave is a registered trademark in the European
Union and other countries.

ISBN-13: 978–1–4039–4745–1 hardback
ISBN-10: 1–4039–4745–7   hardback

This book is printed on paper suitable for recycling and made from fully
managed and sustained forest sources.

A catalogue record for this book is available from the British Library.

Library of Congress Cataloging-in-Publication Data
De Nooy, Juliana.
  Twins in contemporary literature and culture : look twice / Juliana de Nooy.
    p. cm.
  Includes bibliographical references and index.
  ISBN 1–4039–4745–7
    1. Twins in literature. 2. Fiction–20th century–History and criticism.
3. Twins in motion pictures. I. Title.

PN56.5.T85D4 2005
809'.933552–dc22   2004066394

10   9   8   7   6   5   4   3   2   1
14   13   12   11   10   09   08   07   06   05

Printed and bound in Great Britain by
Antony Rowe Ltd, Chippenham and Eastbourne

On our own, you wouldn't look at us twice. But, put us together…

ANGELA CARTER, *Wise Children*

Contents

List of Illustrations

Acknowledgements

This project has spanned several institutional affiliations. It would never have reached completion without a research fellowship from the Centre for Critical and Cultural Studies at the University of Queensland (Australia), which offered not only time away from teaching, but a quality research environment. My special thanks to Graeme Turner, Andrea Mitchell and Mark McLelland.

At the time I joined the Contemporary Studies programme at the Ipswich campus of the University of Queensland, the project consisted of a collection of disparate research papers, and I particularly wish to thank Leigh Dale for the opportunity and encouragement to draw these lines of enquiry together into the present book.

The project started during a postdoctoral fellowship in the then Department of Romance Languages at the same university, and I am grateful to many colleagues there for feedback in seminars and on drafts, for research assistance, and for providing a stimulating intellectual environment: to Peter Cryle, who offered invaluable advice on drafts and on the orientation of the book, to Peter Cowley, Anne Freadman, Joe Hardwick, Diana Jones and James Wheatley; to Ross Chambers when he was Visiting Fellow; and above all to Bronwyn Statham for research assistance that culminated in the co-authorship of Chapters 3 and 4. Barbara Hanna, my research partner on another project, has most generously lent an intelligent ear and eye to this one.

The research for Chapters 3 and 4 was supported by an Australian Research Council Small Grant. Earlier versions of Chapters 3, 6, 2 and 4 were published in *Continuum: Journal of Media and Cultural Studies* 12 (3) 1998 (http://www.tandf.co.uk/journals); *Essays in French Literature* (38) 2001; *AUMLA* (97) 2002, and *Scope: An Online Journal of Film Studies* (November) 2004, and in each case reviewers made constructive suggestions that were implemented. My thanks to these journals for permission to reproduce material and to the editorial team at Palgrave and their readers for further useful advice.

The 1997 conferences of the Australian Society for French Studies and of the Australasian Universities Language and Literature Association provided a sounding board for the project in its early stages, and contributors to the Balzac-L discussion list offered thoughtful suggestions for the corpus.

Finally, I would like to thank the following for granting permission to reproduce film stills in this book: Universal Studios, Frank Henelotter, Umbrella Entertainment, Twentieth Century Fox Television, and Columbia Pictures Industries Inc.

And to Guy for listening and sharing in so many ways, and to Caroline and François for defying narrative patterns and providing a welcome distraction from the project, thank you.

Introduction

My children are twins, and acquaintances often imagine that this book was prompted by their arrival. Far from it: the book was conceived well before they were, and early versions of some chapters had already appeared as conference papers before my twins made an appearance with two banana-shaped patches on the pregnancy scan. Rather their arrival proves the dangers of becoming too absorbed in a research project: it really does colonise your life. As my colleague Peter Cowley exclaimed at the news: 'Just as well you weren't studying stories of abduction by aliens...'

In fact the seeds of the book were sown in the early 1980s, in work for an honours dissertation, when I struggled to find non-dialectical narratives about same-sex couples, that is, stories in which the pair was not largely defined by an opposition between characters. The search led me to Michel Tournier's novel *Gemini*, and to the suspicion that narrative punishment was meted out to characters that chose a partner too like themselves. Other projects – academic and personal – intervened, and it wasn't until the mid-1990s that I returned to a version of this question, with a rather different approach. Its pursuit evolved into what is now Chapter 2, on surviving sameness.

In the course of my hunt for stories of resemblance, I collected a corpus of contemporary tales of twins and doubles and was astounded by the vast number and variety of films, novels, newspaper articles and documentaries about twins, and by the fact that certain stories were being told over and over again. Why, I asked myself, are there such clusters of texts that tell of the stranglehold of brotherly love, of the evil twin who steals her sister's lover, of the homicidal mutant twin, of the reunion of twins separated at birth, of twins divided by warring nations, of confusion between lookalike twins? Why do these stories need to be retold now and how they are being transformed in the telling? What do our narrative uses of twins reveal about contemporary culture?

Twins in Contemporary Literature and Culture addresses these questions. Clearly, twins are being used to work through some important preoccupations, some quite specific to late twentieth-century culture. In particular, some of the most insistent retelling of twin tales today uses twins to explore questions of gender and sexuality. Other sets of stories relate to new ways of thinking about national and personal identity. I make no claim to exhausting the cultural uses made of twins (there is no limit to the ways in which twins can be harnessed by the imagination!), preferring to concentrate on some particularly revealing storytelling habits.

Chapter 1 outlines the scope of the study and offers a theoretical framework for studying both the diversity and repetition of twin tales. Rejecting the premise that there is a single, underlying meaning to the appearance of twins in our storytelling, it proposes an analysis in terms of particular conjunctions of gender and genre rather than treating twins as a unified thematic. Twins are used for different purposes in different narrative genres. While they are equally available to provide intrigue in horror, comedy, crime and romance, they tend not to fulfil the same function in each case. They do not provide a single key to contemporary culture but multiple entry points. The chapter also situates the book in relation to various existing studies of twins and doubles, challenging critical work that suggests that twentieth-century narratives represent the decline into triviality of a great Romantic theme. On the contrary, the examples studied throughout the book attest to innovation and vitality in the refashioning of twin tales for new audiences.

Chapters 2 to 7 each offer a reading of a particular concentration of twin tales, before analysing in detail a story that attempts to shift a repeated pattern. Chapter 2 ('Twins and the Couple') explores the difficulty of surviving sameness in twin narratives, for outside comic genres, stories of twins and doubles are short on survivors. This is not only the case in tales of deadly rivalry between good and evil twins, but also in stories of twins as soul-mates, partners in life, whose relationship of resemblance dooms them to sink into stagnation and perish. Tales of the death of soul-mate twins have been pervasive in Western imaginative discourses throughout the last century, crossing cultures and genres, and harking back to the myth of Narcissus and its use by Freud to describe a pathological state. Clearly they reflect a moral imperative regarding our choice of partners, yet there are good reasons for wanting to tell other, less lethal stories about couples defined by their resemblance. In a reading of three novels relating the life of male twins who form a couple – Patrick White's *The Solid Mandala* (1966), Michel Tournier's *Les Météores* (1975), and Bruce Chatwin's *On the Black Hill* (1982) – this chapter investigates the possibility of telling such stories differently. The twins in each case form a same-sex couple who must negotiate the pitfalls of narcissism. The unfolding of these narratives resonates with the development of contemporary discourses of gay identity, and points to a rethinking of what constitutes a viable relationship. If coupledom has traditionally been understood as a synthesis of differences into oneness, the novels allow us to glimpse its reconception as a relation in which sameness and difference are mutually entailing.

Chapter 3 ('Twins and Sexual Rivalry') turns to female twins, rare in literary history but abundant in twentieth-century popular film, especially in the 1940s and 1990s. The overwhelming majority of these films are thrillers involving deadly rivalry over a man between good and evil identical twin sisters. Moreover, these sisters are always split along the same predictable line – a version of the virgin/whore dichotomy. What is it about this story that it still needs to be told so frequently? How has it been reworked in the wake of the sexual revolution and feminism to appeal to a contemporary audience? And why might we want to tell sister stories differently? Here it is revealing to study a film that transposes gender in the tale of sexual rivalry. Like so many twin sister films, Tim Hunter's *Lies of the Twins* (1991) is a story about jealousy between twins over a love interest, but in this highly unusual case the virtuous fiancé and sex-driven homebreaker are twin brothers. Viewing *Lies of the Twins* as a role reversal exposes the cultural myths underlying female twin films and suggests strategies for rethinking the dichotomy that continues to pervade them. Twins may be commonly employed in film to incarnate the binary oppositions that dominate our thinking, but this chapter shows that they can also be used to question them.

If twin sister thrillers invariably work through fantasies of female sexuality, post-1980 horror films featuring male conjoined twins also impose a compulsory figure. Chapter 4 ('Twins and the "Crisis of Masculinity"') takes a close look at films by Cronenberg, Romero and Henenlotter together with a parody of the corpus in *The X-Files* to demonstrate the systematic representation of this twin relation as maternal. At a time of destabilisation of traditional masculine identities, conjoined twins in the horror genre provide an ideal opportunity to feminise the male body. Joined and disjoined, the brothers' bodies are displayed as umbilically linked, and monstrously so. One bond dating from the womb – twinship – is used to substitute for another – the mother-child dyad – in a surprisingly consistent way. This is but a recent pattern among twin films, and yet its strength is evident when we find the theme of maternity surfacing in conjoined twin films in genres other than horror. The Polish brothers' *Twin Falls Idaho* (1999, 'a different kind of love story') is a case in point: unable simply to ignore this convention, it is obliged continually to deflect it. The examples point to a highly specific cultural use of twins at the close of the twentieth century.

The focus on gender continues in Chapter 5 ('Twins and the "Gay Gene" Debate'), which examines two very different uses of twins to talk about sexual identity: twin studies research on homosexuality and queer comic fiction in the shape of Robert Rodi's *Drag Queen* (1995), a gay parody of long-lost twin tales. While the former uses twins to engage in the nature/nurture debate over homosexuality (revitalised by media interest in the 'gay gene' hypothesis), the latter rewrites the very terms of this debate. *Drag Queen* rehearses a timeworn tale – twins separated at birth are reunited – to unsettle the gay/straight, male/female binaries underpinning the twin studies. Gay lawyer Mitchell and flamboyant entertainer Kitten Caboodle may be identical twins, but are far from exactly alike. Their story illustrates the problems with categorising sexual orientation in an either/or fashion – *either* heterosexual *or* homosexual – as twin studies tend to do. And it questions the usefulness of understanding identity in terms of *either* a core of being *or* self-invention. As such the novel serves as a commentary not only on debates about heredity and environment, but on current tensions in ways of conceiving of identity.

The extensive use of twins to depict fissures in national, ethnic or cultural identity is the focus of Chapter 6 ('Twins and Nations'). The tradition goes back to ancient myths of the founding of cities and civilisations by rival twins such as Romulus and Remus, Jacob and Esau, and reflects the perennial conflicts dividing peoples. Unlike these legends of fraternal twins, twentieth-century narratives of such conflicts most commonly feature identical twins: the 'brotherhood of nations' is represented in terms of an underlying sameness beneath superficial cultural differences, whether in Cold War Europe or across the India/Pakistan border. The assumption of resemblance as the basis for harmonious relations between cultures is, however, problematic in a postcolonial world of hybrid identities and multi-ethnic nations. This can be seen in Marie-Thérèse Humbert's novel *A l'autre bout de moi* (1979), in which the twinship of Creole sisters reflects the cultural tensions dividing the island of Mauritius. Here conflicting discourses of subjectivity put the twins' resemblance in doubt, and in doing so allow a glimpse of a more sophisticated concept of cultural identity, based on shifting identifications rather than common traits. Surveying together the uses of twins to tell tales of nations shows shifting understandings of the origins of communal strife and the preconditions for peace.

Chapter 7 ('Twins as Doubtful Doubles') focuses on two instances in which twins and doubles are openly mocked as hackneyed narrative devices, and yet are simultaneously used to create a highly innovative novel in one case, screenplay in the other. When, in Nabokov's novel *Despair* (1965), Hermann Karlovitch meets his own spitting image, a perfect double he could kill in order to claim his own life insurance, the catch is that he alone can see the resemblance. A parody of literature of the double, the novel is widely regarded as a symptom of its decline. However Nabokov's joke can be seen to herald the emergence of a distinctly postmodern discourse of the double in which likeness is uncertain and subjective, a discourse evident in novels by Amis, Auster, Kristof and Monette, and in films by Fassbinder and Buñuel, with perhaps the most memorable incarnation of the unlikely lookalike being Danny de Vito and Arnold Schwarzenegger in Reitman's *Twins* (1988). *Despair* thus represents a moment of newness as much as a reckoning with the past. Spike Jonze's *Adaptation* (2002) is a twin film that sheds light on this process of repetition and renewal. Screenwriter Charlie Kaufman puts himself in the film together with a fictional identical twin brother, and plays ironically with the notions of triteness and novelty in self-referential commentary on cinematic ploys and clichés. If the twin plot is predictable, its grafting on to the film adaptation of a botanical study is not. The ironic quotation and recontextualisation of the twin motif exemplifies a postmodern approach to originality. The film thus explicitly engages with questions underlying the various narrative uses of twins explored in this book, asking what is entailed in retelling a familiar tale, and how it can be put to new purposes. It makes us wonder whether identical twins themselves, in their sameness-and-difference, might not serve as a contemporary metaphor for creativity.

The final section (Chapter 8 'Twins and Problems of Representation') brings the threads of discussion together. It starts by sketching parallels between some rather disparate twin tales by Angela Carter, Margaret

Laurence and Marilyn Bowering. Each uses twins to disturb the genealogical line and question notions of legitimacy. This pattern mirrors the
unruly history of twin tales, which takes multiple directions across a wide
variety of genres, and never more so than in the late twentieth century.
The clusters identified throughout the book do not indicate one persistent theme or a single overriding meaning for the profusion of twin tales
in contemporary culture. They do however point to a concentration
of cultural energy in certain domains. Unlike earlier manifestations, contemporary twin tales tend not to evoke questions of righteousness, the
duality of man, or the relation between material and spiritual dimensions. Instead their focus is more often directed towards questions of
gender, relationships and identity – whether personal, cultural or sexual.

These emphases are unsurprising when we note the obsession with
the refashioning of the self in an era of hyper-individualism, and when
we consider the importance, in Western cultures, of debates over
gender roles, the redefinition of the family, sexualities and the hybridisation of national cultures at the close of the twentieth century. The
question remains as to why twins stand out as a particularly appropriate figure to embody these issues. Is it merely because twins are readily
available as metaphors for the self in conflict, for the couple, for any
duality? Here we might look to theory, for it is hardly coincidental that
the motifs of doubling and repetition have figured prominently in psychoanalytical and philosophical discourses during the last half-century.
The elaboration of Freud's legacy by Jacques Lacan led to the 'split
subject' being seen as the norm of selfhood rather than the exception.
Gilles Deleuze pointed to repetition as the key to understanding difference. Jacques Derrida explained self-presence – the notion that one
is present and identical to oneself – as an illusion created by the
infinitesimal discrepancy in time and space between instances of
the self. More recently, Judith Butler has theorised gender identity as
an effect produced by the reiterative performance of gender roles.

Tales of identical twins usefully foreground questions of reiteration and
splitting, and thus provide an ideal opportunity to explore these concep-
tual shifts, which underlie the questions relating to identity and difference raised in some of the chapters. No less important than this
theoretical dimension, however, are the specific problems of representation that twins are used to address: how to depict soul-mate relationships,
the ideal woman, bodies that inspire horror, homosexual stereotypes,
ethnic tensions, the writer. In each case, the insistent repetition of a given
twin tale indicates a cultural hotspot, a point at which the desire to tell
the same story again confronts the need to tell it differently.

1

Look Twice: Narrative Uses of Twins

At first glance: a profusion of twin tales, a multitude of meanings

Twin tales are told and retold with astonishing frequency in contemporary culture. Newspapers give front-page prominence to accounts of the birth or surgical separation of conjoined babies, to twins dying of simultaneous heart attacks or bicycle accidents, to twins in crime and twins in sport. The reunion of twins separated at birth and the coincidences that mark their lives are the subject of feature articles and television documentaries. Scientific journals tell stories of twins raised apart and twins raised together. And these are only the tales that claim factual status. Narratives of twins also abound in all manner of imaginative creations. They populate short and feature films in the genres of comedy, drama, thriller, horror, sci-fi, porn, film noir, children's films, action and auteur cinema, and appear regularly in fiction ranging from police procedural novels to picaresque historical volumes, from the Bildungsroman to lesbian satire, from Booker Prize winners to supermarket romance novels.

In addition to these public genres of story-telling, twin tales are recounted in conversation. As a frantic mother of new-born twins, venturing out with the double stroller, I was constantly treated to anecdotes and life histories of twins from complete strangers. The author Michel Tournier recounts similar experiences and puts them down to the mythic nature of twin tales:

A myth is a story that everyone already knows. When I was writing *Gemini* I replied to those who enquired about the subject of my next novel: it's the adventures of two absolutely identical twin brothers.

1

At once my interlocutor's face would light up. Twin brothers? As a
matter of fact, he knew some! Two identical brothers. When one
caught a cold in London, the other sneezed in Rome. How many
times did I hear that kind of anecdote! It was pointless for me to
go into the details of my project. People knew them already, and
recited them to me in advance. I congratulated myself: it was proof
that my subject was of a mythological nature.   (Tournier, 1977:
189, original italics, my translation)

If Tournier's point is that a myth is a story that is always already
known, he demonstrates that it is also a story that demands constant
retelling. What is it about twins that fascinates us to the point that we
are prepared endlessly to rehearse tales of intertwined lives? Are we
merely repetitive, even compulsively so? *Twins in Contemporary Litera-*
ture and Culture examines recent novels and films featuring twins. It
takes a second look at stories that at first seem familiar, that appear to
be already known (evil twin steals lover; stranglehold of brotherly love,
and so on), and asks why they need to be retold and how they are
transformed in recent retellings.

It would be convenient to find a single answer to these questions, to
find that these stories all ultimately come down to the same underlying issue. Indeed over the years several critics have done so, regarding
twins as a subset of the figure of the double which they see as representing either the narcissistic defense of the ego (Rank, first published
1914), the projection of the unconscious (Tymms, 1949), an attempt to
cope with mental conflict (Rogers, 1970), the second self embodying
the quest for self-realisation (Keppler, 1972), the refusal of the real
(Rosset, 1976) or the incomplete self (Hallam, 1982).

It is not by chance that these studies of literary doubles are predominantly psychoanalytical: the topic of twins and doubles appears made
to order for a psychoanalytical reading, with its easy links to the mirror
stage, narcissism, the uncanny, separation anxiety, sibling rivalry, the
false self, projection of the unconscious, and exteriorisation of inner
conflict. Yet, too often, relying on the explanatory power of psychoanalysis allows the reader to ignore its story-telling side, to overlook
the following kind of yarn – exemplary in its modelling of aspects of
the fairy-tale:

I once knew two twin brothers, both of whom were endowed
with strong libidinal impulses. One of them was very successful
with women, and had innumerable affairs with women and girls.

The other went the same way at first, but it became unpleasant for him to be trespassing on his brother's preserves, and, owing to the likeness between them, to be mistaken for him on intimate occasions; so he got out of the difficulty by becoming homosexual. He left the women to his brother, and thus retired in his favour. (Freud, 1953–74 Vol. 18: 159)

The anecdote appears in a footnote to one of Freud's case studies. The 'once' (upon a time), the opposition of sexual options, and the prominence of fraternal rivalry, confusion in amorous encounters, and renunciation lend the anecdote as much to literary analysis (alongside George Sand's *La Petite Fadette* for example) as to psychoanalytical. Narratives of twins and doubles are not confined to incidental footnotes and case studies in psychoanalytical texts: consider Freud's account of the child's libidinal development and nostalgia for the lost mother that underpins his theory of primary narcissism (Freud, 1953–74, Vol. 14: 73–102), Lacan's tale of the toddler's jubilation before the mirror (1977) and Dolto's of his sorrow (1987). A whole series of stories is constituted by Dolto's reworking of Lacan's rewriting of Freud's retelling of Ovid's tale of Narcissus. Rather than viewing these as master patterns determining cultural discourses across time, it is possible to regard them instead as narratives in their own right, equally worthy of textual attention.[1] With their own specific genre conventions, they circulate in parallel and even converge with literary and popular discourses at particular moments in history. A classic example is the intersection of late Romantic prose fiction and the rise of psychoanalysis: moral and medical discourses mingle with the supernatural to produce Stevenson's *The Strange Case of Dr Jekyll and Mr Hyde* or Poe's 'William Wilson,' stories that anticipate the development of theories of the unconscious. Here cultural production finds itself remarkably in tune with the theoretical developments of the time, but as we shall see, this is not the only occasion of complicity between theoretical and literary (or filmic) discourses. The chapters that follow will therefore look to psychoanalysis less for catch-all explanations than for further evidence of patterns in story-telling habits.

The meaning of twins (or doubles, or mirrors, or shadows, or fission, or fusion, or repetition, or the number two), like all meaning, is situation specific. Anne Freadman demonstrates this apropos of coiffure: the cutting of hair cannot simply be taken as a symbol of castration, as Freud suggests (Freud, 1953–74 Vol. 11: 96, Vol. 21: 157), but acquires meanings particular to times and places. If cutting off one's tresses could signify self-mutilation in 1869 (Freadman, 2001: 225), by the 1920s 'the haircut had lost its power to act as a sacrifice or a loss, or even as an aggressive act in a private sexual dynamic. It had become a style, a fashion, a rule of conformity' (226). A parallel argument can be made regarding twins in cultural production. Identical and conjoined twins offer counter-intuitive images of one being in two bodies and two beings in one body, and thus may be seen to lend themselves to explorations of the nature of the self. However there is seemingly no limit to the cultural purposes to which twins can be put. Pressed into the service of the imagination, twins can be used to signify not only the unconscious, the divided self, narcissistic love, death, and fear of sexuality, but also the nation, the couple, fertility, eroticism, chance, life choices, uncertain paternity, writing, reality versus image, monstrosity, race relations, sexual difference, indeed any kind of difference, any figure of the Other (another ethnicity, gender, class, sexuality) and any duality, and to explore nature/ nurture debates in any field.

The present book, then, refuses to regard the profusion of literary/ filmic twins as the symptom of a single deep-seated anxiety that carries across genres and eras. It will arrive at no single answer as to why twin tales are so insistently retold. For although the coherence of the topic of twins at first appears a given, a second look at the corpus reveals that this is not a unified topos.[2] Stories of twins are remarkable not only for their number and frequency, but for their diversity. Identical, non-identical, conjoined, mutant, telepathic, homicidal, buddies, tricksters, soul-mates, long-lost siblings or jealous rivals, twins populate stories that may share very little in terms of plot, character, genre and audience. Consider, from 1990s films, the Jackie Chan vehicle *Twin Dragons* alongside Michael and Mark Polish's *Twin Falls Idaho*, or, from novels of the same decade, Arundhati Roy's *The God of Small Things* together with Patricia Cornwell's *From Potter's Field*, Danielle Steel's *Mirror Image* and Bryce Courtenay's *Tommo and Hawk*. The stories available are not variations on a theme, but a whole variety concert.

A closer look: family resemblances

Amidst this apparently infinite variety, however, insistent patterns occur. Just as in nineteenth-century prose fiction the frequent appearance of the uncanny (invariably male) double anticipates the rise of psychoanalytical theories of the unconscious, so patterns peculiar to contemporary culture emerge. A set of late twentieth-century novels recounts the shared life/death of soul-mate twins and suggests that cultural energy is being directed into redefining what constitutes a viable couple. A crop of early 1990s thriller films uses twin sisters to rework a particular myth of female sexuality, rewriting the virgin/whore dichotomy – without however abandoning it – for an audience less convinced of the value of virginity. Post 1980s horror films portray the relation between conjoined twin brothers as maternal, feminising the male body at a time when masculine identities are in crisis. Multiple research papers in behavioural genetics use twins to inquire into the causes of homosexuality as it ceases to be viewed as pathological. Phantom twins represent the divisions of Iron Curtain Europe in film and fiction as communist regimes are about to fall, pointing to an elusive relation between a Cold War East and West that do not simply mirror each other. Tales of twins raised apart highlight the underlying sameness of cultures in conflict with one another and testify to a belief in the superficiality of cultural difference. Meanwhile postmodern twins question the very notions of sameness and difference as they slip in and out of resemblance with each other.

Clearly twins do not have the same meaning in each of the clusters identified: they are not called upon to do the same representational work in horror films as in research papers; and female twins and mixed sex twins are not put to the same narrative purposes as male twins. Yet within each cluster, representations are surprisingly consistent. In other words, regularities tend to appear as a function of genre and gender.

If we compare these sets of texts to patterns in the nineteenth-century literature of the double, the divergence in preoccupations is noticeable. The dualities are different. Gone are the theological overtones, the exploration of the relation between material and spiritual worlds, in favour of a concentration on more human relationships. The moral dimension is muted and the social amplified. Contemporary twin tales converge around questions of gender and identity, whether personal, cultural or sexual. A comparison at this very broad level, however, can only lead to the most general of conclusions regarding the changes wrought by a turbulent century. More revealing are the cultural battles being fought out over more specific issues – over understandings of the couple, the ideal woman, the male body, gay identity, national identity, the creative self – tussles represented by particular patterns among twin tales and the challenges to them. These are the focus of the chapters that follow.

The book examines the tensions played out in contemporary narratives of twins and doubles (insofar as the latter overlap with twin tales) in literature and popular culture. It eschews study of a presumed general theme of twins in favour of analysing distinct sets of recurring twin tales and their significance. Innovations occur from time to time in the retellings, and the chapters linger on texts that depart from familiar tales in some way to see what is at stake, why a particular story needs to be retold differently, what pressures it is under. These are extremely useful texts for identifying cultural hotspots and crises of representation, for the innovations attest both to the difficulty of shifting narrative habits and to the importance of doing so.

The book does not attempt to cover the full range of recent twin tales but concentrates on some particularly compelling interventions in narrative routines. The first such intervention (Chapter 2) concerns the survival of the twin couple: against tradition, the twins in Bruce Chatwin's *On the Black Hill* overcome the threats to their relationship and survive together to the age of eighty. In Chapter 3, Tim Hunter's *Lies of the Twins* challenges the conventions of thriller films by dividing men rather than women in terms of sexual activity. In Chapter 4, the Polish brothers' film *Twin Falls Idaho* struggles to portray the permeable male body other than as an object of horror and a violation of gender boundaries. Robert Rodi's comic novel *Drag Queen* turns the tables on twin research in Chapter 5, defying the belief that homosexuality could represent a single category of sexual identity. In Chapter 6, a novel of Creole twins in Mauritius, Marie-Thérèse Humbert's *A l'autre bout de moi*, allows us to glimpse an understanding of cultural identity that is not dependent on resemblance among members of a culture. And Spike Jonze's film *Adaptation*, in Chapter 7, uses twins to question prevailing myths of creativity and divisions between high and low culture. Each of these texts puts a new twist on a familiar twin tale, and in doing so, resists a received idea of identity or of relationships.

Genre and gender: twinned constraints

A close look at each cluster of twin tales reveals that they tend to be highly coherent in terms of genre and gender, to the point where the representation of twins of a given gender (such as female) in a given genre (such as thriller films) seems to lend itself to the rehearsal of a certain cultural concern (such as fidelity), virtually imposing a particular tale, hence that feeling of having read or seen it all before. The stories accorded detailed attention in this book are those that put pressure on these familiar nexuses of genre, gender and topos to transform existing models.

Critical work linking genre and gender has proliferated since the early 1970s (Eagleton, 2000: 250), primarily linking the gender of the author and the choice of genre. My study considers another point of intersection: the genre conventions giving rise to gendered patterns of representation in twin tales. Although this line of enquiry is distinct from a focus on the gender of the author, the two are not unrelated: obviously the gender of the author has a bearing on the choice of gender (and exploits) of characters, the genre of the narrative and its purpose. It is far from incidental, for example, that when Marilyn Bowering raises the spectre of twin brothers firing at each other from enemy aircraft in *Visible Worlds*, her story refuses to conform to the 'boys' own' template and offers an alternative tale of female endurance and lost children. Neither is it by chance that the representation of twin sisters as one virginal and one voracious is found most consistently in films directed and produced from within the predominantly masculine structures of the studio system.

The focus on the intersection of gender and genre highlights the narrative habits that shape the retelling of twin stories. It enables us to ask how gender representations are called into question by shifts in genre and, conversely, how generic conventions are challenged by shifts in gender. And it allows questions to be raised regarding, for example, the representation of masculinity in horror movies and the fact that female twins are found in such a narrow range of film genres. In this way, rather than providing sociological explanations of change, I will be grounding my readings in intertextual networks (literary/filmic traditions) and accounting for textual innovation in terms of the manipulation of genre constraints and of the representations they support.

Such an investigation requires underpinning by a theory that considers genre to be under constant renegotiation. Freadman and Macdonald's work questions traditional ideas of genre as fixed models of textual production. In their detailed exposition of the concept and uses of genre, they argue that genres are not simply sets of rules. Rather they take form as 'regularities of practice, subject to deliberate modification on occasion,' yet with the inertia of ingrained habit (1992: 9). These regularities give rise to reader expectations that are crucial in determining not only interpretation but the production of further examples of a genre. And among these are gender expectations. One of the ways in which a text may address genre-related expectations is through 'not-statements': texts position and define their genre by invoking and explicitly distancing themselves from neighbouring genres (Freadman, 1988). The novels and films studied in the chapters that follow provide numerous examples of such self-positioning against the patterns of particular genres, in order to shift certain stories as they are retold.

Exhausting twins

The chapters outlined above make no claim to an exhaustive exploration of contemporary narrative uses of twins and doubles. Firstly the clusters of texts chosen, while not always culturally specific, are limited to those that engage with a Western tradition: the occasional European art-house film finds its way into an overwhelmingly North-American corpus of films; anglophone and francophone novels are studied against the background of a wider European tradition. The wealth of narrative material from non-Western societies, from indigenous and other Asian, African, Pacific and South American cultures, brought to light by ethnologists and scholars of religion, has not been examined (and the 'Twins' issue [1994: Vol. 19: 2] of the journal of myth and tradition, *Parabola*, gives an idea of the scale of such a venture). Secondly, even within the cultural limits I have set myself, the sheer volume of twin tales published annually precludes assembly of a comprehensive corpus.

It would nonetheless be possible to identify and study further patterns of twin tales: in action films for example, in pornographic film and literature, in detective fiction, in science-fiction, in reports of legal cases, in tales of incest, in tales of twins as authors, in children's literature, or in Booker Prize winners set in India. The very notion of exhausting the topic, however, runs counter to the thrust of the book. The possibility of accounting for twin tales as a whole presupposes the idea that they constitute a unified topos, an idea that I challenge. Aiming for exhaustiveness would mean marking out the limits of contemporary narrative uses of twins, whereas I argue that there are no structural or imaginative limits to potential uses, but that each application will involve the negotiation of discursive habits, the manipulation of generic conventions established to a greater or lesser degree. Despite the recurrence of particular narrative routines, twin tales are continually mutating: each repetition offers the opportunity for difference; each new text has the potential to revise a template. There is thus no reason why twins could not be harnessed in film, fable or front-page report to represent, say, weather patterns (Tournier's *Les Météores* provides a foretaste), the nature of writing (as in John Barth's *Sabbatical*), technological change (the link between the double and the machine is a longstanding one, see Coates, 1998: 2), or worker alienation (*Fight Club* comes close). In order to do so, however, there is a need to acknowledge and deal with an accumulation of pre-existing stories that together exert a certain pressure to conform.

The chapters, then, do not constitute a typology of twin tales – structural or thematic – in the manner of the studies by Keppler (1972), Dolezel (1985), and even Doniger (2000). Part of the delight of the texts I have chosen to study in detail is the way in which they are *un*true to type, and refuse to be typecast. Rather than adopting the restraining and unifying model of a typology, where the focus is on the typical, each chapter pays close attention to a text where a given formula is in flux. Topography might be a more useful model, in that it involves detailed description of localities. *Twins in Contemporary Literature and Culture* is self-consciously selective, investigating loci where late twentieth-century twin stories proliferate, looking out for changes in the landscape, and explaining these shifts in terms of the interrelation of gender, genre and topos. Chapters therefore have a dual emphasis, demonstrating not only recurrence but variation, exploring both the conventions that shape twin tales in various genres, and the points at which these constraints are strained. This reflects the double imperative driving the retelling of twin tales: there is the need to tell these stories again, and the need to tell them differently.[3]

Looking back: existing studies of twins and doubles

Important studies of twins and doubles in myth and literature, not only from literary disciplines but also from the fields of anthropology, ethnology, psychology and religion, appear at intervals to span the entire twentieth century: from Rendel Harris's 1903 volume, *The Dioscuri in the Christian Legend*, through Otto Rank's psychoanalytic study (1914)[4] and Ralph Tymms's psychological one (1949), a spate of texts in the 1970s and 1980s, to the recent massive tomes by Hillel Schwartz (1996) and Wendy Doniger (2000). So why do we need another one? The short answer is the scarcity of detailed work devoted to more recent twin narratives, and presumptions by a number of critics that twentieth-century doubles are somehow less interesting than or merely derivative of earlier representations. The short answer does not, however, do justice to the work that has been done and on which this book builds, so the remainder of this introductory chapter will be devoted to an examination of existing studies, their scope, their usefulness, in some cases their limitations, and the ways in which this book departs from them.

Although my project focuses specifically on twin tales, studies of doubles are highly relevant to it, since at various points in time, certain topoï of twins and the theme(s) of the double have been intertwined.[5] This is certainly the case in the late twentieth century, confirming Stewart's social research, which highlights the Anglo-American tendency to associate twinship above all with notions of identical appearance and behaviour (2003: 119–25, 157–60). In the present study, the twin as double looms large in the third, fifth, sixth and seventh chapters, although it scarcely figures in the second and fourth chapters, which explore other relations between twins. This contrast is consistent with René Zazzo's analysis in *Le Paradoxe des jumeaux*. Zazzo distinguishes between the theme of the double and that of the couple in narrative uses of twins (1984: 81–2, 160), and shows that the predominance of one or other of these two themes in twin tales varies at different historical moments. Coates distinguishes between twins and doubles in a different way. He suggests that '[w]hereas twins are staple figures of comic literature, which feeds on the confusions their similarity generates, the Double recaptures the image of the twin for non-comic literature: the Double is the emissary of death' (1988: 3). While this generalisation can be argued for much pre-twentieth-century literature (especially theatre), it is belied by the longstanding connection between twins and death (explored in Chapter 2 below). Moreover, the distinction is blurred in more recent texts, in which twins assume many of the tropes of earlier doubles. Indeed, of the twins featured in the present study, only one set is comic (Chapter 5). Twins and doubles are, then, not interchangeable, but related to a greater or lesser extent in particular periods and genres.

Several studies engage with the definition of the double, a vexing issue given that almost any relation of resemblance and/or opposition may be used to identify a double. As Guerard notes, '[t]he word *double* is embarrassingly vague, as used in literary criticism' (1967: 3). Although I shall evoke stories and studies of doubles where relevant, I shall restrict my primary corpus to tales of twins for reasons of economy and coherence.

If twins preoccupy the contemporary imagination, as their frequent appearance in recent films and novels suggests, a survey of the literature shows that twins have prompted fear and fascination since mythological times. However, just as they have not necessarily played on the same anxieties, or evoked the same laughter or yearnings in different times, places and genres, neither have they been uniformly present throughout history. Tales of twins and doubles are noticeably abundant in myth and legend, in the theatre of antiquity, and at two periods during modern times in Western literature: the seventeenth and nineteenth centuries.

The contrast between their manifestations in these latter two periods is sharp. In English Renaissance and French Classical theatre, twins appear above all in comic theatre. Shakespeare and Molière find an antecedent in the Greek comedies of Menander and the Roman plays of Plautus. Exploiting the generic constraints and possibilities of playhouse performance, they stage comedies of confusion in which twins, lookalikes and doubles (divine or mortal) substitute for one another in amorous intrigues and are falsely accused of another's misdeeds. Key twin comedies are Shakespeare's *Twelfth Night* and *A Comedy of Errors* (the latter based on Plautus's *Menaechmi*) and Molière's *Amphitryon* (based on Plautus's play of the same name). Then, after a relatively idle period of a century or so, doubles (more often doppelgängers and half-brothers mistaken for twins rather than twins per se) regain prominence across Europe, tending to meet a tragic end in Romantic and *fin de siècle* prose fiction and gothic novels (for example by Jean Paul [Richter], Chamisso, Hoffmann, Hogg, Dostoevsky, Stevenson, Maupassant), and in the work of Edgar Allan Poe in America.

Criticism follows suit, focusing primarily on these periods and genres.[6] Shakespeare's twin comedies are often studied alongside his plays featuring non-twin doubles (such as *The Two Noble Kinsmen* and *The Two Gentlemen of Verona*), for example by Jean Perrot (1976), for whom the double falls '*sous le signe des jumeaux*' – under the sign of the Gemini – as the title of his book suggests. However, if, for Perrot and Zazzo, twins are the source of certain themes while doubles are the reflecting image, for scholars of nineteenth-century literature, twins represent a subset of the broader category of doubles. The Romantic era is glorified as the 'heyday' of the double (Herdman, 1991: x; Tymms, 1949: 120) and twins are subsumed under this motif, which is viewed as 'a central theme' of the period (Herdman, 1991: x). Consequently, there is a great deal of criticism pertaining to nineteenth-century doubles and in which the representation of twins is a secondary concern.

In terms of the sheer number of narratives, twentieth-century twins and doubles are more abundant than their predecessors, yet they are often seen as a footnote to the history of the double. Although well-served by Irwin's (1975) analysis of Faulkner and Slethaug's study of postmodern American fiction (1993), twentieth-century doubles have received scant attention in comparison with the concentrated focus on nineteenth-century literature, and are in fact dismissed by some critics: their lack of coherence is seen as evidence of the weakening of the nineteenth-century theme, and their very proliferation is deemed a trivialisation.

The double in decline

Tymms, in an admittedly dated study, frets over the trivialisation of the double, which occurs, he argues, when the figure does not function as a vehicle for psychological analysis (1949: 8, 109, 119). During its Romantic apogee, on the other hand, the double was used to embody the unconscious self. Rogers concurs with Tymms's judgement and similarly privileges the psychological. He valorises the 'latent' double over the 'manifest' (which we may presume to include identical twins) (1970: 4), and draws attention to the difficulties faced by post-Freudian authors in 'transcend[ing] the limitations of representing doubles in an overt manner' (1970: 162). It seems that they are almost obliged to descend into self-parody, exemplified by Vladimir Nabokov's *Despair*, considered by Rogers as 'ultimately not satisfying' (Rogers, 1970: 171).

The object of Coates's study is post-Romantic literature, but mostly *fin de siècle*, with relatively few twentieth-century examples. Coates echoes Tymms and Rogers when he writes of the predicament of successors to Joseph Conrad and Henry James: 'As the doctrines of Freud become more widely known, however, the dividedness of the self becomes a truism. Hence its representation becomes trivial [...] and ceases to carry any literary information' (1988: 34–5). And in further comment on the increasing banality of the figure, he suggests that 'the appearances of the Double made possible by film [...] remove the Double to the realm of technical trickery' (1988: 35).

Herdman similarly shows nostalgia for the nineteenth century, and in keeping with the discourse of *fin de siècle* decadence laments the decline of the double: 'The motif does not die with the nineteenth century, but its treatment in the last decade shows it in a state of declension from the fullest development of its potential' (1991: x, cf. 143, 145). Although he recognises that the double survives the turn of the century with altered emphases, his thesis precludes the possibility that it might flourish. For if the vitality of the literature of the double depends on the interpenetration of moral/spiritual and psychological discourses (x, 19, 145, 151), then, once again, post-Freudian avatars are at a distinct disadvantage. Herdman too regrets the 'relapse of the double theme into comparative triviality' at the close of the nineteenth century (1991: 144).

In the light of these analyses, the abundance of twentieth-century twin tales could perhaps be regarded as a response to the post-Freudian limitations described: if representing psychological doubles openly has become problematic, identical twins are a plausible substitute. They can be shown to mirror each other overtly, and their mirroring can embrace a moral perspective.

Meanwhile, if the theme of the double is considered to have become hackneyed (Rogers, 1970: 2), the same can certainly be said of the oft-repeated complaint of its twentieth-century trivialisation. Jonze's film *Adaptation* offers a less serious commentary on the perceived slide of the double into triviality. It alludes self-reflexively to the status of the double as a disreputable device of fiction (cf. Tymms, 1949: 15), with its discriminating screenwriter protagonist fretting over the cinematic clichés produced by his identical twin screenwriter brother who enjoys popular success (see Chapter 7 below).

The bulk of the critical texts on the double, then, from Rank and Tymms onward, reserves the place of honour for Romantic doubles, often showing little sympathy for postmodern playfulness and seemingly immune to the sway of poststructuralist discourses of identity. This occurs even in quite recent criticism. In 1995, a flurry of analyses was published to coincide with the setting of the double as the topic for the French *agrégation* in literature (a national competitive examination for entry to secondary and tertiary teaching posts). The syllabus comprised texts by Hoffmann, Chamisso, Dostoevsky, Maupassant and Nabokov. Nabokov, the only twentieth-century representative, is seen from the outset as the one who 'liquidated' the theme (Troubetzkoy, 1995: 7). For Troubetzkoy, Nabokov's text marks 'the fall of the empire of the double' (Troubetzkoy, 1996: 189, cf. 205), delivering the final blow to a once-great theme, in decline since the end of the nineteenth century. Although he gestures towards the double's later productivity (1995: 17), citing Coates, he stops short of elaborating on the directions this might take.

Coates is in fact ambiguous on this point, for he starts out suggesting that 'following the turn of the century the Double atrophied as a literary trope' before revising his thesis to the effect that the double had assumed a new form, 'that of the second-person pronoun' (1988: 65), and briefly exploring this use. One of the rare critics to argue explicitly against the discourse of decline is Hallam, who cites and refutes Field's comment that '[t]oday the theme has very few advocates in literature [...] and is generally regarded, with some justice, as a quaint and curious chestnut of the Romantic era in literature' (Field, 1967: 220, cited Hallam, 1982: 11). Hallam points to the use of the double by 'innovative writers like Joyce, Mann, Kafka, Woolf, Faulkner, and Borges,' although he still attributes the success of their inventions to the groundwork done by their nineteenth-century predecessors (1982: 11). Similarly, Miller, whose book includes a chapter on twins and discusses a number of twentieth-century texts, views these examples through the prism of a nineteenth-century 'heritage of romantic duality' (1985: 417, cf. 29–38). Although he in no way dismisses contemporary doubles, he sees continuity between them and their more exalted forebears: 'Dualistic works of art [...] continue to appear, and the new works have done little to deny or efface the old' (1985: 418).

It is curious to observe that many of these writings were published in the years following a period when the figure of the double had been not only ubiquitous but a tool of some leverage in literary theory, under the impact of contemporary psychoanalytical theory and philosophy. We need only think of the profound influence of Lacan's theory of the mirror stage (1977 [first published 1949]), with its conception of the speaking subject as a divided unity, or of Kristeva's semiotic/symbolic divide through which she elaborated the existence of an inaccessible otherness within the self (1984 [1974]), or of Derrida's demonstration (with respect to citation) that in order for something to be identical to itself, it must be able to be repeated/duplicated (1982 [1971]: 307–30). Indeed Descombes (1979) characterises modern French philosophy from Kojève to Derrida and Deleuze as primarily concerned (like the double) with problematising the opposition between sameness and otherness.[7] That literary uses of the double should continue their putative decline at a time when the double attained such imposing status in theoretical work is difficult to believe. There is every reason to suppose that these theoretical breakthroughs were accompanied by novels, plays and films in which the double figures in ways specific to the close of the twentieth century, just as Maupassant's and Stevenson's texts heralded Freud's. Coates alludes to this – albeit briefly and somewhat regretfully – when he writes of the contemporary social context in terms of multiple fissures within the self, of entire series of reflecting surfaces, and of fragmented super-egos that function to preclude the emergence of a solitary double representing death, self-knowledge or self-betrayal (1988: 35).

Happily, Gordon Slethaug's *The Play of the Double in Postmodern American Fiction* (1993) pursues this argument in a sustained way. Slethaug studies novels by Nabokov, Thomas Pynchon, John Hawkes, John Barth, Richard Brautigan, and Raymond Federman and relates them to the poststructuralist rethinking of binary categories by Lacan, Barthes, Derrida, Foucault and Kristeva (19–30). He argues that the postmodern literature of the double is distinguished by a move away from the double's 'traditional dualistic moorings' towards a new playfulness and an interrogation of 'selfhood, language, and culture' (197, cf. 30). Postmodern authors are said to use the double to explore in particular 'a divided and discontinuous self in a fragmented universe,' the constructed nature of human reality, and 'the inevitable drift of signifiers away from their referents,' preoccupations that Slethaug sums up as 'the split sign, the split self, and the split text' (3).

Slethaug's book is important in providing the first full-length study of the contemporary double in its own right, rather than as a leftover from nineteenth-century fiction. To do so, Slethaug focuses on novels by recognised American literary authors, but his thesis can be extended to the work of writers such as Paul Auster, Martin Amis, Marie Redonnet and Madeleine Monette (cf. Chapter 7 below). Whilst my study is related in purpose to Slethaug's, it approaches the question somewhat differently: firstly in examining twin tales, a corpus that intersects only partially with that of the double; secondly in paying as much attention to popular film and prose genres as to literary fiction; thirdly in looking for clusters of similar tales, denoting a concentration of cultural energy around certain questions; and fourthly – a consequence of the clusters found – in foregrounding issues of gender.

Not a trifling matter

Two further studies of a less literary nature make valuable contributions to the field. Like Slethaug's book, they neither mourn the passing of a previous era nor dismiss late twentieth-century cultural production as a poor relation. Moreover they do not consider popular culture a trifling matter. Wendy Doniger (2000) juxtaposes B grade movies with ancient and medieval sources in *The Bedtrick*, and Hillel Schwartz (1996), in *The Culture of the Copy*, contemplates not only literary examples but rubber sex dolls and hair-perm and motorcycle advertisements featuring twins. Both consider the supposedly trivial worthy of serious attention and a sign of vigour rather than decline.

In contrast with Herdman, Schwartz affirms that the double has remained a central theme – nay an obsession – in contemporary culture, that it is at the root of 'our most perplexing moral dilemmas' (1996: 11). Living in the culture of the copy requires us to revise old ideals of authenticity as singularity and (in a move reminiscent of Derrida's elaboration of *différance*) to conceive of an authenticity defined by doubleness (Schwartz, 1996: 17). For in a world of multiple copies without an original to anchor them, doubleness no longer signifies duplicity. Schwartz's postmodern eclecticism allows him to analyse reproductions of all kinds, not just twins and doppelgängers, self-portraits and store mannequins, but Warhol's soup-cans, forgeries and photocopies, placebos and prosthetics, fake flowers and flight simulators. Narratives are not the focus of this miscellany, but it nonetheless provides a useful entry point for understanding twin tales about doubling and cloning.

Doniger's book, on the other hand, is devoted to a particular set of narratives, namely stories 'of going to bed with someone whom you mistake for someone else' (2000: xiii). All of these concern doubles of one sort or another, and many involve twins. Doniger organises her vast corpus – drawing on Sanskrit texts, the Hebrew bible, Greek and Latin literature, German and French stories, Hollywood films and assorted other tales – according to plot and theme in a self-consciously structuralist manner, in order to undertake a 'broad comparative enterprise' (xviii). She asks questions across eras, cultures and genres, seeking if not universal meanings then at least 'cross-cultural [...] meanings for the bedtrick as well as for the concepts of sex, love, and knowledge that undergird it' (xxi).

These two books are impressive quasi-encyclopaedic studies, and both Schwartz and Doniger achieve the latter's aims of delighting, demonstrating a point, and dazzling with erudition (Doniger, 2000: xxvi–xxvii). In each case there are partial overlaps with the questions driving this book, in that twins as copies and as sexual usurpers appear in several chapters. However, while Doniger and Schwartz draw attention to continuity in the recycling of motifs and themes, I point to rifts and shifts that occur in retellings. The divergence of our aims comes back to that double insistence driving the retelling of certain tales. Whereas Doniger demonstrates the need to keep telling the same story, the ease with which we resort to it, the continued sympathy for particular speaking positions, I explore the difficulty of telling it differently, of diverging from a persistent story-line. I ask what precisely is involved in some of those shifts that Doniger accommodates as variants of the theme. This requires lingering over some particularly telling retellings, not widely studied elsewhere, over the detail of their differences.

Convergences of genre and gender

Although Doniger explores gender asymmetry in bedtrick stories, and Herdman comments in parentheses that 'sisters are a rarity' in the Romantic corpus (14), rarely are gender issues associated with genre in the literature. Nonetheless, a small number of critics usefully link topos to genre and gender in their studies of literary twins and doubles.

On the one hand there are insightful analyses of quite particular conjunctions, usually with a feminist purpose. Joanne Blum notes that 'the tradition of the double has been largely a male one' and that 'the type of double reflected in their texts is, almost without exception, a single-sexed one' (1988: 2). She describes the male/female double in nineteenth- and twentieth-century women's fiction as an effort to transcend traditional gender roles: 'male and female selves overreach their culturally prescribed gender identities to relate to one another in such a way that the boundary between self and other becomes blurred' (1988: 1). Valérie Raoul (1996), poring over a century of French-Canadian women's writing, brings together genre, gender and culture. She identifies a particular treatment of the female double in the genre of the fictitious diary that overturns the novelistic tradition of the (male) double as a threat to selfhood: a female narrator is able to mourn the death of a beloved friend through continuing the writing she has left behind, and through the resulting fusion of identities. A third example is Lucy Fischer's analysis of the representation of female twins in women's melodrama of the 1940s (1989: 172–215, discussed in Chapter 3 below). Such studies do not attempt to account for the same range of twin tales as the present one, but support its argument by providing further instances of a specific articulation of genre and gender determining the representation of twins.

On the other hand, some of the wider studies of twins and doubles make more general links between genre and gender. Otto Rank details some of the rich history of twins in myth and legend, in which rival twins are linked to the founding of cities and civilisations, sometimes tragically: Romulus and Remus, Zethus and Amphion, Jacob and Esau (1973: 90–7). It is left to René Zazzo to note that these legendary twins are invariably fraternal: both male and non-identical (1984: 143). Genre and gender are further linked to topos when he explains the absence of identical twins in myth by the fact that foundational myths use twins to raise the question of social identity rather than personal identity or singularity of being (1984: 83).

While Rank notes the frequency with which twins appear in comedies of confusion (1973: 89), Zazzo finds patterns in the genres and periods in which non-identical and identical twins appear: 'To find identical twins in ancient literature we need to switch from tragedy to comedy' (1984: 155). He notes, however, that identical twins in nineteenth-century prose narratives rarely signal comedy, and are instead used to represent themes earlier associated with non-identical twins and the theme of the couple, such as jealousy or the mystic bond of soul-mates till death. Zazzo interprets this as an elucidation of coupledom through exploration of the double (1984: 171). He also signals the importance of incestuous mixed sex twins in nineteenth-century and *fin de siècle* narratives (1984: 171), a topos that continues to flourish a century later, a notable instance being Arundhati Roy's breathtaking *The God of Small Things* with its tale of 'two-egg twins' and forbidden loves.

Perrot, however, goes furthest in using the concept of genre as an organising principle in his study of twin tales. In following the 'chain' (1976: 9) of literary twins from Plautus to Poe, he describes the links of the chain in terms of genre transformations. Submitting the myth to the constraints of new genres has resulted in the reformulation of those genres: 'each particular text tends to subvert the model it has adopted' (1976: 14). Thus Charles Perrault bent Roman comedy to the constraints of the popular children's tale, where it assumed the pedagogical function formerly reserved for tragedy (1976: 11). Thus the use of the double in Poe's short stories represents the displaced obverse of Shakespearian theatre (1976: 11, 217).

Perrot's use of genre to explain the transformation of stories is productive. Less useful, although perhaps predictable in a 1970s structuralist study that engages with the theoretical writings of the day, is the premise of the unity and centrality of his object of study. The 'myth of twins' is said to be singular and to occupy 'a privileged position in the cultural sphere of the Western world' (1976: 7). If the myth represents the backbone ('l'axe vertebral,' 1976: 7) of a binarised worldview, this appears to be due to some kind of unchanging deep structure, flexible perhaps but enduring. Perrot maintains that the twins myth has served as the medium for genre transformation (1976: 13): although flexed to fit new constraints, 'the original matrix' (1976: 218) remains constant. The 'chain' of the myth's existence is therefore necessarily linear and continuous.

Like Perrot, I propose to use genre to explain some of the transformations in late twentieth-century (and later) twin tales, focusing on the impact both of the choice of genre on the (re)telling of a story, and of the particular story on generic conventions. Unlike Perrot's, however, my study presupposes neither a single twins myth open to reworking nor a single chain of twin stories. It refuses the centrality and continuity of Perrot's model of the twins myth, and rejects the metaphor of the chain in favour of finding multiple strands, discontinuities, split ends and crossovers. Like Angela Carter's *mise en scène* of twins in *Wise Children*, with its false paternities and adoptions, it disrupts the attempt at a genealogy of literary twins.

Looking forward

Far from having merely declined from a nineteenth-century Dostoevskian apogee to become a facile narrative device in the twentieth century, as a number of critics have contended, the figure of the double, frequently in the form of the twins, has proliferated in popular and elevated forms. Less unified than their Romantic antecedents, twins today come in more than one gender and multiple narrative genres. But this disunity does not constitute a dilution: there is concentration at a local level (the horror film, the novel of soul-mates, the sociological research paper), where certain tales demand constant retelling.

This insistence is not however the product of a particular anxiety that carries across genres and eras: significance is situation specific. The appearance of twins and doubles in narratives does not simply signify the narcissistic defense of the ego, the projection of the unconscious, an attempt to cope with mental conflict. Nor does it necessarily embody the quest for self-realisation, the refusal of the real, or the incomplete self. Rather it acquires meaning in the context of historically precise conjunctions of genre and gender.

The chapters that follow originated as reflections on distinct corpora of twin tales: a set of novels here, a cluster of films there. Their lack of relation intrigued me: Chatwin's twins had so little in common with Rodi's, de Loo's with Humbert's, the filmic brothers of *The Krays* with those of *Double Impact*. Yet within clusters certain tropes reappeared insistently. Neither the divergences nor the convergences were adequately explained by existing studies of twins and doubles, few of which offered sustained attention to contemporary texts and several of which dismissed popular representations altogether. I thus decided to draw my analyses of twin tales together to argue for a broader understanding of the ways in which twin narratives play out in contemporary culture. This book is the result. It invokes genre to account for diversity and repetition among twin tales.[8] And in its attention to the possibilities and difficulties of shifting generic constraints, it offers an understanding of what is at stake in twin tales that depart from familiar patterns.

May the following analyses of the adventures of Benjamin and Lewis Jones, of Rachel and her twin lovers, of Blake and Francis Falls, of Mitchell and Kitten, of Anne and Nadège, of Charlie and Donald Kaufman find an echo in the reader. And may the literary and screen twins that succeed them continue both to divert us and to divert from the narrative paths that have been laid.

2
Twins and the Couple: Surviving Sameness in Novels of Twin Lives

The Bloomfield's closed circle

They say truth is stranger than fiction. In any case, the same narrative problems arise in the telling of it. Let me start with the tale of the identical Bloomfield twins, William and John, who lived, worked and died together. Born three minutes apart, they died only two minutes apart, aged 61, of almost simultaneous heart-attacks. But how do you tell a story of resemblance, a story where nothing manages to drive the two apart or dialecticise the relation into an opposition between contrasting twins?

The story as told in the *Australian* newspaper and in Brisbane's *Courier Mail* is one of the closed cell of perfect identity. '[T]he twins lived in a world of their own, totally self-sufficient in each other's company,' 'oblivious' and 'impervious' to others (Montgomery and Walker, 1996). '[C]loser than a married couple could ever be,' with 'no need for close friends,' the 'reclusive' 'soulmate[s]' 'learnt to ignore the outside world'; 'no one could penetrate their inner circle' (Russell, 1996). The lack of any access to the closed world of the twins makes it hard to tell a tale of their life together.

So what can be told? There is a tale available, that of their death, and there are models for it. The story is thus told as a Romantic tale of decadence and decay in the best tradition of Edgar Allan Poe. In Poe's 'The House of Usher,' a genteel pair of pallid, strikingly similar twins, Roderick and Madeline Usher, languish in their crumbling mansion as their premature death approaches, a simultaneous demise that marks the end of the dynastic line and precipitates the collapse of the house that shrouds them. Like the Usher twins, the Bloomfields 'came from an aristocratic family' (Russell, 1996). They 'were their parents' only children and grew up in decaying splendour in one of Hobart's stately homes' (Montgomery and Walker, 1996). There is a faintly *fin de siècle* feel to the descriptions of their lifestyle (which – not incidentally – also correspond to a gay stereotype): 'cultured, elegant dandies who enjoyed dressing up' and 'loved attending [art] exhibitions in expensive, fashionable clothes,' they wore fluffy tailor-made bow-ties, and shared a passion for art and fine food, but were heard to mumble morbidly about dying. In a conclusion worthy of Poe, there were problems telling the twins apart at their death. Since they carried their papers in the same leather pouch, 'the only clue as to who was who came from the 'W' and 'J' monograms on their underwear' (Russell, 1996).

But the problem that interests me is not that of telling twins apart but of telling them together. The Bloomfields were in their 60s when they died. Unlike the Usher twins, theirs is a somewhat early, but not a particularly untimely death. And yet, closure, decay and the inevitable course towards death seem to be the constants of the stories we tell about sameness. I suspect, however, there is an alternative, potentially more radical story about this couple that we do not know how to tell, or for which we do not have readily available models. This chapter is about the difficulty of telling such a story. And at stake is the question of the viability of a certain understanding of coupledom: a couple relation not defined by contrast and the synthesis of differences into oneness.

The wages of twins

Stories about twins appear short on survivors. From Romulus and Remus to popular film today, a high proportion of twin tales conclude with the death of one or both twins. Certainly twins escape with their lives in comedies of confusion (whether ancient, Shakespearian or contemporary), but in these genres they have no life together. Indeed, as René Girard remarks, they are usually separated at birth and, in plays, never appear on stage together until the very last scene (1981: 66–7). Similarly, stories of the reunion of twins raised apart tend to end with both twins alive (see Chapter 5). Twins who are not separated early, on the other hand, twins whose lives are entwined are frequently doomed.

Why is it that narrative resolution so often spells untimely death for these twins? Is it because twins threaten our notions of discrete bodies and indivisible individuals? Or because they disturb the social order by disturbing the opposition between same and different, between self and other? Is it because they challenge the canonical couple, the marriage of complementary others that they are sacrificed in stories? No doubt it is for all of these reasons ... but not all at the same time. The deaths are different – as are the forces leading to them – in different eras, in different genres. This chapter surveys the major threats to the narrative survival of twins in ancient, Romantic and contemporary tales and discusses the significance of the deaths they represent, before examining some attempts to rewrite the fate of the twin couple in the latter half of the twentieth century.

Legend abounds with stories of fratricidal rivalry, which threatens the life of several of the mythic twin founders of cities and nations: Remus dies at the hands of Romulus over the site of Rome; Proëtus and Acrisius of Argos quarrel in the womb and continue to war against one another. Where it does not lead to death, such rivalry may force twins apart – to the point where Esau and Jacob found separate nations – as a means of survival.

As Zazzo points out (1984: 154–5), these stories relate attempts to re-establish a social order that is threatened by the conflicting claims to power represented by twin leaders. Death thus serves to restore equilibrium. Girard goes further in associating twins and death in his analysis of the theme of enemy brothers. He claims that twins threaten the social order through their very existence, for their shared position within the family (and indeed their family resemblance) blurs the distinctions on which peace and order depend. This erasure of difference inevitably gives rise to sacrificial violence (1977: 49–67).

Among ancient legends, a more optimistic view of fraternity is offered by the story of the Dioscuri, Castor and Pollux. Of the 'heavenly twins,' only one – Pollux – was born immortal. The mortal Castor is killed, not at the hands of his twin, but in battle against another set of twins. Such is the love between the brothers that Pollux pleads with his father Zeus to be allowed to share his own immortality with his twin. The request is granted and the twins thereafter take it in turns to die, such that there is always one in the underworld, and one in the living world.[1] While marked by the death of a twin, this most widespread of twin legends[2] is a tale of the partial survival of a twin couple.

Fast-forwarding past the Renaissance comedies of confusion to the concentration of twin tales in nineteenth-century fiction, we find that here too a form of fratricidal rivalry leads to the demise of twins, but that its sense is somewhat different. Unlike the fraternal twins of legend, usually divided by appearance as well as by tastes, Romantic twins and doubles are often outwardly identical, but diametrically – even diabolically – opposed in character. The divide is primarily a moral one. A persecuting double in the form of an evil twin (Tupper's *The Twins: A Tale of Concealment*, 1849), doppelgänger (Dostoevsky's 'The Double', Hogg's *Private Memoirs and Confessions of a Justified Sinner*) or spirit (Maupassant's 'Le Horla') struggles to usurp the life of the protagonist, a struggle often culminating in a murderous suicide whereby one twin, in trying to kill the other, ends up killing himself (cf. Rank, 1971: 33). Poe furnishes the classic example of the simultaneous death of identical rivals in the tale of 'William Wilson': William's life of vice, debauchery and intoxication is hindered by his namesake and likeness, born on the same day, who is endowed with a highly developed sense of morality. This double dogs William and intercepts his plans, admonishing him in a whisper, until the day William stabs him repeatedly with a rapier. His dying words, which somehow speak through William's own voice, reveal the intertwined fate of the two: 'in my death, see by this image, which is thine own, how utterly thou hast murdered thyself' (Poe, 1965: 325). Persecuting doubles and deadly twins harking back to the Romantic tradition continue to populate contemporary popular genres, especially thrillers.[3]

Unlike the foundation myths, these tales are linked to questions of personal rather than social identity, and the threat portrayed by the double is above all a threat to selfhood (as Rank, Tymms, Rogers and Keppler emphasise). The issue of twins as a couple, the possibility of any relationship beyond the desire for mutual extermination, rarely arises as the struggle between moral forces is played out. Indeed in many cases it is unclear whether there are indeed two characters, or whether the 'twin' is a projection of the repressed other half of the protagonist's own self.

There is, however, another twin topos dating from the nineteenth century that spotlights the twins as couple, and it too remains insistent throughout the twentieth century. Once again, Poe provides a template: 'The House of Usher,' echoed in the Bloomfield story, tells of a twin death very different from that of William Wilson: soulmate twins, turned toward each other rather than the outside world, sink into stagnation and perish there. Their house collapses into the still mirror-like lake that surrounds it. Perrot argues that the Usher twins die from being 'enclosed in that dead-end situation that is the twin condition' (1976: 162). Whereas the otherness of the other twin is magnified in the stories of rivalry, here it is suppressed to maintain resemblance.

This is not death by opposition but death by a suffocating sameness, an implosion rather than an explosion of the couple. We recognise this scenario as one of narcissism. Poe's tale predates the psychoanalytical use of the term but anticipates fully its connotations of decay, sterility, insularity, and nostalgia for the lost Eden of the womb. It was towards the middle of the nineteenth century that the Narcissus myth came to be associated with sexual psychology and pathologised.[4] Following Freud's 1914 study, narcissism was used to denote not only auto-eroticism, but an early stage of psychical development, and the choice of a love object who resembles oneself – past, present or future – in some way (Freud, 1953–74, Vol. 14: 73–102). Freud explicitly linked forms of narcissism with homosexuality, hypochondria and melancholia, whereby a libidinal investment turned inward rather than outward accounted for a morbid withdrawal from the outside world. These elements reappear insistently in tales of twin couples spiralling inwards to self-destruction.

Not twins, but twin-like, are the pale, quasi-identical sister and sickly brother in Cocteau's *Les Enfants terribles* (novel 1925, film 1949), whose intense, tortured relationship is played out in the cluttered single room they shared in childhood, which they recreate in the grand gallery of an eighteen-room mansion. Here Elisabeth's jealous attempts to keep Paul to herself result in their double suicide. The implication of incest is less covert in S. Corinna Bille's short story 'Le noeud' (1974): equally pallid and totally absorbed in one another, the young brother-sister twins drown intertwined in the still waters of the lake. Elliot and Beverly Mantle, the twin brothers of David Cronenberg's film *Dead Ringers* (1988), illustrate perfectly the dangers of the suppression of difference with their regression to infantility and early demise in a claustrophobic, intra-uterine world.[5] And Oswald and Oliver Deuce, the increasingly resemblant twin zoologists in Peter Greenaway's terminally titled film *A Zed and Two Noughts* (1985), become so obsessed with rotting flesh that they set cameras to photograph their own suicide and decomposition. In Marie Redonnet's play *Tir & Lir* (1988), the indistinguishable Mab and Mub, increasingly bedridden, rot in the squalor of their small room, mirroring the death of their twins Tir (after the amputation of his gangrenous legs) and Lir (confined to bed with venereal disease).[6] Marjorie Wallace's biography *The Silent Twins* resonates with its fictional counterparts: June and Jennifer Gibbons are seen to slide from elective mutism and self-imposed physical confinement at home (where they 'rot in their stinking little room with its piles of crumpled paper and bits of half-eaten food,' Wallace, 1986: 77) to indefinite confinement in Broadmoor prison hospital.[7] A 1994 post-script recounts Jennifer's self-predicted death from heart failure at the age of thirty on the day of their release (Farmer, 1996: 275–8; cf. the documentary films of *The Silent Twins*, 1985, 1994).

Over the course of the twentieth century, the twin protagonists of these stories become increasingly indistinguishable: the brother/sister pairs (necessarily fraternal, although portrayed as alike) giving way to identical (and therefore same-sex) twins in the more recent examples. The spectre of incest is raised more insistently with regard to the mixed sex pairs. The story, however, is strikingly similar in both cases: immobility and isolation leading to death and decay as life and blood sap away. This has become the most readily available topos for representing the fate of twins who form a couple. Death here is the 'solution' to a relationship question, not an identity question, and decrees that same and same cannot live and love together. As Jean Perrot suggests, 'the identical, trapped in a reflective relationship, has no future other than that of irremediable destruction (self-devouring)' (1976: 55).

It is perhaps because the topos resonates with pervasive psychoanalytical discourses of narcissism that it can found in virtually all non-comic narrative genres (short stories, plays, films, novels, biographies, documentaries and newspaper articles are cited above) and crosses through Western cultures (French, Swiss, Canadian, British, Anglo-Dutch and Australian writers are represented in this chapter). Clearly this influential topos reinforces traditional taboos in meting out narrative punishment for incest. However the insistence with which it is used – particularly with same-sex twins – in the last quarter of the twentieth century suggests that something more is at stake in portraying the failure of like and like to survive together. This period saw a rethinking of the nature of the couple through, for example, the questioning of traditional (polarised) gender roles and the rise of gay pride. In more abstract discourses, it saw feminist psychoanalysts and philosophers (Irigaray, Cixous) questioning whether the passage from primary narcissism to the symbolic order should be celebrated, and poststructuralist theorists (Derrida, Deleuze) embracing doubleness as the norm and condition of existence rather than as an aberration or threat. The time was ripe to revisit the topos of the twin couple and re-explore models of coupledom. In many cases, and notably those cited above, this exploration ultimately reaffirms the ingrained idea that sameness spells death: differentiate or die! We are led to understand that partners in life must complement not mirror each other.

There are, however, a small number of twin tales that attempt to tell such a story differently, that challenge the scenario to varying degrees. It is to this possibility that I now turn.

I propose to trace the problematic in three novels, and the choice of genre is pertinent. Although, as we have seen, twins are doomed in a range of narrative genres, the particular problem of telling a story of sameness is exacerbated in the novel, for narrative time introduces change and difference. Put simply, things happen – and happen to disturb resemblance. The length of the novel – as opposed to the newspaper column, the short story, or even the feature film – thus increases the difficulty of sustaining a story of a twin couple, making the problem a narrative one as much as a psychological one.

It is significant that arguably the three most renowned twin novels of the later twentieth century, all by major literary figures, explore the relationship between male twins who form a couple. The novels in question are Patrick White's *The Solid Mandala* (1966), Michel Tournier's *Les Météores* (1975, translated as *Gemini*, 1981), and Bruce Chatwin's *On the Black Hill* (1982), and each traces the lives (or life) of twin brothers. With the exception of Mark Twain's *Those Extraordinary Twins* (conjoined but not a couple), *The Solid Mandala* appears to be the first novel of same-sex twins who live out their lives together. Indeed its closest – perhaps the only – antecedent seems to be the Dioscuri legend. And yet, within sixteen years, two more such novels are published by feted authors – Tournier and Chatwin – before the topos is taken up in the auteur cinema examples of *Dead Ringers* and *A Zed and Two Noughts*. Clearly, something about the union of twin brothers has caught the imagination of the times.[8]

The three novels come from different countries (Australia, France, Britain), but I submit that history (their different decades) separates them more than geography. White, Tournier and Chatwin (all three widely travelled) draw on a common pool of cultural material: each of the three explicitly positions his text as a reworking of the Dioscuri myth; White refers extensively to Greek legend and Dostoevsky; and Tournier's novel adapts a multitude of twin legends from the history of Western civilisation.[9] All three thus situate their writing within and against a broader Western literary tradition.[10] And if White's twins are anchored to an outer suburb of Sydney and Chatwin's to an isolated farm in the Welsh hills, while Tournier's chase each other around the globe, all three novels develop parallel thematics of space (confined/outward-looking). The vastly different geographical settings are used to similar purposes.

Although from different national cultures, White, Tournier and Chatwin share a somewhat loose subcultural affinity. It is hardly coincidental that all three novels are written by gay or bisexual men, and that the twins in each case form a same-sex couple. The sexual dimension of the relation between the brothers is explicit in Tournier's novel and alluded to in White's. Chatwin's is coyly non-committal on this point, although the twins share a bed until their death. A version of the story relayed orally was apparently considerably gayer (Clapp, 1997: 198–9), and indeed Chatwin is said to have toyed with 'Mr and Mr Jones' as a possible title, gesturing to a form of same-sex marriage (197).

Although White's autobiography explains that Waldo and Arthur, the twins of *The Solid Mandala*, represent the two halves of himself (1982: 146), issues of identity are overshadowed by the relationship between the brothers, who form one of the 'monumental couples' (Indyk, 2003) that dominate White's novels. Moreover, White identified most clearly with Waldo ('Waldo is myself at my coldest and worst,' White, 1982: 146–7), and at times referred to Manoly Lascaris, his partner for almost fifty years, as a solid mandala, thus associating him with Waldo's twin Arthur.[11] Parallels can thus be drawn between the twinship and the life-long couple formed by White and Lascaris.

Tournier is the most explicit in drawing an analogy between homo-sexuality and twinship. In *Le Vent Paraclet*, he claims provocatively that homosexuality as practised by singletons can only ever be an im-itation of the relation between twins (Tournier, 1977: 254–5), echoing Paul in *Gemini* (1981: 278).[12] Paul's flamboyantly gay uncle Alexandre embodies this view with his fascination with copies and his efforts to dress his lover to resemble himself (1981: 177–9, 239, 298). This view of homosexuality, which collapses same-sex relations into sameness, is vigorously rejected by many working in queer theory, who emphasise diversity both within and between sexual relations of all colours. However the status of sameness in same-sex relations remains an issue. Joseph Bristow, for example, in his introduction to *Sexual Sameness*, stresses the tension between sameness and difference that characterises the politics of gay and lesbian criticism (1992: 1–8). And Leo Bersani, who similarly introduces sameness into the title of his book *Homos*, argues that '[h]omosexual desire is desire for the same from the per-spective of a self already identified as different from itself,' suggesting that it 'presupposes a desiring subject for whom the antagonism between the different and the same no longer exists' (1995: 59–60).

The question of negotiating resemblance within a couple (or a coupling – Bersani in particular is no advocate of the couple) thus has particular resonance in gay studies and queer theory, where the question of sameness arises in a troubled and complex way. Gay studies, however, is a relatively recent field of enquiry, and queer theory even more so. This brings us back to the historical developments (in the form of discursive shifts) that I suggest are more significant than cultural origins in separating the texts.

The possibility of a convergence in the representation of twins and gay couples is historically specific. It relies on an understanding of sameness and difference as mutually entailing rather than opposed, of sameness as a form of difference. This understanding, illustrated by Bersani above, is a far cry from conceptions of homosexuality of eighty years earlier, whereby sexual 'inversion' (a woman's soul in a man's body or vice-versa, cf. Ellis, 1915) produced pseudo-heterosexual same-sex couples in a dialectical synthesis of opposites.[13] Vincent Descombes, in *Le Même et l'autre*, argues that the problematisation of the opposition between sameness and otherness is a defining character-istic of modern French philosophy, and illustrates it with a duplicate title page, showing that in order for two entities to be alike – even exactly alike – they must be other than each other (1979: 7).[14] The influence of poststructuralism in the academy has increased the cur-rency of these ideas: since the 1970s, we have learnt to talk glibly about the split subject for whom the self is partly other; to denounce the nostalgic search for the unified subject in favour of the *différance* between instances of the 'same' self; and to deconstruct oppositions by demonstrating the underlying sameness of contradictory terms. And the rethinking of the relation between sameness and difference has been embraced by postmodern popular culture: the poster for Reitman's film *Twins* (1988) features Danny de Vito and Arnold Schwarzenegger, identically dressed, with the tag-line 'not even their mother can tell them apart.'[15] Thus new discourses have come to rival the dialectical world-view of the advancement of (hi)stories through the resolution of oppositions.

Patrick White's 1966 novel pre-dates poststructuralist and postmod-ern discourses. Tournier's and Chatwin's novels, on the other hand, are contemporaneous with their development and, I suggest, reflect them to some extent. White, Tournier and Chatwin were working with similar narrative materials and referred to a shared tradition of twin tales. However, new ways of conceiving of the couple (and therefore of twinship) became possible – 'thinkable' – in the years separating the novels. For this reason, I shall deal rather briefly and selectively with *The Solid Mandala*, highlighting aspects that relate to the other novels, and reading it as an indication of the narrative solutions to the impasse of narcissism that were possible in 1966. I shall then pick up these threads and trace their development in Tournier's *Gemini*, before concentrating at some length on Chatwin's novel and on its reworking of the material, for *On the Black Hill*, although it reads as the least fanciful of the three, constitutes the most radical rewriting of the narrative fate of twins.

Patrick White: Arthur, Waldo and the marbles

In *The Solid Mandala*, Arthur and Waldo Brown live together, breathe as one (White, 1966: 30, 33, 76), and share a bed until they are in their seventies. Like Castor and Pollux, they are not identical twins, and like Madeline and Roderick Usher, their world eventually implodes. On the one hand, the very fact that they reach old age together already constitutes a considerable challenge to the traditional twin topoï I have described. On the other hand, like the Bloomfields, they hardly epitomise the viable couple. Somehow they have survived, but without ever having had a future. Together with a couple of mangy old dogs, they live their entire lives in Terminus Road in a house that disintegrates around them. And like their street, their life goes nowhere: hand in hand they walk down the road and back again.

But stagnation is not the only threat to their existence. Waldo sees himself as the intelligent, literary one and insists on his difference from his twin, but in fact Arthur mirrors him and shadows him in his pursuits. Waldo feels persecuted by this 'double,' dreams of shaking off his brother, and when he realises that he cannot escape from Arthur, dreams of killing him. He dies while mentally trying to destroy his twin, and his death is a sort of suicidal murder – a hatred that chokes him to death. Even in death, Waldo is 'still attached to Arthur at the wrist' with fingers like 'steel circlets' grasping his brother (295). Distressed that he was unable to prevent Waldo's death by hatred, Arthur flees and Waldo's body rots in the rotting house and is partly eaten by the dogs. He thus succumbs to both of the classic threats to twins: murderous rivalry that turns back upon himself, and decay.

Arthur, on the other hand, transcends these dangers. Arthur is the *idiot savant* whose simple-mindedness betrays a naïve wisdom. Soft and round and loving, he is concerned to maintain twinship, but not as an exclusive or closed relation. He seeks wholeness and oneness with his brother, but a oneness that is much more inclusive than narcissistic unity, a oneness that embraces others, for all his relationships are open, shared. He finds symbols of what he seeks in marbles, which are like solid mandalas, protective circles of fullness and totality (238), microcosms of the world, mystic images of harmony. Arthur has several precious marbles, including one for Waldo and one for himself. The centre of his own is a double spiral that 'knit[s] and unknit[s] so reasonably' (281), like his relation with his brother. Waldo's marble is quite different, with 'a knot at the centre, which made [Arthur] consider palming it off, until, on looking long and close, he discovered the knot was the whole point' (228). In fact, the marble is in the image both of Waldo, 'born with his innards twisted' (32), and of Waldo's relation with Arthur: Waldo, who cannot knit and unknit twinship, who cannot disentangle himself other than destructively.

Arthur wants to share wholeness and fulfilment, even cosmic understanding, with his brother and with others. He sees 'that the knot at the heart of the mandala, at most times so tortuously inwoven, would dissolve, if only temporarily, in light' (273) and finds himself '[o]ffering the knotted mandala. While half sensing that Waldo would never untie the knot' (273).[16] But Waldo refuses Arthur's gift of a marble, and it is as if he rejects the offer to share in his brother's immortality. For we gradually realise that Arthur (who secretly pores over Dostoevsky) figures the divine idiot. Arthur remains after Waldo's death, knowing that he was not intended to die. In a final apotheosis as he is taken to the asylum, he rises God-like, Christ-like, like the red disc of the sun. But unlike Pollux, he is unable to share his divinity with his brother. Despite their longevity, the Brown Brothers are failed Dioscuri.

This is a very partial retelling of *The Solid Mandala*.[17] What I wish to draw from it is a reading of the image that features in the title and its use to suggest a possible way out of the stultifying closure of the twin relation. *The Solid Mandala* is less obviously about sameness than Tournier's and Chatwin's twin novels. Waldo and Arthur are not identical – indeed they are opposites in many ways – and yet they are doubles, like the two halves of the self that White claims they represent. Their relation is dialectical – Arthur strains to achieve the wholeness of synthesis from opposition – and yet their mirroring of one another produces the suffocating narcissistic environment that kills Waldo. The book is not a rethinking of the canonical couple – the union of complementary others – and yet Arthur's gift of the mandala and all it represents will find echoes in the solutions proposed by Tournier and Chatwin to the problem of surviving sameness within a couple. The offer of the marble with its ephemeral knot can be seen as a (thwarted) attempt to maintain the wholeness and unity of twinship (its closure) while at the same time opening it (embracing others, integrating the outside world into its microcosm). This is Arthur's visionary solution to the narcissistic insularity of the twin relation: to make a mandala of it. It fails to save them, however, for it is a solution of cosmic proportions, and Waldo is only too human.

Michel Tournier: Jean-Paul and the elastic bubble

Michel Tournier's *Gemini* reads as a massive thematisation of twinship, quoting and recycling the history of the Western imagination of twins.[18] Its protagonists, Jean and Paul, are so alike that they are collectively called Jean-Paul and the name is conjugated with a singular verb, as if they are indivisible.[19] The 'geminate cell' (Tournier, 1981: 196) of their existence is a biological cell that Jean comes to see as a prison cell. It protects the perfection of their resemblance from differentiation and safeguards their relationship, 'which unites like with like' (198), from otherness. Its closed circle is also represented as a sealed glass bulb (200, 330) and as an egg. Self-sufficient, inflexible and fragile, it isolates them from the rest of the world. Full and heavy like the silence of their perfect communion ('dialogue of silences, not of words' 133), it admits of no story unless it is disturbed.

For within the hermetic cell of this twinship, there is no need for mediation of any kind. There is thus no noise. Following Michel Serres (1982), Ross Chambers describes 'noise' as the 'interference' in the system that prevents perfect and direct communication (1991: 30–1). Noise interferes with the immediate transmission of thought and ideas such that they require interpretation. Noise thus provides a place for the reader, and for storytelling. And as Chambers points out, the noise of communication, its interpretability creates 'room for manoeuvre.' Room for manoeuvre is precisely what is lacking in Jean-Paul's twin cell.

By protecting the twins from differentiation and noise, the cell resists the passage of time. In a full writing out of the narrative problems posed by twinship, we read: 'The geminate cell is the opposite of being, it is the negation of time, of history, of stories' (Tournier, 1981: 196, translation modified, cf. 1975: 274).[20] In its timelessness, it resists not only stories, but life itself: 'There is marble and eternity in ovoid loving, something monotone and unmoving which is like death' (1981: 199).

Clearly, if the embryonic story of this twinship is not to be stifled or *étouffée dans l'oeuf*, then the cell must be prised open. It is shattered by Jean, who becomes engaged and then flees his brother when Paul breaks up the engagement. Jean travels endlessly and without destination, seeking rupture, solitude and otherness, seeking lightness and emptiness after the density and inertia of life with Paul. Each new experience is an attempt to maximise difference from his twin. Paul, however, self-appointed keeper of the cell and indeed his brother's keeper, dreams nostalgically of repairing the cell. To maintain their perfect identity, the sedentary Paul is obliged to pursue. In order to restore resemblance, he tries to experience whatever Jean experiences, but Jean puts a world of difference between them.

The pursuit of one twin by the other resembles to some extent a Derridean *décalage*, a discrepancy, a deferral, a gap of *différance* between two instances of the same (Derrida, 1982: 1–27; cf. Rosello, 1990: 160), and here we see a vivid reflection of the poststructuralist discourses contemporary with the novel. Paul's journey is prompted by dissymmetry: he falls forward into movement when he tries to lean on his absent brother, and the ensuing chase continues to be characterised by this lopsided gait.[21] In fact the brothers were always *différant* in this sense – Jean's clock always chiming just before Paul's (Tournier, 1981: 127), Jean 'irreducibly ahead' of Paul (328) – but the separation in time and space as they race around the world makes it impossible to ignore (cf. Maclean, 2003: 67–8, 85–6). This representation is not, however, ultimately sustained. The conclusion to the novel recuperates *différance* into a synthesis of opposites: the similarity of the twins turns to contrast in order for Paul, still nostalgic for the twin cell, finally to achieve a permanent oneness with his brother.

As Jean travels, he loses weight – even corporeality – to the point where Paul hardly recognises a portrait of him. The twins become increasingly antithetical. Paul finally understands that his dream of repairing the heavy, brittle cell that once enclosed them is impossible, and that the cell must be transformed into something lighter, more elastic, and able to encompass distance. This transformation, however, requires suffering, just as glass becomes pliable only when heated to an unbearable temperature (Tournier, 1981: 309). Such torture occurs when Paul loses an arm and a leg tunnelling under the newly erected Berlin wall. But this mutilation is in fact merely a physical realisation of Paul's existing condition, for Jean's absence was already a metaphoric amputation. Jean meanwhile has completely disappeared and Paul accepts that his brother no longer exists as flesh and bones. Paul's absent limbs, on the other hand, tingle as though they are there, and he realises that this phantom part of his body is in fact Jean, now physically incorporated into him: 'I know it, this left side of mine which moves, wriggles and pushes out prodigious extensions into my room, into the garden and soon perhaps into the sky and sea. It is Jean, now become a part of his identical brother' (447). (Jean-)Paul's limbs are extensible: they stretch out infinitely into the room, the garden, the cosmos. His body starts to resemble an elastic bubble: 'I am in a bubble – which expands and contracts. I am that bubble. Sometimes its outer membrane collapses flaccidly and clings to my body, fitting my own skin, at others it swells out, enveloping the bed and invading the room' (439). Like the mandala in White's novel, the bubble becomes a microcosm of the universe: 'My injuries are the narrow scene within whose confines I must rebuild the universe' (440). At the conclusion of the novel, Paul is no longer suppressing difference and otherness in order to maintain resemblance. Indeed the twins can scarcely be said to resemble each other at all at this stage. Rather Paul embraces a world of difference as his phantom limbs project outwards ever farther, embodying his lost twin and the distance between them. Paradoxically, however, he maintains the nostalgic ideal of wholeness and oneness in the image of the bubble that envelops this projection and thus contains the twinship.[22]

Paul has accomplished what Arthur Brown could not: otherness is absorbed into the twin relation to preserve it and the twins are definitively united. Resemblance has been sacrificed in order to achieve it, but the dialectical synthesis of the two brothers is presented as a triumph. Their unity, however, is no longer of this world. As in the Dioscuri myth, the absent Jean shares his immortality with his earthly brother[23] ... or with what is left of him, for the apotheosis takes a terrible toll. The twins are aged only thirty at the conclusion of the novel, and one is missing, presumed dead, while the other is a double amputee. Only half a body remains from the original two, and while his spirit spreads into the universe, Paul is largely unable to communicate with those who nurse him: 'for a long time now my words and my screams have ceased to reach those around me' (439). Like the original Gemini, Jean-Paul has become a celestial body: the fused couple has no mortal viability. The perils of narcissism may have been side-stepped, but this is no model for flesh and blood survival.

Bruce Chatwin: Lewis, Benjamin and the eggs

It is difficult to appreciate just how unusual Bruce Chatwin's *On the Black Hill* is, for it reads so plausibly. Lewis and Benjamin Jones live together on their Welsh farm, form a couple, and share what had been their parents' bed for forty-two years, until one dies at the age of eighty. The twin relation not only survives, but the twins look to the future. And they live, not in Terminus Road, but at a farm known as 'The Vision.' This story of longevity and of looking forward is not, however, made from radically new materials, but recycles elements with which we are already familiar.

As children, Lewis and Benjamin Jones are identical to the point of being indistinguishable. They share and swap everything, including their names on occasion. They share a secret language and have trouble learning the difference between 'yours' and 'mine.' But living as they do in the world, the twins, like Tournier's Jean-Paul, cannot avoid the slight differences brought about by the passage of time and (hi)story. Benjamin's childhood illness makes him more homey: he bakes cakes, dresses up in his mother's clothes, and becomes his mother's favourite. And being conscripted and tortured as a conscientious objector during the First World War does nothing to make him more outgoing. Lewis, on the other hand, takes an interest in aviation, especially air disasters, and dreams of travel. Like Jean in *Gemini*, he seems to be more oriented towards the outside world than his brother. He has the urge to wander and in particular to wander towards women. And like Paul, Benjamin, the stay-at-home, is devoted to keeping the twins together. Even as children, when Lewis speaks of marrying, Benjamin bursts into tears. As he grows up, Benjamin still wishes to live permanently with his twin.[24]

In adulthood, twinship is threatened in the time-honoured ways. There is the stagnation and sterility entailed in the refusal of otherness: already at the age of twenty-two, Lewis and Benjamin 'behav[e] like crabby old bachelors' (Chatwin, 1982: 131) who have passed directly from childhood to old age. They travel no further than the chapel, and even the local village represents enemy soil: 'Since the day of the peace celebrations, the twins' world had contracted to a few square miles' (131). Although they receive bicycles from their mother for their thirty-first birthday and gradually 'extend[ ] their range' (161), Benjamin in particular mistrusts 'anyone "from off"' (176–7). Rather than venturing into society, they gradually increase the size of the farm: Benjamin and his mother buy land 'as if with each new acre they could push back the frontier of the hostile world' (173). Just as they reject the outside world, they refuse the passage of time: 'Deliberately, as if reaching back to the innocence of early childhood, they turned away from the modern age; and though the neighbours invested in new farm machinery, they persuaded their father not to waste his money' (131). They resist all forms of change: 'time had stood still, here, on the Radnor Hills' (157).

The closure of their relation does not however spare them the anguish of a fratricidal antagonism that turns back upon itself. This antagonism is born of jealousy, but the jealousy is one of possessiveness, rather than of rivalry. When Lewis has to work on another farm, Benjamin pines: 'He hated Lewis for leaving and suspected him of stealing his soul' (99). But the hatred recoils on Benjamin and, in what appears to be an attempt at suicide, he almost dies, which brings Lewis home. Similarly, every time Lewis follows a girl, the possessive Benjamin does his best to disrupt the affair. When Lewis finally loses his virginity, it causes the most severe rupture between the twins. There is a fist fight, and Lewis has to leave, for 'Benjamin's love for Lewis was murderous' (181). Punishing himself, Lewis tries to slash his wrists. In both instances, murderous intent and suicidal attempt are intertwined.

In recycling elements that are common to so many twin stories, it is as if Chatwin is working through a tradition and writing out the problems of the move he is making. It is as if he is telling the story of the difficulty of telling this story. For somehow, the twins manage to deal with these threats and not only survive but ultimately thrive together. At a thanksgiving service at the end of the novel, the chapel is filled with the results of the harvest. We see the culmination of a life that is clearly considered to have been fruitful and profitable. This result has not been easy to come by, but the twins' struggles are obviously all worth it in the end. A future is explicitly attributed to them: at the end of their life, 'they knew that their lives had not been wasted and that time, in its healing circle, had wiped away the pain and the anger, the shame and the sterility, and had broken into the future with the promise of new things' (14). This sentence, which anticipates the story about to be told, makes reference to the dangers to twinship of both anger and sterility. In a sense, the story will be about overcoming these impediments. And if, as we have seen, narrative time threatens the twin relation by introducing change and difference, we are given to understand that it can also resolve these problems. But how? The search for an answer will take us along a circuitous route.

Single egg twins

Chatwin's twins live in a very circumscribed area from which they are loathe to stray, and so it is not surprising to find a recurring image of wholeness, unity and closure to match the Bloomfields' circle, Arthur Brown's marble-mandala and Jean-Paul's cell-bubble. At the beginning of the courtship of the twins' parents, Mary looks up to where Amos points: 'She heard a soft crack and saw a yellow smear on the toe of her boot. "Oh no!" she cried. "Now look what I've done!" Her foot had crushed the nestful of eggs' (Chatwin, 1982: 24). It seems you cannot make a relationship, any more than an omelette, without breaking eggs. Mary breaks out of her solitude, and leaves the isolation of her previous nest. Along with the eggs, she breaks class barriers, prompting the clergyman, when she informs him of her engagement, to spill his breakfast egg down his cassock. Eggs are closed to safeguard their contents, but must not remain so indefinitely or preservation gives way to putrefaction. And eggs are fragile – they are hardly an appropriate image for long-term survival. *On the Black Hill* is full of broken eggs.

A feud develops between 'The Vision' and 'The Rock,' a neighbouring farm. Mary tries to patch up the quarrel when she sees her neighbour, Aggie Watkins, selling eggs in town, but Aggie, full of venom, spits at her. Half crazed, Aggie continues her cry 'Fresh eggs! Fresh eggs!' (75), but when someone stops to buy, she protects her eggs even from this incursion. The eggs remain whole, unsold. The divide between the families continues. Years later, Mary again sees Aggie and her eggs in the street, but this time Aggie is sobbing. Illiterate, she believes the card she has received is news that her son has died in battle. But Mary explains that it's a Standard Field Service Postcard, and that her son Jim is fine. Aggie

> dropped her basket, and the two women flung their arms round each other's necks, and kissed.
> 'Now look what you've done,' Mary said, pointing to the egg-yolks smeared over the shiny wet cobbles.
> 'Eggs!' said Mrs Watkins, disdainfully. (96)

The isolation of whole eggs is scorned, for friendship depends on breaking the shell.

Things are not quite so simple for the twins, however, for whom a relationship with an outsider is not simply a case of coming out of one's own shell, but of breaking the shell that protects the twin relationship from difference:

> The twins' first memory [...] was of the day they were stung by the wasp.
> They were perched on high-chairs at the tea-table. [...] Mary was spooning egg-yolk into Lewis's mouth and Benjamin, in a fit of jealousy, was waving his hands to attract attention when his left hand hit the wasp, and was stung. [...] from then on, they associated eggs with wasps and mistrusted anything yellow. (42)

Whereas their mother enters the egg-and-spoon race at the local fair and keeps bees, the twins mistrust opened eggs and are frightened of being stung. They shy away from relationships and infiltration from outside. When a bossy woman at the fair scrutinises them and finds a tiny mole behind Benjamin's right ear, a mark of difference, the twins bolt in terror.

We could call this time the whole-egg phase of their twinship. It lasts throughout their childhood. They seek to maintain an unmediated, noiseless relation and, in a refusal of otherness, eliminate any third party. As small children, they sacrifice their toy: 'they decided that he, too, had come between them. So the moment Mary's back was turned, they sat him on the bridge, and tipped him in the brook' (44). But this was not just any toy. It was a Humpty Dumpty: in trying to preserve their oneness, they give an image of own inevitable fate – the egg that couldn't be put together again. Then a baby sister arrives, and the twins do not want her either:

> They had pestered their mother to give them a baby sister; and when, at last, she arrived, they climbed up to the bedroom, each carrying a coppery chrysanthemum in an egg-cup full of water. They saw an angry pink creature biting Mary's breast. They dropped their offerings on the floor, and dashed downstairs.
> 'Send her away,' they sobbed. (Chatwin, 1982: 45)

Certainly the twins are jealous: their mother is the only third person with a place in their life, for she initially provides a protective nest for their twinship. Their rejection of Rebecca goes further than this, however. For like the egg-cups that they finally balk at offering her, a relation with their sibling would not simply hold their twinship in place, but would allow its fragile wholeness to be opened up and consumed.

Nonetheless, the twins do not live in a world where eggs can remain whole and timeless, sealed off from the outside. As mortals, their world is one where eggs are and must be broken, a menacing prospect while the twins are caught in the nostalgia for impossible unity, but a fact that they ultimately learn to accept and even turn to their advantage. Before they can achieve this, however, they must pass through a painful and destructive, egg-breaking phase of twoness, in which third parties are no longer excluded by the twins but come between them. For Lewis, a third person is a means of distinguishing himself from his brother, of maximising difference in a way that sets up an antagonistic relation.

The sting and penetration of the wasp are echoed during early adulthood in the hurt Benjamin suffers through Lewis's sexual encounters with outsiders. It is no coincidence that when Lewis flirts, 'the girls egg[ ] him on' (88). At the market one day, Lewis finds himself next to a long-legged woman. 'On her arm was a large wicker basket. A younger man was with her and, when he let fall a couple of eggs, she pushed the sunglasses up on to her forehead and drawled in a gravelly voice, "Darling, don't be so hopeless..."' (173). Joy and Nigel are very much outsiders to the community, bohemian artists who come to rent a farm in the area. Joy is far from worried by the prospect of a few eggs broken, of a new conquest, and indeed takes it upon herself to seduce Lewis. Lewis ignores the yellow warning sign – or is perhaps attracted to it – and loses his virginity. This occasions the previously mentioned rupture between the twins. Mary explains to Lewis: '"You can't come home yet. It's terrible to see your brother in such a state." Benjamin's love for Lewis was murderous. Spring came. [...] It still seemed that Benjamin's anger would never die down' (181).

The twins are only finally brought back together by the death of their mother. This is fitting, for in fact Mary has played a crucial role in triangulating the twinship and ushering in the phase of antagonism. Mary wants both to have grandchildren and to keep the twins for herself. So she perversely encourages the stay-at-home Benjamin to marry and forbids the more outgoing Lewis. The twins compete for Mary's love and she exploits this. Lewis suspects Benjamin and his mother of conspiring against him, and the relation is explicitly described as a triangle 'of son, mother and son' (172). In her fantasy death scene, Mary sees the twins 'standing, symmetrically, on either side of the bed' (156).

From two to three

Mary's death, half-way through the twins' life, marks the beginning of a third stage, and even a stage of threeness, in which third parties cease to be threatening. At first it looks like a return to the first stage of indistinguishable sameness: in the evening following the funeral, Benjamin has laid out two identical nightshirts from among their late father's clothes, and after their bath (and thenceforth every night for the rest of their lives) they sleep together in their parents' bed, '[u]nited at last by the memory of their mother' in a way that they could not be during her life (Chatwin, 1982: 183). When the Second World War arrives, it 'washe[s] over them without disturbing their solitude' (183). Now '[t]heir wrangles were over. They were inseparable now as they had been before Benjamin's childhood illness' (203). However, they do not simply retreat happily into narcissistic isolation. Even were it possible to rebuild their egg-shell, they have no nostalgia for its sterility, for its lack of future. On the contrary, solitude now dismays them.

The sameness that defines them at this stage does not suppress the noise of otherness. In fact the twins now welcome others into their life. Manfred, a German POW, is assigned to work on the farm: 'A third cap in the porch, a third pair of boots, a third place at table – all helped remind them that life had not entirely passed them by' (188). Lotte, a Viennese Jew, similarly comes from far outside their Welsh village, but 'earned her place as the third person in their lives and ended up extracting their most intimate secrets' (192). She persuades Benjamin to let Lewis buy a tractor, introducing time and technology to the farm. The tractor becomes Lewis's woman, another third party (201).

Lotte, who studies twins, tells of how Castor and Pollux 'both popped out of the same egg,' just as Lewis and Benjamin did (192). Popped out, and presumably broke the egg to do so. And by this stage in the novel Lewis and Benjamin have come out of their shell. They are no longer trying to push back the boundaries of the outside world. But even so, they still feel too closed in on themselves:

> The day of their sixtieth birthday was almost a day of mourning.
> Each time they tore a page from the calendar, they had forebodings of a miserable old age. [...] How was it possible, they wondered, that they had come to be alone? (203).

Their solution is to continue to bring others into their life. The most important of these is Kevin. The twins discover that they have a great-nephew, grandson of their sister (who had been expelled from the family home by their father for being pregnant). As children they rejected their baby sister, but they embrace Kevin and paradoxically it is for precisely the same reason: he brings otherness into an otherwise closed relation. He is the source of much happiness, and becomes their heir. Kevin is their future.

But this threesome does not turn into another form of closure. The twins continue to make friendships with others. They find a new friend in Nancy Bickerton, whom Lewis as a child had wanted to marry, now the only survivor of a family of local gentry. There is also Theo, an ex-hippy, a tent-dweller who, although very unlike the conservative Welsh farmers, nonetheless becomes a close third: 'For all their differences, Theo and the twins were devoted to one another' (Chatwin, 1982: 233).

The threesomes formed in this way do not reproduce the triangular relation with the mother that caused antagonism. If thirdness is explicitly what saves the twins from stagnation, they use this otherness very differently from when their mother was alive. Third parties are no longer excluded as dangerous elements that might come between the twins (the first phase), nor are they used to prise apart the twosome (the second phase). Rather, they are accepted as the noise in the system that allows the twins room for manoeuvre, as the noise in their relation that makes them participants in life ('remind[ing] them that life had not entirely passed them by' 188) and opens up their life into a tellable story. What makes the story tellable is what makes the survival of the twin relation possible. Third parties become the means for maintaining the twinship through time, in a way that intersects – but does not coincide – with work by René Girard and Eve Sedgwick.

Girard (1965) and Sedgwick (1985) examine the classic triangle of rivalry between men over a woman. Girard shows not only that mimetic desire gives rise to resemblance between rivals, but also that the antagonism produces an intense bond between them that eclipses their attachment to their common object. Sedgwick goes further to argue that the rivals tend to use the woman, the third term, as an unavowed means of mediating the homosocial relation between the men. Thus the third term, the object of desire, while apparently driving rivals apart, actually serves to bring them together. It is the means of their relation. Siobhan La Piana takes this yet a step further in the direction of *On the Black Hill* when she affirms that twin narratives 'make[ ] transparent the homosocial desire that exists in all such triangles' (1990: 28). Analysing the films *A Zed and Two Noughts* and *Dead Ringers*, she suggests that the rivalry underlying the mediation can be eclipsed by the perfect resemblance of twinship (28).

In *On the Black Hill*, it is as if Lewis and Benjamin (who already start out with resemblance and an intense bond) gradually take these arguments on board and make them work to their advantage by learn-ing to bypass rivalry. At the end of the novel, the third party has ceased to be an object of desire for Lewis (the threesomes are not erotic triangles), and has ceased to be a threat to twinship for Benjamin. Third terms are recognised as the means of survival for their relation. However, the mediation in *On the Black Hill* goes beyond the 'traffic in women' (Rubin, 1975) that characterises patriarchal heterosexuality for Sedgwick, that is to say, 'the use of women as exchangeable, perhaps symbolic, property for the primary purpose of cementing the bonds of men with men' (Sedgwick, 1985: 26). Unlike *Dead Ringers* and *A Zed and Two Noughts*, the novel does not fall into the pattern identified by La Piana whereby the brotherhood of twins is used to 'overpower and objectify women' (1990: 32).

A clue to this important difference is already to be found in Sedgwick's careful word choice: 'cementing.' Patrick White uses this same metaphor in *The Solid Mandala* to make a similar – although ungendered – point about the role of third parties in sustaining relationships. Early in the novel, Mrs Poulter and Mrs Dun discuss the twins on the bus: 'The private lives of other parties act as the cement of friendship. The Brothers Brown could be about to set the friendship of the friends' (White, 1966: 14–15). Cementing indicates that third parties are used – even exploited – in order to fix bonds. However, as we have seen, this is precisely *not* the key to twin sur-vival. As Tournier's *Gemini* warns us, twinship already constitutes a rigid, heavy bond. There is no need to fasten it further, thus con-demning the twins to death by stagnation. Indeed, immobilising bonds could well be the diagnosis of the problem with the threesomes in twin stories of stagnation. Maria-Barbara, Jean-Paul's mother in *Gemini*, rarely stirs from her *chaise longue*. She is the 'maternal plinth' (1981: 261), the stable base for the twins during their youth, ensuring continuity and identity. But in reinforcing the closure and immobility of the twin cell, she also hinders its long-term survival, and the twin-ship ruptures soon after her disappearance. In *A Zed and Two Noughts*, Oliver and Oswald become indistinguishable through their relation with the bedridden Alba, whose legs are both amputated. As La Piana remarks, Alba 'brings the twins together, makes them love each other through her body' (1990: 31). However, this mediation too im-mobilises the twinship, turning it in upon itself, and Alba's death is immediately followed by that of the twins. In these cases, the third term of mediation is used to maintain resemblance by containing otherness within a closed circuit.[25]

The situation is rather different at the conclusion of *On the Black Hill*, where there is no single third cementing sameness, but a series of others. Kevin and the friends of both sexes who represent third parties for Lewis and Benjamin open up the twinship, and expose it to the otherness that can allow it to survive in (narrative) time. The relation of sameness thus passes through a number of detours. The dead end becomes a passage. Sameness and difference have ceased to represent mutually exclusive categories.

This effect is achieved because the mediation in *On the Black Hill* is not an attempt to shore up the circle of twinship. In fact, the proliferation of third parties in Chatwin's novel comes to replace the nostalgic ideals of oneness and completeness. Lewis and Benjamin Jones do not try to put Humpty together again. This contrasts sharply with *The Solid Mandala* and *Gemini*, in which Arthur in one case and Paul in the other seek to repair the rupture of the twin relation by recreating its roundness. In these two texts, twinship is idealised as totality in the microcosms of Arthur's mandala and (Jean-)Paul's bubble.[26] Arthur and Paul strive to include the whole world in their circles. The microcosm spells safety: after all, if everything is inside, there can be no threat from outside, for there is no outside. The dream of wholeness and the desire for closure are thus perpetuated. And through solidity in the one case and elasticity in the other, Arthur's marble and (Jean-)Paul's dilating bubble are enduring, able to defy the vicissitudes of historical time. Unlike these representations of wholeness, those in Chatwin's novel are fleeting. What is closed breaks open. The bubbles in *On the Black Hill* do what bubbles do best: they burst. But then again Chatwin's twins do not aspire to immortality. Their survival is a very mortal one.

Lewis is fascinated by airships, the least solid of aircraft. His scrapbook is full of air disasters, the bursting of these and other bubbles. At the thanksgiving service at the end of the novel, the minister declares: 'Our life is a bubble. We are born. We float upwards. We are carried hither and thither by the breezes. We glitter in the sunshine. Then, all of a sudden, the bubble bursts and we fall to the earth as specks of moisture' (Chatwin, 1982: 246). For the characters in *The Solid Mandala* and *Gemini*, bubbles and baubles that encompass the world without breaking are the solution to the problems of twinship, but at the price of not really belonging to this world. In *On the Black Hill*, life involves breaking eggs and the risk of bubbles bursting.

A high-point, perhaps the culmination of the life of the Welsh twins, is a ten minute joy flight over their farm, a present from Kevin for their eightieth birthday. After Benjamin's initial terror, he is excited to see his land, to recognise a friend waving. Lewis gets to hold the controls, and follows instructions to do a figure-of-eight, then another big loop. 'Not until he had handed back the controls did Lewis realise that he had written the figures eight and zero in the sky' (Chatwin, 1982: 241). These figures of course celebrate the twins' eightieth birthday. However they also put two contiguous loops alongside one big circle: two representations of the twin relation, but no longer competing with each other. Traced in the sky and allowed to fade away, they are neither constraining nor enduring.

> And suddenly he felt – even if the engine failed, even if the plane took a nosedive and their souls flew up to Heaven – that all the frustrations of his cramped and frugal life now counted for nothing, because, for ten magnificent minutes, he had done what he wanted to do. (240)

Lewis Jones manages to fulfil his dream of flying without flying away from his brother. He manages, for a divine moment, to do what had seemed impossible. But these twins come back down to earth. This is not a Dioscuri story of the sharing of immortality. Neither totality nor eternity is offered, just ten minutes of bliss.

The passage of time is emphasised in *On the Black Hill*. More than eighty years are carefully inscribed in the story. Unlike the inalterable twins of the Castor and Pollux clock against which the time of the novel is measured, Lewis and Benjamin are not heavenly twins, but mortal. And the time in which they live not only describes a 'healing circle' but also, like a bubble, 'br[eaks] into the future' (Chatwin, 1982: 14). It seems that the twins' future depends on accepting breakage without nostalgia so that time can 'wipe away' the pains of the past (14). Their survival depends on renouncing closure and learning to manoeuvre through time, difference and noise, through the very stuff of stories.

From the moment of the birth of twins, time introduces *différance* and *décalage* – that tiny discrepancy, gap or time lag – for one twin is always born before the other. Lewis, the first-born, remains a step ahead of his brother, even in death. On the day of Lewis's heart attack, 'Benjamin had rolled up his shirtsleeves and was scouring egg-yolk from the plates. In the stone sink, rings of bacon fat had floated to the surface. He was very excited about Kevin's baby boy' (247). Coping with egg-yolk has become a daily, breakfast occurrence, but the yellowness is still able to herald danger. The rings of fat are prosaic reminders of the circles of time that break into the future, of the bubbles of life that glitter and burst: Lewis's life, Kevin's baby's life. There is a surge of pain in Benjamin's chest and he knows it is Lewis. This is the price of mortal existence, but at a ripe age. Outside, a vapour trail bisects the sky: not the happy fleeting circles of the joy flight, but something tearing the sky apart.

Benjamin too is bisected. At first, after Lewis's death, 'he could hardly even button his shirt-front' (248). He cannot put the two halves together again. Yet he does not pine away or suicide to end the story. One night, he wanders off and is found next morning at the graveyard, gazing at his reflection in the blank half of the newest tombstone. The graveyard becomes his second home. But Benjamin is not pursuing his brother. He is merely continuing to do what he has learnt: maintaining the relation through yet another form of mediation, establishing communication across another interval, through another detour between them. 'He seems to be quite happy as long as he can spend an hour in the graveyard each day' (249).

Telling twins together

New stories are not made from radically new materials. Yarns are spun from existing stuff, the familiar thread twisted anew. A sediment of stories needs to be sifted and shifted, before Chatwin's twins can look to the future in their old age. In the second half of the twentieth century, the narrative tradition of doomed twins is repeatedly negotiated. White's and Tournier's novels put pressure on the tradition, sustaining twinship for some sixty years (White), or for more than 600 pages (Tournier, French edition). But White's twins eventually succumb to stagnation and fratricide, while Tournier's only escape the dangers of narcissism by turning sameness into opposition, and even then the twins' survival is doubtful. Ultimately, the only image of hope they offer is for shared heavenly (rather than earthly) existence through a synthesis of differences.

Chatwin, on the other hand, reworks the story of sameness until it becomes tellable as a story of survival. Lewis and Benjamin Jones confront and conquer the threats that loom over textual twins. This is achieved by reconceptualising the sameness that defines them, such that it no longer excludes difference. The twin pitfalls of stagnation (the suppression of difference in order to maintain a stultifying sameness) and antagonism (a magnification of difference that conceals and denies similarity) are both products of a binary opposition between sameness and difference. And Lewis and Benjamin suffer from both dangers. They learn, however, to integrate difference into the circuit of sameness without short-circuiting. Reflecting poststructuralist and postmodernist critical discourses that challenge a dialectical world-view, their twinship is reconceived as a mediated non-oppositional relation that allows respect for the other within the same.[27] This is what allows Chatwin's twins to survive sameness.

On the Black Hill thus offers an alternative both to narcissistic stalemate and to dialectical opposition as the fate of the same-sex, lookalike couple, and it provides a model for narrating a form of coupledom in which roles need not be clearly differentiated. Perhaps then, there are other, more optimistic stories to be told of the Bloomfield twins, with whom we began this chapter, or indeed of other couples who might identify themselves in terms of shared traits. One of the Bloomfield articles quotes Mal Bennett from their favourite restaurant, one of several people who became 'part of their family' (Russell, 1996). Perhaps he knows enough to tell a story in which the egg – their closed circle of silence and decay – is broken open and made into an omelette.

3
Twins and Sexual Rivalry: Recasting the Wicked Sister in Thriller Films

Isabella Rossellini stars as Rachel Marks, a top West Coast fashion model searching for a more satisfying life. Her journey brings her to the office of therapist Jonathan McEwan (Aidan Quinn), an honest, sensitive and loving man. The two fall in love and all is well until Rachel becomes bored. Then she meets James, Jonathan's identical twin brother. Identical in all but character. James is dangerous, untrustworthy and irresistible. Rachel finds herself torn between the caution and the thrills. As she continues down this difficult road, her life begins to swing completely out of control.

So reads the synopsis on the cover of the video of *Lies of the Twins* (Tim Hunter, 1991). Seen it all before? Well, yes and no. The alternative between the 'good' twin and the 'bad' (between the sensitive and the sensuous, between the homemaker and the homebreaker), the impossibility of telling them apart on occasion, the jealousy that drives one twin to steal the other's partner and makes them rivals to the death in love: these are all familiar to us from films such as:

- *A Stolen Life* (Paul Czinner, 1939)
- *Cobra Woman* (Robert Siodmak, 1944)
- *A Stolen Life* (Curtis Bernhardt, 1946, remake)
- *The Dark Mirror* (Robert Siodmak, 1946)
- *The Guilty* (John Reinhardt, 1947)
- *Dead Ringer* (Paul Henreid, 1964)
- *Twins of Evil* (John Hough, 1971)
- *Sisters* (Brian De Palma, 1973)
- *Dark Mirror* (Richard Lang, 1984, remake for television)

- *Killer in the Mirror* (Frank De Felitta, 1986, remake of *Dead Ringer*)
- *Mirror Images I* (Gregory Hippolyte, 1991)
- *Twin Sisters* (Tom Berry, 1992)
- *Single White Female* (Barbet Schroeder, 1992)
- *Doppelganger: The Evil Within* (Avi Nesher, 1992)
- *Thicker Than Water* (Marc Evans, 1993, for television)
- *Mirror Images II* (Gregory Hippolyte, 1993).[1]

However *Lies of the Twins* is the odd man out in this list, precisely because its twins are men.

What is it about this story that it needs to be told and retold with frantic frequency? To what can we attribute the sudden abundance of these films in the early 1990s? More pointedly, why might we want to tell this familiar story differently? What is involved in transposing the tale to tell a story of *male* twins? What kinds of lies does *Lies of the Twins* expose? This chapter explores the gender asymmetry to be found in popular twin films, and analyses the way in which a particular myth of female sexuality was reworked in the 1990s Hollywood revival of the 1940s twin sister plot. The characteristic division of women into virgins and whores clearly needed updating for a new audience for whom virginity was somewhat less of a prize. Apparently, however, the categorisation was far too powerful to abandon entirely. *Lies of the Twins* is a particularly useful film to study in this light. As a role reversal, it both rehearses and shifts the conventions of female twin films, and in doing so, suggests strategies for rethinking the pernicious dichotomy that pervades them.

Gender in twin films

Statistically, one in approximately eighty births is a twin birth, such that twins represent about 2.5 per cent of the population (Zazzo, 1984: 72).[2] While no precise figures are available for comparison, twins certainly abound in film production, featuring in hundreds of films across a range of genres. While the (frequently mutant) twin wreaks homicidal havoc in horror (*Basket Case I* and *II*, *The Dark Half*, see Chapter 4 below), twins separated at birth team up in action films (*Double Impact*, *Twin Dragons*) and in comedy (*Twins*). The intense relationship between soul-mate twins provides substance for drama (*On the Black Hill*, *The Krays*, *Dominick and Eugene*) and leads to stagnation and decay in art-house films (*Dead Ringers*, *A Zed and Two Noughts*; see Chapter 2). Confusion between lookalike twins is a staple of comedy and a popular device in most other genres, but it is worth noting too the number of films involving non-identical twins (*Twins, Dominick and Eugene, A Zed and Two Noughts*).[3] Recurrent thriller scenarios involve the hunt for the murderer of one's twin (*Jack's Back*, also the action film *Maximum Risk*) and – of most interest to us here – the struggle between good and evil twins (*Take Two, Raising Cain, Lies of the Twins*).

All of the examples just cited are recent films about male twins. This wide range is not found among films featuring other twin pairs. Indeed, the use of twins in film is strongly gendered. Despite comprising over a quarter of twin births, twins of mixed sex are strangely absent from film (exceptions being *The Prince of Tides, This World Then the Fireworks*). On the other hand, there are plenty of twin sister films, but these form a rather homogeneous corpus in comparison to twin brother films. Male twins and female twins are more or less equally represented in number, but not in kind.

Firstly, as far as we can ascertain, *all* twentieth-century female twin films feature identical twins, who (once they are past adolescence) are played by the same actor.[4] And secondly, apart from the occasional comedy of confusion (such as *Big Business*) and the recurrent 'family entertainment' plot of twin girls matchmaking for their parents (*The Parent Trap* and its remakes),[5] the overwhelming majority of these films are thrillers involving deadly rivalry between good and evil twin sisters. Moreover, these sisters are always split along the same predictable line – a version of the virgin/whore dichotomy. In fact, of all the thrillers/ psychological dramas about female twins and doppelgängers available, we found only two where the twins were *not* distinguished to some extent on the basis of their sexual proclivities (*A Kiss Before Dying* and *The Lookalike*).[6] Clearly, the conventions for the filmic use of twins are functions of the interaction of genre and gender.

Evil twin sisters

Female twins and doppelgängers are virtually absent from legend and literary history, even during the Romantic era. In their studies of twins and doubles in myth and literature, René Zazzo (1984: 143) and John Herdman (1991: 14) both comment on the rarity of twin sister stories. Meanwhile the lack of examples in Otto Rank's study speaks for itself: the medieval 'Le Lai du frêne' is the only one mentioned, and then in a section that only appears in the French edition (1973: 100). Robert Rogers, on the other hand, identifies a tradition of 'good angel/bad angel' pairs of female characters in nineteenth-century literature (1970: 29). Although these are not twins,[7] they clearly pave the way for the filmic representation of good and bad twin sisters.

For twin sisters have become standard fare in twentieth-century film. There are two privileged moments of this phenomenon: the 1940s woman's film and, following a couple of 1980s remakes of the earlier films, 1990s thrillers. Most of these stories involve a contest between a good and an evil twin – or more simply the 'good girl' and the 'bad girl' – and the problems of telling them apart. One particularity of female twin films is the frequency with which the bad girl steals her sister's husband. Indeed, this is often her primary aim.

Lucy Fischer analyses three woman's films from the 1940s (*Cobra Woman*, *A Stolen Life* and *The Dark Mirror*) in which female twins are 'rivals for the affections of an eligible man' (1989: 178). In these films, the 'good girl' is passive, self-sacrificing, sweet, demure and truthful, while the 'bad girl' is a *femme fatale* – sexy, deceptive, competitive and bold. A further dimension of either insanity or supernatural evil often adds to the bad twin's wickedness. As Fischer remarks, 'the good and bad twins in the films seem like nothing so much as dichotomised male projections of opposing views of the Eternal Feminine' (191), that is to say, the traditional dichotomy of the virgin and the whore. The dénouement of these films (the evil twin dies and the good twin gets back her man) reinforces the idea that good girls are preferred by men in the long run, and that modesty and virtue are desirable attributes.[8]

Fischer's essay concludes with a study of two films that resist this tradition: the experimental *The Bad Sister* (Laura Mulvey and Peter Wollen, 1983) which valorises the point of view of the rebellious bad sister, and *Sisters or The Balance of Happiness* (Margarethe von Trotta, 1979) which questions the division of roles and argues instead for their synthesis. Elsewhere, Fischer also suggests that *Desperately Seeking Susan* (Susan Seidelman, 1985) functions as a rewrite of the canonical good girl/bad girl dichotomy of the 1940s twin dramas (Fischer, 1990). A comedy of confusion rather than a thriller involving deadly rivalry, *Desperately Seeking Susan* shows good girl Roberta finding her desiring self and a desirable male by playing the part of her bad girl double, Susan. Rather than representing the good girl's reward, the wayward husband is ditched. Sisterhood prevails. Typical of comedies of confusion (from the Shakespearian comedies to recent popular twin films such as *Big Business*) is the film's resolution whereby neither twin dies and identities are re-established and stabilised by each twin having her own partner. *Desperately Seeking Susan's* twist on the tale is that Roberta and Susan were not doubles/twins to begin with.[9] In fact, none of the three recent films studied by Fischer involves twins, but Fischer makes her point about the possibility of telling sister stories and good girl/bad girl narratives differently.

However, soon after the time of Fischer's writing, which coincided with a couple of remakes of earlier wicked twin sister films, a whole new crop of female twin films emerged. To the set of films listed at the beginning of the chapter, which includes only films where the twins are in conflict over the same man, we could add *Double Vision* (1992) and *Double Edge* (1992), making a total of eight good girl/bad girl twin films from 1991 to 1993 including five in 1992 alone. These films are all thrillers of one kind or another: *Doppelganger* leans towards the horror genre; *Mirror Images I* and *II* fall clearly into the porn category. They are far from experimental and, unlike Fischer's choices, are all directed by men. However, almost all these films follow *Desperately Seeking Susan*'s lead in suggesting that something is missing from the good girl's life.[10] That the good girl/bad girl narrative should have been reiterated so frequently at this time clearly indicates that this important cultural myth needed reworking for a 1990s audience.

Revamping the ideal woman

The 1990s thrillers invariably begin by reproducing the traditional dichotomy of the virgin and the whore, most frequently in the form of a faithful but frigid, frilly wife and a sexually insatiable call-girl cum deadly killer, (un)dressed in slinky black. (Both twins almost always have a father fixation). However, unlike the 1940s films, the 1990s films do not conclude with a simple triumph of virtue. Rather than virtue being rewarded, the virtuous twin's disinterest in sex needs to be cured. The elimination of the bad sister is not enough. The good girl needs to realise that she is only half a woman. In order to become whole, her repressed sexuality must be assumed. She must become a synthesis of the two twins, combining moral rectitude with a sexual appetite. In a number of films (*Twin Sisters, Mirror Images I* and *II*, *Double Vision*), this is achieved by playing the role of her sister and pretending (at the very least) to be a prostitute. It seems you can never tell when your sweet wife will start playing the whore. But is it possible for a wife to assume the sexiness of her hooker twin without also acquiring her deadliness? Perhaps not: husbands seduced by the wicked sister tend to be appropriately punished in the 1990s films, as the new whole woman emerges from the wifely twin. There is sometimes even an element of doubt over the identity of the surviving sister, and the suggestion is made that now that the two halves are one, it hardly matters which twin remains. The frisson of danger lingers around the now sexy (ex-)wife, who could easily revert to the stiletto-heeled, hairpin- or knife-wielding castrating whore.[11]

One could be tempted to see the image of this new synthesised woman as an improvement on the ideal woman of the 1940s.[12] It would, however, be an error to regard these films as in any way rejecting or going beyond the virgin/whore dichotomy. On the contrary, they still seem to be prompted by the problem identified by Freud in 'A special type of choice of object made by men' (Freud, 1953–74 Vol. 11: 163–76), that of reconciling the tension between maternal and erotic images of woman, the same problem that Wolfenstein and Leites considered pervasive in film in 1950:

> The difficulty of choosing between a good and a bad girl is one of the major problems of love-life in western culture. The problem is to fuse two feelings which men have found it hard to have in relation to the same woman. On the one hand, there are sexual impulses, which a man may feel to be bad, and which he may find it hard to associate with a woman whom he considers admirable. The image, and the actuality, of the 'bad' woman arises to satisfy sexual impulses which men feel to be degrading. On the other hand, there are affectionate impulses evoked by women who resemble the man's mother or sister, 'good' women. A good girl is the sort that a man should marry, but she has the disadvantage of not being sexually stimulating.
>
> There are various possible solutions to this conflict. The attempt may be made to satisfy one of these impulses at the expense of the other, to satisfy them both but in different directions, or to combine the two impulses in a single relationship (1950: 25–6).

Both the 1940s and the 1990s female twin films can be seen as attempts to solve the same conflict, opting respectively for the first and the third of the solutions mentioned.

Wicked twin brothers

By contrast, in films about male twins, the good twin/bad twin dichotomy is configured quite differently. Rather than the virgin and the whore, male twins tend to be distinguished on the basis of attributes such as lawfulness, altruism, family values, worldliness and physical prowess. *Jack's Back*, for example, contrasts an altruistic, civic-minded medical student with his ex-marine twin who has a vaguely specified criminal past and is familiar with the underworld of petty crime. *Steal Big Steal Little* pitches compassionate, family-oriented Ruben against his corrupt and greedy twin Robby. *Maximum Risk* involves an honest cop/gangster pair. In *The Dark Half*, a family man must prevent his sadistic, boozing alter ego (the psychic vestige of his unborn twin) from committing further murders. And in *Raising Cain*, a respected psychologist, loving husband and devoted father adopts one of his multiple personalities – an aggressive, violent 'twin' – to murder women and steal their children. The hustler is a favourite bad boy figure: in action films he is a kickboxer contrasted with either a concert pianist (*Twin Dragons*) or an aerobics instructor (*Double Impact*). In *Twins*, a decidedly unathletic small-time hustler teams up with his genetically perfect twin: strong and true but hopelessly naive. Even in *Dead Ringers*, where the twins are much less clearly delineated, they are still distinguished along similar lines: Elliot's worldliness (both in attaining professional prestige and in finding bedfellows) is juxtaposed with Bev's altruistic commitment to research. Sexual shyness occasionally comes into the equation, as in *Dead Ringers*, where it does not dominate, or in *Equinox* in which a Mafia underling brushes with his excruciatingly timid twin, who, as is often the case with antithetical female twins, is sexually fearful.[13] However, in general, the dichotomy between male twins does not oppose sexual appetite to sexual inhibition, innocence or circumspection. The contrast between the family man and his evil twin (as in *The Dark Half* and *Raising Cain*) is more likely to be made on the basis of violence than of sexual behaviour.

Although we can distinguish a good twin and a bad twin in these films, the bad boy is frequently not so much wicked as just a little wayward. Furthermore, in many of these films, the twin relation is not predominantly one of rivalry, but involves a large element of cooperation. Certainly this is the case in the comedies and action films (*Twins, Twin Dragons, Double Impact*), but is also true of thrillers and horror films like *Jack's Back, Basket Case* and *Dead Ringers*. The deadly antagonism between good and evil twins, omnipresent in female twin films, is not the only scenario among the lads: brotherhood frequently triumphs.[14] Meanwhile sisterhood among filmic twins is virtually absent. And where there *is* mortal combat between brothers, it is very rare to find it shaped as competition over a love interest.[15] In sharp contrast to the number of female twin films rehearsing this story, there are very few examples among recent male twin films. There is *Take Two*, but in this film it is the *good* twin who falls for his brother's wife and attempts to save her from him.[16] There is *Dead Ringers*, but from the start Elliot's desire to share Claire with Bev is never a contest for her love but an attempt to preserve a symbiotic twin relation based on the identity of their experiences, and his death is not the result of a fratricidal struggle.

And then there is *Lies of the Twins*. In this male twin film, the brothers are distinguished as much by their attitude to sex as by their altruism: the bad boy steals his brother's de facto; and the twins fight to the death to possess her. *Lies of the Twins* is thus highly unusual among male twin films, but reworks all the classic elements of female twin films.

Erotic triangles

Of course, this is not to say that men are never rivals in love. Indeed René Girard's *Deceit, Desire and the Novel* and Eve Sedgwick's *Between Men* examine celebrated literary examples of such triangles. Another famous literary case to which we will have occasion to return is Tolstoy's *Anna Karenina*. When Anna leaves her husband for lover Vronsky, she is shunned by society and forbidden from seeing her son. Sleepless with unhappiness, she turns to opium before finally throwing herself under a train. *Brief Encounter*, *Dr. Zhivago* and *From Here to Eternity* are examples of classic films showing a woman torn between two men, between husband and lover, duty and delight. However, the male rivals in love are rarely represented as brothers, let alone twins. In fact, Girard and Sedgwick show the extent to which the (increasing) resemblance between the rivals is dissimulated in such texts. On the other hand, as we have seen, rival women are regularly portrayed as virtually indistinguishable: as twins, they are hard to tell apart, and can be mistaken for one another.

This is a significant difference, for whereas the man over whom the female twins tussle has a perfect excuse for his infidelity – he was seduced by a woman who was the spitting image of his wife – the female object of male rivalry has no such justification. Female twin rivals provide their man with an improvement on the excuse of being led astray by the temptress: he can hardly be blamed if the siren he beds looks exactly like his wife, if indeed she seems to be merely the dark side of his enigmatic woman. Women, however, have no excuse for waywardness, and cannot simply be tricked in this way into infidelity. Instead they are faced with clear-cut moral choices, the consequences of which are fully understood. For women in this position, there must be no ambiguity in the distinction between virtuous sobriety and sinful pleasure, no hint that husband and lover are in a sense the same man in a different light. Anna Karenina has no-one to blame but herself.

Lies of the Twins: a role reversal

It is against this background of films and other narratives that we propose to read *Lies of the Twins*. This is a film that reproduces the idiom of twin films but does so in a way that reads against the standard stories of male and female twins and rivals. Most obviously, this appears as a gender reversal: like so many twin sister films, this is a story about jealous rivalry over a love interest, but here the twins are brothers. However, the film also points to competing strategies for the interpretation of twins and, by extension, twin films: strategies we might call psychological and discursive.

Jonathan and James McEwan are identical twin psychiatrists, both played by Aidan Quinn. They cannot be distinguished physically, although close attention reveals that James wears a gold ring most of the time. Jonathan is devoted to his job, donating his services one day a week at a public clinic, and ready to make sacrifices in his personal life and even to interrupt romantic evenings to be available to his patients. Rachel has difficulty in dragging him away not only from his patients but from his lecturing and research for a night of sex and romance. James, on the other hand, is keen to take time off in the middle of the day for sex with Rachel and is interested in variations on standard routines: sex on the car bonnet under the flight path near the airport; anal sex in a seedy downtown hotel. His interest in his profession is said to consist primarily in 'act[ing] out his own manipulative fantasies with clients,' and we certainly see a sadistic side to him in his dealings with Rachel. And unlike the monogamous Jonathan, James has an unspecified number of girlfriends. Although James is self-seeking and somewhat violent in contrast with Jonathan's altruism and equanimity, interest in sex seems to be the main basis for distinguishing between the twins. The dichotomy between virtue and debauchery as represented by Jonathan and James is probably as close as we are likely to get to a male equivalent of the virtuous wife and the whore.

Does this indicate a split in the male psyche, as psychoanalytical interpretations of the double often suggest?[17] Or are the twins evidence of a female split, and conjured forth by Rachel's conflicting desires for stability and excitement?[18] Above all, we would argue that they represent a rewrite: a quotation and displacement of a familiar duality. For Jonathan and James are not the only pair of characters in the film. Equally important is the relation between the two fashion models, Rachel (Isabella Rossellini) and Elle (played by Iman). And the close-ups that sweep up Rachel's body to her face, the prominence of sequences involving modelling shoots and the obtrusive sound of cameras clicking on the soundtrack all draw attention to the fact that, in an important sense, this is a film about images of women.

The film's opening sequence shows the two women engaged in a poolside conversation about Rachel's new romantic interest, Jonathan. The conversation ends with Elle's question 'When do you move in?' to which Rachel replies, 'As soon as he asks.' Cut to a garden wedding scene. The very pale Rachel is a traditional bride all in white, the white flowers in her hair adding to the virginal look. She smiles in the direction of Jonathan entering the garden from her right. Enter from left, on the same axis as Jonathan, Elle, whose name is a third person pronoun – the archetypal other woman. Elle is black and dressed in black. Jonathan and Elle both stride toward centre. But this is not Jonathan and Rachel's wedding (they do not marry, but rather live together) and Elle is not the evil twin ready to pounce on the unsuspecting husband. Rachel is at work, modelling, and this is a shoot. And Elle and Jonathan do not confront each other but each meet and have a conversation with Gil, the women's agent. The filmic conventions of black and white clothing to denote and distinguish good and evil characters, which date back to the hats in westerns, are regularly reproduced in female twin films.[19] Here, however, they are quoted and displaced. They work in this film as a kind of 'not-statement' (Freadman, 1988): this is *not* a good girl/bad girl film; it positions itself in relation to and against such films. Elle is never a rival but a friend, and far from playing the 'bad girl,' advises Rachel to play it safe. Rachel and Elle, as *not* good/bad girl twins, are the foil against which we understand Jonathan and James.

In this film then, the other woman is not an enemy to eliminate. In fact, she is a supportive listener. And not only does *Lies of the Twins* open with a tête-à-tête between Rachel and Elle, but the final conversation in the film is another exchange between the same women on the same subject. This framing shows us the storytelling situation: this is a story told by a woman to a woman. It is a woman's story, possibly a feminist one.[20]

Ross Chambers, in *Story and Situation* and *Room for Maneuver*, shows how a story can figure its own reading. Elle, as listener, as addressee of the story, is one such figure for reading, although, as we shall see, not the only one. Her feedback to Rachel shows that she, like the rest of us, is familiar with twin stories. She knows how they tend to end. Thus she advises caution regarding bad boy James ('You stay away from James'), is aware that psychiatrists often turn out to be mad doctors ('Maybe he [Jonathan] needs a psychiatrist'), and affirms that the ideal is now a synthesis of sweetness and sexiness when she quips, 'Maybe these days it takes two of them to make one real man.' Elle even nudges the action on to a classic dénouement by providing Rachel with its means: the gun with which one twin will kill the other. She figures our expectations. And when the ending veers away from the predictable pattern, she's as delighted for Rachel as we are (we, the authors of this chapter, at any rate).

Rachel turns to Elle for advice when she is faced with the choice between the stability of Jonathan and the excitement of James. All else is equal. Torn between a good boy and a bad boy that you can hardly tell apart, what's a girl to do? Before she can decide, Rachel must discover the secret of the twins' estrangement, a secret called Sandra Shearer – the name of a woman, and the name of a story. Finally, Sandra's mother recounts this story of crime and punishment to Rachel. Ten years earlier, Sandra had been in a similar predicament to Rachel's. As Jonathan's fiancée, she was seduced by James. When Jonathan could not forgive her, she attempted suicide. Now a living vegetable, the only reminder of her former attractiveness is her black hair – cut into a fringed bob identical to Rachel's.

Clearly, turning the tables such that the virgin/whore dichotomy is for once applied to men is not sufficient to remove the labels from women. Even when transposed on to men, the virgin/whore opposition is reflected back on to female characters. Thus in the Sandra Shearer story, it is not the bad boy but the woman who is punished for adultery. Just because here the men are divided into faithful fiancé and philanderer doesn't mean that the woman can escape the good girl/bad girl routine.

Sandra Shearer may be the twins' secret, but variants of the story are well known under other names. When Rachel seems to be following this script, losing sleep over the dilemma of choosing between the twins, Gil, her agent, recognises it instantly: 'Enough of this Anna Karenina!' Gil is the other important figure for reading (in) the film, and through this exclamation he offers Rachel some very helpful advice: pick another story, play another role – which ultimately Rachel does. Gil as reader invites comparison with the traditional figure of the doctor in the woman's film. In the garden wedding shoot at the beginning of the film, he provides Jonathan with a job description: as an agent for fashion models, he becomes 'their father, their friend, their confessor, their confidant.' As Jonathan notes, in some ways he is like a doctor or psychiatrist, but with very beautiful clients. Gil's reply puts Jonathan back in the patient position – 'Sometimes beautiful women attract the wrong kind of men, don't you think?' – and from the start the two professions are seen to be in competition. Later, Gil will say to Rachel: 'I know he's a shrink but .... if you have a problem, you come to me, alright?'

According to Mary Ann Doane, the doctor is the traditional figure for reading woman in the woman's film. Moreover, in female twin films, because the twins are identical, 'a psychiatrist is needed to *see through* the surface exterior to the interior truths of the two sisters' (Doane, 1984: 74).[21] In other words, the doctor is the one who is able to diagnose the good or evil lurking deep beneath the deceptive sameness of the twins' appearance. In *Lies of the Twins*, however, it is the doctor twins who need to be deciphered and diagnosed. James nonetheless continues to speak from a position of presumed authority, and alludes to the hidden truth of the subject with comments such as 'In sex we become our true selves,' even locating Rachel's beauty at a level beneath the skin ('Your true talent is bone structure'). Meanwhile, in a *mise en abyme* of our interpretative situation, Gil presents a theory of reading that cuts across the doctor's to engage with the specificity of film. Gil's way of reading stands in neat contrast to a psychoanalytical X-ray vision of truth: 'I only know the surface, just what I can see. [...] I deal with surfaces every hour. And you can look at a surface and tell a great deal. And after all, that's what we have to look at, isn't it?' Rather than deep feelings or expressions of true selves, Gil sees the 'transparency of emotion in your face.' Whereas the medical practice of reading requires arcane knowledge and uses institutional authority to deliver weight to its pronouncements on hidden truths of character, Gil's reading practice, whereby he looks carefully at the images before him, is available to all. In particular, it is available to film-viewers who, like Gil with his photographic images, have only the surface of the screen to look at. And it is available to Rachel. This point in the film marks the low point in her career – the twins are interfering with her work to the point where she is stood down from modelling until she sorts herself out – but Gil's comments also mark a turning point in that they provide Rachel with the means to read and solve her problem. For as we shall see, it is by no longer seeking invisible inner truth but by focusing on the surface as Gil does – by focusing on the identical appearance of the twins – that Rachel extricates herself from her predicament.

In fact, the importance of surfaces and images and their relation to truth has been in play throughout the film and is merely made explicit by Gil's theory of reading. The very first shots in the opening sequence show Elle in the limpid waters of the swimming pool, in which depth is not hidden but transparently clear. Only a slight refraction – a quirk of light – distinguishes surface and depth. Beside the pool, anchored by bowls of fruit, is an assortment of glossy magazine covers featuring the models. The camera lingers on these and then on the two models, languishing poolside, in such a way that the images on screen appear as further posed shots, continuous with the cover photos and still lifes. At regular intervals during the film we see the models at work, posing, quoting the clichés of twin films in a distancing and even parodic way. Thus Rachel at different moments portrays both the schoolmistress and the leather-clad bikie. And counterbalancing the wedding shoot, Rachel is all in black with the car and motorbike while Elle is a blonde in a silver jacket. Good girl and bad girl roles and images are equally available to be assumed by the same woman on different occasions. Rather than evidence of a deep psychical split between dark desires and innocence, the choice of costume represents culturally determined discursive possibilities.[22] And if Gil remarks to Rachel, 'That girl's not you, she's an image,' there is no suggestion that a 'real you' exists or what it might be, for what we have – 'all' we have – are images, surfaces. Thus, even when the models are not at work – reclining around the pool, taking in the art exhibition, Rachel lying on the psychiatrist's couch although she was told it wasn't necessary – their stylised bodily attitudes present us with yet more poses.

Even James reinforces this idea at one point. After her first experience of anal sex, Rachel says, 'I feel like I've dissolved; I feel that there isn't any me any more,' to which James replies, 'Where did you get the idea there was any you to begin with?' If, as he stated earlier, we become our true selves in sex, then the truth of the self is that there is no self.

Through juxtaposing sequences from Rachel's professional and personal lives, the film shows the circular relation between images and identity. In one instance, good boy Jonathan's comment 'I like sexy schoolteachers' is taken up in the shoot of Rachel as pert schoolmistress with adoring pupils: that is to say, Jonathan's sexual fantasy is seen to prompt the image. However, images are equally cues for sexual behaviour. Thus Rachel's languorous modelling on the car and motorbike is a rehearsal for bad boy James' seduction on the car bonnet. Clearly images, fantasies and behaviour, Rachel's modelling and 'real life' are not essentially different, but feed into each other and work together in elaborating and maintaining identities.[23] Like Rachel, Jonathan and James are not making up the script as they go along but are participating in available scenarios. And Rachel shows that she is equally capable of playing leading roles in a number of dramas. The parallels between Rachel's modelling and her relations with the twins show that we cannot look through deceptive poses to see the real person, but rather that Rachel's character is as much a textual surface as her magazine spreads are.

Rachel thus blurs the divide between image and reality, between surface and depth, between lies and truth, in favour of a discursive understanding of the self. And her disturbance of classic dichotomies extends to that between beauty and brains. Rachel is no bimbo: she knows her Voltaire, uses Latin expressions and shows a knowledge of foreign languages (and there too, clear divides are not maintained: JONATHAN. – 'So you speak five languages?' RACHEL. – 'I mix different languages'). She is moving into the business side of modelling, undertakes library research on twin phenomena, and quotes Dr Gail Minor's 'postfeminist' book back to its author.

The latter exchange is a revealing one. Firstly, Dr Minor shows that she has a script all worked out for Rachel's life. Rachel refuses it, but having no readily available substitute story, can only do so rather tersely:

> DR MINOR—A model?
> JONATHAN—Well not for long.
> DR MINOR—Are you taking courses or are you planning another career?
> RACHEL—No.

Rachel, however, retaliates with her own recognition of a role. Dr Minor's catty dismissal of modelling as a serious career for a woman while she fawns on Jonathan invites the following reading:

> RACHEL—Do you know what I like best about your book? It's when you talk about the need for we older women to accept ourselves and

not fall into what I think you call the pathetic trap of constant
flirtation in order to gain reassurance of our desirability.

Dr Minor, in falling into this 'pathetic trap,' is acting out a common
story. The fact that she has identified it and analysed its power does
not protect her from rehearsing it. Rachel complains to Jonathan:
'They don't think what I do is real. They talk to me like I'm a pet.' The
film makes the point that the role-play involved in modelling is no less
real and no less scripted than the everyday role-play we all engage in as
we participate in stories that shape our lives. As for being a pet, well
pets need not be servile – Rachel's next shoot has her modelling with a
tiger.

If Rachel dismantles oppositions, James has a stake in maintaining
them. After all, he has a big investment in the good twin/bad twin scenario. His explanation of the twin relation aims to distinguish clearly
between the brothers. But while insisting on their profound psychological difference, he shows Rachel photos that do nothing to support his
argument. He has to point himself out: 'I'm on the left, always. See,
there's always one dominant twin, Rachel, usually the first born. [...]
The problem for Jonathan is that we're not identical.'[24] On the other
hand, the problem for Rachel (and for the viewer) is that they are
indeed identical: 'He called and he said, "It's Jonathan." It was his sick
idea of a joke. For a moment, I did not know. I really did not know.'

James argues for a fixed polarity for each twin: dominant/weak,
exciting/predictable. Clear binaries such as these make for clear-cut
choices and James seeks to persuade Rachel that she is free to make
an informed choice between dating him and settling for Jonathan.
To some extent, this is to present Rachel with the Anna Karenina
dilemma: women must make fully conscious choices and pay dearly
for them. However *Lies of the Twins* does more than put Rachel in a
position to choose: it re-examines the whole notion of choice. Thus
James' insistence on Rachel's control of her destiny is coupled with an
attempt at seduction that undermines it: 'You're a free agent, you're
free to go, you're free to stay, in fact you're free tonight, aren't you?'
Rachel's free choice is even less obvious when James declares imperi-
ously 'I'll decide when it's over.' Later, when Rachel refuses to see him,
he makes the dubious assertion that 'Nothing will happen to you that
isn't an expression of your own desire.' The psychiatrist's supposedly
superior insight into Rachel's deep desires tells him that 'no' really
means 'yes.' While insisting that Rachel is free to choose, James claims
to know what she wants better than she does.

In female twin films, men tend not to find themselves in Rachel's situation. They tend not to be told that they are in a position to make a well-informed choice. Indeed they are usually able to avoid this predicament by proposing the classic male excuse for infidelity – being duped and seduced by the evil temptress. The plea is made all the more plausible through the twins' resemblance: the siren transformed herself into the image of their wife. Because *Lies of the Twins* reverses gender in retelling this familiar twin story, Rachel tries to take this line. After all, James impersonated Jonathan on a couple of occasions and sent flowers with merely his initial to indicate the donor. But while the Bette Davis characters from earlier films are prepared to swallow this excuse from unfaithful husbands, it won't wash with James. He shows a sudden concern to make an honest woman of Rachel:

> RACHEL—You tricked me into hurting him enough already.
> JAMES—How could I trick you? When you knew who I was already. You just can't be honest with yourself, can you?

Although Rachel is aware of which twin she is having sex with (in moments of passion, she calls out the appropriate name), she has a more subtle understanding of her capacity for free choice in this situation: 'You know, it's like a drug. You know it's going to kill you but you see it laid out there and you find yourself going toward it as if you had no will. And I hate him then, I really do.' She tries to resist, with some success:

> ELLE—How long has it been now?
> RACHEL—Since you left. Three weeks and he hasn't called.
> ELLE—How about calling him?
> RACHEL—I fight it and I'm getting stronger every day.

But, like Anna Karenina on morphine, Rachel gets hooked on James. It starts interfering with her professional life: turning up for work with dark rings under her eyes, she is asked, 'Do you think we're shooting a spot for a rehab centre?'

The drug metaphor exposes not only the dynamics of freedom and enslavement but the fact that James is a bad habit. And habits – whether drugs or discourses – are persistent. Even Gil's helpful advice 'Enough of this Anna Karenina' is followed by 'Take a pill if you have to, but sleep!' which was of course precisely how Tolstoy's leading lady tried to fix her insomnia. Anna Karenina is obviously a hard discursive habit to kick. Gil's solution is at best a methadone programme. The substitute story he suggests still involves dependency. His words about surfaces, on the other hand, are more empowering, as we shall see.

Rachel decides to level with both twins, and then leave town. Having been threatened by James, she packs a gun. Arriving at James' office, she is confronted by both twins, both claiming to be Jonathan. For the first time, all three characters are together. The triangle is clear: the symmetry of the split screen with one twin on each side (Figure 3.1) and the reverse shots of Rachel establish its three points. From the twins' point of view, all Rachel has to do is to choose the real Jonathan. But the scene is shot primarily from Rachel's point of view as she swings her head, looking from one twin to the other, and neither she, nor we, can tell them apart. We do not see James' gold ring in this scene or for the rest of the film. Wonderful of course to be in the position of choice – and with such a wide range to choose from! The joke is on us as we try in vain to distinguish Aidan Quinn from Aidan Quinn.

Figure 3.1 Aidan Quinn plays Jonathan and James McEwan in *Lies of the Twins*
Source: © 1991 Universal Studios All Rights Reserved

But aided by Gil's theory of reading – what you see is what you get – Rachel looks at the surface rather than probing it for the hidden truth of good and evil. She sees what the camera sees, what we see: 'Stop. I don't care who you are. I don't love either of you. You're the same person in a different light. You can't love anybody but each other. I was just a mirror between you.'

The unstated basis of female twin films – indeed of the virgin/whore dichotomy more generally – is the fact that, in Lucy Fischer's words, 'the same woman can be regarded in contradictory ways' (1989: 190). But unlike the majority of female twin films, *Lies of the Twins* is refreshingly upfront in exposing the sameness of its antithetical twins. In turning the discourse around to focus on male twins, *Lies of the Twins* draws attention to the transparent truth that the twins are the same. The obvious fact that we are usually seduced into forgetting is that good boy and bad boy are played by the same actor, just as Rachel plays good and bad girls for the camera. And just as Rachel's photographic images reflect different fantasies, so the twins are 'the same person in a different light.'

As for 'You can't love anybody but each other,' Rachel understands as clearly as Eve Sedgwick that the seemingly enviable situation of being courted by two rivals leaves her only a supporting role in a drama being played out *between men*. She is merely an object of exchange used to mediate the competitive twin relation. Any doubt as to the accuracy of Rachel's reading is put to rest when the twins violently shove her aside to grapple with each other. If Rachel will not choose, they will sort it out between themselves and make the choice for her. There's a shot. Rachel blacks out. When she comes round, one twin is dead and one is left. He says he's Jonathan and adds: 'It's just me now.' Rachel need only accept him as the winner of a contest in which she is the prize. Lingering doubts about the true identity of 'Jonathan' – James may still be lurking under that face – could only pep up the relationship.

But the teasing uncertainty of this nonetheless predictable ending doesn't tempt Rachel. She doesn't fall for the line 'It's just me now.' There are plenty of others. The binary choice that the twins sought to impose was never the only game in town. She explains to Elle that she's off to Europe for work, earning pots of money.

RACHEL—I couldn't go back. In a way I loved them both, especially Jonathan, but I really didn't know them, until the end and then it was too late. They could never get free of each other.

ELLE—Men!
RACHEL—Jonathan spoke about the great souls and James only liked the gutter. In the end...
ELLE—Yes?
RACHEL—In the end, I go back to work and go out with a rock star.

The ending Rachel chooses is that of a modern fairy-tale that valorises the professional activity of women. It fulfils all the formal requirements of a happy ending – fame, fortune, success and romance – however it seems to be grafted from some other story on to this one. It is as if Rachel picks up and adapts the ending from another script in another genre. With the reversal of gender, the female twin thriller ceases to provide an adequate template for telling the story of sexual rivalry, and *Lies of the Twins* is obliged to borrow from other genres of representation – notably fashion photography – that impose alternative conventions for reading. Through changing her interpretative practice, Rachel effects a shift away from the good twin/bad twin story. Rather than learning the deep truth of good and evil and of her own desires, she sticks with the surface, even the superficial – money, fame, modelling – and it suits her just fine. In the final scene, Rachel leaves flowers on 'James's' grave. 'Jonathan' rubs a strangely ringless spot on his finger and smiles, unseen. But who cares which twin survived – Rachel is moving on.

Lies of the Twins thus concludes in a satisfyingly different way from other stories of twinship and rivalry. Whereas female twin films tend to address the dilemma of the good girl/bad girl choice in their conclusions, either through the triumph of virtue or the synthesis of sweetness and sexiness, *Lies of the Twins* exposes rather than resolves this dilemma. It exposes the pretence – the lie – that there is any real choice involved in choosing between the good and the bad. If Wolfenstein and Leites identify three solutions to the good girl/bad girl question, *Lies of the Twins* offers a different response: torn between the virtuous fiancé and his wicked twin, Rachel ultimately turns away from both twins. She refuses to be forced into making binary moral choices or into accepting choices made on her behalf. For her, ultimately, it's double or nothing where the twins are concerned, and if it interferes with her work, better that it be nothing. Rather than solving the good boy/bad boy dilemma, Rachel recognises it for what it is and manages to walk away from it. She stops probing it as an inner conflict and treats it as a bad habit. The recognition of the split as a discursive rather than a psychological issue makes it possible to refuse and retreat from the dichotomy.

Lies of the Twins rewrites the classic dénouement of female twin films (the romantic reward of the good twin) and also positions itself against the story of woman's downfall (the Sandra Shearer/Anna Karenina story) by insisting on an interpretative practice informed by work on photography. Thus when a powerful story starts colonising her life, Rachel brings to bear the skills of her trade – an understanding of the composition, use and circulation of images – in order to shift its ending. In this sense, Rachel, too, is a figure for reading (in) the film, one who reminds us that our interpretative practice opens a space for telling stories differently.

Twins and the split image of woman

Twins are commonly employed by the imagination to incarnate the binary oppositions that dominate our thinking. Given the range of possibilities, the narrowness of the portrayal of female twins in film is remarkable. Invariably the stuff of thrillers, twentieth-century twin sister films repeatedly play off a wifely and a wanton twin, rivals for the attention of a man.

Fifty years of social change separate the swarm of twin sister films in the 1990s from their 1940s precursors. The sudden rush to retell the sister story towards the close of the twentieth century indicates a pressing need to rework certain aspects of the tale of the chaste woman and the hussy. In the process a clear moral tale becomes a little muddied, but the underlying myth – that women are defined and divided by their sexual behaviour – survives. Bolstered by centuries of tales of fair maidens and treacherous temptresses, the division is not easily relinquished. If the 1990s' heroines manage to incorporate both dangerously alluring voluptuousness and virtue, it is important to understand that this is not a rejection of the virgin/whore opposition itself, but a refinement in its application. The split does not lose its power to divide. The new imperative is for one woman to be able to fulfil both roles on occasion.

Lies of the Twins is alone among 1990s twin films in going further in its repudiation of the myth, but in order for this to occur, the gender of the protagonists is transposed. The film does not address the customary female split but figures a parallel male one. It is as if the virgin/whore dichotomy can only be depicted as a false choice when it is transferred to a non-traditional object. Only where the myth has no hold can we walk away from it.

Despite its innovative twists and our optimistic reading of them, *Lies of the Twins* hardly marks a turning-point in popular film representations of gender roles. Its departure from the tried formulae of twin films is subtle. Despite the preceding decades of feminism, it marks not a dismantling of the virgin/whore dichotomy in popular film but a somewhat tentative challenge to its continuing power. We are left to wonder whether a future spate of female twin films will ever manage to recast the wicked sister.

4
Twins and the 'Crisis of Masculinity': Patterns in Body Horror Cinema

Conjoined twin brothers in horror

In the decade preceding the revival of wicked twin sister films discussed in Chapter 3, we start to find another recurrent pattern in film, this time involving brothers, but not just any twin brothers. From the early 1980s until the mid-1990s, conjoined twins (once known as 'Siamese' twins due to the celebrity of the nineteenth-century brothers Chang and Eng) repeatedly appear in the horror genre. This in itself is not surprising, given the history of their depiction as monsters of one sort or another. What is surprising is the insistent way in which the brother story is used to tell a mother story. The brothers' bodies are shown to be umbilically connected, and the twin relation substitutes for another relation dating from the womb: a maternal one.

The emergence of this striking pattern can be related to more general developments in the horror genre in the 1980s that reflect the destabilisation of traditional masculine identities: the male body is ruptured, becomes permeable, even feminised. At the same time, the pattern is a highly specific configuration of era, genre, gender and topos. The representation of the twin relation as maternal does *not* occur before this period, or in prose genres,[1] in film genres other than horror, with female twins, or with non-conjoined twins. During the 1980s and 1990s, however, conjoined twin brothers can be seen to provide a particularly clear opportunity for film-makers to feminise the male body, to display it as monstrously maternal. The topos seems to lend itself to the rehearsal of cultural anxieties concerning masculinity.

The intertwining of the theme of maternity and the topos of conjoined twins is evident to a greater or lesser extent in *Basket Case* (Frank Henenlotter, 1981), *A Zed and Two Noughts* (Peter Greenaway, 1985),

Dead Ringers (David Cronenberg, 1988), *Basket Case II* (Henenlotter, 1990), *The Krays* (Peter Medak, 1990) and *The Dark Half* (George Romero, 1993). Although these films range from art-house to schlock classics, they are all associated to a degree with horror. During this period, the link between conjoined twins and the maternal becomes prevalent in horror to the point where it is parodied in an episode of the cult television series *The X-Files* (1995), and where an attempt to refocus the story of fraternal attachment as a love story (*Twin Falls Idaho*, Michael and Mark Polish, 1999) requires constant deflection of the motherhood story.

This chapter discusses the gendering of conjoined twin films, traces the representation of fraternity as maternity in the most overt examples, and relates it to the evolution of the horror genre. Then, in a reading of the way in which *Twin Falls Idaho* seeks to distance conjoined twins from horror, it demonstrates just how insistent this pattern has become by the end of the twentieth century.

Genre and gender

Although the birth of female conjoined twins is considerably more common than that of their male counterparts (70 per cent of surviving sets are female [Sanders, 2003; cf. Bryan, 1992: 59]), there are very few films featuring female conjoined twins, and those that do exist follow the virgin/whore pattern analysed in the previous chapter. The rare examples include Brian de Palma's *Sisters*, in which sweet Danielle and murderous Dominique are separated by Dr Emile. Avi Nesher's *Doppelganger* similarly involves bodily joining and disjoining, although the lookalike in this case is an alter ego rather than a twin. While these two films tend towards the horror end of the spectrum, they share concerns that are entirely continuous with those of the twin sister thrillers in which good girl/bad girl twins are deadly rivals over a man. Even the pornographic film *Joined: The Siamese Twins*, constrained by the video classification system to eschew the violence of the thrillers, manages to dichotomise its conjoined twins as sexually adventurous and sexually reticent.[2]

On the other hand, late twentieth-century films exploring the physical attachment (and detachment) of male twins' bodies share their own set of concerns, not only distinct from those of female twin films but setting them apart from other male twin films in their focus on maternity and their proximity to the horror genre. *Dead Ringers*, *Basket Case* and *The X-Files* are the most revealing examples, and allow us to analyse the ways in which the twins are connected both to each other and to cultural developments in the 1980s.

Dead Ringers (Cronenberg): 'a view from the womb'

Dead Ringers (1988) may seem an odd inclusion in this corpus, for each of the twin gynaecologists, Elliot and Beverly Mantle, ostensibly has his own, intact body. Fantasmatically, however, the two bodies are inextricably joined. Thus in Beverly's nightmare, the twins are connected by a band of flesh resembling a giant umbilical cord passing from one belly to the other, that Claire, the woman who comes between them, severs with her teeth. Additional footage, not included in the final cut, apparently even shows 'a quarter size parasitic figure of Bev growing out of his own abdomen' (Humm, 1997: 82). Furthermore, Beverly claims not to possess an individual nervous system, while Elliot states: 'Whatever goes into his bloodstream goes directly into mine.' Playing doctor in the most deadly way at the end of the film, Beverly operates on Elliot with instruments supposedly designed 'to separate Siamese twins.' Resonating with repeated verbal references to the original Siamese twins, the final shot has the moribund twins in foetal position, joined like Chang and Eng at the chest.

As several critics have pointed out, however, the fusion and division of the brothers in fact involves another fantasmatic figure, absent from the film – the mother. Linda Badley notes that the film crew dubbed their work 'Foetal Attraction' (1995: 132). Drawing attention to the twins' blood-red robes, the claustrophobic interiors bathed in filtered amniotic-blue light, and the intra-uterine nature of both their domestic environment and their professional activity, she argues that the film is a 'view from the womb' (132). Drugged, the twins regress to an increasingly infantile condition. The rare view of the outside world is terrifying: Beverly's failed attempt, at the end of the film, to exit the narrow confines of the twins' environment finds him in a telephone booth planted in an overwhelmingly open space in front of their building. Speechless and unable to escape to a life with Claire, he returns to death in the twins' apartment. As he has previously commented, 'separation can be a terrifying thing.'

From the womb, the omnipresent mother is not visible. Her role can even be denied, as occurs both in the twins' fantasised umbilical link to each other and in their use of reproductive technology. As gynaecologists, they specialise in female fertility, and their perspective is so restricted to the womb that they do not 'do husbands' or childbirth.

Gender instability emphasises the possibility of the twins usurping the mother's position: the feminised names Bev and Elly prepare the way for Beverly to use gynaecological instruments on his twin, thus (lethally) superimposing a female anatomy on Elliot. As Badley writes: 'Their professional and personal lives are devoted to the construction of intricate systems that substitute for the mother, separate from her, or both' (1995: 133).

There is a wealth of critical work on the film, focusing on the representation of twin separation as separation from the mother and its attendant anxieties. Maggie Humm leans on Melanie Klein's argument that 'the maternal controls the processes of separation and identity' (1997: 77) to examine the film's representation of male infant anxieties and their role in the construction of masculine gender identity: 'In *Dead Ringers* the mothering body is [...] the very source of male desire and identity, the matrix through which male subjectivity is established' (60). Marcie Frank refers to the way in which 'Cronenberg construes [the twins'] separation paradigmatically as the separation of mother and infant' (1991: 460). Barbara Creed focuses on the film's depiction of male hysteria as a defence against symbolic castration, 'that is, the castrations or separations which occur in the infant's early history and which the infant experiences as a loss of something which it feels is an integral part of its own body – such as separation from the womb or loss of the mother's breast' (1990: 129). What these analyses have in common is a tendency to view the maternal dimension of *Dead Ringers* as an idiosyncrasy of Cronenberg's films.[3] Considered alongside *The Fly*, *The Brood*, *Scanners* and *Videodrome*, *Dead Ringers* does indicate something approaching an obsession with reproductive processes. Yet, if we examine *Dead Ringers* together with other films exploring the same topos, we find that Cronenberg's representation is not so idiosyncratic, and that the relation to the maternal body is a recurring theme in films involving male conjoined twins. Significant elements of *Dead Ringers* are anticipated by some less than auteur cinema horror: *Basket Case*.

Basket Case (Henenlotter): keeping a lid on it

Duane Bradley carries his twin brother Belial around in a wicker basket (Figure 4.1). Belial (a Biblical name for the personification of evil) is a monstrously deformed 'parasitic' twin, a head and arms that was once attached to Duane's right side.[4] In their adolescence, while their motherly aunt was away, their father had them separated in a clandestine

Figure 4.1   Belial in *Basket Case 1*

attempt to give Duane a normal life he did not seek. With remarkable resilience, Belial survived being put out with the garbage, and became a homicidal mutant of superhuman strength. *Basket Case* (1981) starts off as a story of revenge as Belial, aided by Duane, sets about killing those who performed their separation. As the film progresses, however, the focus shifts to Duane's attempt to escape from the twin dyad by means of his relationship with Sharon. What is interesting is that this attempt is represented in terms of the separation of mother and infant.

Whereas *Dead Ringers* is marked by symmetry and similarity, Bev and Elly both living in a foetal environment and usurping the maternal role in their work, the obvious asymmetry of the twins in *Basket Case* calls for a division of labour: Belial receives Duane's maternal ministrations. Belial's existence is foetal (he prefers the dark, enclosed space of the basket), as is his appearance, dominated by a frequently blood-smeared, disproportionately large, squashed head. Moreover, he is infantilised firstly by his aunt and then later by Duane. Duane turns out to be something of a maternal mixed bag. At times he is the stereotypical 'bad mother,' feeding Belial a diet of junk food, losing him and his basket, and leaving him with a non-functioning television as babysitter while he goes on a date with Sharon. At other times, he is nurturing and rehearses a familiar maternal discourse. Sensitive to the jealousy and fear of abandonment that has prompted Belial's toddler-style destructive rampage in the hotel room, Duane cuddles him on his lap and reassures him: 'I'm not deserting you. I just needed some time to myself. I'd never desert you after all we've been through. We'll always be together.'

Although the maternal role is clearly assigned to Duane, the existence of both twins is marked by womb-like confinement, and here the resonance with *Dead Ringers* is clear. The seedy Hotel Broslin (tracking shots emphasising its long, narrow, tunnel-like passages and staircases) is dark and claustrophobic, as are the bar where Duane recounts his life story, the cinema where he loses Belial and the offices where the murders are committed. The only exceptions to the otherwise enclosed spaces of the film – Duane and Sharon's sightseeing tour of New York and a dream sequence in which Duane runs naked down the street to Sharon's apartment – both come to represent the possibility of Duane's independence from his twin. And just as Beverly, in the concluding scenes of *Dead Ringers*, is unable to function in the open spaces outside the uterine world of the twins' shared lives, just as he is ultimately unable to commit himself to a relationship with Claire, Duane too is unable to fulfil the promise of these excursions into the open spaces beyond the twin relation. Sharon poses precisely the same threat to the twin relation as Claire does, offering the twins the possibility of separating from each other but ultimately causing them to self-destruct in the same way. When Duane finds Sharon killed by Belial, he launches an enraged attack on his twin. They struggle, eventually falling from the window to their presumed death, their bodies rejoined as before at Duane's abdomen, nicely anticipating the return to the conjoined position of the bodies in the final scene of *Dead Ringers*.

Unlike the invisible but omnipresent maternity in *Dead Ringers*, the mother role in *Basket Case* is aligned with Duane. His striving for independence is portrayed as a separation not from the mother but from the mother role in relation to his barely formed brother. In pursuing Sharon, Duane seeks release from his confinement – in both the spatial and obstetric senses of the word. His struggles are however in vain: Duane is unable to be delivered of his foetal twin, who reattaches himself to Duane's abdomen. What the two films thus share is a preoccupation with the twins' conflictual desire for and fear of separation and, in representing that conflict, both take the relation to the maternal body as paradigmatic. In each case, through portraying the fraternal relation as umbilical, the topos of conjoined twins is used to allude to the spectre of male maternity.

Basket Case II: coming up for air

With predictably miraculous hardiness, Duane and Belial survive their fall to feature in an equally low-budget sequel, *Basket Case II* (1990), that reinforces this representation as it recounts another story of failed separation. For a while, independence seems attainable: Duane and Belial are taken in by a community of 'freaks' living in the home of Granny Ruth, a 'freaks' rights' activist. Here, Belial finds not only a new home outside his basket (the nursery), but a new mother (Granny Ruth) and the possibility of a new and different life, paired up with Eve, a shy, head-and-two-limbs creature as foetal as himself. The diminished importance of the basket marks the attenuation of the umbilical link between the brothers. Duane, relieved from his fraternal/maternal responsibilities, can finally hit the road. And who better to accompany him than the apparently normal Susan.

Susan however insists that although they are alike, neither she nor Duane belong to the normal world outside. And at the film's conclusion she reveals her own freakishness, explaining, 'I'm pregnant. I've been so for the past six years.' She lifts her shirt to reveal a long, re-sealable opening in her abdomen from which a squalling amphibian emerges. As the reptilian foetus returns inside her body, she blithely informs Duane that he isn't ready to be born yet but has to 'come up for air' sometimes. If Duane reacts with horror, it is not only at the revelation of Susan's freakishness, but at the sudden realisation that he and Susan are indeed alike in their abnormality, that their sameness lies in their monstrous maternity. If her pregnancy involves the repeated birthing of a monster child, a continuous, impossible process of separation, Duane is reminded of his own maternal attachment to his baby-like brother, who pops in and out of the security of the basket. There is, of course, only one way to 'make things right': Duane must (re-)enact his maternity, reincorporate his brother's body into his own, which he does by sewing the reluctant Belial back on to his side. Jolted by the image of Susan's permanent pregnancy, and of a creature unable to leave the womb, Duane recognises his inability to sever the umbilical link with his brother and reverses their illusory separation. 'It's alright,' he shouts wildly, 'We're back together again.'

The X-Files: staying out late

The representation of the conjoined twin as a foetus hesitating at birth reaches its culmination in an episode of *The X-Files* entitled 'Humbug'

(1995), in which no attempt made to conceal the dynamics (and trauma) of maternal-infant separation. If, in both *Dead Ringers* and *Basket Case*, the brother story is a cover for a mother story, then 'Humbug' blows that cover. In clearly portraying Lenny and his conjoined twin brother Leonard as mother and baby, 'Humbug' is marked by a degree of parodic self-reflexivity and explicitness in its representations of the fraternal as maternal that is not present in the other examples.

In this episode, Scully and Mulder find themselves in Gibsonton, investigating a series of murders in which the fatal 'entry wound' is a deep, gaping puncture in the victim's abdomen like a slit between two puckered lips. Gibsonton, the traditional off-season home for sideshow performers, is a carnivalesque community, home to such human curiosities as The Alligator Man, contortionist Dr Blockhead and his omnivorous side-kick The Conundrum. It is at the funeral of the murdered Alligator Man that Scully and Mulder first encounter Lenny and Leonard. Lenny has what appears to be an infant, cutely dressed in a tiny suit, clasped against his breast, nuzzling into him (Figure 4.2). But this is no new-born: rather Lenny turns out to be mothering his parasitic conjoined twin brother, Leonard. A further encounter reinforces the feminised image of Lenny when he knocks at Scully's door early one morning in his dressing-gown. His body is soft, and the bulge of his brother's body protrudes from his gown. Scully cannot help staring, while Lenny's eyes are drawn to the cleavage revealed by Scully's gaping robe. Conscious of the other's gaze, each hurries to cover the exposed flesh. The two bodies – the monstrous and the feminine – are clearly parallel in the way in which they attract the gaze.[5]

As to the identity of the killer, tracks suggest that the killer has a tail of sorts, and can squeeze through a dog-flap. The mysterious clue linking all the murders is a trace of blood, curiously always at the opening through which the killer enters rather than exits the scene of the crime. The explanation is revealed when alcoholic Lenny is locked up to dry out. We see him all alone in his cell: where Leonard is usually perched, we find a wound, and there is blood around the window bars. The Sheriff is horrified: 'They extracted the twin!' Scully, however, knows better: 'No, the twin extracted itself. [...] This wound is identical to the other victims' wounds, with one exception – he's not bleeding.' Indeed the wound has no discernible effect on Lenny's health. Neither is Leonard a victim: rather the blood on the bars points to the escape route of this half-formed creature. Once more, the conjoined twin is revealed to be a homicidal mutant. Scully's diagnosis?

Figure 4.2 Conjoined twins Lenny (Vincent Schiavelli) and Leonard in the 'Humbug' episode of *The X-Files*

'I have a feeling that Lenny has an internal anomaly that allows his conjoining twin to disjoin.' Sure enough, when Lenny dies soon after, Scully's hypothesis is confirmed: the autopsy reveals 'offshoots of the oesophagus and trachea that almost seem umbilical in nature.'

Unlike Belial in *Basket Case*, Leonard is not simply attached to his twin by tissue that can be severed to effect separation. The relation is more like Susan's ongoing pregnancy – the little monster who has to 'come up for air sometimes' – with the difference that Leonard is distinctly detachable, able to 'crawl outside [Lenny's] body and then go gallivanting around town.' In fact, Leonard occupies a space reminiscent of Belial's basket – a kind of marsupial pouch on his brother's left side, below the ribs, with a long, vagina-like opening. Like Duane in *Basket Case*, Lenny is very clearly maternal in his relationship with Leonard. But when the basket is replaced by a pouch, this adds a very distinct and bodily feminisation. The sign of his twin's detachability is not a scar but an orifice. Furthermore, Leonard's umbilical 'tail' (hence the unidentified tracks) and blood-smeared body (hence the mysterious blood traces) suggest that he is part-foetus and that, despite repeated birthing, he is far from ready to leave the gestational pouch definitively. In fact, his murders are attempts to burrow into imagined pouches in other bodies. As Lenny explains soulfully, 'I don't think he knows he's harming anyone. He's merely seeking another brother.' Fearing that his inadequacy as a brother/mother is what drives Leonard away, and yet over-protective and possessive, Lenny echoes a classic maternal discourse of reproach and self-reproach, and insists that Leonard always comes back. This time, however, he does not return. We glimpse him escaping from the jail, umbilical cord trailing, and taking refuge in the narrow passages of a hall of mirrors before venturing outside to be devoured by The Conundrum. His fatal/foetal desire to re-enter a brother's belly is fulfilled.

Horror and the male body

The texts of our corpus have so far all been associated to some extent with the horror genre, but the trademark irony of *The X-Files* allows us to view 'Humbug' as a commentary on the conventions of the genre. Firstly, there is the very use of conjoined twins: the predictability that they should be the central figures and that one should be the murderer.[6] And secondly, in portraying their fraternal relation so clearly as a maternal relation, the 'Humbug' episode self-consciously engages with a usually implicit – even covert – aspect of their representation in late twentieth-century horror. This foregrounding of conventions allows us to raise explicit questions about genre and topos. Why do conjoined twin brothers feature so prominently in 1980s and 1990s horror? What makes them such suitable material for a maternal makeover at this time? Finally, what would it take to shift this pattern and make a film of joined brothers that takes the story away from horror?

The horror film is loosely defined by the centrality of a monstrous character (Russell, 1998: 252), and conjoined twins are readily perceived as candidates for this role. Indeed historical studies suggest that a large proportion of so-called monsters – notably the two-headed and multi-limbed varieties – were in fact conjoined twins. Thompson's survey *The Mystery and Lore of Monsters* (first published 1930) gives examples of such monstrous births from the Roman and early Christian periods, followed by a multitude of representations of so-called double-headed monsters and creatures with extra limbs or a head at their abdomen from the illustrated volumes of Conrad Lycosthenes, Fenton, Ambroise Paré, Pierre Boiastuau and Fortunio Licetus in the sixteenth and seventeenth centuries (Thompson, 1968: 30–62). Wonders of the eighteenth century to which crowds flocked included 'a monster with one head and two distinct bodies, with four arms, hands and legs' (66), and it was only during that century that Caspar Friedrich Wolff suggested the principles of embryology to explain the existence of such creatures (Thompson, 1930: 70).

The overrepresentation of conjoined twins in accounts of monsters was mirrored in their omnipresence in nineteenth- and twentieth-century carnival freak shows, which allowed the public to experience that mixture of fear, disgust and attraction occasioned by the presence of the monstrous. Fiedler identifies the horror film as heir to the now defunct freak show, in that it provides a similar opportunity to gaze upon the monstrous with impunity (1981: 315). Horror films are now the only place where 'freaks' can still be shown.[7]

Most recent studies of monstrosity define the monstrous and explain its cultural importance in terms of a violation of boundaries (Fiedler, 1981; Kristeva, 1982; Halberstam, 1995; Cohen, 1996). Monsters represent an unholy hybridity, a 'category crisis' (Garber, 1992: 16). Certainly, conjoined twins fit this definition: they disturb the borders between self and other, one and two, whole and part, autonomy and dependence. And yet, in our corpus, their representation confounds another, unexpected borderline involving gender: brother/mother. While the notion of boundary challenging explains the link between conjoined twins and horror, it falls short of accounting for the representation of the conjoined twin relationship as maternal.

Julia Kristeva's *Powers of Horror* (first published 1980) is valuable here, for it links the violation of boundaries with the relation to the maternal body in early psychosexual development. Kristeva explains that 'abjection' – our reaction of horror – stems from a breakdown of the distinction between self and other. Thus we react with disgust at what transgresses the borders of the clean-and-proper body (vomit, pus, excrement), at what disturbs the boundary between inside and outside, between me and not-me (corpses, decay). She argues that these distinctions (self/other, inside/outside, proper/abhorrent) in fact elaborate a more archaic division that must be made between one's own body and the mother's in order to establish oneself as a separate entity. Thus Kristeva posits that horror in the most general sense harks back to the ambiguities of separation from the maternal body.

Now, the disturbance of bodily limits is a given with conjoined twins. And splitting them means separating two beings together since the womb, like the infant/mother dyad. The topos thus lends itself to the theme of establishing identity through difference, viewed by psychoanalysts such as Kristeva as inevitably based on the separation from the mother as other and giving rise to separation anxiety.[8] And yet the repeated use of conjoined twins in horror films to invoke an abject maternity is not simply the result of a developmental parallel between twin individuation and mother/infant separation, for it is only *male* conjoined twins that impose exploration of the maternal, while virtually all female filmic twins succumb to the virgin/whore dichotomy: there are no nurturing twin sisters.[9] Clearly it is the relation between the male body and the maternal function that arouses horror in the 1980s and 1990s.

It is useful to consider Badley's and Halberstam's accounts of the evolution of the horror genre at this point, for while they do not coincide, they both point to a focus on gender ambiguity in late twentieth-century horror films. In line with rising public anxiety about the 'crisis in masculinity,' they see gender confusion as having the capacity to terrify during this period.

Halberstam describes a shift from the violation of racial, species, class and nationality boundaries in nineteenth-century gothic monsters towards a crisis of gender and sexual identity in contemporary horror. She puts this largely down to the triumph of psychoanalytical interpretations of 'subjectivity as sexual subjectivity and identity as sexual identity and monstrosity as sexual pathology' (1995: 24).

Badley, on the other hand, explains the shift she identifies in terms of the waning of Freudian psychoanalysis, yet still arrives at gender disturbance as a central concern in contemporary horror. She suggests that early horror is traditionally explained in psychosexual terms, with the emphasis placed on its supernatural aspects – the unconscious, psychological terror, the uncanny. On the other hand, post-1980 horror, she argues, can be seen in terms of a discourse of the body: the body is opened up and transformed, displayed in all its monstrosity (1995: 5–31). It is worth noting that the topos of conjoined twins lends itself to both these understandings of horror, offering both the uncanniness of the fabled telepathic relation between twins and the possibility of the gruesome division of their bodies. Badley's characterisation of recent horror, however, sheds even greater light on the filmic representation of conjoined twins when she suggests that male maternity actually typifies post-1980 horror. The late 1970s, she argues, saw a discursive shift from the Freudian psychoanalytical model of the self to an understanding of the self as embodied, and the 1980s horror boom articulated the accompanying crisis of identity through an iconography of the monstrous. The focus on the supernatural was replaced by a graphic physicality and especially by grotesque bodily transformations, frequently producing gender ambiguity (Badley, 1995: 26). Most notably, horror films started to feminise the bodies of their male protagonists, to expose them as 'hysterical' (105–6). This metamorphosis is figured in depictions of the hypermasculinised 'hard body' as permeable, as a focus of invasion. In particular, it is transformed into a maternal body 'through which the male subject confronted or "gave birth to" the soft bodied "feminine" in himself' (106). Badley suggests that it is this association between the male body and the maternal function – the monstrousness of male maternity – that is at the heart of the 1980s transformation films (126). If traditional masculine identities were in a state of flux at this time, men's bodies were mutating in parallel on screen.

There is, then, critical work linking recent horror and its representation of the monstrous body with the violation of gender boundaries and explaining the phenomenon in terms of contemporary cultural anxieties. Badley goes so far as to identify male maternity as symptomatic of recent horror. The coherence of our film corpus, however, indicates a pattern that is at once more specific than the characterisation of an entire genre and yet wider than the kind of personal obsession attributed to David Cronenberg. Male maternity may be distinctive of 1980s horror, but conjoined twins – invariably joined via the belly and facing the anguish of separation – provide a particularly clear opportunity for exploiting it.

The pattern we have identified is thus the product of a particular conjunction of topos (conjoined twins), gender (male), genre (body horror) and era (post-1980), and through repetition it acquires a certain discursive power during the 1980s and 1990s. So much so that the theme of maternity becomes difficult to avoid when portraying conjoined twin brothers in film, even when the twins appear in genres other than horror. *The Dark Half* is a limit case in which the most tenuous bodily attachment between brothers still invokes the maternal, while *Twin Falls Idaho* attempts to take the story in a different direction and to rearticulate the twin relation.

The Dark Half (Romero): in denial

The Dark Half (1993) sits precisely at a point of tension between thrillers and horror, between narratives of good and evil brothers and stories of conjoined twins, between the macho and the maternal. Thad Beaumont and his alter ego George Stark are only physically connected in the most minimal sense, and yet this vestige of corporeal connection together with the proximity to the horror genre seem to make it impossible to avoid representations of their relation in terms of maternal attachment.

The film is not obviously about conjoined twins. As a child, Thad Beaumont suffered from severe headaches accompanied by auditory hallucinations. The cause was eventually discovered and a 'very rare sort of tumour' was surgically removed from his brain. Consisting of 'en eye, part of a nostril, [and] two teeth,' the 'tumour' turned out to be the vestiges of an unborn twin, 'absorbed into the system,' that somehow 'got itself going again' and started to grow.[10] Now married with small twin sons, Thad is a college English professor who writes best-selling, violent, sleazy novels under the pseudonym of George Stark. In order to frustrate a blackmail attempt, Thad decides to reveal the true identity of George Stark and retire the pseudonym. Faced with the prospect of his own 'death,' Stark comes to life with a vengeance, colonising the foetal remains and becoming Thad's homicidal double.

Nor is *The Dark Half* obviously a film about maternity. Despite his beginnings as a foetal twin, Stark is certainly not infantilised. On the contrary, the character is hypermasculinised: drinking, smoking, violent, foul-mouthed and sadistic, he relishes in his gratuitously violent murders. In this case, the 'beast inside' – Thad's 'dark half' – is certainly not a baby. Although physically identical right down to their fingerprints, Thad and George are poles apart: while Thad is conspicuously depicted sharing childcare responsibilities, George is a thoroughgoing tough guy. The ready availability of this contrast between the caring, respectable, unassuming Thad and the vulgar, violent George Stark suggests that this film sits comfortably with male twin films in other genres. Moreover, the relationship between Thad and George has none of those nurturing aspects that were so apparent in *Basket Case I* and *The X-Files*. Yet even in this film the appearance of male conjoined twins imposes consideration of the maternal. For even in *The Dark Half*'s determinedly masculine, hard-bodied world, Thad's means of escaping from George Stark involves a repeated (and somewhat unconvincing) denial of his own maternity.

From the very beginning, the scenario of Thad's 'tumour' is a very clear example of a feminisation – indeed, literally, a hystericisation – of the male body: Thad's body harbours a growing foetus. The organ that nurtures the foetal twin is not however the womb we might expect. Unlike the brother emerging from the pouch in *The X-Files*, or from below the rib cage in *Basket Case*, or from the belly in *Dead Ringers*, the vestige of Thad's twin is lodged in the brain. The site of gestation has shifted upwards. As Vern Bullough (1973) notes, hysteria was once thought to be due to a disturbed uterus wandering through the body. In these terms, the vertical migration of the unabsorbed foetal twin to Thad's brain – his wandering would-be womb – is a form of male hysteria.

It is significant that the foetus is a cerebral one. Thad does not share the same sort of obvious bodily connection with Stark that is apparent in the other films of our corpus. Indeed he is at pains to deny such a bond. Thad comes to understand his alter ego twin as an intellectual invention – 'a conjuration, an entity created by the force of [his] will,' and the mode of their connection is primarily psychical, mediated through writing as Stark's thoughts are channelled through Thad's hand.

The denial of a visceral bond is however undermined through the competing metaphors of creativity that pervade the film. On the one hand, Thad, when writing as George, uses long, black pencils, phallic weapons viciously sharpened to the point where they can and do maim. At the same time, Thad himself describes his writing as a kind of birth: 'It's not coming out of me easy,' he comments. More significantly, George Stark's creation is re-interpreted to Thad through gestation and birth metaphors. When Thad visits the doctor who removed his 'tumour,' he is told that his parents had insisted on its burial in the family graveyard plot. The tissue has the status of human remains, like a miscarried foetus or a stillborn baby. The morning after the first murder, the local gravedigger finds a hole in the grave site with hand prints around the edge 'as if someone buried alive dug his way out.' The second twin has pushed his way into the world. Later, the local police investigator confronts Thad with the preposterousness of his assertions that the murders were committed by his pseudonym: 'Maybe you'd like to tell me where this guy came from, Thad. Did you just sort of give birth to him one night? Did he pop out of a damn sparrow's egg? Exactly how did it go?' George Stark is characterised as Thad's offspring, borne of his body as much as of his pencil.

In *The Dark Half*, then, there are not the obvious indices of maternity that are present in the rest of our corpus (the professional and personal obsession with reproductive processes, the distinctly foetal mutant twin, the quasi-marsupial pouch). Nonetheless, the traces of conjoinedness in horror mean that that we once again find an insistent maternal dimension to the representation of the relation between the brothers.[11]

Twin Falls Idaho (Polish brothers): deflecting the maternal

The Polish brothers' 1999 film *Twin Falls Idaho* presents itself in terms of its difference. The tagline to the film's title is 'a different kind of love story,' and the review quoted on the poster reiterates the claim: 'However many films you may have seen, you probably haven't seen anything like *Twin Falls Idaho*.'[12] Certainly the film is not your standard romance, and as a love story, we might expect a sharp contrast with the horror films studied. Separation from this corpus, however, seems to involve revisiting many of its tropes.

From the earliest sequences we see the narrow hotel corridor and the dingy exiguity of the hotel room. One face and then the other peeps through the bathroom door. Blake and Francis Falls, conjoined laterally at the thorax, do not venture outside except at Halloween, and their indoor existence is emphasised through the use of sepia tones, and green and blue lighting. Only once do they find themselves in the brightly exposed open space of a city park, and the experience is distressing. The film recounts the triangulation of the twinship: Penny enters their life, and while Blake falls for her and imagines a life away from his brother, Francis grows jealous and contemplates his abandonment. Meanwhile, their quest to find their lost mother, along with half-articulated allusions to an abandoned child and a joking reference to the abject maternal make motherhood an underlying issue throughout the film.

Clearly the film rehearses some of the conventions we have identified for the depiction of conjoined twin brothers: the dark confined spaces, the stark contrast between inside and outside, the monstrous body as object of a voyeuristic gaze, the woman who comes between the twins, the maternal dimension. It does not, however, simply reiterate them. There is an important difference in the portrayal of the twin relation between this and the other films in our corpus: the fraternal relation is never represented as maternal or as substituting for the mother. In *Twin Falls Idaho*, the undercurrent of allusions to motherhood is clearly associated with mothers, not brothers, while the brothers' relationship is repeatedly characterised as marital.

This does not however mean that the film is simply able to ignore the representational conventions established for the topos. On the contrary, it is continually obliged to deal with them. This is obvious firstly in the generic positioning of the film. *Twin Falls Idaho* is described as a drama and a love story, but this does not simply eliminate the horror genre: rather the film positions itself as patently *not* horror. Anne Freadman (1988) emphasises the importance of 'not-statements' in her theorisation of genre, demonstrating that cultural practices define their genre by explicitly distancing themselves from neighbouring genres. The regular use of conjoined twins to represent horror means that *Twin Falls Idaho* must continually reassert its status as other than horror, which it does by repeated references to and deflection of the genre.[13]

Thus the camera lingers voyeuristically on the joined chests as Penny's doctor friend examines them, but Miles is patently *not* wielding a scalpel ('Relax, I'm not a surgeon,' he says) and is far from keen to see them separated. Even the emergency surgery late in the film to separate the twins eschews the gruesome in favour of a poetic dreamlike sequence. Misshapen bodies are highlighted in the film, but are far from confined to the twins: from the taxi-driver's steel claw hand from which Penny recoils in the opening sequence to the ex-circus dwarf who leads Penny to Blake's van at the end, unconventional bodies abound. At a Halloween party, the twins stand out only for the excellence of their 'costume' among the carnivalesque party-goers, who include a half-man-half-woman and 'Siamese' twins in red Chinese outfits tied together with ribbons. Split screens are used to show the variety of disguises.[14] The gay host, on learning of the twins' conjoined condition, exclaims 'the horror!' imagining that one twin might be gay and the other straight, and insists that he is a freak too. As a culturally sanctioned freak show, the party works as a commentary on the conventions of horror, in contrast to the principal narrative. Finally, the story that might have been the basis for horror – the story of gestation in a cow's belly – is clearly a joke.

The second, related way in which the film needs to displace conventions is in the representation of the twin relation. Although Blake takes care of his sick brother, this nurturing is not figured as maternal. On the contrary, there are explicit references to the twinship as a marriage. After examining the brothers early in the film, Miles takes Penny aside: 'You see two people depend on each other for survival – makes you feel kinda queasy, huh? Quite a marriage.' And as Blake says goodbye to Penny, he adds with the trace of a wry smile: 'Maybe I'll call you – when I'm single.' Later the exploitative Jay wants to offer them tabloid fame by inventing 'the most famous divorce case of all time.' And their charismatic neighbour Jesus, marriage celebrant cum revivalist preacher, sees their relation as the ultimate wedlock: 'I like what you two represent: two folks living in harmony. [...] You two symbolise peace and love, like you're the biological realisation of togetherness. [...] Divorce is not even an option in your marriage.'

The conspicuous repetition of the conjugal analogy serves to distance this portrayal of conjoined brothers from the others we have studied. The analogy is reinforced when Blake and Francis do a magazine romance quiz interpreting give and take in relationships, and during the bitter fight when Francis accuses Blake of falling in love, and Blake accuses Francis of jealousy. Furthermore, the twin relation is portrayed as a partnership of equals. It resembles their musical duo, Blake and Francis each using one hand to play a guitar. As Miles remarks when surgery seems imminent: 'Two single dollars put together into one bill, worth twice its value – tear it in half and you don't get two single bills. The bill loses all its value. The strength is in the bond of two. They need each other to live as one.' The parental does not enter the equation.

Similarly, the possibility of their separation is never seen in terms of birth/emergence, unlike infantilised Beverly propelled outside, Belial peeping from his basket, Leonard protuding from the pouch, and Stark emerging from the hole in the ground in the other films of our corpus. Instead, it is seen as a divorce, and the metaphor is one of bisection. Blake reminisces about their youthful desire to separate:

> Every dollar was fifty cents. When we were little, we used to search for train tracks, every city we'd visit, and when we found 'em, we'd lie down, a rail would split between us, and we'd wait for a train. Francis used to say, 'Blake, do you hear the train?'

When the operation to separate them finally takes place, we see a hallucinatory fantasy. A grainy film, fading to white, shows Blake and Francis unattached, cycling on a cliff edge in circles and figures of eight on separate old-fashioned bikes. Having traced these symbols of their relation and separation, Francis cycles away, waves goodbye across a gulf between two cliffs and disappears. Francis has gone over to the other side, and Blake remains. This is parting, not parturition.

Lastly, the use of confined spaces is not linked to a uterine metaphor. There is nothing foetal about the claustrophobic scenes in the hotel. Rather, together with the bars that frame the twins' faces at the peephole in the hotel door, the grill fence of the city park through which passersby gawk at them, and various verbal references, they allude to the caging of freaks.

Twin Falls Idaho thus sets itself apart from the other films in our corpus by positioning itself against the horror genre and avoiding any hint of the maternal in its representations of the twin relation. Curiously, however, there is still a focus on maternity in the film. It is as though merely abstaining from representing male maternity is not enough to dispel a now compelling convention. Maternity must be seen to be firmly re-anchored to the feminine.

Early in the film we learn that there is something to discover about Penny. Miles' remark is unfinished: 'If you ever want to find out how he's doing, or some information...' and his words echo later to Penny in front of the mirror. Who is 'he'? And for what does Penny need to make amends ('I need something to level my karma') by tending to Blake and Francis? Penny's secret haunts the film. Her lawyer/pimp Jay sheds some light, when he too takes Penny's solicitude for atonement: 'Just because you had a retard ... ok, you couldn't take care of it, you did the right thing, you got rid of him, but you can't replace him with those freaks in there.' Penny's secret is a son that she tries to forget she had. Although Penny's capacity for childcare is somewhat doubtful (she is at a loss when asked to buy food for the twins), her caring gestures towards the brothers are interpreted by both herself and Jay as substituting for a maternal relationship with her disabled son. If motherhood is a theme of the film, in *Twin Falls Idaho* it is deflected back where it belongs – on to the mother.

This is not the only instance of feminine refusal of and confrontation with the maternal role. The brothers know that Francis' health is failing, and they are in town with the express purpose of finding the mother who abandoned them, known to them only through a name on their adoption certificate: Francine Ross. At Halloween, the only night they can roam freely, they go trick-or-treating and call on Francine, who registers shock but recovers momentarily:

> FRANCINE—You two boys have made a really great costume. It kind of frightened me. I thought you two were real.

FRANCIS—You look real too.
FRANCINE—Real?
BLAKE—... like ... our mother.

The dish of sweets crashes to the floor, and Francine gasps 'I'm sorry, I'm sorry' as she slams the door.

Even before this encounter, however, Francine's experience is a subject of speculation. Penny's friend muses: 'Could you imagine being their mother?', and the failed reunion is followed by a scene where a story – clearly endlessly rehearsed to comic effect – is told to explain (or to avoid explaining) the absence of a mother. Penny's enquiry ('Did your mother have to put up with shit like that when you were kids?') is met with 'We didn't have a mother.' When Penny insists, Blake continues with 'We don't have a human mother' and the brothers jointly tell of being transferred to a cow for the last one and a half months of pregnancy, the punchline being a moo-like 'Maaaa' from Francis.

The unanswered questions about Penny's child and Francine's desire to avoid the inevitable confrontation with her sons become important linked issues in the film. It is Penny who begs Francine to visit the twins in hospital as Francis lies dying. Both women are in tears as Francine describes her decision to give up the twins and the anguish that has never left her, and we understand Francine's story as a commentary on Penny's. And just as Penny avoids receiving information about her son, Francine feels she cannot go to the hospital. Eventually, however, she yields, and Francis is reunited with his mother before he dies.

If Francine is finally able to accept her maternal role after denying it for so long, we wonder whether Penny will not do likewise, but the question remains open, and the film concludes with the possibility that Blake's grieving might eventually give way to romance with Penny. Motherhood is thus a crucial theme in the film, but remains firmly linked to mothers.

Shifting the pattern

If twin sister films invariably work through fantasies of unbridled female sexuality and virginal virtue, late twentieth-century filmic narratives of conjoined twin brothers also impose a compulsory figure: a mother story of sorts. In these films associated with the horror genre, the fraternal relation inevitably substitutes for the maternal. David Cronenberg's twin gynaecologists may have attracted the most critical attention in this regard, but they are far from alone in their fraternal/maternal attachment.

With bodily limits already blurred by an archaic joining going back to the womb, the topos of male conjoined twins provides an ideal opportunity to hystericise the male body, to linger on its instability and permeability, to depict it as maternal. Employed in this way, it speaks to the preoccupation with gender ambiguity said to be characteristic of post-1980 horror and reflecting a crisis in masculine identity.

However, the striking coherence of our horror corpus – the insistence and predictability with which the foetal brother appears – is only partially accounted for by such broad characterisations of horror genres. Atypical of filmic representations of twins generally, and not paralleled in horror films of conjoined twin sisters, the representation of brother as mother is a product of a particular conjunction of topos, gender and genre. Its force at the close of the century is such that the theme of maternity still needs to be addressed when a film featuring conjoined twin brothers attempts to shift the genre away from horror. Thus the self-styled love story *Twin Falls Idaho*, unable to simply escape or ignore this convention, must continually deflect it. Its protagonists are obliged to negotiate not only their own fraternity, but also the fact that they form part of a broader filmic fraternity of conjoined twins, occupying a privileged site for exploring the separation of self and (m)other.

5
Twins and the 'Gay Gene' Debate: When Queer Comic Fiction Meets Behaviour Genetics

A queer twist on twin tales

> The reunited twins story is a venerable chestnut in journalism, one of those rare and quirky good-news items that is guaranteed to gain international exposure, along with stories of pets that have tramped across the country to find their masters. (Wright, 1997: 33)

Reunited twins may be a news story, but they are hardly a new story. The minutiae of lives – habits found to be shared, extraordinary parallels or contrasts in experiences – may differ from case to case, but the tale is predictable enough to be parodied, an opportunity taken up by Robert Rodi in *Drag Queen* (1995). Queer rather than quirky, conspicuously comic, the novel puts a gay spin on the long lost twin tale, putting its characters in a spin in the process.

Twins separated at birth – what might be gained from a gay retelling? To answer, we need to read intertextually, juxtaposing this tale with others. As Wright points out in the quotation above, reunited twin stories are common in journalism. They also feature in plays, novels and films, and these represent the more obvious comic antecedents to Rodi's novel.[1] There is, however, another entire field and method of research devoted to versions of this story: twin studies. Although the genre of writing associated with it – the research paper in behaviour genetics – is only partly narrative, it will prove a useful foil against which to read *Drag Queen*.

Twins confront us with questions of identity, and perhaps none more confronting than sexual identity. Sexual identity is the focus both of many twin studies and of Rodi's parody, and it is both productive and revealing to read *Drag Queen* as a tacit engagement with such studies, for the novel unsettles the premises of much of the research. Studies comparing rates of homosexuality among different types of twins seek to determine whether sexual orientation is social or biological in origin and feed into debates about the naturalness or otherwise of same-sex relations. They tend to rely, however, on some overly neat distinctions – between heterosexual and homosexual, between same and different – that the novel puts into question.

The chapter starts with improbable tales of identical twins of mixed gender, which appear in both fiction and research. It then studies the way in which twins have been mobilised in research work to support the very structure that they seem to defy: the binary opposition that divides same and different, self and other. The chapter points to the uncertainty of the binaries underpinning twin studies before scrutinising the categories of sexual identity made available in the research papers, and unmade in Rodi's novel. In doing so, it underscores the tensions between the various understandings of identity and the self that vie for acceptance in contemporary culture.

Identical, except ...

Monozygotic (literally single egg) twins are usually referred to in English as identical, and come into being when an embryo splits into two, in effect cloning itself. This would appear to rule out the possibility of mixed gender identical twins. In the cultural imagination, however, such pairs are not hard to find. They may stretch the limits of *vraisemblance*, but are readily available for comedy, whether in Shakespeare's *Twelfth Night*, or some four centuries later in Mabel Maney's *Kiss the Girls and Make Them Spy: An Original Jane Bond Parody*.

I remember being constantly asked if my baby son and daughter were identical twins. When I repeated that they were of mixed sex and invited the asker to ponder the implications, the response was often: 'yes, of course, but apart from that?'[2] It was as if sex/gender were a kind of add-on or overlay to an underlying physiology and psychology, such that twins could be identical in every way except sex. Boy/girl identical twins are easily conceived in the public imagination, if not *in utero*, and provide an opportunity to pursue the fantasy of imagining oneself as a member of the opposite sex.[3]

There is, of course, a notorious case of such twins in the social research literature: the 'John/Joan' case made famous by John Money (1972) and exposed by researcher Milton Diamond (1997) and later by journalist John Colapinto in *As Nature Made Him: The Boy Who Was*

Raised as a Girl (2000). In 1963 one of a pair of identical twin baby boys had his penis burnt off in a botched circumcision and was subsequently castrated and raised as a girl on Money's advice. The gruesome accident provided an opportunity for Money to test his theory that children were born psychosexually neutral, that gender identity was learnt rather than innate and indeed remained malleable during the first eighteen months of life. The fact that the accident had befallen a twin was a useful coincidence in research design, for the identical twin brother could serve as the control subject. For many years, reports indicated the supposed success of this experiment: the castrated twin was said to delight in feminine pastimes and appearance. Its disastrous consequences for the entire family eventually came to light, however, along with the fact that in the meantime 'Joan' had undergone a double mastectomy and phalloplasty in order to become David, male once again.

This is but a recent chapter in the shady history of twins research. For although undeniably beneficial in the isolation of genetic factors contributing to certain diseases, twins research has its sinister side, having, as Wright notes, 'been born in Galton's aristocratic notions of the natural worthiness of the English upper class, taken to its evil extreme by Nazi eugenicists, and too readily used by American scientists to rationalise racial injustice' (1997: 30; cf. Schwartz, 1996: 30–6).

Like so much twins research, both the John/Joan experiment and the exposure of its failure have been used to weigh into the nature/nurture debate, here in relation to gender identity and gendered behaviour. Each has come down clearly on one side or the other: where Money claimed 'nurture,' Colapinto retorts 'nature.' It is ironic that identical twins – who confound the opposition between same and other, the binary at the basis of all oppositions – should so frequently be harnessed to uphold dichotomies. A number of supposedly clear binaries are in play in this case: male/female, masculine/feminine, nature/ nurture. And the experiment as a whole depends on yet another opposition: twin studies methodology is founded on a neat, watertight distinction between identical and non-identical twins. Results are even formulated in terms of percentages for concordance and discordance, that is, sameness and difference. The disturbance of the opposition same/different by the very existence of identical twins is occulted: sameness and difference become calculable percentages.

John/Joan is not the only case of genetically identical (monozygotic) mixed gender twins in the scientific literature. In fact, although seemingly impossible, at least three instances have been recorded. Wright explains that in each case one twin was an XY male while the other had an X but no Y chromosome, creating an intersex condition known as Turner's Syndrome whereby an apparent female presents ambiguous sexual development (1997: 99; cf. Bryan, 1992: 65). Such cases (and the rise in intersex activism) remind us that male/female is not a simple binary (cf. Fausto-Sterling, 1993; Kessler, 1998). At the same time, they question an even more fundamental opposition in twins research: that between identical and non-identical twins.

Despite its dualistic title, Lawrence Wright's book *Twins: Genes, Environment and the Mystery of Identity* works to deconstruct this and other binaries underpinning much twins research, notably the nature/nurture dichotomy. He contends that identical/non-identical is a misleading nomenclature by which to distinguish types of twins (1997: 95), in that resemblance among both monozygotic (MZ) and dizygotic (DZ) twins occurs along a continuum.[4] 'Clearly some identical twins are more identical than others' (96), he affirms: '[f]raternal twins can be so similar that they believe they must be monozygotic, while identicals can be dramatically discordant for facial features, such as cleft lip or palate' (96). MZ twins may be born from entirely separate placentas, while in rare cases the placentas of DZ twins merge (90). Wright indicates the wide range of ways in which monozygotic twins may differ from each other, being 'genetically identical but biologically different' (98). Sources of difference for MZ twins include: the timing of the twinning process, twin transfusion syndrome, unequal prenatal nutrition, the attachment of the placenta(s), chromosomal changes, and distribution patterns of the X chromosome in MZ twin girls (Wright, 1997: 91–9; cf. Farber, 1981: 9).

Wright, however, goes further, putting a question mark over the whole monozygotic/dizygotic opposition. As he notes, 'the most fundamental proposition of twin science is that fraternal and identical twinning are entirely separate processes' (1997: 84). He reports, however, that the one egg/two egg categorisation is called into question by geneticist Charles Boklage, who wonders whether the two forms of twinning have something in common, for there is evidence that both kinds of twins are more like each other than like singletons. Boklage suggests 'a third type of twinning, in which fraternal twins derive from a single egg, one that splits *before* conception, so that the same egg is fertilised twice' (Wright, 1997: 85).[5] Such a process 'would confound comparisons between identicals and fraternals, undermining the whole structure of behaviour genetics' (85–6).

The deconstruction of the oppositions underpinning twin studies does not stop there. Early pregnancy scans (transvaginal ultrasounds at five weeks) increasingly reveal multiple pregnancies that show up several weeks later as single gestations. The so-called 'vanishing twin' syndrome (of which Schwartz traces the mythology, 1996: 19–21) is now believed to be extremely common, with a conservative estimate of 15 per cent of the population consisting of apparent singletons who are in fact survivors of a twin pregnancy (Wright, 1997: 77). Considerably more startling is the possibility of human chimera: Boklage cites instances of individuals carrying two different blood types and speculates that in these cases fraternal twins may have merged in the womb to become a single person (Wright, 1997: 83).[6] The dividing line between singletons and twins seems less than clear.

The final chapters of Wright's study demonstrate the complexity of the interaction between genes and the environment, both in the individual and in human evolution. He outlines arguments that suggest that not only our perception of our experiences, but even our environment may reflect a genetic disposition, for as we grow older we tend increasingly to produce our own living conditions. These arguments question the possibility of usefully distinguishing genetic from environmental factors and echo the misgivings expressed by Farber in *Identical Twins Reared Apart: A Reanalysis.*[7] Farber casts doubt on a further opposition at the basis of many twin studies: that between twins raised together and twins raised separately. These apparent poles of difference conceal a great deal of variation both in the degree of separation, and in the twins' awareness of the twinship (1981: 15–21).

Lookalike twins: are they the same or different? The question could lead us to ponder the mutual exclusiveness of the categories that govern our thinking about identity, to question the self/other opposition. More commonly, however, embedded in a network of suspiciously neat binaries (identical/non-identical, monozygotic/dizygotic, singleton/twin, genes/environment, together/apart), twins have provided researchers with an opportunity to reinforce binary thinking. One field where this is particularly obvious is the study of sexuality.

Quest for the 'gay gene'

Doubts and queries such as those outlined above have not derailed the huge research enterprise of twin studies. The largest concentration of such research occurs at the University of Minnesota where, by 1997, intensive studies of some 238 sets of multiples reared apart had been conducted under the direction of Thomas Bouchard. Many of the cases received extensive press coverage, not least because of the extraordinary specificity of the similarities between some of the twins: resemblances ranged from nail-biting, giggling, nightmares, preferred brand of beer, to what they named their dog, and even the fact that they had undergone vasectomies (Wright, 1997: 38–58).[8]

This level of detail can be contrasted with some of the twin studies published on homosexuality. For one abiding use of twin studies has related to the 'gay gene' hypothesis, the idea that homosexuality may be genetically determined and therefore inherited. The quest for the gay gene, which has gained momentum in the last twenty years, arouses ambivalence in queer circles. As Eve Sedgwick points out, more important than the outcome are the motivations driving the research: gays may rejoice at homosexuality being judged 'natural,' but given the lack of public enthusiasm for boosting numbers of gays and the medical paradigm of gene therapy, the quest may lead to prevention or 'treatment' options (1990: 42–4; cf. LeVay, 1996: 255–71; Haynes, 1995: 110).

Twin studies are a major tool in this quest, and Geoff Puterbaugh's *Twins and Homosexuality: A Casebook* (1990), a collection of research papers first published from 1952 to 1985, chronicles their use. All report on twin studies that ascertain the concordance rate for homosexuality among monozygotic and dizygotic twins, and the framing of the papers in Puterbaugh's introduction indicates his purpose: the collection is intended to emphasise the importance of a genetic component in male homosexuality.

Striking is the binarism of these studies: subjects are expected to fit neatly into the categories homosexual or heterosexual, and any ambiguity is seen as problematic. Sexual histories that disturb the clarity of the divide are classed as 'bisexual,' irrespective of whether or not the label corresponds to the subject's self-description, as in the following quotation from a University of Minnesota research team's paper, first published in 1985: 'One member of pair 4 had a homosexual affair, which was intense and prolonged, so that we regard her as bisexual, although she describes herself as exclusively heterosexual since her second marriage in her late twenties.' (Eckert *et al.*, 1990: 129). Here it is assumed that there are only two conceivable forms sexuality might take, with at a pinch the possibility of alternation between the two. This lack of options exacerbates the difficulty of determining how the twins fit into the overarching binary of concordance and discordance. The same paper discusses a pair of male twins, one of whom regards himself as exclusively homosexual and the other as exclusively hetero-sexual, however the latter's affair with an older man when in his teens allows the researcher to put a question mark over this case: 'Whether to count [this] pair concordant or discordant or partially one or the other, is problematic' (132). In other words, despite the contrasts in the twins' self-description and sixteen years of monogamous marriage versus a series of homosexual relationships, the researchers with their limited categories cannot decide whether they should tick the boxes 'same' or 'different' with regard to sexuality. We are a long way from the detail of the study of twins who both married women called Linda and had a dog called Toy (Wright, 1997: 39).

Many recent studies use similarly limited/limiting classifications: although King and McDonald (1992) and Kendler *et al.* (2000) rely on self-description by informants rather than inflicting unwanted labels on them, only three categories are offered in each study (homosexual/ gay, heterosexual, bisexual) and in the second these are then collapsed into two – heterosexual and other. Those who do not identify as het-erosexual are lumped together in a homogenising of the Other. Certainly Kendler *et al.* acknowledge that 'the assessment of the com-plex phenotype of sexual orientation with a single item is far from ideal. Sexual orientation involves, at a minimum, dimensions of sexual fantasy, attraction, and behavior, none of which was explicitly cap-tured by our single item' (2000: 1846). While this admission at least indicates awareness of the problem, identifying sexuality through a tick in one of two or three boxes is a common methodology even in recent twin studies of homosexuality. And of course such methodology fits the social fantasy of homosexuals and heterosexuals constituting entirely separate groups of people.

While media interest and much of the work of the Minnesota project have focused on an extreme level of detail and nuance in similarities between twins, down to the name of the women they divorced and the crooking of their little finger, twin studies researching homosexuality have tended to focus on the most general level of likeness. Aston-ishingly unconcerned with the fine detail of sexual attraction is the following 1980 experiment on a pair of male monozygotic twins:

> The subjects' penile volume responses were recorded by a method described previously while they were shown thirty 10-sec segments of moving pictures, ten of nude men, ten of nude women, and ten of landscapes. The segments were presented in random order at 1-min intervals. (McConaghy and Blaszcynski, 1990: 85)

Only one of the twins claimed to be homosexual and the stated aim of the experiment was to find out whether the ostensibly heterosexual co-twin was telling the truth. But how much does this blunt instrument tell us about sexuality? What kinds of men and women were shown, indeed what kind of landscapes? What positions, activities, body parts were represented, suggested or highlighted? As Sedgwick remarks,

> It is a rather amazing fact that, of the very many dimensions along which the genital activity of one person can be differentiated from that of another (dimensions that include preference for certain acts, certain zones or sensations, certain physical types, a certain frequency, certain symbolic investments, certain relations of age or power, a certain species, a certain number of participants, etc. etc. etc.), precisely one, the gender of object choice, emerged from the turn of the century, and has remained, as *the* dimension denoted by the now ubiquitous category of 'sexual orientation.' (1990: 8, cf. 22–6.)

Concordance data on dimensions such as those Sedgwick suggests are scarce to say the least in published twin studies on sexuality.

Happily, there are exceptions to the dichotomising into het and homo. Heston and Shields' 1968 paper refuses simply to muster all same-sex experiences together, and discusses similarities and differences in relationships, attitudes, partners and sexual practices between two pairs of homosexual twins in the same sibship (1990: 54–8). More recently, the large studies conducted by Bailey and Pillard (1991) and Bailey *et al.* (1993) use Kinsey's 1948 seven-point scale to rate both sexual behaviour and fantasies (although results are still grouped into the broad categories 'heterosexual' and 'homosexual,' the latter including homosexual/gay and bisexual), while Whitam *et al.* (1993) use an eighteen-page questionnaire on sexuality and the Kinsey scale to determine concordance or partial concordance.[9] A couple of methodological critiques have appeared: Byne and Parsons question the widespread assumption that 'homosexuality is a unitary construct that is culturally transcendent' (1993: 229); Haynes critiques the binarism of twin studies into homosexuality, promoting use of the Kinsey scale and concluding with the caution that 'there is evidently great plasticity in orientation, as one moves from one point on the sexual continuum to another, for differing lengths of time, and at different periods of one's life' (1995: 111). Finally Kirk *et al.* (2000) use multiple measures of sexual orientation (behaviours, attitudes and feelings), creating the conditions for a more nuanced statistical analysis.

Kallmann's 1952 study found 100 per cent concordance between monozygotic twins for homosexuality. These results have never been replicated, and the sampling and methodology have been harshly criticised and are generally considered to be seriously flawed. In the intervening years, twins concordant or discordant for homosexuality have appeared in research papers in varying proportions. My interest in these studies is not in their results – most of those published in the 1990s indicate that monozygotic twins are twice as likely to be concordant for sexuality as dizygotic twins (cf. LeVay, 1996: 175) – but in what those results are taken to mean. What does it mean to say that homosexuality is genetic to a (greater or lesser) degree? Wright quotes Pillard in conversation on this question: 'Is it a propensity to like somebody who is sort of the same as you versus somebody who's different, or to like a man versus a woman, or to be very sensitive or what? [...] It's hard even to speculate because we don't know that much about how genes affect behaviour' (Wright, 1997: 73). It is in addressing this question – the meaning of the quest for the gay gene, a question generally passed over in silence in the research literature – that Robert Rodi's gay retelling of the reunited twins tale proves useful. For while Rodi's characters could be recruited to support the conclusions of twin studies showing monozygotic concordance for homosexuality – they're both gay on the Kinsey scale – his novel demonstrates, in human detail both dazzling and drab, just how little that tells us.

Rodi's *Drag Queen*: multiple gay identities

Robert Rodi's parodic novel *Drag Queen* can be read as a comedy of confusion in the tradition of *Twelfth Night*, with more than a trace of the Tootsie strain of cross-dressing comedy. Its humour draws both on confusion between twins of mixed gender (or gender expression), and on non-recognition of the same face gendered differently. The author is clearly on to a winner with these themes: twin comedies have a history of success going back well before Shakespeare to Plautus and Menander, and the (straight) cross-dressing comedies *Some Like It Hot* and *Tootsie* were voted the two funniest American movies of all time by the American Film Institute in 2000. As a gay variation on the reunited twins theme, *Drag Queen* fulfils its dust-jacket promise of hilarity, so if we return to the question driving this book and ask what is at stake in this retelling of a familiar twin tale, one response might be to see it as a story (re)told for maximum laughs. And yet, an important element of this comic tradition is strangely missing from the book:

the 'bedtrick,'[10] often the principal source of mirth in such comedies. There are no duped wooers or bedfellows in *Drag Queen*, which should alert us to the possibility of reading this parody in terms of other genres. Taking my cue from the references in the book's early scenes to television documentaries about twins, I propose to read the novel as an implicit commentary on twin studies of homosexuality. If twins are our window on to 'the mystery of identity' (Wright, 1997), Rodi's novel uses twins to explore a range of contemporary understandings of sexual identity, allowing the narrative to be read as an unstated intervention into the gay gene debate.

For into this debate swings Mitchell Sayer – well not exactly swings, trots more like it, taking especial care not to disturb his immaculate appearance and pristine townhouse, distressed and preoccupied at the discovery that his lapis lazuli letter opener is not in its proper place. Caricatures are the stock in trade of parody, and from its first page *Drag Queen* introduces us to a gay stereotype: the obsessively neat, successful professional with impeccable taste, in awe of his mother. The novel opens with a transparently contrived revelation to unleash the plot and wreak havoc in Mitchell's circumspect and tidy life. Mitchell's wealthy society mother announces her intention to join a Tibetan convent and confesses to Mitchell not only that he was adopted, but that he has an identical twin brother. Mitchell's immediate reaction to the disclosure is to reflect on his sexuality and wonder how identical his co-twin might be in this regard. And he refers to 'some so-called news magazine show in which it was reported that identical twins – even long-separated identical twins – almost always possessed identical character traits' (Rodi, 1995: 8). In other words, his first reaction is to relate his situation and sexuality to a popularised version of twin studies. His second reaction is to admit to himself 'an incestuous element to this speculation' (9) and compare this fantasy of the only child to the disgust of gay friends at the thought of sex with their brothers. His response reflects research findings on sexual relations between male identical twins: that twins reared together are never sexually attracted to each other, while homosexual twins raised apart typically report attraction to their co-twin, a pattern Puterbaugh puts down to 'a near-universal pattern of incest-avoidance' (1990: xiv; cf. Wright, 1997: 46).[11]

Rodi's text thus engages early with patterns revealed by twin studies on homosexuality. This continues during his first contact with his twin, by telephone, during which Mitchell again refers to the television show and its mythologisation of research on identical twins (19) and speculates on his twin's sexuality: after hanging up, Mitchell 'reflected with pleasure on the conversation – on Donald's lilting tone, peppered with "honeys" and "dolls." There was no doubt about it: Donald was gay' (21). And if Donald, like Mitchell, is gay, then obviously they must be very much alike. But the book quickly turns the tables on twin studies narratives. For at the first face to face meeting of the twins, Mitchell is confronted not with his mirror image, not with someone 'exactly like him' (8), but with Donald's alter ego Kitten Kaboodle, flamboyant drag queen and singer at the Tam-Tam Club. This is not the recognition scene he had rehearsed; this is not what the infotainment programme had led him to expect.[12]

Rather, the confrontation raises the question of the extent to which Mitchell and Kitten can be regarded as belonging to a single category of sexual identity. And that question leads to another: just how meaningful is it to discover that monozygotic twins tend to be concordant for homosexuality, that a gay twin is statistically likely to have a gay co-twin? In fact it is precisely as (un)revealing as finding out that identical twins are concordant for heterosexuality, when you consider the range of partners and partnerships than can be encompassed within this broad category. The very different gay stereotypes assigned to the two brothers make the point that sharing a hypothetical gay gene might be largely irrelevant in determining sexual identity. Rather a genetic disposition will be expressed through the cultural options available, which vary historically and geographically. The het/homo divide unquestioningly accepted in Puterbaugh's collection of twin studies and indeed more generally in our culture is a fairly recent invention, as Foucault (1976), Katz (1996) and other historians of sexuality have argued. Since sexual behaviour cannot be isolated from the cultural positions through which we engage in it, presumably, before the late nineteenth century, a 'gay gene' (and indeed a 'straight gene') would have produced quite different identities and conduct again from those represented by Rodi's pool of players.

The range of gay identities Rodi invokes is more varied than the polarities represented by Mitchell and Kitten. Just in case the reader was tempted to binarise homosexuals into outrageous drag queens and anally retentive aesthetes, there is Mitchell's leather-man friend Simon, who represents another gay subculture, fiercely virile and contemptuous of the drag scene. Here are three contemporary cultural options for a gay gene to pursue, sufficiently different to empty meaning from the notion of genetic determination.

Stereotypes – not unlike twin studies – thrive on clear-cut categories, preferably two: us and them. It is ironic that a genre that trades in stereotypes, namely parody, may function to undermine their application, as Rodi's novel does. Rodi is not out to dismiss stereotypes, but to displace them. If Mitchell sees Kitten as 'the living embodiment of every cliché straights had about faggots' (28), clearly the same could be said of Mitchell himself and of Simon. All three are not just 'out,' but are out-an-out caricatures. However the combined effect of the three characters is such that none can be seen to represent single-handedly the category 'gay.' Rather they expose the tensions within a supposed community.

In *Declining the Stereotype*, Mireille Rosello argues that if stereotypes cannot be eradicated (1998: 128), they can perhaps be 'declined.' Sometimes, however, declining in the sense of simply refusing is neither possible nor indeed strategic, and so Rosello invokes the linguistic sense of declension: to decline a noun is to recite all its possible forms and variations. She suggests that attention to the formal characteristics of a stereotype can work to deprive it of some of its harmful potential (1998: 10–11). *Drag Queen* is not unlike a declension of the gay stereotype – a focus on all its possible forms and variations – for Rodi's strategy is to complicate stereotypes by multiplying them. Rather than contesting a gay male stereotype by making Mitchell less prissy, he does the opposite, pushing Mitchell's character as far as possible into the caricature of the fastidious fop, but at the same time introducing the equally clichéd but widely divergent gay characters of ultra-masculinist Simon and histrionic Kitten. Not even the drag queens are a homogeneous bunch, Kitten sharing the classification with thick-set Amazonian bouncer Carlotta. If, for twin studies researchers, 'homosexual' is the answer to a question, for Rodi it needs a follow-up question – 'what sort?' – in order to be meaningful. Rodi's readers know (or learn) that homosexuality is not a single sexuality let alone a monolithic lifestyle. Rodi's sharp wit contrasts with the bluntness of the research instruments used in so many of the twin studies pertaining to homosexuality. While the latter tend simply to binarise sexuality into homosexual/heterosexual, Rodi disrupts the dyad through the proliferation of identities.

Rosello warns, however, that the multiplication of images is not sufficient to counteract the power of stereotypes, and we can extend the application of her logic to the power of the het/homo binary:

It is true that the strength of stereotypical images often comes from their uniqueness, because uniqueness begs for simple equations (community x = delinquency), but the grammar or syntax of the stereotype can survive even if plurality is introduced. 'All Arabs are ...' can be followed by several adjectives or nouns, even contradictory sets of words. When the grammar of stereotyping is combined with diversity, a list results that adds the force of a litany to the rhetoric of formulas adopted by stereotypes' (1998: 72).

She suggests that what is additionally required, in order to discredit and disarm a stereotype, is attention to its formal characteristics, through, for example, ironic repetition and carefully framed quotations (1998: 11).

Rodi obliges: when Mitchell first sets eyes on Kitten and sees 'the living embodiment of every cliché straights had about faggots' (1995: 28), he does not simply see a stereotypical drag queen, but a quotation of someone else's pernicious stereotype, dangerous to himself. And in order to see her this way, he must align himself momentarily with a straight line of sight, while simultaneously distancing himself from it. This split or stereo perspective is the very definition of irony, and alerts the reader to Mitchell's initial blindness to his own conformity to a cliché that is only apparently benign.

Rodi's quotation of stereotypes undermines not only the clichés themselves but the classificatory system that spawned them. All three main characters see themselves as the epitome of gayness. However all three have different preconceived ideas about who rightfully belongs in the category 'gay' and who does not. Having struggled for acceptance as a gay corporate lawyer, Mitchell discovers his own prejudices about how gays should comport themselves. He rejects Kitten's cavorting as unbecoming to any self-respecting gay, but Mitchell is not the only one to impose a straight-jacketed view of the authentically gay. Perhaps leather-cinched is a more appropriate metaphor in Simon's case. Simon is far from reticent in rejecting Kitten and her kittenish ways, excluding femininity of any kind from gay membership and even seeing drag queens as a different species altogether: 'They're not a third sex, they're a second species. Something vital is missing, something – something *human*' (51). From within the ghetto, Simon repeats the ultimate statement of exclusion and excuse for atrocities: the Others are so different that they can no longer be classed as human beings. And yet, the reporting of his speech ('Tweak. Tweak.') is continually interrupted ('Tweak. Tweak.') by the distracting and potentially arousing way in which Simon pulls at his unpierced nipple, an intrusive reminder of Simon's sexuality and the fact that he too belongs to a group that has been persecuted as less than human. And when his little tirade is immediately followed by a scene in which his friends chant '*Simon says, Simon says*' (52) we see how transparently formulaic his rendition of the division into us/them, same/other, human/inhuman has been.

No-one is, however, categorically innocent. Even Kitten, the victim of these exclusionary classifications by Mitchell and Simon, is caught out with her categorising. Unlike the others, she does not reject particular forms of (homo)sexuality. It is not that her use of the label 'gay' is too narrow, rather it is too wide. She does not exclude, but includes too readily. She is being courted by Zack Crespin, an old frat brother of Mitchell's, but when she broaches the subject of his gayness, Zack pulls her up short:

> '*I'm not gay*. I love women. *Love* 'em.' he shrugged. 'Probably more than any guy you'll ever know. Been with all kinds – fat, skinny, black, white, old, young. Hell, it's tough for me to think of a type of chick I *don't* want to screw.' He turned to her. 'Which is pretty much why I'm with you, kid. To me, you're just one more kind of chick – a chick with a dick.' (146)

Even Kitten has fallen into the trap of using categories with overly tidy edges. Zack does not fit neatly into a simple homo/het binary, and there are more possibilities than simply straight or gay. If Mitchell, Kitten and Simon complicate the dichotomy by multiplying gay stereotypes, Zack disturbs it by straddling the divide. And yet all these characters would be expected to tick the same box on the behaviour geneticists' questionnaire. That Mitchell, Kitten, Simon and Zack are all considered gay men at least some of the time, gives an idea of the range of paths a 'gay gene' might take.

Mitchell's encounters with his twin force him to reconsider his definition of gayness. He confronts this question as he surveys the clientele of Dreamweaver's bar, trying to determine gender and sexuality: 'He couldn't decide if this place was straight or gay, camp or hip, or something else he didn't yet know the name of' (89–90). 'Queer' is of course the name that springs to mind, a more nebulous and inclusive term than gay. Queer is an unstable category, its diverse membership united only by a lack of identification with normative sexual identities, and to some extent *Drag Queen* recounts the queering of Mitchell's outlook.[13] Would queer then be a more appropriate umbrella term for describing Rodi's characters? Is queerness what Mitchell and Kitten share in the way of sexuality? If so, this would suggest that twin studies researchers might do better to seek a queer gene – some loosely defined propensity to stray from the straight and narrow – than a gay one. But the quest for a queer gene is doomed before it starts. However non-specific in referring to sexual practices, the term queer is highly culturally specific in its usage. And no, Mitchell and Kitten could not be said to share queerness. Like 'gay,' the term 'queer' is problematic in its application to Rodi's characters: Mitchell, for most of the book, is emphatically not queer; womaniser Zack is unlikely to accept the label; and Simon recoils from any contiguity with drag queens. Only Kitten/ Donald uses the epithet in self-description when posing as Mitchell – nearly blowing the cover, for it is not a term by which Mitchell refers to himself (242).

The difficulty arises from the fact that although queer confounds the either/or constraints of the homo/het binary, it does not escape binaries altogether, and in fact exists by virtue of an oppositional relation with the term straight. Halperin makes this clear when he writes:

> Queer is by definition *whatever* is at odds with the normal, the legitimate, the dominant. *There is nothing in particular to which it necessarily refers*. It is an identity without an essence. 'Queer,' then, demarcates not a positivity but a positionality vis-à-vis the normative – a positionality that is not restricted to lesbians and gay men but is in fact available to anyone who is or who feels marginalized because of her or his sexual practices […]. (Halperin, 1995: 62)

The queer/normative opposition is embodied by the flamboyant drag queen/respectable gay lawyer pair. Mitchell is the epitome of the straight gay. However much he may pride himself on being out of the closet, he is censorious and uptight. He is a suit (albeit an Armani one), committed to his career in corporate law, and reluctant to rock the boat. Deeply shocked at Kitten's capers, he immediately wishes 'to straighten out Donald (so to speak). Get him off this drag thing and into a real, respectable lifestyle' (28), and vows 'to salvage his twin from a life of irrelevancy and buffoonery' (95). At the very least she should wear 'normal clothes' (36) to their meeting. And he is no less shocked at the Simon's leather-club antics. For Mitchell, being gay means being invisible, fitting in as much as possible: 'He'd devoted his life to proving to straight people that gays were no different from them, that they were just as serious, just as hardworking – just as, in a word, dull' (28). His character epitomises Bersani's paradox of gay presence/absence (1995: 31–2, 67–8), whereby increasing mainstream acceptance of gays (the gay presence) has been achieved by blending in with the crowd, and disavowing any specific cultural presence (the gay absence). Mitchell is, then, the straight gay who finally comes across to meet his queer twin on her own ground, however straight/queer is not a binary the book leaves intact, for Zack is the queer straight.

If sexual identities such as gay and queer are questioned in Rodi's novel, gender identities – male/female, masculine/feminine – are even more explicitly disturbed. Predictably, gender categories are most obviously blurred by Kitten Kaboodle, who hovers between the roles of Mitchell's brother and sister (91). Mitchell asks why she does not have The Operation, revealing his assumption that drag queens are men who want to be women, and a lack of imagination as to alternatives to these two genders. But it is Simon who takes the straight line to the point where it turns back on itself. Distancing himself from any hint of gay effeminacy, Simon proposes an exaggerated divide. In an effort to eliminate any cross-contamination of gender, Simon's club Darklords has 'an entirely gay membership' and 'gay' here excludes drag queens: 'We don't have any truck with the feminine, Mitchell – the irrational, emotional, anti-intellectual feminine' (104–5). Mitchell's flight from the threat Kitten poses towards the hyper-masculine Darklords is a parody of homophobia, as Mitchell is persuaded that drag queens are not human but 'walking agents of chaos': 'Men should be *men*, Simon. Women should be women. Confusing the two – that's an act of sedition. Of anarchism' (104). However the gender divide is already crossed in Simon's discourse when he explains that the '[m]asculine concepts like order, tradition, hierarchy' (105) he reveres are embodied in a queen – the British monarch. Once again, Simon mouths patriarchal platitudes about the vague threats to the social order posed by the disturbance of the opposition between masculine and feminine, while unable even to separate the two in ideal form. And Mitchell, who allows himself to be seduced both by the club's ethos and by one of its members, Kip, soon discovers that Kip with his weakness for Broadway musicals is a queen at heart: 'the insidious tentacles of the feminine' reach into even 'the most ultra-masculine enclave' (121).

Gender identities are further disturbed by Mitchell's manipulative sister Paula and colleague Zoe, both of whom are much more closely aligned with the drag queens than with other female characters. Donald (Kitten in mufti) understands Paula 'instinctively' and 'admire[s] her instinct for getting what she wanted' (241). A mere pawn in Paula's scheme for self-advancement, 'Donald shut his eyes and wondered, Is this how Mitchell feels when he can't get rid of Kitten?' (230). Paula is 'all sharp angles and hard edges,' one of those women 'so powerfully beautiful they could actually afford to act mannish' (163), a masculine drag queen.

Zoe is similarly larger than life and over-colourful, both in her dress (lime-green and bejewelled, 160) and in her plot to muscle in on Mitchell's position at the office. In her perfidy she is explicitly aligned with Regina Upright, the chanteuse who pushes Kitten from her slot at the Tam Tam Club. The twins realise that their lives are running in parallel: each is being stabbed in the back by a female rival from the same (that is, drag queen) mould (187). More dramatically, Zoe is dragged off the street as a drag queen when Mitchell's misguided plan to have his twin kidnapped and 'deprogrammed' goes awry. Zoe is mistaken for Kitten, abducted and subjected to aversion therapy for drag queens over twelve hours, and has to be groped at the crotch before her captors will accept their error. A supposedly 'natural' woman, Zoe is to all intents and purposes indistinguishable from the line-up at the Tam Tam Club.

In a series of classic deconstructive moves, binaries – male/female, homo/het, gay/straight, queer/straight – are transposed and undone. Presumed contraries coexist and oppositions are realigned as Rodi's characters complicate and disorganise apparently discrete categories of identity. In addition to perturbing the pigeon-holes, the novel canvasses several contemporary interpretations of sexual and gender identity: is it what's in your genes? or what's in your jeans? or how well you carry off the performance? We have seen that *Drag Queen* problematises the genetic explanation (or at least oversimplified versions of the gay gene hypothesis), and mocks the kind of biological dualism that blithely aligns genitals with gender. Its engagement with the notion of identity as performative is more complex, and leads us to a discussion of competing conceptions of the self in contemporary culture.

Dragging for identity

Identical twins routinely raise the question of identity, and we shall see that *Drag Queen* recycles the conventions of twin comedies in order to engage with competing discourses of the self. As the story unfolds, the novel shifts from a tension between constructivist and essentialist positions towards a more fluid understanding of selfhood. The tension and its resolution are played out in the evolving relationship between the twins.

The gay gene hypothesis relies on a premise of sexual identity as hardwired and immutable. Mitchell (who sees eye to eye with the television documentary on twin resemblance) subscribes to this view, and interprets his sexuality through the 'coming-out' discourse: his gayness had always defined him, and was finally acknowledged publicly when he came out (8). It is part of his core identity, a true self that must not be denied, a notion reflected in Mitchell's promise to himself, on coming out, to tell the truth without exception from that day on (74).[14]

If Mitchell sees himself as truthful and true, he considers Kitten to be both a liar and a fake, her dress a costume and her persona a pretence. He accuses her of living a lie (73), of running away from her real self (208). Kitten, however, turns Mitchell's true/false distinction around: rather than representing the fake to Mitchell's real, Kitten *en grande toilette* claims to be an original to Mitchell's copy. She is a creature of her own creation, one of a kind (204), while nondescript Mitchell is a greyscale photocopy of an identity, 'a big gray absence of a person' (209, cf. 241). Explaining her disinterest in sex reassignment surgery, she remarks: 'Kitten was one hundred percent my creation. So, why would I want to get some surgeon involved, make him partly responsible for her?' (207). Although Mitchell impugns her claim to uniqueness, saying she looks 'like Ivana Trump's stunt-double' (64), Kitten succeeds in rewriting Mitchell's dichotomy real/pretence as original/copy and then switching the content of the categories. Rather than drag queens, for Kitten it is copycats such as lip-synchers and conformist lawyers who are the ones with no real self, with a derived identity.

From Kitten's perspective, lies – such as the melodramatic life-story Kitten tells a journalist (68) – are an important aspect of self-invention. Along with clothes and coiffure, they are the construction materials for the self. Self-construction is an iterative process: 'I start over every morning. Build myself up from scratch.' (36). Hair in particular effects the passage from one identity to another: 'Donald took his long blond wig, bent over, and affixed it to his scalp. But it wasn't Donald who stood up and tossed the silken tresses into place; it was Kitten Kaboodle, the Doyenne of Despair' (38).

Kitten places her self-creation in a female tradition of stardom: in the Golden Age of Hollywood, while male actors 'were all so natural,' able simply to draw on a longstanding masculine iconography of the heroic, female actors had to construct their characters from scratch (205). The lack of any female iconic tradition other than 'the Virtuous Wife and the Whore' was compensated for by outrageous theatricality.

Female historical figures found themselves in the same position of having to invent themselves. The link to drag is made explicit in the discussion of Elizabeth the First: 'Probably the first drag-queen role model in history. *Everything* about her was the most fabulous artifice, and she carried it off like some legendary Warner Brothers movie idol' (206). Thus Kitten sees artifice as the prerequisite for originality, not its antithesis, while seeming naturalness (*à la* Gary Cooper, Spencer Tracy and Jimmy Stewart) consists merely in adopting existing personas.

Kitten's identity is thus a performance in the Hollywood mould, and it needs to be constantly rehearsed for others: 'She had an uncanny feeling that she was in a movie, playing a part. Must remember to act like I feel something, she told herself. [...] It helped her acting to have an actual audience.' (115) Although these are her thoughts when she hears of her adoptive mother's death, it applies more generally to her sense of self. Kitten's identity is both formed and performed in relation to an (often anonymous) audience.

Thus far, the twins appear to represent the diametrically opposed poles of essentialist and constructivist accounts of identity formation, the poles of nature and nurture so important to twin studies research. Mitchell focuses on the nature of identity (his own true nature) while Kitten is more interested in its cultural construction. Mitchell sees identity in terms of being, Kitten in terms of doing. As you might expect with identical twins, however, the opposition is undermined. There is an underlying sameness to the two interpretations.

Kitten's position for most of the novel is in fact paradoxical, for she wields the discourse of self-creation at the same time as she invokes the 'real me.'[15] 'This is me, this is the way I am. I could pretend to be something I'm not for you, but I wouldn't ask *you* to do that for *me*' (61), she tells Mitchell. To create Kitten, 'I kept dressing and acting out until I reached a point where I felt like me – the point where I became Kitten' (207), she explains, and soon after she repeats to her twin that Kitten, not Donald, is 'the way I really am' (209). Despite the avowed self-construction, Kitten's sense of self is not so far from Mitchell's. She too supports the idea of real and fake selves, and Donald – her persona when in masculine attire – is the fake. Only when wounded by Regina's perfidy is there a moment where Kitten doubts her self: 'And this indeed was the measure of her despair: that for the first time in her life, she felt more comfortable as Donald' (179). It is as if there is at all times a pre-existing interior self that the visible self-creation needs to match.

Kitten, then, although a constructivist, is still far from subscribing to Judith Butler's concept of performative identity. In *Gender Trouble* (1990), Butler argues that gender is a highly regulated cultural performance, and that the repetition and continuity of this performance create the effect of gender identity: 'acts and gestures, articulated and enacted desires create the illusion of an interior and organizing gender core' (1990: 136). Rather than stemming from a pre-existing essence of the self, our sense of self is produced by copying the performance of others in (among other aspects) gender expression. Butler goes on to suggest that drag queens, in flaunting this process, expose the imitation that passes for the real, the contrived artlessness of the spectacle of the 'natural' woman: 'The parodic repetition of "the original," [...] reveals the original to be nothing other than a parody of the *idea* of the natural and the original' (1990: 31) (and indeed this is precisely what occurs when Zoe is mistaken for a drag queen). Thus drag queen is to 'natural' woman (and even to straight-laced lawyer) '*not* as copy is to original, but, rather, as copy is to copy' (1990: 31).

If Mitchell proclaims the truth of his gay self, Kitten too aspires to realness. Indeed both twins lay claim to superior authenticity in their identity. There is, however, little chance of either of them winning the debate, for despite their stated views, they embody Butler's argument: as identical twins they undo the hierarchy of original and copy, being genetic copies without an original blueprint. Although clones of one another, neither twin provided the model. As if to emphasise this fact, there is no record of which twin was born first (78). No hierarchy can be established. These twins were born double, neither more authentic than the other.

The twins only start to rethink their positions, however, as events unfold towards the end of the novel and the conventions of comic twin tales are brought to bear on questions of sexual identity. Classic twin scenes are those in which one twin dresses up as the other, one is mistaken for the other, one recognises (him/herself in) the other. Rodi defers these until quite late in the novel.

Comedies of errors

In most twin comedies, confusion between lookalikes reigns from early in the text, and is then resolved in the conclusion, in which identities are sorted out. In *Drag Queen*, however, such confusion – constantly expected – is delayed. When Kitten flounces into Mitchell's office, there is no possibility that she will be taken for Mitchell and asked to negotiate real estate deals. And Kitten's agent is similarly unlikely to ask Mitchell to model his hands as Kitten does. These twins are, then, not unwitting doppelgängers, mistaken for one another. But the moment of high farce inevitably arrives towards the end of the book. It is preceded by Mitchell's plea to see his twin in male garb, a request that makes explicit what Mitchell desires from his twin: to see himself in/as another:

'[...] What if I come over tomorrow, after work, and we just go out for a couple of drinks? With you as you.'
'You've already *met* me as me.'
'You know what I mean. With you as *me*, then.' (188)

The request is not to 'come as yourself' but to come as Mitchell, as Mitchell's self, to be identical to Mitchell. Donald obliges, and so the two players are finally seen to resemble each other uncannily, with only Kitten's long fingernails distinguishing them: 'He looked amazingly, astonishingly, like Mitchell' (202). This is the first time Mitchell has been able to recognise himself in his twin. Several drinks later, under Donald's deft hand with make-up and under protest, Mitchell is transformed and recognises his twin in himself: 'I ... I'm Kitten! he realized with horror' (212). Mitchell's giddy moment is not the vertiginous experience of seeing double, but the disconcerting one of seeing Kitten and Donald simultaneously. Paradoxically, in order to resemble his identical twin, Mitchell has to be made up to look quite unlike himself, while Kitten too has to change appearance to something that feels decidedly uncomfortable, and unrecognisable as herself.

In initiating Mitchell's makeover, Donald reasons that the only way Mitchell will ever understand his perspective is by seeing it from the inside. Little does he guess that he too will experience a new way of seeing. Being dressed as Donald (that is, as Kitten in drag) paves the way for change, splitting Donald and Kitten and allowing them to be seen as two characters. Mitchell's twin is referred to as Donald (and with masculine pronouns) throughout the latter part of the novel, opening up other possibilities for understanding Kitten's identity.

The clowning begins when an urgent call from Mitchell's boss sees Donald take his place in corporate negotiations, while Mitchell finds himself performing Kitten's routine at the Tam-Tam to save her job. Interestingly there is no bedtrick involved in the confusion of identities, no substituting one for the other in romantic encounters. Rather this is a 'worktrick,' in which each attempts to embody the other's professional persona.

Convinced of the constructedness of Kitten's self, Donald at last realises the performative nature of Mitchell's identity when he has to carry it off. 'When was the last time I was out in this identity?' he muses, but then realises: 'Of course, he wasn't going anywhere as Donald, now. He was going as Mitchell' (222). His way of assuming a masculine identity is to play Mitchell, carefully hiding his tell-tale fingernails, the key to twin recognition in *Drag Queen*.[16] The supposed naturalness of Mitchell's lawyer figure is shown as something that does not come naturally, but requires stagecraft.[17] Donald's point of reference for doing Mitchell is television: 'He'd seen enough episodes of "L.A. Law" to fake it.' (248). But faking it means that he still clings to the notion of the real self.

That changes, however, when Donald (as Mitchell) watches (Mitchell as) Kitten on stage: 'and there in the bright blue spotlight appeared a vision of – himself. His *other* self. Kitten!' (245). Kitten drifts from being the essence of self to the 'other self' to an identity increasingly detached from her creator. Donald surprises himself by 'taking mental notes, like, *Vibrato on the first note in the phrase instead of the last; I'll have to try that*' (247), learning how better to perform Kitten's identity from Mitchell's reinvention. Mitchell, in jollying up the hitherto tragic stage persona with a rendition of 'Put on a happy face,' produces a Kitten no less real. The song functions as a refrain, alluding to a performative notion of identity, and the possibility of self-transformation. Meanwhile Mitchell, through his (literal) performance of Kitten, experiences a drag self that no longer seems untrue, and Donald even begins to enjoy butch role-playing, using his lowest register to come on to queen Marina (243). By the time Mitchell's boss attempts to re-establish identities – 'Which one of you is Mitchell Sayer?' (251) – neither twin claims the identity to they were so attached at the beginning of the novel, and neither twin has an investment in the authentic self. Mitchell proudly declares: 'Don't look at me. *My* name is Kitten Kaboodle' (252) while his brother introduces himself as Donald.

The twins have moved from their polarised viewpoints to sharing a revised conception of identity, one symbolised by a recurring image in *Drag Queen*. Relatively early in the novel, while Kitten is being interviewed for a magazine story, something seemingly extraneous occurs outside the window to interrupt both the interview – Kitten blurts out 'Is that a body in the river?' (67) – and the novel, in that the event is never connected with the plot. Concurrent with the progress of the interview are attempts to recover the body. The two are only loosely associated in the text: firstly by Mitchell's desire to 'trade[ ] places with the corpse' rather than answer questions about his connection with drag (68) and secondly by the journalist's comment 'Fascinating,' for 'it wasn't clear whether she meant Kitten's story, or the crane the police boat was now positioning above the floating corpse' (69). Mitchell's wish is at first glance simply another way of saying 'I'd rather be dead.' But the parallel between Kitten's fiction of the twins' family origins and the floating corpse makes Mitchell's apparent death wish worth pursuing further. Kitten fishes for a life-story to suit the occasion, while the anonymous floating body the police are fishing out is severed from a life-story. Both give rise to speculation and invention. Both avoid any anchoring of identity. If we reinterpret Mitchell's comment along these lines, the wish to trade places with the corpse becomes a desire for a floating identity. This wish, we shall see, is ultimately fulfilled.

This interpretation is reinforced elsewhere in the novel. Being made up feels like Shiatsu for Mitchell: 'Feels a little bit like I'm floating [...], floating above a big forest' (211). The sensation accompanies his transformation into Kitten, his drift from one identity to another. Gazing upon his unfamiliar reflection feels 'curiously lightening' (213) as he slips anchor from his habitual straight-laced self.

Donald experiences a similar sensation when Mitchell appears on stage as Kitten, for he is suddenly dissociated from the persona he has created: 'He felt suddenly weightless, as though he were dissipating, turning to fog. [...] Yet he looked down at his feet [...] still solid, still here. He hadn't dissipated at all' (245). The creature he had crafted and whom he saw as his real self has somehow ceased to occupy the core of his being. He now glides unattached, open to other possibilities of selfhood: 'Let Mitchell be Kitten from now on; Donald would take over as Mitchell' (248). Previously his essential self, Kitten is suddenly seen as an identity that can be adopted by others, that can even be lent, a floating identity.

Donald raises the anchor on Kitten, allowing her to become a floating identity in the most literal way (atop a float in the Gay Pride parade), and to be adopted by Mitchell. Mitchell (who has quit his straight job and is now working for gay and lesbian clients) replaces Donald (who has been knifed protecting him at the club) as Kitten Kaboodle on the Tam-Tam parade float. Donald, arm in sling, looks on with delight. He is planning his first holiday, both from Chicago and from Kitten – now that Mitchell can continue the role in his absence. And as the float passes, Simon is left speechless with confusion at the now virtually interchangeable twins, who drift in and out of resemblance. Kitten has learnt to play Donald, Mitchell has learnt to play

Kitten, and both have learnt to enjoy it. No longer the truth of self, nor a creation to match one's core being, identity is now viewed less earnestly as something to (role-)play with, and something from which you can even take a holiday.

Traditionally, twin comedies move from confusion to clarity. *Drag Queen* inverses this order: only at its conclusion can the twins be mistaken for each other. This comedy produces rather than resolves errors. Conventionally, the dénouement serves to re-establish identities and stabilise them through the romantic pairing off of each twin with a separate partner, thus resolving the bedtrick(s) characteristic of the genre. *Drag Queen* offers no such stabilisation of identity – its purpose was never to calm gender or identity anxieties. It ends with Donald, Kitten, Mitchell, and Simon – characters whose differences earlier represented tensions and discontinuities that were papered over by the label 'gay' – all present at the parade. They do not, however, simply appear under one banner, in some kind of gay synthesis. Rather the parade gathers a multitude of banners in a celebration of diversity. And if the twins have become more similar, this does not mean that they have both attained some definitive (genetically programmed?) gay identity. Rather, through their relationship, they have each dissolved their ideas of the definitive self. It is their new enthusiasm for metamorphosis that makes them interchangeable at times.

Parody and purpose

In her discussion of drag as parody and its potential for destabilising heteronormative identities, Judith Butler asserts that 'the task is not whether to repeat but how to repeat' (1990: 148). The repetition that is parody can serve many purposes, not all of them transgressive. What purposes then does Rodi's retelling serve as he transposes a familiar tale?

Not just a gay version of a comic tale, Rodi's parody adapts a particular set of narrative habits to queer purposes, engaging the potential of twins to destabilise oppositions and identities. The conventions of the long-lost twin narrative play into Rodi's hands as he light-heartedly undoes the dichotomies masculine/feminine, male/female, gay/straight, same/different, identical/fraternal, nature/nurture, oppositions underpinning the earnest enterprise of twins research.

The use of twins in the quest for the gay gene invites us to dwell on the question: do you become gay or are you born that way? Reading *Drag Queen* as a commentary on such twins research allows us to open up such questions. Rodi makes us ask 'just which way do you mean?' by laying out some of the disparate ways in which a putative gay gene might express itself. But he goes further in engaging with the overarching nature/nurture debate that prompts twin studies. Through the story of Mitchell, Donald and Kitten, he suggests that the question is not whether nature, nurture or some combination of the two makes you who you are. For such a question implies that 'who you are' is clear and steady, and can be contained in a case file based on an interview or a set of questionnaires. Rather, *Drag Queen* raises the possibility that 'who we are' depends to some extent on the day of the week and the floating identities and stories we fish out for ourselves. Rodi is less interested in whether nature and/or nurture moulds identity than he is in the possibility of slipping out of the mould, whatever its provenance. As such, he engages with a discourse of identity that moves beyond debates between constructivists and essentialists towards a postmodern fluidity of the self.

6
Twins and Nations: Tales of Cultural Divides

National fissures

In 1997 a television news item signalling the fiftieth anniversary of the partition of India and Pakistan included a cameo piece: twin brothers, long separated by the border, were reunited to blow out the candles on their fiftieth birthday cake.[1] A perfect coincidence, of course, but also a perfect illustration of the way in which twins are so readily called upon to represent divided nations. The divisions in question may be across or within borders: external (a nation divided from its neighbour, as in this example) or internal (a nation fractured by political, ethnic or class divisions).

However, although twins regularly function as a metaphor for these national fissures, they do not always function in the same way. The use of twins to symbolise nations may be perennial, but it is not unchanging. Ancient stories of the founders and rulers of cities and civilisations provide the earliest examples of such twins: Romulus and Remus at the site of Rome; Zethus and Amphion building the walls of Thebes; Eteocles and Polyneices elected co-kings of Thebes; Acrisias and Proëtus dividing Argolis into the kingdoms of Argos and Tiryns; Atreus and Thyestes as rival heirs of Mycenae; the biblical twins Esau and Jacob begetting the two nations of Edom and Israel. These twins are fraternal rather than identical and often embody opposed talents and social principles: the hunter and the herdsman (Esau and Jacob), the labourer and the musician (Zethus and Amphion) (Zazzo, 1984: 146–54). Most notably, however, they are hostile rivals to the point of fratricide, Zethus and Amphion standing alone among these legendary twins in governing together peacefully. Twins in foundation myths disturb the principle of primogeniture, the right of the first-born son to rule

(Zazzo, 1984: 154). The equality of the twins puts a question mark over the legitimacy of power: the authority of the ruler is split at its source – his birth. The rivalry and antagonism of these twins suggest a fundamental division threatening societies at their very origin, an obstacle that needs to be overcome – usually by the death of one twin – in order for social cohesion and order to be achieved.[2]

In modern twin tales of nations, on the other hand, twins tend to represent the solution rather than the problem. Rather than creating division, they provide a means for surmounting it. Typically, this plays out as a triumph of sameness over difference, hence the prevalence of identical twins. However, once again, we find that twins – even twins used to represent nations – do not constitute a single topos.

This chapter traces some of the principal patterns found among modern twin tales of divided nations, and focuses on the importance of sameness and difference in each case. It then turns to a lesser-known novel by Mauritian author Marie-Thérèse Humbert, which departs from these patterns, not through a shift in genre or gender, but through a change of topos. In *A l'autre bout de moi*, Humbert adapts a classic twin tale to illustrate the dangers of privileging resemblance and unity as the pre-requisites for harmonious relations in this postcolonial world of hybrid identities and multiethnic nations. In the process, she questions the very nature of resemblance and the role it plays in the formation of identity.

'Siamese' nations

Most overtly allegorical in modern twin tales of cultural divides is the appearance of conjoined twins to symbolise nationhood. Unlike the rival twins of ancient legend, conjoined twins are used to portray not so much national division, as national unity over division. In 'America's "United Siamese Brothers,"' Alison Pingree analyses early nineteenth-century pamphlets and biographical articles about Chang and Eng, the twins from Siam, to demonstrate that these most famous of conjoined twins were appropriated as a symbol of unity among the American states following the Civil War. Publicity pamphlets for the brothers show the image of 'an eagle, sporting a banner reading "E Pluribus Unum" in its beak, with the motto "'United We Stand'" inscribed below' (1996: 92). During this period of uncertain union, the twins were depicted as the incarnation of the political ideal of a unity encompassing difference and plurality. Tellingly, Darin Strauss's fictional biography of Chang and Eng (2001) also highlights the parallels between the brothers' inescapable fraternity and the political tensions of the newly-United States of America. Far from triggering battles for supremacy, as in ancient myth, twins are here seen to embody the solution to the rivalry and fratricide of civil war.

Further north, John Ralston Saul uses conjoined twins as an emblematic image for his study of Canada at the end of the twentieth century, *Reflections of a Siamese Twin* (1997). In doing so he alludes to Jacques Godbout's novel *Les Têtes à Papineau* (1981): Charles-François Papineau is the name (laden with references to Quebec history) given to conjoined twins sharing a body, but with two heads, one anglophone, one francophone, who debate the possibility of separation.[3] Surgery takes place but enables only one twin to survive: the anglophone Charles F. Papineau, who writes that he is unable to complete the text because he no longer understands French. Here the elimination of one twin heralds not harmony but loss.

If twins pose a threat to the social order in ancient legend, these allegories offer conjoined twins as a hopeful image of peaceful if sometimes difficult cohabitation. Curiously, in these tales, it is their dissimilarity that is emphasised. And yet, unlike the mythic rulers, they are not fraternal twins. Conjoined twins of necessity share identical genes, and so it is significant that in invoking them to symbolise nationhood it is not their sameness but their difference that is foregrounded.

The border between them

In contrast, differences are downplayed and sameness is emphasised in the twins story most readily available for use in contemporary tales of nations – that of the reconciliation of twins raised apart. Separated early in life, living parallel but contrasting lives on opposite sides of a border, such twins finally meet and rekindle a relationship across the frontier. Here again, twins suggest the possibility of overcoming divisions. The topos appears across genres and is easily transferred geographically. It can be used to sum up, in a few moments of news footage, fifty years of India-Pakistan relations (as illustrated in the introduction to this chapter) or to explore at length the legacy of World War II, as we shall see. Although usually male, the twins may be of either sex, in keeping with the plot (combatant male twins in nations at war, for example) or with a tradition of gendered representations of the nation. They are almost never, however, of mixed gender, for what remains constant is the need for, if not an identical pair, then at least twins who are interchangeable in some way.

The documentary film *Oskar and Jack* (1997) recounts the life stories of a pair of identical twins raised apart and reunited late in life through the Minnesota twins project directed by Professor Bouchard (see Chapter 5). If Oskar and Jack were considered the most newsworthy of all Bouchard's research subjects, it is due to their potential to represent nations. In 1979, when their reunion took place, newspapers (shown in the documentary) bore the headline 'Twins! Nazi and Jew.' Born in Trinidad to a Jewish father and German mother, the twins were separated soon after birth in 1933 when their parents split up, Jack growing up a practising Jew in Trinidad, Oskar a German in a family with strong Nazi sympathies. Their first meeting, in their twenties, faltered over political differences and was marked by mistrust, but later in life, they arrive at mutual understanding achieved through the sharing of their stories. In the documentary, each twin tells of his childhood fear/fantasy of meeting the other in combat during World War II.[4]

The topos of twins separated by a border is equally available for fictional use. Like *Oskar and Jack*, Tessa de Loo's novel *De tweeling* (1993, *The Twins*, 2002) explores the different perspectives from which twins separated in childhood experience Nazism. After the death of their parents, Anna and Lotte are raised apart by different branches of the family, Lotte in the Netherlands, where she becomes engaged to a Dutch Jew, Anna in rural poverty in Germany, where she marries an SS officer. Both lose their partners during the war. Some forty years later, the two elderly women meet again by chance at a health resort. Each recognises her own suffering during the war, but Lotte in particular resists reconciliation, believing that Anna was not merely a victim of circumstance but was complicitous in inflicting the misery endured by the Dutch. Only through the forced exchange of narratives does each sister arrive at a grudging understanding of the hardship experienced by her twin and by the nation she represents.

These twin tales echo historical novels and films of brothers at arms on opposite sides (Confederate and Yankee, roundhead and cavalier, loyalist and republican Irish brothers) in which brotherhood triumphs over enmity and sameness is (re)discovered across difference. The topos is clearly available for adaptation to a range of conflicts, and one can equally imagine twin stories waiting to be told about Israeli and Palestinian, Serbian and Croatian, North and South Korean, Iraqi and American twins. If the story is somewhat predictable, the interest lies in the allegorical detail, in the embedding of the twin tale in specific national histories.

Although de Loo's twins are not identical (Lotte's weaker health is the pretext for the sisters' separation), the same premise of sameness underlies all these stories.[5] The use of twins raised apart as a trope for life on two sides of a border depends for its force on the image of an arbitrary separation creating difference where there was none: 'there but for the grace of God, go I.' Only the luck of the draw seems to designate who will adopt which religion or political position, who will be the victim and who the perpetrator. Oskar and Jack make this evident as they focus on small discrepancies between them as babies that might have led a parent to choose one twin over the other. Lotte's conviction that she would have acted differently in her sister's place loses its certainty. Apparently irreconcilable differences are belied by the shared heritage of the twins, and the peoples of warring nations are mirrored in each other. Twins, then, offer the possibility of seeing the life one might have lived, but for circumstances, here geographical ones.[6]

A more ambiguous and innovative use of twins separated by a border as a figure for national fissures occurs in Agota Kristof's trilogy of novels: *The Notebook, The Proof* and *The Third Lie* (first published 1986, 1988, 1991). It starts with a tale of twins evacuated to a village at the frontier between East and West, as the iron curtain drops. One twin manages to cross the border to the West. Inconsistencies multiply, however, and successive narratives indicate that most of the events recounted are fabrications, although the relentless, everyday cruelty, the amoral acts of survival, vengeance and possessive love belie a truth that goes beyond the circumstances of events. The tissue of lies leaves the reader unclear, for much of the trilogy, as to whether there are in fact twin brothers or whether one (but which one?) is an invention of the other. The phantom twinship makes the trilogy hover between classification as a tale of twins or a tale of doubles. Is there one? Are there two? Is there a relation(ship) across the border, or merely the illusion of one? Although there is an exchange of (multiple and conflicting) narratives, this is no story of a celebration of brotherhood. In a departure from the usual tale of the triumph of sameness over difference, Kristof depicts unhealing wounds and insurmountable obstacles to reconciliation.

Changelings

Although internal fissures in national identity may be represented by twins raised apart – greedy gringo/warm-hearted hispanic in the film comedy *Steal Big Steal Little* (1995), decadent bourgeois/bomb-throwing revolutionary in the Hungarian art-film *My Twentieth Century* (1988)[7] – another common topos is that of babies swapped at birth, of change-lings. Hospital error sees Etienne, in the film *The Third Walker* (1978), brought up in a French-Canadian family rather than with his English-speaking twin in the next village. Changelings are, however, more often doubles, metaphorical rather than biological twins. Thus the children of Salman Rushdie's *Midnight's Children* (1981) are boys born at the same instant: midnight on 15 August 1947, the moment of birth of India as an independent nation. Separated by class and religion, they are immediately swapped in the cradles in a disruption of that separation.

Midnight's Children builds on an extensive narrative tradition of twins/doubles of differing social standing who change places. Among its more famous literary precursors are two of Mark Twain's stories. In *The Prince and the Pauper* (first published 1882), lookalike boys, each envying the other, swap places and become trapped in the other's role. Each becomes wiser before the prince regains the palace and the pauper returns to a somewhat improved position among the common-ers. 'Pudd'nhead Wilson' (first published 1894) adds race to the equa-tion in its story of the cradle swap of the slave's child and the master's heir (apparently half-brothers). The wickedness of the usurper shows that he is unfit for any but the slave condition to which he is eventu-ally returned when the true identity of the rightful heir is revealed. In concluding by swapping characters back to their original stations, Twain's texts use the double ultimately to reaffirm the status quo. In 'Pudd'nhead Wilson' in particular, a similarity of appearance obscures more profound social divisions. Nonetheless, in *The Prince and the Pauper*, and indeed in the majority of more recent examples, such as Martin Amis's *Success* (1978), the ease of interchangeability indicates an essential sameness concealed by superficial class differences. The double therefore serves to question, sometimes discreetly, sometimes quite plainly, the existence of social inequalities.

This latter perspective is the theme of the documentary *Twins in Black and White* (1998), which recounts the experiences of sets of twins with different skin colour. Just as skin colour varies among brothers and sisters in ethnically mixed families, so fraternal twins can be born with colouring different enough for one to be seen as black, the other white in social situations. The film highlights the impact this difference – literally skin-deep – has made on the twins' lives and on their relationship with each other. Here too, the emphasis is on the

circumstantial nature of social divisions, in contrast with the fundamental sameness evoked in our culture by the idea of twins, whether
identical or not.[8]

A double-take on identity

Twins raised apart across borders, changelings that cross class or
cultural barriers, the forced cohabitation of conjoined twins: these are,
then, the conventional modern patterns for telling national stories
through twin tales. Each in its own way proposes twinship as a way of
overcoming division, either through unity (conjoined twins) or resemblance (changelings and separated twins). Rather than representing the
source of strife, as in the foundation myths, twins now offer a readily
available image for the solution to strife, for peaceful coexistence.
Marie-Thérèse Humbert's novel *A l'autre bout de moi* (literally *At the
Other End of Me*, 1979),[9] follows a rather different path, whereby
the ideals of unity and resemblance, far from healing divisions, exacer-
bate tensions with tragic consequences. At the same time, the twin
viewpoints presented in the novel allow us to glimpse alternatives to
these ideals.

The twins in *A l'autre bout de moi* are depicted somewhat ambiguously:
are they similar or dissimilar? Are they the problem or the answer? Is
twinship an impediment to or a model for identity formation? Humbert
departs from the patterns sketched above in order to tell a tale of
Mauritian twins that doubles as a tale of national identity in crisis. And
in doing so, she reveals competing discourses of individual and cultural
identity. To write of the island of Mauritius and of its complex intereth-
nic relations, Humbert could have chosen to tell of pale twins brought
up separately in white and coloured families, or of Indian and Chinese
babies swapped in the cradle, or even perhaps of conjoined French- and
Creole-speaking twins of unequal strength and power.[10] But she didn't.
Neither, however, did she seek to tell a startlingly new story. On the contrary, she chose a classic twin tale: twins – here mixed race sisters –
growing up together and struggling to survive stagnation and rivalry.
'The theme of adversary twins' is evoked on the cover of the novel, situating it in a narrative tradition, and the topos is used to explore the
dividedness of a hybrid identity and the search for an identity of one's
own. This search is first and foremost a personal one for the narrator,
Anne, but, as Shakuntala Boolell (1997) points out, the parallels between
Anne's predicament and the situation of Mauritius are such that it can
be read as an allegory for a national quest for identity.

As we saw in Chapter 2, tradition dictates the death of one or both twins as the dénouement to this story. And this is indeed what happens: one twin must die before the other can accept and recognise her own identity. Identity is an ambiguous term, paradoxically denoting both oneness and twoness: the individuality of a single entity and the identicalness of two.[11] In the novel, twoness is sacrificed and synthesised into oneness. Wholeness and indivisibility are sought at any cost. A terrible price is paid to acquire an identity of one's own. The personal drama can be read simultaneously in national terms: it warns us of the model of assimilation and synthesis into One – whether the unified person or 'one nation.'[12]

On the one hand, then, the novel serves as a cautionary tale. It also, however, gestures towards an alternative model for the understanding of self and nation. Another discourse of subjectivity, only half-articulated in the text, exposes common assumptions about the relation between sameness and difference. It points to a less destructive conception of identity – personal and Creole – and is the focus of the analysis that follows. The problem of surviving sameness, raised at the interpersonal level in Chapter 2, is here posed on a national scale.

Identity and the identical: Humbert's *A l'autre bout de moi*

The undecidability between the twoness and the oneness of identity – between the identical and the individual, the split and the whole – characterises the figure of the double and is the pivot on which Humbert's *A l'autre bout de moi* turns. To say that Anne Morin, the narrator of *A l'autre bout de moi*, is haunted by a double would not be strictly correct. Rather, her story is that of being herself relegated to the role of the double. She sees herself as the mere shadow of her vivacious twin sister, Nadège, and without an identity to call her own. In fact she is doubly positioned as the double: not only is she the pale imitation of her sister, but she belongs to a group who are the shadow of white society, a dark imitation. Neither black, nor Indian, nor Chinese, her family are counted among the 'almost-whites-but-not-quite' (Humbert, 1979: 22), a barely classifiable group with no clear identity of their own, who ape the whites without hope of being fully accepted by them.

Resemblance is thus the nub of Anne's problem. Anne sees identity in terms of oneness threatened by twoness and tells the story of her attempt to extricate herself from her role as shadow and arrive at an individual identity of her own. In order to escape both from her sister and from her off-white skin, she becomes prim and proper, an assiduous churchgoer, and seeks to marry the son of a white bourgeois family. The colourful Nadège, meanwhile, keeps company with darker-skinned Mauritians – whether black, Creole, Indian or Chinese – and represents everything that Anne rejects in herself. Nadège has a secret Indian lover, Aunauth, who struggles to increase the political power of the non-white community. When Nadège falls pregnant, Anne unleashes her hatred, in which she finally recognises the part of self-hatred. To mollify her twin, Nadège has a backyard abortion and dies as a result. Only then does Anne accept the other side of herself, her Creole heritage, represented by her sister. Although she is traumatised by the death of Nadège, it is only through the elimination of her twin that she manages to synthesise the two halves into one whole. And then she not only accepts her skin colour, but speaks with Nadège's voice, even takes Nadège's place beside Aunauth. Anne's solution is to live Nadège's life as her own, to become the original of which she had felt herself to be the copy. The threat of the double is suppressed and the twins become one: shadow and original coincide.[13]

Anne's narration is not, however, seamless, and if we resist the temptation to construct its coherence, if we refuse to read the narration in the image of the conception of identity as wholeness that it explicitly promotes, then we find it undermined by traces of more sophisticated discourses of identity. Anne relates the remarks of other characters, in particular Nadège and Aunauth, and she herself makes occasional observations that sit uncomfortably with her project of undivided selfhood. These moments enable us to put pressure on the narration, to read it against the grain. They fracture the telling, and if we position our reading in and across the fissures, we find an alternative understanding of identity, less deadly, produced by but repressed within the text.[14]

Anne's narration hinges on her reading of her resemblance with her sister. She sees herself as an exact copy of Nadège, but a carbon copy, a lacklustre mirror image, a poor quality photo (121), perfectly similar ... but lifeless:

> although our faces with their regular features, were trait for trait almost perfectly alike, Nadège always had a sort of special radiance you couldn't explain. It was about me that people exclaimed, 'My God, you look so much like your sister!' Never the other way round. (35)

She speaks of 'the dull shadow that was me' (419), as if she has no self but is merely a reflection. This portrait of the twins, trapped in a mirroring relationship, leads inexorably to Nadège's death. And yet, right from the beginning, little clues appear that allow us to doubt Anne's assessment of her predicament and to start to unhinge her reading. Are the twins really identical at all? At their birth, the midwife declared that they were fraternal twins, but Anne dismisses her opinion: 'our resemblance was so great that people generally maintained that she'd made a mistake' (Humbert, 1979: 35). But who are these 'people'? Not their father, for whom Anne resembles her mother (370). Certainly not Nadège, for when their cousin Arnaud fatuously pretends to confuse them to amuse his audience, she exclaims: 'Blockhead! has anyone ever mixed us up before?' (386). The answer to this rhetorical question is, of course, that someone *has* confused them: Anne herself has been having trouble distinguishing them all along. But she is perhaps alone in this. Aunauth, serial lover of the twins, spells it out most clearly: 'whatever you thought, you're not like Nadège. [...] really Anne, even physically, you never resembled Nadège more than a sister who looks like another sister. As for me, I never saw you as identical' (368).

Aunauth's interpretation cuts across Anne's narration. It is an isolated point of rupture in a story that continues right up until the final paragraphs to speak of similarity: 'my profile [...] so like Nadège's' (462). As such it provides an opportunity for the reader to consolidate any doubts about the narration and a position from which to resist the telling. The passage jostles the narration in more ways than one. It is one of only half a dozen moments in the novel where the enunciation of the text is made explicit, and we glean some details of Anne's situation in the present of her writing. At the outset, she and her partner have found refuge in exile in the suburbs of Paris (11–14, 100), but forced to confront the past through the chance viewing of a snippet of television and through the flow of writing it unleashes, Anne feels the need to return to her birthplace, and narrates the final third of the novel from Mauritius (315–463). But it is only when Anne quotes his refutation of the idea of her resemblance to her sister that we realise that Aunauth is the man at her side throughout the telling, and that she has taken her sister's lover, her sister's place. This is therefore a passage of revelations, not the least of which is that the twins are far from identical in eyes other than Anne's.

Anne's first reaction to Aunauth's statement is to want to protest. Then she realises that his opinion is in fact 'redemptive' in requiring

Anne to reconceive her identity such that it is not dependent on her sister's (368), so she refrains from appealing against his judgement. She does not however integrate its consequences into her narrative. She never refers to it again and simply reverts to reiterating her belief in her indistinguishability from her twin (seeing the resemblance as increasingly pronounced, seeing Nadège when she passes the mirror, 450). Following Aunauth's statement, Anne continues to relate her story with scant reference to her present situation – after another short exchange with Aunauth (372) there is but a fleeting comment (389) – and without allowing his insight to colour her telling. His words remain an unresolved challenge to the coherence of Anne's story.

Why does Anne insist on absolute resemblance, whereas we might interpret her relation with her twin as a form of identification? If she insists on her similarity to her sister, it is because the premise of sameness is her only way of accounting for her perceived lack of identity both personal (she is the copy of her sister) and cultural (she is one of the 'almost-whites' who mimic the white bourgeois community, 39). This impression of lack is in turn dependent upon a certain conception of identity: identity as centred, whole, circumscribed and independent – in other words, identity as something like an island.[15] Unfortunately it seems that the island must needs be a desert island before Anne can claim it as her own.

Anne sees Nadège as occupying a place 'at the centre of a mysterious circle that set her apart' (36) and seeks a similar space for herself where she can stand alone. She wants to be at the centre of her own island, with a centred self, rather than being at one end of a shared space. To achieve this, she must first leave Nadège's magic circle. Separating from her sister becomes her primary aim (367, 419). Anne is locked into a view of the self whereby shared space and mirrored identity exclude selfhood. And all she manages to occupy is 'a very small space [...]. Just my size' (193).

Although Anne regards Nadège as standing alone in the centre of her own circle, Nadège does not seem to share this view, and Anne manages to let slip through her narration reports of Nadège's less destructive understanding of identity. A comparison of the sisters' remarks about mirrors is instructive. We have already mentioned that Anne sees herself as a dull mirror image. As she stands before the looking-glass, she believes Nadège to be substantial enough to warrant reflection, whereas her own image eludes her: 'When I look at myself in the mirror, it's you I see' (121). In fact, she believes that she *has* no reflection of her own, because she *is* a reflection, that there is nothing of her to reflect but a mere play of light and shade. Nadège, on the other hand, less anxious about identity, has a very different attitude towards mirrors and reflections:

> She never ever looked at herself anywhere but in the eyes of others, distracted by these chance mirrors like a child with the changing colours of a prism, perpetually playing at creating new shades, in turn intrigued, captivated, indignant or charmed by these external reflections, and thus constantly wandering further from herself. There's nothing less imaginative and less true than a mirror! she would declare scornfully. (419)

While Anne peers in vain into the mirror, waiting for her Self to appear, Nadège looks at herself and even *for* herself in the gaze of the other. Unlike Anne, she is not threatened by seeing herself as a reflection; on the contrary, she rejoices in it. For when she looks at herself in others' eyes, she sees not a simple copy, but rather a shimmering and ever-changing image, coloured by myriad refractions. Nadège's practice takes her away from any supposed centre. Her identity – both personal and Creole – is not fixed or anchored, but based on identification with multiple images. It is not constituted by a stable centre but by a set of relations tending outwards. Nadège is drawn out from herself toward her reflections, and importantly experiences no loss of self in the process.

This is the alternative to Anne's island view of identity: Nadège sees her identity – and one could make the case for Creole identity more generally – as based on relation. This relational view – identity as an open set of identifications, of relations between – coincides with the models being elaborated in psychoanalytical stories of identity development around the time of the novel's publication. According to Lacan, as toddlers we accede to a position as subject by assuming doubleness, by identifying the mirror image as 'me' (1977). Thus, having an identity to call one's own requires in the first instance an investment in a specular image – an identification. But identity is not simply acquired once and for all in a single step, and Julia Kristeva's work extends the importance of identificatory mechanisms in the constitution – and continuous renewal – of the self. Well before the mirror stage, she sees the imaginary mobilising 'a whole array of identifications' (1995: 103) for the developing subject, giving rise to 'a kaleidoscope of ego images that build the foundation for the subject of enunciation' (104).[16] From this period onwards, she argues, the life of the psyche depends on it remaining open to identifications. To cease this process of projection and investment of the self in the other is to risk stagnation and moribundity (1987: 15). To this way of thinking then, multiple images of the self mirrored in the other are not threats to identity but constantly constitute it. It is in the course of identifying with them that we acquire identity.

The prismatic image Nadège has of herself is multi-coloured rather than imitation white. Nadège finds herself reflected in – and projects her own likeness on to – people of all colours. She is perfectly capable of passing between cultures – between the Chinese shopkeeper's yard and the Hindu festivals of the village, for instance. And if she sees herself in the eyes of whites too, unlike Anne she also sees *them* in herself, mirrors them back with a tinge of colour. When the white girls at school ask if she is one of them, so as to know whether they should play with her, Nadège replies, 'We aren't white, but neither are you: someone told me there was black blood in your family' (Humbert, 1979: 94). She is able to reject the role of shadow for the almost-whites and to see whites and creoles as doubles of each other. She perceives the paradox that the place and the supposed purity of white society depend for their existence on a relation (of exclusion) to the would-be-whites. In other words she accepts the relational and mirroring nature of the various identities on the island of Mauritius. She understands that no community carves out a place for itself other than through mechanisms of identification and exclusion.

Nadège, then, does not confuse likeness with a constricting sameness. She seems to comprehend that likeness – whether between individuals or groups – rather than undermining identity, is the very basis of it, and that identification with others, far from being an impediment to identity, is the means of achieving it. Although she eschews the conventional looking-glass, she echoes Lacan in appreciating the role of the mirror in the formation of identity. Her use of other people as mirrors involves not just reflection, but also projection of and identification with images. Nadège's child-like amusement before her animate mirrors reminds us of the toddler who learns to recognise himself as other, as a reflected image, in order to achieve a sense of self.[17] This is what Anne cannot see: resemblance as a projected (rather than reflected) image, identicalness as a form of identification. Not having Anne's investment in sameness, Nadège is enlivened by a constantly othered image (a capricious reflection) requiring her continually to redefine herself. Her identity is constructed through successive identifications – it's all done with mirrors. As such, it is not menaced but rather constituted by doubleness.

It is worth remembering that for Lacan's toddler, the jubilatory moment of recognition, when he assumes the mirror image as his own, is the first instance in which he has a sense of his separateness as a subject. Primarily this is a question of separation from the mother. But what happens when that mirror image is not recognised for what it is, is mistaken for another? It is interesting to ponder the case of identical twins where the likelihood is that the mirror image will be taken to be the twin rather than the self. Anne, it seems, has never been able to assume her mirror image as her own, and consequently has never had a sense of self. As for separateness, Anne's narration gives expression to her tortured, simultaneous identifications with and rejections of her mother, characteristic of the failure to tear oneself away from the mother-child dyad. But Anne also seems mired in another dyad, just as inextricable as the mother-child one, for she is unable to separate from her womb-mate, her twin sister.

Nadège, on the other hand, clearly made the break and made these relationships workable long ago. Indeed, so well has she learnt the lessons of the mirror that she is impatient with the idea of simple duplication and has moved on from the conventional looking-glass when seeking confirmation of her sense of self, which she now finds in less predictable identifications.

Nadège knows her face as her own, *because* it is reflected in other faces. Meanwhile Anne considers her face not her own because it is too much like Nadège's. It is only when her sister becomes faceless, so to speak, that Anne can possess her own face. When Nadège reveals her pregnancy, Anne slaps her violently, leaving her dazed, stupefied. Triumphantly, Anne observes: 'before this expressionless mask, I finally had a face' (Humbert, 1979: 427). When Anne sees her own reflection, she feels she *is* a reflection. Only when she has no reflection – in front of a blank face – does she finally believe that she has any substance.[18]

The tension between the twoness and oneness of identity is never resolved in Anne's narration. They remain incompatible. Her articulation of the identity problem is always in terms of doubleness, of the mirror that blurs rather than clarifying her image. When she reminisces, she realises that she never sees herself in the past: 'I see *us*, a plural me, or perhaps a plural Nadège, [...] like a trick photo, a double click on the same exposure. I see myself in duplicate, I see us in duplicate, [...] – 'I' only exist as a couple' (75). Anne focuses on her resemblance to Nadège as the source of her difficulties, however it is not as if she is alone in being perceived as double. In fact, far from being peculiar to her by virtue of her twinship, duality appears to be a general condition in the novel. Nadège is the image of her father: 'his female double' (223). Paul Roux, Nadège's suitor, seems to split in two when in conversation, now loquacious, now reticent (285). Suzanne, the Chinese shopkeeper's wife, gives the impression of being 'a poorly dubbed actress, as if the voice and gaze didn't match' (161). And her husband, Ah-Ling, is no more the unified subject than she is, for he seems a different person according to whether he is serving blacks, Indians, whites, mulattos (68). Anne complains of her lack of unity and of seeing herself as double, and yet other characters do not simply coincide with themselves. In fact, Anne could say that she sees them in duplicate. They, however, seem unperturbed by their status as doubles and/or fragmented subjects.

Anne relates these impressions but does not relate them to herself. Her predicament – '«*je*» *n'existons qu'en tant que couple*' ('"I" only exist as a couple,' 75)[19] – appears as singular to her as her self seems duplicate. Nevertheless, what Anne perceives as her dilemma can be recast as its solution if we follow Nadège's model of identity. If identity is not a solitary state but is based on relation, then doubleness becomes the answer to Anne's problem, for twoness (the specular relation) makes it possible to assume oneness (identity through identification). Twoness and oneness cease to be mutually exclusive.

Doubleness presents a solution too to Anne's supposed lack of cultural identity, for if Creole appears to be an in-between identity, in fact none of the island's cultures are clearly distinct, not even the insular white community. From this perspective, Creole identity ceases to be merely off-white. Creole and white become doubles of each other and, like Ah-Ling, mirror in turn the gamut of Mauritian cultures.

Nowhere land

Parallelling the contrast between the island view and the relational conception of identity is a tension between alternative spatial representations of twinship. Both a womb and a nowhere land (*'pays de nulle part'* 267, 339) are invoked to situate Anne's relation with her sister. They are not contrasted in the novel but coexist in Anne's discourse as if they were coherent with each other. If, however, we tease out the implications of each space, it becomes clear that the two have vastly different consequences for the continued viability of the twinship. The tragic events of the novel's dénouement seem to follow the inevitable logic of the womb metaphor, but uncoupling the images reveals a less destructive interpretation – available to Anne but ignored – of the twin relation and, by extension, of the twins' cultural identity.

Like the island of Mauritius, lapped and caressed by the swell of the sea, the twins' childhood was as if bathed in warm, gentle waters that wrapped around them like a cloak (72). But as in all amniotic idylls, this dark Eden carries the threat of expulsion from the womb. In Anne's dream,

> The water starts to gurgle and eddy, [...] come back to me! warm water, gentle water, so like the hot tears that clad my first sorrows; but no, the water keeps receding, leaving a great emptiness around me, in me; nothing remains of me but a long shudder and all I can do is fall, [...]. And then comes the light, a terrible light that strips me bare and rends me, [...] there is no longer peace, nor warmth, where am I then Nadège? (72–3)

The breaking of the waters heralds the fall from grace into the exposure of daylight. But the dread inspired by birth is in this case less an anxiety about separation from the maternal body than a fear of separation from the sister beside her in the womb. In the dream, Nadège reassures Anne: 'You are next to me' (73).

Anne is thus torn between antithetical desires. On the one hand, she seeks to flee her sister and find her own space, to flee her colour and join the white elite. On the other hand, to do so requires that Anne tear open the comforting, aquatic envelope of her shared embryonic identity. Aunauth is again the sole character to articulate the contradiction: 'Despite all your efforts to the contrary, you dreamed obscurely of finishing the incomplete design, of forming a single entity with Nadège' (368). The tug-of-war is evident in the violence needed for Anne finally to break away.

There are several uterine spaces shared by the twins in the novel. The reassuring confines of Ah-Ling's shop enclose one such space. A sensuous nook of smells and tastes and colours, it 'shielded' and 'nourished' their childhood (62). In Anne's dream it cradles them like 'a womb in the sea' (73). At the novel's conclusion, however, its roof is ripped open in a hurricane. For the womb is not for indefinite sojourn or its cocoon becomes constrictive, its waters stagnant, its silence deathly.

Built on the ruins of an old cemetery, the Morin family's dilapidated home with its dark stillness is such a womb/tomb: the house that 'surrounded our childhood with its walls of rotten wood' (15) is seen as 'a sort of stronghold where silence would come and condense' (17), and where 'everything would slowly die in the sultry closeness' (205). As we saw in Chapter 2, such images are typical of novelistic representations of the twin relation as a shared sphere of deathly silence and heavy plenitude, timeless and immobile like an unbroken amniotic sac. And if the twin relation is conceived as quasi-uterine containment, then ultimately the only alternative to a stillborn future is the rupture of the sac.

Anne, who sees her twinship in this womb-like way, is drawn as if by the force of the metaphor towards rupture. And in her attack on Nadège, she achieves it decisively. The confrontation takes place in the village of Cassis, whose very name whispers repeatedly to Anne of breaking (*casser*, 383), and the rift between the siblings is like a birth for Anne, who takes her first searing lung-full of unpaired existence: 'And this sudden breaking in me, this intense burning sensation, as if, for the first time, my lungs filled with air' (383). The breach occurs when Nadège reveals her pregnancy and Anne realises what the birth of a brown baby will mean for her plans for marriage into the white bourgeois community. Anne slaps her face with full force and screams at her in a frenzy, airing her broken dreams and bitterness, and towards the end of her tirade goes as far as wishing for the death of the foetus: 'qu'il crève,' she cries, 'I hope he dies' (428). As a direct result, Nadège aborts. *Crever*: to burst, to die. Along with the twinship, another sac is punctured. But Anne doesn't stop there. Her peroration – 'Foetus! Horrible foetus! Die!' (428) – is directed not towards Nadège's baby but aimed quite clearly at Nadège herself, huddled on the sand in a foetal pose, 'her head hidden in her folded arms, her legs tucked under her' (428). Sadly, Nadège does just that. Skewered by the knitting needle, she is aborted as much as her baby. Anne's words reveal her conception of the twinship as an overcrowded uterus. If abortion is the elimination of a body colonising the womb, in this case the foreign body is that of the twin. Twinship, the baby and Nadège – all three perish. And Anne is born, but born of Nadège's death.

Inherent in the idealised space of the womb is, then, the threat of imminent rupture. The womb, however, represents for Anne not only the terrain of the twinship, torn between white and coloured visions of its destiny. The island of Mauritius itself, the warm, wet cradle of the twins is portrayed as a circumscribed amniotic space from which Anne is ultimately expelled. Fractured like the twinship along colour lines, in the aftermath of Nadège's death and Aunauth's implication in the tragedy it is rent by political tensions, and Anne and Aunauth have little option but to abandon the island.

There is, however, another representation in the novel of the space shared by the twins. It relies on a metaphor of land or country and thus conjures up the possibility of extrapolation to a less constraining model for cultural affiliation. Anne describes a psychical space, another part of herself that is not easily located or accessible, but hovers *à l'autre bout de moi*, at the other end of herself. She writes of a *pays de nulle part*, a nowhere land to which she is transported by music, death and suffering, and which links her to her mother, her sister and her childhood: 'When I'm hurting I always think I'm in nowhere land, at the other end of me, far, far away, where the waves pound continually and drag me away from my body' (339). This unfathomable space of otherness within herself is less amniotic than semiotic, in the Kristevan sense of the word. Kristeva's semiotic is a modality where feeling rather than thinking prevails, where waves of sensation wash over the body in an infinitely repeatable rhythm of separation and fusion. Governed not by reason but by the rhythm of bodily drives, it harks back to a time before the emergence of the thinking and speaking subject, a time of symbiosis with the mother (and quite possibly with a twin). Unlocatable, inaccessible to the intellect, and inadequately described by language, the semiotic can however be accessed by the social/speaking/reasoning subject through aesthetic, emotional and sensual experience (Kristeva, 1984: 25–30). Thus listening to Rachmaninov offers Anne a fleeting chance to 'to leave, to go far away, to the Nowhere Land we used to play at visiting in our childhood, but above all, to be assured of returning' (Humbert, 1979: 267–8). And it is in this nowhere space at the furthest reaches of herself that Anne connects with her sister: 'at the other end of me, the only zone where I could ever meet her' (428).

Although Kristeva uses Plato's term of the *chora* (an amorphous, nourishing, maternal receptacle) to describe the pre-linguistic functioning of the semiotic, there is an important difference between her conception of the semiotic and the womb-like spaces that harbour the twin relation elsewhere in Anne's narration. In Kristeva's theory, the split between the semiotic and symbolic is in no way definitive. It is not a matter of choosing between two discrete modalities, of moving from darkness into light. The symbolic (social structures, language, reason, identity) needs to be constantly renewed by the eruption of semiotic energy. And having been swept away in a semiotic tumult of music, colour, ecstasy or pain, the subject must be able to regain the possibility of intelligible speech and the relative stability afforded by the symbolic. As Anne puts it, she must be assured of her return. There is thus an ongoing dialectical relation between the semiotic and the symbolic rather than the destruction and abandonment of one mode in favour of the other (cf. de Nooy, 1998: 29–43). It is this aspect of the 'nowhere land,' the fact that it need not be relinquished for Anne to retain her social identity, that sets it apart from the amniotic spaces in the novel.

If I insist on this difference between semiotic and amniotic representations of twin-spaces in the novel, it is because the former holds out some hope of a continued existence for the twin relation (and indeed for the twin), whereas the very image of the latter invites rupture. The semiotic nowhere land at the other end of the self is an alternative representation of twin space readable in Anne's narration. Less clearly circumscribed than the island of identity, its limits less constraining than the womb, it allows for a to-ing and fro-ing between the sensual and the social, between drifting and anchorage, between the dissolution and reconstitution of the self, and allows therefore for mobility between cultural identities. Indeed identity becomes defined by movement rather than place. And if the nowhere land represents an otherness within, it cannot be abandoned. In another dream, Anne hears Nadège try to convince her of this lesson. Nadège calls out to her 'sister sitting at the other end of me, so lost and so near': 'There is no elsewhere. [...] We are already so far away when we want to embrace, solitary islands, drifting toward the receding horizon of our desire' (266). There is nowhere to escape to, she intimates, away from Mauritius, away from our relationship. Exile is doomed. We are already enough like islands without trying to isolate ourselves further. Reaching out is what is important. Once again, the discourse ascribed to Nadège is one of being-as-relation rather than identity-as-island. We can see that the two definitions of identity (as island, as relation) and the two spatial representations of twinship (womb and nowhere land) work in tandem to reinforce the same contrast between understandings of selfhood and cultural identity (self-contained or relational). Now this is Anne's dream, not a reported conversation, so the words supposedly from Nadège's lips are in fact bubbling up from that other region of herself, from the nowhere land. Will she heed them? Will she make them hers? The words reach her 'from a land too remote' (266): they are too foreign to be integrated into her world view. They remain '*sans suite*' (266) in both senses of the expression: disjointed and without impact or follow-up. It is only later – too late – when Nadège's voice has become her own (12), that she understands something of this discourse.

The realisation begins when Anne strikes Nadège with her diatribe and realises that 'the woman at my feet that I was staring at in atrocious, savage satisfaction, was myself' (428). Anne is forced to confront the fact that what she rejects – Nadège's colour, culture and desires – is integral to herself and hence inescapable. It is Anne's self-hatred that causes Nadège's death. When she later analyses her behaviour, she admits: 'Perhaps I was also rebelling against myself, a certain part of myself' (426). She is finally able to identify with that other part of herself, the foreignness within that she projected on to Nadège and thus kept so long at bay. She articulates her discovery – 'I am now convinced that there is no shadow behind us that is not our own shadow, no ghost within us that is not in our image.' (153) – and reiterates it, highlighting it as the major lesson she has learnt from the tragedy: 'To be separate from her, to be, at any price, that's what I wanted. I didn't yet realise that what that made me renounce, because it was too like me, was often the most authentic part of myself' (419).

This is not however the sole lesson she learns. When she strikes Nadège, she not only sees that her twin represents a part of herself but also realises that separating from her sister is no guarantee of an independent identity. For her show of anger and disgust is made possible through the intervention of another figure: 'at the moment when I'm about to shout my disgust at Nadège, that warm look settles on me, Mother's gaze, which merges into mine' (425–6). Her only means of breaking free of Nadège is to identify with her mother, the woman she struggled to repudiate: 'Yes Father, I finally have my identity. You remember, you said it yourself one afternoon: you are of your mother's breed!' (425). Thus when Anne finally manages to achieve her 'own' identity, it is not independent of the play of mirrors, of identifications and attachments. It is not singular, separate and self-sufficient. In fact it is no less double than before.

In this one crucial episode, Anne accepts the part of both Nadège and her mother in herself. The extent to which she revises her understanding of identity in order to do so, however, seems to be minimal. We see this in the aftermath of a further moment of self-recognition that occurs beside her father's deathbed. Anne is struck by the revelation that her antagonism towards her sister was in fact rivalry for her father's love (454).[20] The fantasmatic solution to the competition – a fantasy that brings Anne a sense of peace – is to take Nadège's place and to be embraced by their dying father while he calls her by both names, Anne and Nadège. In other words, the solution is a synthesis of the sisters. And this imagined synthesis is then realised by Anne as she takes on aspects of Nadège's life.

Anne believes that she has learnt, but in fact she hasn't learnt so very much. She has learnt to accept those parts of herself that she once rejected and projected on to Nadège, but she has not learnt that this was possible without eliminating her sister. She has learnt to recognise her resemblance with her mother and her love for her father, but they both had to die for her to attain this understanding. Anne cannot accept her own identifications as a basis for identity until the objects of identification are out of the way. Once she thought of herself as merely a reflection of others. If she finally achieves a sense of self, it is in no small measure because those she mirrors have gone. It is as if her entire family has to perish before she can synthesise their attributes into an identity she can call her own. The island view of identity as whole and separate prevails.

In the cataclysmic conclusion to the story, a cyclone ravages the area, uprooting the olive tree that shaded their house and tearing the roof from Ah-Ling's shop. With its 'eviscerated carcass' (461), it is as if the shop's belly has been torn open. The gutting of their former shelter, their 'womb in the sea' (73) means that the rupture of uterine spaces is complete. Anne emerges whole and new from the destruction of her family circle.

Although it cuts a swathe through the cane fields, the gale does not sweep away previous habits of thought. Anne's reaction to the shop's demise is to imagine that it will regrow just as it was (461–2) and in the meantime to look for a substitute, 'another refuge my size' (458). Ultimately such a refuge is exactly what she finds, a nest just her size and shape: the hollow space left by the disappearance of her twin. Anne glides into Nadège's silhouette in Aunauth's doorway, fills Nadège's shelf with her own things, occupies Nadège's place in Aunauth's bed, takes over her voice. She slips into Nadège's identity as if it were a discrete, enclosed space, a hollow that she no longer has to share with another, for her twin has been incorporated into herself.

Anne and Aunauth escape to Paris, only for Anne to learn that there is no escape, no elsewhere. Finally, then, she understands Nadège's words and feels able to return to Mauritius. She now accepts her Creole inheritance and her ties to her birthplace. But her mother, father and sister are all dead. If she is finally able to live contentedly in Mauritius it is perhaps because she has the island to herself.

Anne's search for self is thus satisfied, but at great cost. Unable to accept an identity defined by doubleness, she pursues individuality with singular determination. Inevitably she must suffer the loss that unitary selfhood demands – the loss of her double, her identical twin. Nadège's vision of identity – a way of seeing oneself in the eyes of others and in constant kaleidoscopic transformation – is glimpsed but is too volatile to constitute the foundations of selfhood for Anne.

Island homes

The dynamics of the twinship portrayed in Humbert's novel reflect some of the cultural tensions dividing the island of Mauritius. Parallel with Anne's search for personal selfhood is her search for cultural identity. As a member of an in-between group perceived to have no identity of its own, labelled 'almost-white' rather than Creole in the text, Anne's options appear to be limited to fusing or breaking with those she shadows, to joining white society (or another clearly identifiable group) or leaving the island.

However, the alternative discourse of identity associated in the novel with the character of Nadège translates into a third option: a more strategic adoption of identity (cf. Spivak, 1987: 205), based on shifting identifications rather than on an insistence on sameness, on common traits. This amounts to an understanding and acceptance of Creole identity as in-betweenness rather than unity, as an identity in motion rather than a definable entity occupying a designated cultural space.

Humbert's novel thus serves as a parable, not only for Mauritius, but more generally for hybrid and diasporic cultures in search of identity. In telling of twins trapped in a mirroring relationship rather than of twins separated by a border and then reunited, Humbert avoids the usual twin topos chosen for parables of national division and substitutes a topos that, although equally familiar, is not normally used in this way. The effect is a tragic dénouement, virtually imposed from the outset by the positioning of the novel as a variation on the 'theme of adversary twins.' Countless retellings of the story of death-by-sameness-and-rivalry make Nadège's fate inevitable.

What, then, might we learn from this parable? Anne lives to regret, and to value what she has lost, but these lessons are a lament, not a blueprint for avoiding her errors. Reading against Anne's narration, however, offers a glimmer of hope. If she were to examine more carefully her impressions of Nadège's sense of self, if she could maintain the connection with the nowhere space she senses as the real space of twinship, perhaps she could relinquish her ideal of self-contained selfhood and the concomitant ideal of clearly-defined ethnicity. Perhaps she – and indeed other island people (I refer to my own country) in search of identity – could see that it need not be a question of finding an isolated and clearly distinguishable cultural self, of eliminating in-betweenness, or of synthesising otherness into a coherent whole. Rather identity might be understood as a way of seeing oneself in others, a way of living doubleness. Then, instead of seeking a snug, smug place just our size, we could look for identity in multiple, shimmering images that reveal us to be in constant kaleido-scopic transformation, and in relations of identification that take us outside of ourselves. Rather than having an island to ourselves, rather than being an island unto ourselves, we might marvel at the changing shoreline, and at what the waves bring to change us.

The uses of twins to represent fissures in national or cultural identity reveal understandings of the causes of and remedies for tensions and conflict among peoples. Tales of rival twin rulers in ancient legend affirmed the necessity for undivided power to unite a nation, while in modern times allegories of conjoined twins suggest that cohabitation, however uncomfortable, is a divided nation's best chance for survival and prosperity. Changelings that cross class barriers and twins separated by skin colour or national frontiers illustrate the arbitrariness of social and geographical dividing lines and make the case that what the two share outweighs their differences.

Twins can also, however, be used to make more subtle arguments about cultural and national identity that go beyond the forging of unity across division, the discovery of sameness across difference, the triumph of our common humanity. Through their problematic rela-tionship, the twins of Humbert's novel demonstrate the pitfalls of the celebration of sameness and unity and offer a vision of cultural belong-ing defined not by bonds of flesh or blood but by the play of light across a face, not by finding common ground but by continually moving between.

7
Twins as Doubtful Doubles: Postmodern Identity, Irony and Invention

Once more with feeling

Umberto Eco identifies as postmodern the need to acknowledge the repetition of past utterances, of familiar plots:

> I think of the postmodern attitude as that of a man who loves a very cultivated woman and knows that he cannot say to her, 'I love you madly', because he knows that she knows (and that she knows he knows) that these words have already been written by Barbara Cartland. Still, there is a solution. He can say 'As Barbara Cartland would put it, I love you madly'. At this point, having avoided false innocence, having said clearly that it is no longer possible to speak innocently, he will nevertheless have said what he wanted to say to the woman: that he loves her, but he loves her in an age of lost innocence. (1985: 67)

Like declarations of love, tales of twins are seen to frequent 'low' genres and employ hackneyed formulae. Already in 1949, Tymms could write that 'doubles are among the more facile, and less reputable devices in fiction' (1949: 15). This judgement has dogged the double and is echoed by Rogers, Coates and Herdman, as they lament the twentieth-century slide of the figure into banality and triviality (see Chapter 1). If anything, doubles in the form of identical twins have come to command even less respect through their proliferation in popular film genres, children's literature and supermarket romances. Eco's solution of ironic quotation is one way in which postmodern twin tales can 'accept the challenge of the past, of the already said,' (1985: 67) and yet – as with a lover's declaration – the effects of the quotation are far from contained by the irony of purpose.

137

This chapter focuses on two instances of the ironic citation of doubles and twins, two ways of confronting the problem of triteness. The first is examined only briefly, in order to devote attention to its legacy, both in prose and on film. Vladimir Nabokov's 1965 novel *Despair* mocks literary uses of the double at the same time as it employs them. It also, however, marks a turning point in the representation of the double. With the benefit of hindsight, Nabokov's joke can be seen to herald the emergence of a distinctly postmodern discourse of the double, explored in various genres in ways specific to those genres. *Despair* thus represents a moment of newness as much as a reckoning with the past. The second text is Spike Jonze's *Adaptation* (2002), a twin film that functions as a mise-en-abyme of this process of repetition and renewal, of the tension between tradition and novelty, and highlights the extent to which these issues need to be addressed as questions of genre. In its use of twins, the film explicitly engages with the major questions of this book, asking what is entailed in retelling a familiar tale, and how it can be put to new purposes.

The undoing of the double: Nabokov's *Despair*

When is a double not a double, and who is in a position to tell? Certainly not the story-teller in the case of *Despair*. Nabokov's novel is the tale of a doubtful double, a double that isn't one. From the opening pages, its narrator, writer Hermann Karlovitch, reveals himself to be both self-deluding and a compulsive liar. He recounts his meeting with a tramp, Felix Wohlfahrt – a happy traveller in both name and nature. In Felix, Hermann sees his own spitting image, and he proceeds to narrate the formulation and execution of his ingenious plan to exchange places with this perfect double, kill him, and then use the corpse to claim his own life insurance. The catch is, however, that no-one other than Karlovitch can see the slightest resemblance. The double in this canonical text of the literature of the double is not one at all.

Nabokov relates Karlovitch's error to the blindness of communism in its disregard of differences (1989: 20, 158–9), however *Despair* is also peppered with ironic references to trite narrative ploys: 'a trick of the trade, a poor thing worn to shreds by literary fiction-mongers' (1989: 43); 'Do you feel the tang of this epilogue? I have concocted it according to a classic recipe' (179); 'Those little tricks, my good man, with life policies, have been known for ages. I should even say that yours is the flattest and most hackneyed one of the lot' (205). With such comments, with its intertextual allusions to Dostoevsky ('Dusty') and Gogol and its parody of the theme, Nabokov's novel is seen by several critics to mark the point of undoing of the Romantic novel of the double, a final point following which the double can no longer be treated with any seriousness in literature. Stuart (1995: 189) considers it a mockery and rejection of the double as a literary device. For Troubetzkoy, if the double was 'put into action by German romanticism,' it suffered a 'spectacular liquidation' by Nabokov (1995: 7). *Despair* represents 'a compendium of all the past figures of the double, at the same time as it delivers a verdict without appeal' (1995: 10). It marks 'the fall of the empire of the double' (1996: 189), 'the final struggle, with Hermann bringing up the rear in the parade of doppelgängers' (1996: 205). Elsewhere, Rogers sees the self-parody of *Despair* as essentially a defensive technique to counter the suspicion with which the double as a literary device has come to be viewed post-Freud. Caricature is the only means remaining for the modern author to 'transcend the limitations of representing doubles in an overt manner' (1970: 162), a treatment that Rogers views as ultimately unsatisfying (1970: 171).[1] And we are left to presume that once this avenue has been explored, the theme of the double has been exhausted.

Having been thoroughly exploited by the Romantics, and then mocked by Nabokov in a final showdown, the double in its late twentieth-century manifestations is consigned by critics to the wastebasket of literary history. And yet it has flourished. How then, have stories of the double appealed their verdict, and defied their dismissal? Let us briefly explore some novels and films from the 1980s and 1990s that echo *Despair* in their uptake of Nabokov's ironic portrayal of the double, before turning to *Adaptation*. The doubles that follow are all doubtful in some way: either their resemblance is uncertain, their very existence is in question, or they are considered of dubious worth or quality. It is the thematisation of this doubt, this dubiousness that draws them together and constitutes the grounds for appeal against dismissal.

The shadow of a doubt: postmodern fiction

Although critics have interpreted *Despair* as symptomatic of the exhaustion or degeneration of the figure of the double, the story of Hermann Karlovitch can also be read as a precursor to a series of postmodern literary doubles, for whom resemblance is in the eye of the beholder and identification is the prerequisite for identity. Thus, against the tide of criticism, Slethaug argues that 'the book is one of the first, if not the first, to interrogate the conventions of the double within contemporary fiction' (1993: 38) in its use of an 'antimimetic' double (188).[2] For Nabokov's tongue-in-cheek take on the double is followed not only by playful fictions but by elegiac narratives that do not attempt to resurrect the Dostoevskian or Poe-etic double, but dignify Karlovitch's delusion, transporting it into the realm of desire.

Marie-Thérèse Humbert's *A l'autre bout de moi* (1979), analysed in the preceding chapter, can be seen as a successor to Nabokov's novel in the history of literary doubles, not in taking on the legacy of the Romantic tradition, but in taking up the figure of the doubtful double, and taking it beyond a joke and beyond the simple diagnoses of error and madness. Humbert suggests that if madness there be in seeing likeness where others see none, then it is a madness of the most widespread kind. Like Karlovitch, Humbert's protagonist Anne is a somewhat unreliable narrator, although the signs are far more subtle. Like Karlovitch, Anne is convinced of her absolute resemblance to her double – her twin Nadège – and is (at least partially) responsible for her death. And in both novels, the likeness is in doubt.

The novels depart from one another, however, in the significance and attribution of the doubt. The narration of *Despair* offers multiple opportunities for the reader to take the reality checks Karlovitch misses, to diagnose his folly and set him apart as singularly deluded. Either Felix is or isn't a double, and the reader is offered a vantage point of superior insight from which to tell. The reader is in no doubt, and the double collapses. In *A l'autre bout de moi*, on the other hand, resemblance is not a clear-cut yes-or-no decision. Likeness comes and goes, now clear, now disturbed, like a reflection in a swinging glass. Opinions on the extent of the twins' resemblance are divided, and have different and far-reaching consequences for the lives of the characters, but are never simply right or wrong. There is no clear line separating reality and desire: identification is a process that flows between them. Likeness and difference are not poles apart, and their confusion is not symptomatic of derangement. Nadège is a doubtful double, slipping in and out of resemblance with the narrator, but although the reader is not offered a position of smug certainty from which to judge the likeness or lack of it, the shadow of doubt does not result in the collapse of the double.

Nabokov's text straddles eras. Written in Russian in 1932, and translated soon after by the author into an English version, of which few copies survived the blitz, *Despair* was retranslated and simultaneously revised in 1965 (Nabokov 1989: xi–xii). Written at the height of the modernist era but rewritten as postmodernist trends were emerging in literature (cf. Troubetzkoy, 1996: 193–5), it opens up a Romantic theme to late twentieth-century reworking. *A l'autre bout de moi* hints at but falls short of embracing a postmodern fluidity of identity (represented by Nadège, but put to death by Anne, the survivor), and a reading such as mine is only possible post hoc. Humbert's novel is, however, followed by some 1980s texts featuring doubtful doubles that lend themselves more easily to the postmodern label, with their playful – although not necessarily comic – self-referentiality, intertextual allusions, plurality of perspectives, and mistrust of the authority and experience of the unified subject. In most of these texts, the textual play is aided by the fact that, as in *Despair*, the protagonist is a writer of one sort or another, exploiting a popular notion of the doubleness of the figure of the author.[3]

Martin Amis' *Money: A Suicide Note* (1984) can be situated in the wake of *Despair*.[4] Through the blur of his addictions to alcohol, cigarettes and pornography, the antipathetic narrator, John Self, fields menacing phone calls from someone who seems to know his every move, like a second Self. Although eventually a diarist, Self is not strictly speaking a writer: he is a man with a story he wants to turn into a Hollywood movie, and he engages an author called 'Martin Amis' to revise the script and enhance its realism and character motivation (1984: 234). In a progressive *mise en abyme*, the title of the film changes from *Good Money* to *Bad Money* to simply *Money*. Low and high genres collide and 'Amis' with his literary pretensions provides the reader with a position from which to interpret the words of his less literate counterpart. The conversations between 'Amis' and Self provide self-reflexive commentary on the distance between educated author and vulgar narrator. Could the second self making the insulting and unsettling phone calls be an omniscient Amis with an author's 'sadistic impulses' (233)? Or the equally knowing reader who, like 'Amis,' interprets Self's narration from an ironic distance: 'you're in on it too, aren't you. You are, aren't you' (268)? Meanwhile, Martina Twain (Martin Mark Two? – 'Maybe she was a joker, just like me' says Martin, 349) gives Self a potted literary education. The caller, however, turns out to be neither Amis, nor the reader, nor Martina, but Self's disgruntled, double-crossing business partner. The hallucinatory double is ultimately revealed as no double at all. The relation of resemblance is as illusory as the moneyed life Self wants so badly to believe is really his. But while all the characters repeat that the joke is on Self, that Self himself is a joke (353), the joke is equally on the reader who followed the interpretative clues, and Amis is the self-declared joker (349).

Like Amis in *Money*, Paul Auster is a secondary character in his own work. Auster's New York trilogy (*City of Glass, Ghosts, The Locked Room*, first published 1985–86) is a textbook example of postmodern literature of the double with its dislocation and fragmentation of characters, plurality of truths, massive intertextuality, and representation of experience as a textual weave. The protagonist of each of the three intersecting tales is a writer. In the first, Dan Quinn writes avowedly intertextual detective fiction under the pseudonym William Wilson (Poe's famous doubled character) – 'What interested him about the stories he wrote was not their relation to the world but their relation to other stories' (Auster, 1990: 8) – before borrowing the identity of 'Paul Auster' to take on a case as private investigator. Private investigators feature likewise in the sequels, and writing becomes analogous to spying as the trilogy plays between the genres of literary fiction, detective fiction and biography. Each protagonist shadows a man, attempting to piece together his life, to the point where one life becomes absorbed into the other's. In each case, in trying to account for – and write an account of – another life, the detective-cum-author becomes the double of his quarry: 'Writing is a solitary business. It takes over your life. In some sense, a writer has no life of his own. Even when he's there, he's not really there. Another ghost' (Auster, 1990: 209). If at the outset there is no obvious relation between the watcher and the watched, the investigator gradually identifies with the object of his attention to the point where there is nothing left of himself or of his previous life. Not even a shadow of his former self, he has become the shadow of the other, his double. Only a complete rejection of writing and reading – tossing the crucial manuscript into the trash – can halt the process. This then is a less jocular – although no less ironic – uptake of the topos of the writer and his doubtful double. As in *Despair*, the writer character takes on – to the point of taking – the life of another who did not resemble him at first.

Although twins appear as a repeated motif in Auster's trilogy (1990: 89, 235, 253, 308) and Amis's novel (1984: 165, 217), these are tales of doubles rather than twins. How then might twins, with their more tangible kinship, incarnate the doubtful double? Agota Kristof's trilogy – *The Notebook, The Proof*, and *The Third Lie* (first published 1986–91) – offers a demonstration. Once again writers (of notebooks, of testimony, of poetry), twins Claus and Lucas relate in large exercise books their experiences as children and adults in iron curtain Europe. Although each bundle of documents tells a coherent story, each succeeding set of notebooks throws doubt on the most basic elements of the story told previously, such as the existence and identity of one or other of the brothers. Only at the very end of the trilogy is the reader finally left to understand that there were indeed two twins. Their story, however, was not told in Claus's and/or Lucas's notebooks: these were the tale of a phantom doubling, a lost but imagined twinship. During the 1980s, then, the doubtful double ceased to represent the undoing of a nineteenth-century theme to become emblematic of a more generalised discourse of identity.

This becomes even clearer when we consider its appearance in a cluster of fiction by francophone women writers. Here a significant and quite specific conjunction of genre and gender indicates that the writer-as-doubtful-double has become a topos in its own right, far removed from its earlier function of providing ironic commentary on the figure of the double. The title of Madeleine Monette's *Le Double Suspect* (first published 1980), names the topos: published in English as *Doubly Suspect* (2000), it could equally be translated as *The Suspect Double*. Valérie Raoul (1996) has analysed the parallels between Monette's text and Francine Noël's *Babel, prise deux* (*Babel, Take Two*, 1990). Both are novels in diary form by Quebec women and trace a particular narrative of female doubling. In *Le Double Suspect*, Manon dies, leaving behind a diary that her friend Anne continues in her place. Writing becomes a mode of mourning, and as Anne writes, she risks melting into the absent beloved who becomes her double. Similarly, in *Babel, prise deux*, Fatima's diary tells of how her dear friend and double Amélia dies before her translation of an author's diary is complete, and Fatima's diary then becomes an extension of Amélia's project. Although not a diary, *Silsie*, by French novelist Marie Redonnet (1990), finds a place alongside these texts. A first person narrative, it commences with the death of Silsie, and follows the narrator as she slips into the place left by her beloved friend. She goes to Dolms, a village whose name is the only word written in Silsie's poetry notebook, but the pages remain unfilled as she founders, merged into Silsie and submerged. Unlike the traditional literature of the (masculine) double, all of these novels begin rather than end with a death. Rather than the 'problem' of the double being 'resolved' by death, here it is the double that goes some way towards healing the sorrow caused by a death. In these texts we find death at the source of a doubling in which resemblance is an uncertain outcome rather than a given. A specifically feminine doubtful double is created through a process of identification-as-mourning.

There exist then several clusters of novels, from the 1980s in particular, that take up where Nabokov left off and leave a question mark over the resemblance and existence of the double. However, whereas Nabokov's doubtful double was seen to represent a final comment on an exhausted theme, the uptakes of this figure testify to new discursive arrangements, whereby the slide into doubleness – the identificatory absorption of one's self into another – is a consequence of writing and may even be an act of love.

A discourse, however, is always written out in a genre of one kind or another. To say that the doubtful double has become a figure of a postmodern discourse of identity, does not mean that it will be represented in the same way in different genres. Its appearance in film, for example, raises representational problems specific to the medium, and that work to distance it from its prose counterparts, as the following brief survey shows.

Schwarzenegger and de Vito, and other unlikely lookalikes

Casting doubt over the resemblance and especially the physical resemblance of characters at first appears to be a particularly novelistic possibility: points of view are juxtaposed within the narration, leaving the reader to question the extent of likeness. The adaptation to film genres seems counterintuitive: how can the question mark over resemblance be sustained on screen, where surely likeness and unlikeness will be immediately obvious? Several filmmakers propose approaches to the problem.

Hermann Karlovitch comments self-reflexively in Nabokov's *Despair* about the inappropriateness of film as a medium for his story, ironically because film would be unable to reproduce the absolute likeness he sees between himself and his double without the traces of the split screen remaining visible (1989: 15–16). Fassbinder nonetheless takes up the challenge and shows the unreliability of Karlovitch's judgement in this case also. Although it is less of a commentary on literary doubles, his 1978 film of *Despair* follows the novel fairly closely. However, whereas in the novel the reader's doubts about the double are not entirely confirmed until the dénouement, the film of necessity demonstrates the lack of resemblance between Hermann and Felix from the outset. The importance of Karlovitch's activity as a writer (and narrator-mediator of the story) is downplayed in the film, such that the viewer is positioned as direct witness to and arbiter of Karlovitch's delusion.

In a later film, however, Fassbinder returns to the question of the doubtful double, and explores it in a far more ambiguous way, situating the viewer equivocally. His last film, *Querelle* (1982), is based on Jean Genet's final novel, *Querelle de Brest* (1953). Querelle and Robert are brothers, and from early in the film explicit verbal reference is made to their similarity, while Querelle denies the resemblance and the closeness of the brothers. On the other hand, there is an uncanny likeness between Robert and Gil, who are in fact played by the same actor (Hanno Pöschl). This similarity, however, strangely passes without comment. Querelle (Brad Davis), who is discovering his pleasure in homosexual relations, is increasingly drawn towards Gil, whom he denounces for a murder he himself has committed. In pursuing Gil, Querelle appears to be projecting his relationship with his twin brother on to his object of love, and there is a suggestion that sameness and even self-love are at the basis of homosexual attraction. Two cases of questionable doubling thus occur in the film: are the brothers as alike as some say? and are Robert and Gil alike in the eyes of anyone but Querelle? *Querelle* plays on these uncertainties, which are never resolved, for it is not clear whether the viewer is in a position to decide or is aligned so closely with Querelle as to share his fantasies.

Uncertainty is increased when the resemblance between supposed doubles is not constant. In Peter Greenaway's *A Zed and Two Noughts* (1985), twins Oswald and Oliver Deuce are played by non-twin brothers (Brian and Eric Deacon) who, although they start out distinct from one another, become progressively more identical during the film to the point where they become indistinguishable ('I can't tell the difference between you any more') (cf. La Piana, 1990: 28–9). The ebb and flow of likeness between filmic doubles is not restricted to art-house cinema: *Desperately Seeking Susan* (Susan Seidelman, 1985) portrays a doubling in which characters identify with and come to resemble one another. In these two films, the viewer is constantly required, if not to doubt her eyes, then at least to revise constantly her reading of the relationship.

At the other extreme of the continuum between sameness and difference, Luis Buñuel alternates actors for the female lead in *Cet obscur objet du désir* (1977). Rather than two characters who resemble each other to a greater or lesser extent, here we have one character, Conchita, played at various times by the equally dark-haired but otherwise not strikingly alike Carole Bouquet and Ángela Molina. The other characters seem oblivious to the changes in Conchita's appearance, and as the film progresses the viewer becomes complicit in this perception of the woman, and is obliged to accept the swap and conflate the two portrayals of Conchita into a single – although divided – character. Is then the split (which corresponds to the split view of womanhood discussed in Chapter 3) the fantasy of the protagonist, Mathieu, or of the viewer? The film leaves the question open. David Fincher's *Fight Club* (1999) offers a masculine rewriting of this split, in a film that similarly invites a psychoanalytical reading, and in which the viewer finally discovers that she is alone with 'Jack' in perceiving him and Tyler as different and separate characters. The lack of resemblance and the apparent objectivity of the viewer's position are revealed as hallucinatory.

Film, then, is not a medium that simply dispels ambiguities of resemblance. Doubt over doubles is not necessarily resolved when characters appear on screen. However, whereas in the novel the doubtful double is repeatedly linked to authorship and the situation of the writer, in film it provides a striking opportunity to play with the positioning of the viewer.

The representation of the doubtful double reaches its apogee in Ivan Reitman's *Twins* (1988), starring Danny de Vito and Arnold Schwarzenegger as the unlikely siblings. The film tells a familiar story of estranged twins – one altruistic, the other a hustler – who team up together. Reitman's twist on the tale is to suggest that such physical opposites as these actors could possibly share any family resemblance. *Twins* occupies the same kind of ironic position in relation to twin films as *Despair* in relation to earlier tales of doubles, and uses the same figure – the doubtful double – to do so. It parodies its predecessors as it shows Vincent (de Vito) and Julius (Schwarzenegger) side by side in matching outfits, with identical gestures and sayings, telepathically connected to one another's thoughts and movements, feeling one another's pain as they go about finding their mother and fortune. The poster for the film, in which the tag-line – 'Even their mother can't tell them apart' – is contradicted by the visible evidence of the identically dressed twins, already provides the distance between two interpretative positions (the mother's, the viewer's) that is the very definition of irony. And yet, at the same time as parodying (male) twin films, Reitman shows that the story does not depend on physical resemblance as much as we might believe. *Twins* could be seen as the twin film to end all twin films. It depends to such an extent on the story of reunited twins being already known that it incarnates its triteness, as if the story is so familiar that only by undoing its essential premise – the likeness of twins – can anything fresh come of it. And yet, rather than the end of the line, the last word in twin films, we find it functioning as a model for its successors when *Steal Big Steal Little* (1995) promotes itself (on the video jacket) as '*Twins* <u>with</u> the resemblance.' As with *Despair*, the undoing of the topos is far from definitive. As *Adaptation* shows, however, it cannot be ignored.

Adaptation (Spike Jonze): Adapting twins

There are no twins in Susan Orlean's book *The Orchid Thief* (1998): flowers, hunters and collectors, skulduggery, passion and botany, certainly, but no twins. Spike Jonze's film based on the book, on the other hand, is a twin film, and so before exploring how twins are used in the film and relating them to the doubtful doubles discussed above, the first question to ask is why they appear at all.

The answer relates to the film's title, *Adaptation* (2002). The adaptation is firstly that of the book, for the story of producing the screenplay is as prominent in the film as the orchids and thief of Orlean's text. References to several other forms of adaptation are, however, also to be found in the film. There are explicit references to evolutionary adaptation (such as that of orchids) with shots of Charles Darwin in his study and voiceovers of his writings. In parallel with evolutionary forces is the necessity for people to adapt: 'Adaptation's a profound process. It means you figure out how to thrive in the world' says Laroche, Orlean's eponymous orchid fancier (35).[5] Successful screenwriting (in the voice of Robert McKee) dictates that characters too must evolve. And – importantly for the purposes of this chapter – genres of writing and the principles that constrain them are also adapted in the writing process, in order for the story – the film – to thrive. Not mentioned explicitly in the film, but pertinent to this study is the adaptation of stock twin stories, for the introduction of twins is what allows this particular adaptation from book to film to flourish.

Why, then, does a book about orchid-hunting and collecting become a twin film? Screenwriter Charlie Kaufman dramatises the process of the book's adaptation and the problems it entails. We shall see that these are problems of genre (how to turn a volume of largely non-narrative prose exploring a fascination with orchids into a fascinating feature film) and problems of oldness and newness (how to avoid repeating the clichés of the past, how to write something new). He also dramatises the solutions he finds for these dilemmas, the most conspicuous of which is the use of twins. Kaufman puts himself into the script,[6] along with his angst, his writer's block, his frustrated love life...and his fictional identical twin brother Donald (both twins are played by Nicolas Cage) in order to 'put in the drama' (70) needed to turn the book into a movie.

'I don't know how to adapt this,' Kaufman the character says to Marty, his agent. His principal difficulty is that 'The book has no story. There's no story!' (51). He wants to remain faithful to the book: 'I wanted to do something simple. Show people how amazing flowers are' (51), 'to create a story where nothing much happens' (68). He wants to avoid turning it into 'an orchid heist movie' or 'a movie about drug running' or 'cram[ming] in sex or guns or car chases. [...] Or characters learning profound life lessons' (5). And yet at the same time he is acutely aware of the need for story. Scriptwriting guru Robert McKee (played by Brian Cox) lectures him that 'first, last, always, the imperative is to tell a story. Your goal must be a good story well told' (64–5). Kaufman's dilemma is not the choice between narrative and non-narrative forms, but finding and elaborating the story that will 'show people how amazing flowers are.' Marty's answer to Kaufman's problem?: 'Make one up' (51) – which is of course what Kaufman the (co)-author of the screenplay does in cloning a twin brother.

If orchids do not lend themselves in any obvious way to dramatisation, twins do. 'That's not a movie,' says McKee when Kaufman gives him an account of the book, 'You gotta go back, put in the drama' (70). Before adding sex and car chases, Kaufman puts in twins. Twins are archetypal story material. The very appearance of twin characters represents the bud of a story ready to unfurl, a story we can already start to predict from the wealth of myth, literature, anecdote and film portraying twins that precedes it. Introducing the Kaufman twins turns Orlean's book into a story, makes it tellable on screen. Twins are the cure for Kaufman's writer's block, allowing him to 'dramatise the idea of the flower' (Feld, 2002: 123), and twins prove themselves to be at least as effective as and far more versatile than drugs, thieves and serial killers for driving a story on film.

In an essay published together with the screenplay, the critic McKee (not the character) identifies the problem as one of genre: while the prose writer can 'dramatize[ ] the invisible, the tides and times of inner conflict,' 'you can't drive a camera lens through an actor's forehead and photograph thought' (McKee, 2002: 133). Kaufman (not the character), however, focuses on the viewer's rather than the actor's forehead. In an interview he explains the need to reach the viewer's headspace such that the film cannot be viewed dispassionately: 'I'm always trying to figure out a way to take a movie from here, out in front of you *[Charlie frames something out in front of him]*, and put it *here [he pulls his hands back even with his head]*' (Feld, 2002: 128). Both of these problems are solved by turning Charlie Kaufman into antithetical twins: on the one hand, inner conflict – Kaufman's relation with himself – is exteriorised and made filmable, and on the other hand, the story of the flower ceases to be an object of detached analysis, and is made to resonate with a particular instance of the human condition – Charlie's self – in all its idiosyncrasy. Kaufman the character looks for the flower's story early in the film:

> 'To write about a flower, to dramatize a flower, I have to show the flower's arc. And the flower's arc stretches back to the beginning of life. How did this flower get here? What was its journey? [...] It is a journey of evolution. Adaptation. The journey we all take. A journey that unites each and every one of us.' (40)

He proposes to film a time-lapse version of the evolution of life on the planet from single cell organisms right through to Susan Orlean in her office, and indeed we see this footage, but it is Charlie Kaufman's personal evolution through his relationship with his twin Donald that brings the story of adaptation from 'out there' to 'in here.' Twins are the means of getting the flower story into the viewer's headspace. Like the insect pollinating the flower – 'By simply doing what they're designed to do, something large and magnificent happens [...] they show us how to live' (23–4) – they give the story life. Donald quotes Orlean's book: 'Sometimes this kind of story turns out to be something more...some glimpse of life that expands like those Japanese paper balls you drop into water and they bloom into flowers.' He looks in her book for '[w]hat turned that paper ball into a flower' (74), for something that might initiate such a transformation. If we look for that trigger in the case of the film, we find it is the use of twins.

Doubtful, dubious and doubting

Although there is no doubt about their resemblance (Nicolas Cage looks astonishingly like Nicolas Cage), the Kaufman twins too are doubtful doubles. Doubt characterises the twinship in several ways: Donald's existence is a subject of speculation; the film abounds with self-reflexive commentary on the questionable quality of popular filmic devices; and finally Charlie Kaufman himself is overwhelmed by self-doubt, partly expressed as a doubt about whether the film we are watching will indeed ever be made. Interestingly, however, *Adaptation* connects more closely with the novels than with the films outlined earlier in the chapter in its use of doubtful doubles to portray writers and the writing process. Indeed its parallels with Martin Amis's novel *Money* are particularly evident: hyper-irony with the insertion of the author as character; the difficulties of writing a film script; highbrow and lowbrow writers as alter egos. In the transfer of this writerly topos to a feature film, *Adaptation* reflects its own preoccupation with the move from print to screen.

Adaptation sees 'real people' (Charlie Kaufman, Susan Orlean, John Laroche, Robert McKee) played by actors (Nicolas Cage, Meryl Streep, Chris Cooper, Brian Cox), actors playing themselves (John Malkovich, Catherine Keener, John Cusack), and a fictional character (Donald Kaufman) appearing both in the credits for co-screenwriting and in the dedication at the film's closing ('In Loving Memory of Donald Kaufman'). Prominent on the *Internet Movie Data Base* messageboard devoted to the film is audience discussion on whether Charlie's twin is 'real' within the fictional reality of the film, or a figment of his imagination, a projection of one of his own voices.[7]

The film opens with a black screen and voiceover representing the thoughts running through Charlie's head: his hypochondria, disgust at his unattractiveness, poor self-esteem, lack of success with women, and general anxiety. From the start we are made to understand that not only is Charlie screwed up, but that the vantage point of the viewer may often be inside his mind. His almost-girlfriend Amelia makes it plain that Charlie's psychological problems are evident to others: 'Okay. Charlie, we're gonna fix you up. We're gonna solve the whole Charlie Kaufman mess once and for all' (13). Amelia sees his taking on the orchid script as a positive step and, in a sentence that deserves to be taken literally, remarks: 'I think it will be good for you to get out of your head' (13). Could Donald be the result of just such a process? The first inkling we have of Donald's existence is when Charlie enters his apparently empty house and shuts the door behind him. As he climbs the winding stairs, we hear Donald's voice recounting the domestic trivia of the day. Donald tends to occupy the upper floor recesses of Charlie's personal space, the space where he writes. It is then small wonder that Donald is seen by some as Charlie's delusion, as an inhabitant of his mind-space, as a character who manages to 'get out' of Charlie's head (particularly since the idea of getting into and out of someone's head was the explicit subject of Kaufman and Jonze's previous film collaboration, *Being John Malkovich*).

The fact that other characters see and react to Donald is presented by one messageboard correspondent as a clinching argument for Donald's filmic reality.[8] The lingering doubt, however, comes as much from the paratext (the credits and dedication) as from the film itself. Whereas a clear line separates, for example, Charlie's masturbatory fantasies from his day to day world and life with Donald, such a line is crossed when the character Donald is given equal status to Kaufman-as-writer-not-character, such that his work figures in the filmography on the DVD of the film, and he is listed as author even in the bibliography to the present book. Similarly confounding are the photos from the filmset showing director Spike Jonze in consultation with Nicolas Cage playing Donald while Nicolas Cage as Charlie Kaufman looks on (Kaufman and Kaufman, 2002: 106, 113). Donald's existence is a subject of speculation not only in the fictional reality of the film but in the world of writers, directors, producers and copyright that frame the film. Our knowledge that in this latter sphere Donald is Charlie's creation, despite the apparent evidence to the contrary, loops back into our reading of the film, making us wonder whether Donald isn't equally Charlie's invention in the story told on screen.

Kaufman's double is equally doubtful in the sense of dubious, arousing suspicions about quality. Unlike Charlie Kaufman, Academy Award winner for the screenplay of *Being John Malkovich*, Donald is an amateur screenwriter of questionable talent and technique: 'I'm gonna be a screenwriter! Like you! [...] I'm doing it right this time. I'm taking a three-day seminar' (10). Donald dreams up a serial killer movie in which the perpetrator suffers from multiple personality disorder and is finally revealed to be all the main characters. His brother responds: 'The only idea more overused than serial killers is multiple personality. On top of that, you explore the notion that cop and criminal are really two aspects of the same person. See every cop movie ever made for other examples of this' (31). Charlie, on the other hand, is trying to write something fresh.

While Charlie scoffs at the (over)use of split personality plots in films, 'multiple personality disorder' can be seen as a diagnosis of the double in *Adaptation*: however well-rounded the character of Donald is, Charlie and Donald are understood to be 'really two aspects of the same person,' with Donald as the artist's lowbrow alter ego. And how would you shoot Donald's thriller? 'Trick photography,' suggests Donald. Using a split screen no doubt. Charlie's verdict on Donald's 'pitch' reflects back on to his own film, and amounts to saying that its use of twins as doubles is the most hackneyed cinematic ploy of them all, even more predictable than the serial killer.

Not only a *mise-en-abyme* of the film, Charlie and Donald's exchanges regarding screenwriting provide a *mise-en-abyme* of the questions prompting this book, namely: how and why are twin stories repeatedly retold? what does it mean to recycle material and what purposes might it serve? and how is the use of twins shaped by genre? Charlie and Donald's lines offer explicit commentary on what it means to retell a familiar story, and how a shift in genre can transform a tale.

Everything old is new again: repetition and adaptation

Like Nabokov's Karlovitch, Charlie is contemptuous of the use of routine narrative devices. He scorns Hollywood clichés ('sex or guns or car chases' 5), yet through Donald's collaboration on the script, manages to include all of these in the film's climax with drug running, alligators, and life-changing conversations to boot. We understand this as the application of McKee's suggestion over drinks that Charlie needs to 'wow them in the end' (70) in order to salvage the project. In a statement that recalls Eco's solution to triteness, McKee (not the character) explains the irony as a case of 'Kaufman get[ting] everything he wants by confessing to the contrivance' (2002: 134). In fact the only contrivance to which he does not explicitly confess is the most obvious one, the use of the identical twin as the author's double.

Rather than merely the repetition of a hackneyed theme, however, *Adaptation* uses twins to thematise the hackneyed. Charlie's twin Donald represents the temptation to put together a script for a blockbuster using pre-packaged plot sequences, cookie-cutter characters, and a liberal dose of gore. He personifies the formulaic writer who achieves commercial success by following a set of rules, indeed a list of 'commandments' (52), about what works, based on what has worked in the past. Charlie is dismissive of the principles Donald is learning and of those who teach them: 'Look, my point is that those teachers are dangerous if your goal is to try to do something new. And a writer should always have that goal. Writing is a journey into the unknown. It's not...building one of your model airplanes!' (12).[9] Even as he resists repetition, however, Charlie's own work is haunted by it. Thus at the very moment that Donald explains his choice of the most facile of symbols – 'the motif of broken mirrors' – to show the fragmentation of his serial killer (51), we see Charlie's face in the mirror at the top of the stairs. The writer(s) of *Adaptation* may not be able to avoid such motifs, but (t)he(y) can at least acknowledge their overuse by attributing them to Donald.

As in so many twin tales, Charlie and Donald are opposites, Donald representing every writing impulse that Charlie rejects in himself. Donald is thus the twin introduced to represent a psychological double in precisely the kind of overt way dismissed by Tymms, Rogers and Coates as banal and trivial (see Chapter 1). Donald's association with low genres is reflected not only in his desire to write a serial killer film but in his physical positioning in relation to his brother: we first see him lying on his back on the floor, having parasitically consumed Charlie's food in the fridge (Donald is staying temporarily with his brother until he finds employment). While Charlie walks in to his bedroom, Donald crawls on all fours to the doorway. As Charlie critiques screenwriting rules, Donald stretches out on the floor again: 'I just need to lie down while you explain this to me' (11), presumably in order to digest both the alimentary and intellectual nourishment Charlie provides (Figure 7.1). At various points throughout the film, Donald lies on the floor while Charlie sits at his writing table, or Donald sits on the floor while Charlie sits on the bed. On the film set and again at a party, Charlie stands while Donald sits. Only towards the end of the film, when Charlie has called Donald in to help with the

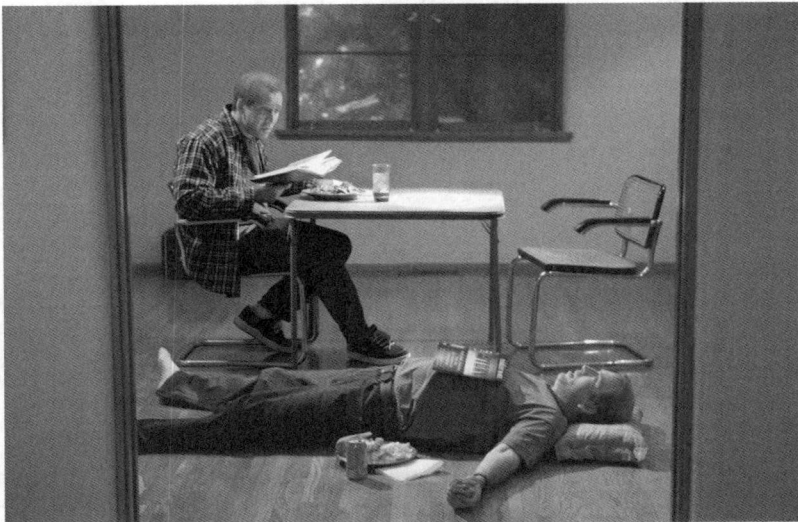

Figure 7.1   Nicolas Cage plays twins Charlie (seated) and Donald Kaufman in *Adaptation*.
Source: © 2002 Columbia Pictures Industries, Inc. All Rights Reserved Courtesy of Columbia Pictures

script, do they start to occupy the same spatial level: both lying, both standing, sitting side by side in the car or in the swamp. Until then, Donald is almost invariably positioned beneath Charlie. Charlie can thus literally look down on his lowly counterpart.

Donald lives off Charlie, recycling his leavings, whether his shrimp cocktails, his throwaway plot lines, or his film industry contacts, but it is above all his repetition of screenwriting commonplaces that earns him his inferior status and Charlie's derision. However, if repetition is a problem for Charlie, no less daunting are the problems of newness. If 'Nobody's ever done a movie about flowers before. So there are no guidelines' (11), then where do you start? His false starts take him on a 'jaunt into the abyss' (67). He simply cannot create something entirely new that will work as a film. Yet if he recycles the old as his brother does, he risks producing the kind of crass commercial screenplay he despises. How then can he reuse something that has been used before? The solution lies once again in the notion of adaptation. Reiteration is already inherent in the very idea of adapting a book for the screen: to adapt is to repeat more or less faithfully in a different genre. Now unlike the rehearsal of clichés, this process is never viewed by Kaufman as repetitive, but rather as producing something quite new. Although the orchid book has already been written, writing it as a screenplay is a leap into the unknown, is something 'Nobody's ever done [...] before' and that has 'no guidelines' (11). The genre shift will require its re-invention. Just as the biological adaptation of orchids can result in 'the strangest and most marvelous forms' (Orlean, 2002: ix), so too can textual adaptation give rise to startling innovation. The concept of adaptation allows Charlie a way out of the binary opposition between the original and the hackneyed.

The lesson of biological adaptation is that repetition produces differ-ence, rather than simply more of the same, an argument also elucid-ated by philosophers such as Derrida and Deleuze. Although Charlie is blind to it at the time, the idea can be glimpsed when he despairs of his brother: 'You and I share the same D.N.A. Is there anything more lonely than that?' (43). Charlie realises that it is possible to be identical to and yet feel he has next to nothing in common with his twin. The point can be extrapolated to the film, which shares the imaginative matter of the book, and yet constitutes a reinvention of that material. And ultimately, the film shows that – like Charlie and Donald – block-busters and ideas films are not made from radically different materials, but from the adaptation of similar materials to a different genre and purpose.

In incarnating a division between serious writing and popular success, Charlie and Donald are reminiscent of the twins of Stephen King's thriller *The Dark Half* and its film adaptation by George Romero, in which bestseller-writer-cum-killer George Stark represents the dark unacknowledged underside of mild-mannered-author-cum-college-professor Thad's personality.[10] Now although Donald embodies only Charlie's baser literary instincts, and not repressed violent tendencies, he does introduce the serial killer motif, and he alludes to the thriller genre in a variety of ways throughout the film. Not only does he position his screenplay *The Three* unambiguously within the genre – 'My genre's thriller. What's yours?' (42) – but there are a couple of moments when he comes across as distinctly menacing, explosive moments that are only defused when, after a pause, he provides an anodyne explanation. Thus he remarks: 'I need a cool way to kill people' and only adds 'for my script' when he notices Charlie's alarm (36). Thus he responds to Charlie tearing down the McKee Ten Commandments he had taped to the wall by looming in the doorway and measuring out the words 'You shouldn't have done that.' The brothers face off until, some instants later, Donald adds 'because it's extremely helpful' (52).

Adaptation thus flaunts and flirts with its proximity to the thriller genre, represented by Donald, without simply joining it. It adapts rather than adopts the thriller. Charlie doesn't respond to Donald's question about which genre he writes in, for at this point he is still trying to produce something completely new, something as yet indefinable. Eventually, however, he appears to accept McKee's pronouncements that 'we must find our originality within [a] genre' and that 'there hasn't been a new genre since Fellini invented the mockumentary' (42). Abandoning his attempts to invent a new genre to accommodate the adaptation of Orlean's book, he agrees to borrow from existing genres (which was of course how the mockumentary came about) by asking the newly successful Donald to collaborate with him on the film's ending. Donald follows the leads Charlie has missed, finding an unarticulated love interest and a drug connection in the book, and taking the script to the point where the car chase, the pursuit through the swamp and the shooting become inevitable.

On the one hand, the contours of the twin plot are predictable here: Charlie's ultimate acceptance of his brother's qualities (personal and artistic) and of the part of himself that they reflect; Donald's death once Charlie has incorporated what his twin represents and become whole. And yet, rather than merely the assembly of a prefabricated twin drama, rather than the rehearsal of elements of a familiar genre in the way that Donald's *The Three* is assumed to be, the predictable plot is paradoxically what shifts the film towards an unpredictable mix of genres. Accepting his dark half, his inner hack, is the mechanism that enables Charlie to include drugs, sex, alligators and car chases into a quirky film about flowers, fascination and what it means to be human, and allows him to finish the script. *Adaptation* ceases to position itself in opposition to the thriller genre and starts to incorporate it. In the process it becomes something that is neither thriller nor contemplative art-film. *Casablanca*, twice cited as the 'finest screenplay ever written' (71, cf. 52), now provides the template: not only was it written by twins (71), but it is defined as a mix of genres (52).

Mixing genres is Charlie's way out of the impasse in which he finds himself, the choice between the impossibly new and the stultifyingly old. In her book, Orlean notes that self-pollination leads to sterile repetition and ultimately extinction. Cross-pollination is not only necessary for survival, but produces new species. With films as with orchids, invention and novelty come from the cross-pollination of existing genres/genera (both genre and genus derive from the Latin *genus*) and, in the case of *Adaptation*, even different genii. Charlie is seen as the genius in the family during the first half of the film (36, 48 although the latter is a fantasy attribution). Gradually, however, just as Charlie makes his first positive remark about Donald's work (with a sincere statement that 'It sounds exciting' 56), people start to recognise the existence of a second genius in the family (56, 65). Finally their differences can be seen as productive, as 'different talents' (74) that can be put to work together to create something strange and marvellous.

The mix of genres means that the clichés from thrillers and twin dramas are employed not only as crowd-pleasers, not only to finish off the film with a bang, but to make possible the illustration of the fascination and passion that are the subject of Orlean's book. They are used to illuminate Laroche's phrase that orchids and insects 'show us how to live. How the only barometer you have is your heart. How when you spot your flower, you can't let anything get in your way' (Laroche 24). Unlike the fascinated orchid-hunter or insect, Charlie is so paralysed by what others think of him that he can neither follow any passion, nor write a film about passion. Charlie imagines Orlean guiding his writing: 'Just find that one thing that you care passionately about ... then write about that' (55). For Charlie, that one thing is human nature, or more precisely his own human nature, his relation with himself. However, it is not until Donald gives him a lesson on love, in a sharing of feelings that could only occur in the life-and-death tension of the manhunt in the swamp, that he can give expression to this passion. That is to say, the tension of the thriller and the story of the synthesis of antithetical twins create the enabling conditions for Charlie to love and write without letting anything get in his way. Shortly before dying, Donald teaches him that 'You are what you love, not what loves you.' (93), and in the closing scenes of the film, Charlie is finally free, able to kiss Amelia, simply because he loves her, to follow his (now mixed) writing instincts, no longer caring what McKee says (99), and to finish the screenplay.

The film is presented to the viewer as the product of the collaboration between Charlie and Donald that it depicts, as the story of its own evolution. This evolution is accompanied by another: that of twins as a filmic topos. Twins are first introduced as typical narrative material, an ingredient to make a story tellable, but one associated with overly familiar plots and imitative productions. In the transformation of the orchid book into a tale tellable on screen, however, something original is created, a singular hybrid. From symbolising triteness and a lack of imagination, twins come to represent the very opposite, the creative process itself.

Reviving the double

Nabokov and Auster, Fassbinder, Jonze and Kaufman are among the cultural heavyweights demonstrating that the double's fall from favour from Great Romantic Theme to disreputable device of fiction did not mark the end of its artistic career. On the contrary, the figure has rebounded with renewed vigour in the late twentieth century – the time of the 'culture of the copy' (Schwartz, 1996). It is even possible to see the double's declining reputation as providing the springboard for its postmodern reinvention: its designation as trite made it recuperable as kitsch.

The recuperation did not, however, stop there. Nabokov's playful displacement of the traditional double gradually evolved into a motif in its own right: likeness as subjective and fluid, as a product of identification. Kaufman's quotation of twins as cliché becomes a commentary on the process of recycling and adapting existing ideas and tropes, of innovating through repeating in another context, a process that sums up the turn away from a modernist approach to invention, from the utopian idea that the totally new is the goal to pursue. Indeed Kaufman's recourse to identical twins per se makes the same point: as the-same-but-different, twins lend themselves to use as a metaphor for repetition-and-difference, as an emblem for postmodern creativity.

8

Conclusion: Twins and Problems of Representation

Feminist diversions

Before bringing the threads of the preceding chapters together, I should like to focus briefly on a recurrent feminist use of twins. The novels concerned – Angela Carter's *Wise Children* (1991), Margaret Laurence's *A Jest of God* (1966), and Marilyn Bowering's *Visible Worlds* (1998) – are too diverse to constitute a cluster. They can however be rather loosely grouped around the fact that each uses twins to disturb the dynastic line.

Twins are particularly suited to this function. Not only does the simultaneous birth of two infants unsettle the principle of primogeniture (see Chapter 6), but a widespread mythic tradition concerns anxiety about paternity. Many cultures have believed that twins could not possibly spring from one father, that two fathers must have been involved. Harris (1906: 7), Rank (1973: 100–2) and Stewart (2003: 6, 18) all refer to the hypothesis of the dual paternity of twins. In Greek myth, one twin had a mortal father, while the other was invariably fathered by a god. In totemic cultures, one father was an ancestral spirit in the form of an animal (Rank, 1973: 102). In other societies, twins have been seen as evidence of adultery on the part of the mother, and Marie de France's 'Lai du frêne' provides a twelfth century literary illustration of this belief. Historically then, twins have been associated with a disturbance of genealogy in a variety of ways.

The novels by Carter, Laurence and Bowering widen this variety, each using twins quite differently. What distinguishes them from the legends above, however, is their purpose: the line of descent is disordered or interrupted as a way of challenging its role in legitimising social existence. The novels are diversions in several senses: not only do they divert genealogy, but they set up genre expectations and then upset them, diverting the course of familiar tales and sometimes deflecting the interest of the story away from twins altogether. And, in the case of *Wise Children* in particular, they are forms of entertainment.

Diverting comedy: Angela Carter's *Wise Children*

Of the three novels, *Wise Children*, a rollicking rendition of a twin comedy, is the only one to allude directly to the myth of dual paternity. Two intertwined families – the legitimate Hazards and the illegitimate Chances – boast multiple twins: at least five sets between them, merry-makers all. The Hazards are a dynasty of celebrated actors, while the Chances make a living where they can find it: as tap-dancers, extras, even strippers. However, as suggested by the surnames and the title, with its allusion to the wisdom of the child that knows its own father, the paternity of the twins and the legitimacy or otherwise of their births and professions are inevitably contested. Similarly contested is the literary pedigree of the text. Ostensibly a novel, it adopts the conventions of theatre (five acts; unity of time, space and action; *dramatis personae* listed as such) and recounts a performance of *A Midsummer Night's Dream*. (cf. Boehm, 1994; Peach 1998: 139). It conspicuously engages with the Shakespearean comedies of confusion with bedtricks, substitute brides, mistaken identity, and misrecognition of parents and children. The theatrical lineage is however as entangled as the families themselves: Shakespearean and music-hall traditions mingle; high and low forms rub shoulders.

The confusion revolves around estranged twin brothers Melchior and Peregrine Hazard on the day of their hundredth birthday and 75-year-old twin daughters (but whose?) Nora and Dora Chance. The expectations generated by the allusions to Shakespearean comedy are that the dénouement will return confused twins to stable perches in the family tree and reveal the truth of fatherhood. These genre conventions are however overturned. The novel settles no questions conclusively but rather emphasises the inconclusive nature of paternity ('a father is a movable feast' 216) and the constructedness of family ties ('Grandma invented this family. She put it together out of whatever came to hand – a stray pair of orphaned babes, a ragamuffin in a flat cap' 35, cf. 189). And finally Peregrine produces yet more twins – baby girls of unknown origin – from his pockets for Nora and Dora to raise through their own invention of maternity/paternity (230).

As Hardin (1994), Webb (1994) and Day (1998: 204) note, Carter undertakes a calculated disturbance of notions of genealogy that challenges not only the organising principle of the patrilineal family, but the legitimacy of the literary tradition. She uses twin fathers to erode the notion of a definitive paternity, twin daughters to undermine the distinction between legitimate and illegitimate, and twin cultural forms (Shakespearean theatre and popular music-hall) to question the authority and ancestry of high culture. The literary canon and the patriarchal family – both bastions of privilege – are shown to be characterised by discontinuity, promiscuity and hybridity.

Diverting romance: Margaret Laurence's *A Jest of God*

Laurence's twin tale is less flamboyant than Carter's, but similarly plays with genre expectations, those of romance in this case, diverting a story to a feminist purpose by interrupting the anticipated genealogy. As Waterston notes in her article 'Double is trouble,' (1990: 83) twins are a persistent motif in *A Jest of God*. Protagonist Rachel is a thirty-four year old 'spinster' schoolteacher in the 1960s, condemned to spending her life looking after her elderly mother. She has an affair with Nick, whose twin brother died in childhood. Nick's twinship is a wound kept open by an aging father who confuses him with his brother. Meanwhile gossip circulates concerning a young unmarried mother who returns to town to bring up her twins, who are '[t]wice as reprehensible as one' baby in the town's eyes (Laurence, 1966: 58). Add to these twins the teenage girls that Rachel labels 'twins from outer space' (12), and the metaphorical twinning of Rachel (whose interior monologue splits into conflicting voices) and of the town (divided into Scottish and Ukrainian families), and twinship becomes a refrain in the novel.

Thus when Rachel's period is late and she fears (and yet hopes for) pregnancy, the possibility that she carries twins seems overdetermined. This would be the 'jest of God' of the title, to make her doubly reprehensible, and then perhaps doubly saved by a future with Nick. But it is not. The growth turns out to be a tumour, and contrary to expectations of a romantic conclusion, Nick is written out of the story completely. There is no reference to him at all by the end of the novel.

And yet the story has a happy ending. With the removal of the tumour, Rachel gives birth to herself as an independent woman. She takes control of her life and ceases to be her mother's pawn. If the 'jest of God' is finally not a twin pregnancy but a tumour, Laurence's jest –

and we should not underestimate its power to disconcert in 1966 – is to substitute self-sufficiency for the birth of twins as the novel's upbeat conclusion. Thus Laurence uses the twin motif – not twins per se, but their absence – to resist the genealogical storyline. The absence of twins where they were expected enables Rachel to refuse the social roles defined for her by the traditional family structure. Rather than her future being defined by her offspring and her place in the dynastic line, Rachel forges her own future.

Diverting adventure: Marilyn Bowering's *Visible Worlds*

Marilyn Bowering's *Visible Worlds* (1998) similarly hijacks the genre/ gender expectations that it sets up. The prologue describes a Canadian football match during which Albrecht finds a map pencilled by his long lost twin brother Gerhard. The map is of Siberia and the Bering Strait, conjuring up visions of Cold War defections to Alaska, and taking Albrecht back to when he collected Soviet POWs in his plane during a prisoner exchange. Football, combat, espionage, escape, airplanes, a brother to track down: all the elements are assembled ready for a Boys' Own story of high adventure. That story, however, is not told. Indeed, if there is an adventure story at all in the novel, it is that of a young Soviet woman, Fika, who crosses the icecap to reach Arctic Canada.

If genre expectations are diverted when Fika's story intercuts Albrecht's, so too are reader expectations of the twin tale rerouted in the novel. When Albrecht takes us back to his childhood, we start to recognise a familiar topos. Albrecht and Gerhard are the twin sons of German immigrants to Canada, growing up between the two world wars. Gerhard is his mother's son, tall, fair and Prussian, a talented musician destined to study in Germany. Albrecht is shorter and darker and resembles his father, a slaughterhouse worker who fought with the Canadian Army. Soon enough we discover that Albrecht and Gerhard spend the war on opposite sides of the Atlantic.

Here we are presented with the germ of a story we know, one that has the clear potential to develop into a full-blown account of brothers separated by country and culture, facing each other across enemy lines. That is not, however, the story that will be told. Rather than a tale of nations and families divided by cultural affiliation, *Visible Worlds* spins a tale about filiation more generally. Although the twins are briefly engaged in opposing armed forces during the war, the main narrative interest is drawn away from the twins and the twinship, and towards a series of children, mostly girls, who become separated from their families: swapped as babies, stolen, abandoned, or lost through mistaken identity. These are never restored to their parents; rather their lives intersect in unpredictable ways. The twin tale unravels; there can be no twin reunion, just a linking of lives through stories. *Visible Worlds* is thus a story of the repeated disturbance of family lines. It trades on the topos of twins that represent divided nations but diverts it to demonstrate the discontinuities that produce families and their histories.

If Carter recycles the Shakespearian tradition of comic twins to disrupt filiation, Laurence does likewise by rewriting the conventions of romance, and Bowering by *not* writing the adventure story she seems to promise. Each reroutes a quite different set of twin tropes to a similar end, exposing genealogy as tenuous and contingent.

The insistent retelling of twin tales

In her work on genre and gender, Anne Freadman writes of genre in terms of problem-solving. She suggests 'that a genre is generated by a problem of representation, and that insofar as it becomes a genre, it represents a set of habits, or a tradition, of solutions to that problem' (1997: 310). Furthermore, in a sentence illustrated to perfection by these novels, she declares that 'No text merely violates its genre, or transgresses its rules. It solves a problem' (1997: 319). Carter, Laurence and Bowering each demonstrate the need to transform a genre – comedies of confusion, the romance novel, the Boys' Own adventure story – in order to represent the family in a way that questions the legitimacy conferred by the patrilineal succession of generations. Solving this problem involves shifting attention from male to female characters and bypassing the constraints of conventional endings, whether children returned to the family fold and embraced by their fathers, marriage and babies, or a hero's return. In each case, a twin tale is diverted from its usual path. Familiar at first, the tale is retold such that it breaks the generic mould in order to rewrite family history. And through such breaks, the history of twin tales itself becomes a tale of borrowings and crossings, of disturbances to the genealogical line.

The urge to break with literary and filmic habits is evident throughout the preceding chapters. Jonze's film *Adaptation* is quite candid in its illustration of Freadman's point. Through self-reflexive commentary on its need to adapt existing conventions in order to turn a book about orchids into a screenplay, it makes transparent the problem-solving nature of its engagement with different genres. However many of the other twin tales that have received detailed attention in this book similarly take a given model but shift genre conventions in order to find a way round entrenched habits of representation. This may involve changing the anticipated gender (a male siren in *Lies of the Twins*, a brother who is also a sister in *Drag Queen*) or nudging the topos along an unfamiliar path (prolonging the life of a twin couple in *On the Black Hill*, questioning resemblance in *A l'autre bout de moi*) or grafting the patterns of one genre on to those of another (drama on to horror in *Twin Falls Idaho*; comedy on to twin research in *Drag Queen*, thriller on to treatise in *Adaptation*).

Reading the tales together as problem-solving interventions in genre routines makes it possible to focus on the kinds of questions twins are being recruited to probe and thus brings us closer to understanding why certain twin tales are so regularly retold in contemporary culture. The problems raised by the films and novels studied in this book are wide-ranging: how to represent a viable long-term relation based on sameness, how to turn the tables on the virgin/whore split, how to depict male bodies when masculinity is said to be in crisis, how to represent joined brothers other than as an object of horror, how to show that not all homosexualities are alike, how to represent a cultural identity that is both hybrid and fluid, how to show resemblance as subjective, how to make a film about an abstract passion, how to portray the contrary impulses driving the writing process.

It is significant that these are *not* questions about the right of the first-born to inherit or occupy the throne, or about threats to the social order. They do not address the relation between man and god, man and animal, mortality and immortality. Nor do they enquire into the nature of the human or the power of the divine. Indeed they barely consider the origins of civilisation or the connection between the material world and spirituality, those preoccupations of past eras at the root of so many twin legends.

Some of the concerns underlying the use of the double in nineteenth-century literature remain important, such as the conflict between conscious and unconscious desires, or between opposing attributes of the self, the incest taboo, the dangers of a closed and narcissistic relationship, the fear of the monstrous. These problems are often, however, raised in different terms in late twentieth-century twin tales, and the main changes can be related to questions of gender and sexuality. Although good and evil twins continue to represent conflicting desires and attributes, the twins are now just as likely to be female as male, and when female, their good and evil is overwhelmingly understood in sexual terms. The dangers of narcissism and incest are increasingly seen through the prism of homosexuality in the exploration of intense relations between twin brothers rather than mixed sex siblings. Psychological thrills have given way to frissons from physicality: horror and fear surge less from twins with supernatural or telepathic connections than from the monstrosity of male bodies that merge. It is not only the Romantic theme of the double that has been reworked to focus on gender issues: the centuries-old comic topos of cross-dressing lookalike twins has been harnessed to explore transgender lives in recent years.

Gender and sexuality are, however, not the only concentrations of cultural energy prompting contemporary twin tales. Intersecting with them are questions of personal and cultural identity. These are prominent in tales of twins who embody different traits, or whose resemblance to each other is ambiguous, in tales of twins of different nationalities, or growing up in different ethnic or social backgrounds. Here competing discourses of identity – identity as unified, coherent and stable versus identity as multiple, fragmented and contradictory – find expression. Dividedness is variously seen as a threat to or a condition of existence.

The emphases I have identified here clearly reflect the profound shifts in twentieth-century discourses of identity and sexuality, connected in latter years with the rise of feminism and the accompanying redistribution of gender roles, the gay rights movement, the postcolonial hybridisation of cultures, the postmodern understanding of the self. These are the areas of investigation that have dominated work in cultural theory over the past three decades. And it is no coincidence that the motif of the double has been so conspicuous in theory during this same period: from Derrida's speculations on *différance* and citation to Butler's reconception of gender as reiterated performance, through the gamut of psychoanalytical ruminations on the mirror and the split self. Omnipresent throughout the humanities since the 1970s are questions relating to the play of sameness and difference, to the relation between self and other.

If twins are similarly omnipresent in narrative genres, however, it is not only because they are able to incarnate these concerns. Crucially important is the fact that their meaning is not fixed, is always 'up for grabs' to a large extent. They are just as available to reinforce traditional dichotomies as to undo them; they can serve to expose masquerade as the exception or the norm, to argue for the overriding unity of the self or its fractured nature, to support a dialectical resolution of conflict or insist on the indefinite deferral of any synthesis. Their importance, then, is as sites of contention in the struggle to claim legitimacy for particular perspectives, and this is what explains the cultural energy they attract.

Hence it is important to resist gathering the tales up under one broad banner as if they could be enlisted together in the march towards a new world view. The big picture of discourses and philosophies, of history on the move, is ultimately less revealing than those clusters of texts where a particular story is insistently repeated with small variations, like a cultural itch that needs constant scratching. That scratching can have purpose. This is particularly the case when certain configurations of genre, gender and topos stabilise, and thrillers of sexy and wifely twin sisters, adventures of brothers fighting in enemy camps, or horrible homicidal mutant twins become trite. For eventually someone scratches through to break the pattern and show up the meanings that were invested in it.

This book has lingered on inventive retellings of this kind, not startlingly new twin tales, but tales that have been recycled and at the same time diverted. The texts in question can be read as exemplary, not in the sense that they are typical of late twentieth-century twin tales – often they are not – but in the sense that, like Nabokov's *Despair*, they provide a possible basis for new generic conventions. In each case, the innovation is prompted by the need to solve a problem of representation – whether of twinship, coupledom, sexual choices, masculinity, national identity, the writing of the self, or the self of the writer – or challenge its habitual solution.

Our need to keep telling twin tales – and to tell them differently – is not therefore driven by a single impulse, but by the stakes of various representations. Let us underestimate neither the importance of these stakes, nor the difficulty of breaking old habits. Representation is the terrain over which cultural battles are fought, and since no representation is definitive, no problem of portrayal solved once and for all, our need to retell and revise the stories currently being told will ensure a plentiful future supply of twin tales.

Afterword

September 2003, Choisy-au-Bac, France. As I check out a pile of children's books at the village library, my son thrusts another into my hands and insists we borrow it too: *Adeline, Adelune et le feu des saisons* (Grosz, 1996). We snuggle up at bedtime to read: once there were two sisters, born within an hour of each other, Adeline as beautiful as day, Adelune as beautiful as night. Adeline's skin turns golden with the sun, while Adelune's remains pale, caressed only by moonlight. In her blood-red dress, her chin stained red with raspberry juice, Adelune imagines suitors admiring her sister and oblivious to her own charms. To rid herself of her rival, she dispatches Adeline on a mission to defy the seasons and find flowers, fruits and berries in the winter snow. With her sunny disposition, Adeline succeeds, and her malicious twin greedily sets out in turn to gather more. Alas, her frosty approach angers the seasons, who send needles of snow in flurries to wound and bury her. My daughter clutches me tightly in fear as Adeline races out into the night, hurrying towards a bright stain on the snow, Adelune's dress.

Neither sister, however, perishes, and the prize of a suitor is deferred indefinitely in favour of the rewards of loving sisterhood. The twins find warmth curled up against each other, and the hour that separated them from birth, the hour of solitude dividing day from night disappears as Adelune discovers the delights of day, and Adeline of darkness. 'And perhaps they are still there today, one beside the other, like two fingers of a hand, admiring the green valley, whence one day will arrive suitors in their dozens.'

At the threshold hour of the bedtime story, between day and night, the fairy-tale appears age-old, and yet it tiptoes towards a revised happily-ever-after, in which the suitor has lost his pivotal position in the twinship, and the stakes of the story have changed. And a future generation of story-tellers absorbs another model and learns to tell and re-tell, to twist and spin tales of twins.

Notes

Chapter 1

1. I have analysed part of this series (texts by Ovid, Freud and Lacan) in an earlier article (de Nooy, 1991b).
2. I take 'topos' to refer not simply to a topic (such as twins) but to its embedding in a particular thematic arrangement or 'place' – conjoined twins, twins as sexual rivals, good and evil twins, the author and his twin/double, the incestuous twin couple, twins in enemy camps, twins separated at birth – which will tend to coincide with its occurrence in a particular genre.
3. The notion of retelling is not intended to imply that at some point of origin there exists a master-story, which is then reproduced in the form of versions of the original. Rather than assuming a hierarchy between renditions, I follow Barbara Herrnstein-Smith in understanding all stories as particular retellings, 'constructed by someone in particular, on some occasion, for some purpose' (1981: 167). Thus telling always involves some retelling, some gesture towards existing stories, and retelling entails both repetition and difference.
4. Rank's 'Der Doppelgänger' was first published in 1914 and substantially revised in 1925. English (1971) and French (1973) translations exist. I shall refer to both on occasion, as the work translated in the French volume includes additional chapters, one of which is devoted to twinship (cf. the publication history detailed in Rank, 1971: vii–ix).
5. The relative coherence of the Romantic literature of the double – or at least of the established canon of works representing it – makes it possible to conceive of The Theme of The Double during this period: a singular theme of a paradoxically singular double. The analysis of contemporary twin tales is a rather different enterprise. Given the diversity of late twentieth-century examples, any such singular Twin Theme in recent literature is unlikely to emerge.
6. An exception is Rockwell's interesting study of resemblance in medieval French romance (1995).
7. See de Nooy (1988, 1991a, 1998) for analyses of the uses of the figure of the double as a theoretical tool.
8. This purpose parallels that of Lucy Fischer in her study of the range of cinematic representations of maternity (1996).

Chapter 2

1. In some versions of the myth, Castor and Pollux are able to remain together, living one day on Olympus and the next in Hades. Harris analyses the 'divided immortality and shared mortality' of the Dioscuri, relating them to other pairs of legendary twins of whom one is immortal and the

other mortal (Amphion and Zethus, Herakles and Iphikles) (1906: 4–5; cf. 1903: 61).

2. Harris (1906) shows the extent of the influence of the 'cult of the heavenly twins' throughout the ancient and Christian worlds.

3. The fratricidal (or sororicidal) twin is amply illustrated in films such as Tim Hunter's *Lies of the Twins* (1991), George A. Romero's *The Dark Half* (1993), Tom Berry's *Twin Sisters* (1992), and Barbet Schroeder's *Single White Female* (1992). The representation of twin rivalry in popular film is discussed in detail in Chapter 3 below.

4. Havelock Ellis (1928) notes that although the Narcissus myth had endured in the popular and literary imagination since Ovid's time, prior to the mid-nineteenth century the figure of self-love evoked the enchantment of youthful beauty.

5. See Chapter 4 below on the amniotic representation of the domestic and professional environment of the twins in *Dead Ringers*.

6. Doubles feature in much of Redonnet's writing: see *Silsie* (1990) and *Doublures* (1986).

7. *The Silent Twins* also incorporates the evil twin theme, thus reflecting both of the major threats to twinship in Romantic and post-Romantic twin tales.

8. Angela Carter's *Wise Children*, recounting Dora and Nora's seventy-five years together on- and off-stage, seems to be the only example of a novel of longevity of a twin sister couple. I have not included it in the corpus for this chapter, for as Boehm (1994) and Peach (1998: 139) show, Carter's rollicking tale openly engages with its Shakespearean comic antecedents, that is to say, a quite different literary tradition from the one to which White, Tournier and Chatwin allude. Moreover, the calculated disturbance of notions of genealogy and paternity (see Chapter 8) overrides considerations of coupledom in Carter's novel.

9. The reworking of Western myths is a defining characteristic of Tournier's novels.

10. It is significant that the twins of each novel are men, and thus inherit a lengthy literary and mythic tradition from which female twins were virtually absent until the twentieth century (see Chapter 3).

11. White writes of 'three solid mandalas' in the Lascaris family, the others being a sister and an aunt of Manoly (1982: 116) and is quoted by friend Elizabeth Knight as referring to Lascaris as his 'solid mandala' (Lawson, 2003). The mandala is a Jungian image of wholeness and perfection (Marr, 1991: 451–2) and White acknowledges the influence of Jung in his novel (1982: 146).

12. In conversation with Zazzo, Tournier distances himself from this view (Zazzo, 1984: 51), and Davis also casts doubt on the seriousness of his statement in *Le Vent Paraclet*, pointing to the 'pervasive irony' of the text (1988: 68).

13. Radclyffe Hall's *The Well of Loneliness* (1928) epitomises this vision of the same-sex couple.

14. This layout is not reproduced in the English translation (Descombes, 1980).

15. See Chapter 7 for an analysis of postmodern twin tales.

16. The image can be compared with the Gordian knot representing the twinship in Bille's 'Le noeud' (1974).

17. In particular, it does not explore the figure of The Writer, for each of the twins is in his own way a writer. This is another recurrent twin topos

and Penelope Farmer, in her anthology *Two or The Book of Twins and Doubles* (1996), devotes a section to 'Authors as Doubles.'

18. Tournier draws heavily on Zazzo's *Les Jumeaux: le couple et la personne* in *Gemini*, as he acknowledges in the conversation prefacing *Le Paradoxe des jumeaux* (Zazzo, 1984).

19. It is difficult not to see an allusion here to Jean Paul Richter, who wrote under the name Jean Paul and introduced the term *doppelgänger* in his 1796 novel *Siebenkäs*.

20. Perrot similarly sees in literary twins the resistance to the passage of time (1976: 218).

21. Derrida develops the notion of a lop-sided step or rhythm – *une démarche boiteuse* – in *Glas* (1986).

22. Mireille Rosello points to this paradox whereby Paul, in order to re-establish sameness, must incorporate difference (1990: 20).

23. There is some doubt over which twin is immortal: is it the ethereal Jean, who fades from this world before inhabiting Paul's absent limbs? or is it, as Maclean suggests (2003: 70), Paul, resurrected after his mutilation and burial in the Berlin tunnel?

24. Helmut von Bracken used the terms Minister for Foreign Affairs and Minister for the Interior to characterise these roles, apparently common in twinships (Zazzo, 1984: 14). The division between a wandering (indeed piloting) twin and his more domestically oriented brother also appears in Corrick's *The Navigation Log* and Bowering's *Visible Worlds*. In both these novels, as in those of Tournier and Chatwin, the traveller is the first to disappear. Only in Chatwin's, however, does the death occur at an advanced age.

25. Although the women are not immobile in *Dead Ringers*, their mediation similarly serves to maintain the closed circuit of sameness. Elliot shares his female bedfellows with his twin, but these exchanges serve as little more than a safety valve for the twins, restoring perfect resemblance (Elliot: 'You haven't had any experience until I've had it'). Difference remains extremely threatening. Although the 'traffic in women' initially succeeds in maintaining twinship, as soon as Claire stops the traffic, refuses to be exchanged and insists on the difference between the twins, the twinship spirals down into death and decay.

26. In Arthur's case, totality is the ideal not only of twinship but of relationships in general.

27. In her analysis of the triangles formed by twins and the woman they love, La Piana similarly identifies a postmodern turn in twentieth-century twin narratives: 'The movement is one from the concept of twins as complementary parts of one whole, a concept which supports rather than questions the notion of the unified subject, to an alternative vision of twins as true reproductions of each other without a source, as simulacra without an original' (1990: 15).

Chapter 3

1. Although the twins/doubles are not clearly rivals in *Sisters* or in *Doppelganger*, they are in conflict over a man, and the good girl/bad girl distinctions are similar to the other films in the list. *Single White Female* is another complicated

case in that the twin relation is displaced on to the flatmate, and the rivalry has a possessiveness not featured in the other films.

2. The proportion varies across cultures (Bryan, 1992: 19-20) and is rising in Western countries due to fertility treatments and the older average age at which women are having children.

3. René Zazzo distinguishes between the theme of the double and that of the couple in narrative uses of twins. These themes have been associated with different genres at different historical moments (1984: 131–74). Films involving non-identical twins and the handful of films in which identical twins are played by different actors – 'real-life' twins (*On the Black Hill*, *The Third Walker*, *Twin Falls Idaho*) or brothers (*The Krays*, *A Zed and Two Noughts*) – tend to explore the relation between the brothers, to address the question of the brothers as couple.

4. In 2002, the Dutch film of Tessa de Loo's novel *De Tweeling* (released as *Twin Sisters*) finally provided a counter-example, with Dutch and German actresses playing the title roles of twin sisters raised in different countries.

5. Erich Kästner's novel *Das doppelte Lottchen* has been filmed repeatedly: in Germany in 1950 and 1994 (as *Charlie and Louise*); in Japan (1952) and Britain (*Twice Upon a Time*, 1953); and most famously in the U.S.A. as *The Parent Trap* (1961), which boasts three made-for-television sequels and a 1998 remake. *Twice Blessed* (1945) and *It Takes Two* (1995) also follow a very similar storyline.

6. Although the virgin/whore pattern can also be found in recent popular fiction (for example Danielle Steel's bestseller *Mirror Image*, which contrasts wanton feminist and devoted wife twins), novels of female twins constitute a far less homogeneous group of texts. The sisters in Terry Prone's *Racing the Moon* (1999), for example, are distinguished by world views and life choices, not sexual proclivities, while Sandra Brown's thriller *The Switch* (2000), avoids the good/bad girl routine as one twin hunts for her sister's killer. Meanwhile, among more literary examples, Alice Thompson's *Justine* (1996) engages head-on with the virgin/whore split in a self-consciously literary rewriting of Sade's Justine/Juliette pair and Angela Carter's *Wise Children* (1991) portrays non-rival twin sisters with an equal interest in sexual subterfuges. The wider range of representations is no doubt due to the fact that while popular films have been predominantly produced through the studio system, the novel is a comparatively low budget production with a history of female participation.

7. Rogers' very wide definition of the double, which goes well beyond lookalikes, twins and siblings, enables him to include pairs such as the Virgin Mary and Eve.

8. Fischer goes on to argue that the twins in fact represent feminised and masculinised images of women. Fischer interprets these films as requiring women to reject their masculine attributes in favour of feminine ones (1989: 172–215).

9. Indeed they fit the pattern of 'doubtful doubles' analysed in Chapter 7.

10. The exception would be *Single White Female*, in which the good girl's life is not depicted as inadequate in any way.

11. *Twin Sisters* and *Mirror Images II*, a tits-and-bums version of much the same tale, include virtually all the elements described in this composite picture of

the 1990s female twin film. The threat of male castration represented by the evil twin is analysed by Barbara Creed in her reading of Brian de Palma's *Sisters* (1993: 131-8).

12. Rogers takes this view in his chapter 'Fair maid and femme fatale' in which he proclaims that 'women in the twentieth century have become whole again.' Rogers argues that the 'virginal maiden/temptress prostitute' dichotomy has waned in serious twentieth-century literature, where it can only appear ironically. With regard to popular genres, although he notes that 'sentimental stereotypes persist,' he cites the image of Doris Day as a new kind of ideal woman: 'clean and yet sexy, desirable and yet not dangerous.' The somewhat tentative, optimistic conclusion he draws is that 'man's attitudes toward women are reaching maturity' (1970: 130).

13. It is perhaps not coincidental that the film is framed as a story imagined by a female journalist.

14. *Keeping the Faith* is exemplary in its portrayal of cooperation between male doubles over a woman. In this film, best friends rabbi Jake and priest Brian have led parallel lives since childhood. Both fall in love with Anna but their conflict is resolved when Brian determines to recommit to celibacy and renounce his love in favour of furthering Jake and Anna's relationship and the possibility of their marriage.

15. Indeed Doniger points to the competing mythology of twin brothers who do *not* replace one another in bed, despite all temptations to do so (2000: 243).

16. In *Take Two*, poor, sincere Barry falls in love with the wife of his rich but unworthy and unloving twin Frank. This is a scenario that Wolfenstein and Leites mention as common in early films such as *The Prisoner of Zenda* and *The Masquerader* (1950: 140-1). It is not representative of recent twin films or even of films from the 1940s.

17. According to Rank's influential 1914 study, the double indicates a splitting of the self as a paranoid defence against the threat of death and the related fear of sexual relations. Following this tradition, Thomas Elsaesser refers to 'the nightmare of the split self' (1989: 28) and traces the legacy of Romantic authors such as Hoffmann and Poe in his work on the fantastic in German silent cinema. More recent films such as *The Dark Half* and *Raising Cain* also inherit from the Romantic tradition and lend themselves to interpretation in terms of a split between the loving father and the fearsome punishing father (cf. Rogers, 1970: 138–160). While it is not impossible to understand *Lies of the Twins* in these terms, the *mise en abyme* of the interpretative situation within the film cautions against this psychological reading, as we shall demonstrate.

18. For Rogers, 'doubling in literature usually symbolises a dysfunctional attempt to cope with mental conflict' (1970: vii).

19. Rogers' chapter on the fair maid and the dark lady discusses the use of colour in representations of the virgin and the whore (1970: 126–37).

20. It is worth noting that *Lies of the Twins* is based on the novel *Lives of the Twins* (revised and published a year later in Great Britain as *Kindred Passions*) by Rosamond Smith (1987, 1988), an alias of Joyce Carol Oates.

21. Cf. Doane (1987: 43). Doane's point is also taken up by Fischer (1989: 187–8) and Creed (1993: 132) in their studies of female twin films.

22. A couple of other poses in the film also deserve a mention for they portray further readily available twin scenarios. There is a shoot in which a white woman lies between two black men, one beneath and one above her, all very lightly clad, a graphic reflection of Rachel's dilemma. Then there is an art exhibition attended by Rachel and Elle. At one moment their two bodies are together framed by an oval sculpture. The two forms enclosed in the one round space constitute a common representation of a stultifying twin relation turned in on itself (cf. chapter 2 above). As Elle remarks, 'It's a hell of a hole.' But the next time Rachel finds herself at the gallery, she is confronted by a painting featuring a large triangle, a further image of her situation.

23. Isabella Rossellini's autobiography (1997) gives ample illustration of modelling as quotation and the use of existing images and icons to inspire photographs.

24. This scene features elements common to many twin stories. Firstly the showing of photographs is usually an important (often revelatory) scene. The fact that James is on the left finds discursive support in the 'Treehouse of Horror VII' episode of *The Simpsons*, involving conjoined twin Barts, where Dr. Hibble remarks: 'Isn't it interesting how the left or sinister twin is invariably the evil one.' As for the insistence that there is always one dominant twin, the competitive aspect of the relation tends to revolve, in female twin films, around the question of beauty rather than achievement: 'Identical twins are never really identical – there's always one who's prettier' (*Single White Female*).

Chapter 4

1. In clear contrast to the conjoined brother films are the appearances of conjoined twins in prose fiction genres. Significantly, the emblematic texts here – from Mark Twain's 'Those Extraordinary Twins' (1899) to John Barth's 'Petition' (1968), Judith Rossner's *Attachments* (1977), and Darin Strauss's *Chang and Eng: A Novel* (2001) – are not horror stories, and there is no proliferation of these tales during the 1980s and 1990s. The examples are overwhelmingly stories of male twins, yet here the relation is not portrayed as maternal, and separation – although a dominant issue – is not figured as separation from the mother. Similarly, Alison Pingree's fine analysis of nineteenth-century biographical accounts of Chang and Eng demonstrates that their connection was represented not as maternal but as a political metaphor, a symbol of the national unity to which the fledgling United States aspired (1996). Both genre and era are clearly key determinants in the representation of the fraternal relation.

2. The representation of twin sisters as virgin and temptress, rivals over the same man, is so pervasive that it dictates female twin stories across most genres. A newspaper article on the death of conjoined Russian twins Masha and Dasha Krivoshlapova headlines 'One was an alcoholic obsessed with sex, the other a stubborn prude' and goes on to tell that their relationship was soured forever when they both fell in love with the same boy (Roberts, 2003).

3. Creed (1990: 125), Frank (1991: 467), Humm (1997: 62) and Showalter (1992: 141) all refer to Cronenberg's preoccupation with the maternal.
4. The term 'parasitic twins' refers to the rare cases of asymmetrical conjoined twins, where one is smaller, less formed and dependent upon the other (Gilbert, 1996).
5. Badley argues that the very way in which the monstrous becomes the object of the gaze already involves a feminisation, for traditionally the (male) gaze has objectified a feminine other (1995: 119–20; cf. Williams, 1984: 87–8).
6. 'The Thing and I' is a segment of a Halloween episode of *The Simpsons* ('Treehouse of Horror VII,' 1996) in which Dr Hibbert separates conjoined twin Barts, one good and one evil. The series is of course known for its self-conscious parodying of both social and generic conventions, so the choice of this scenario to caricature the horror genre is significant: not only is Halloween seen as quintessential horror, so too are conjoined twins and the possibility of their separation. They are associated with the genre to the point where they are able to represent it.
7. It is worth noting that *Basket Case II*, 'Humbug' (*The X-Files*) and *Twin Falls Idaho* all provide commentary on the place of monstrosity in the post-freak-show era. Each depicts the carnivalesque community as a refuge from the humiliations of what amounts to unlimited public exhibition in everyday life.
8. In the psychoanalytical literature, Marjorie Leonard (1961) draws attention to the parallels between the process of separating from the mother and that of separating from one's twin to establish individual identity (cited Stewart, 2003: 66–7).
9. Rogers, in his study of the 'fair maid and *femme fatale*' opposition in the literature of the female double, interprets the virgin/whore dichotomy as a splitting *of* the mother (1970: 126–37). This can be contrasted with the conjoined twin scenario we are examining which involves a splitting *from* the mother.
10. Although this may seem far-fetched, there is a very rare form of conjoined twins, the foetus *in fetu*, that occurs when 'an imperfect fetus is contained completely within the body of its sibling' (Gilbert, 1996; Bryan, 1992: 64). Rare, but not unknown: in 1997 Cairo doctors reportedly operated on an Egyptian teenager with abdominal pains and discovered an underdeveloped twin foetus lodged next to his kidneys. Eighteen centimetres long, weighing two kilograms, and with a head, an arm, a tongue and teeth, the foetus had apparently been feeding off his brother throughout his life. The fully-formed teeth were those of a sixteen-year-old ('Oh, brother!'). Fiedler discusses further examples (1981: 223–5), and both he and Farber refer to the difficulty of differentiating between teratomas (cysts containing skin cells, nervous tissue, teeth, and so on, which may derive from development of an unfertilised egg, a kind of oocytic twin) and foetuses *in fetu* (Farber, 1981: 7).
11. Two further films – *A Zed and Two Noughts* (1985) and *The Krays* (1990) – confirm this insistence. Neither is clearly a horror film, but each flirts with the horror genre: Peter Greenaway's art-house drama *A Zed and Two Noughts* focuses relentlessly on death and decay, while blood is used to represent both the relation between the twins and the violence of their lives in

Peter Medak's fictionalised biography of the gangster Kray brothers. Both films incorporate images of conjoinedness, and there is a strong emphasis on the maternal in each case. In *The Krays* this takes the form of continual references to hatching, birth, abortion, dead babies, and to men as child-like, and is clearly associated with the role of Violet, the all-powerful mother worshipped by her twin sons, who never really separate from her. Given her omnipresence, the twins have no opportunity to usurp the maternal role. The proximity to the horror genre and the occasional allusion to joined bodies again seem to impose a maternal theme, but since neither horror nor conjoinedness define the film and its characters, maternity is firmly anchored to the mother.

The dense and complex *A Zed and Two Noughts* is a more ambiguous case, not least because of the difficulty of defining its genre. Here the possibility of conjoinedness is more salient in the twin relation, and once again, references to pregnancy, abortion, egg-hatching and childbirth pervade the film. Alba is the maternal figure generating most of these, but it is noteworthy that Oliver and Oswald wish to appropriate her corpse on her death, and ask to be re(con)joined using the placenta from her abortion. In this film, the indeterminacy of genre is reflected in the shifting assignment of the maternal.

12. Review attributed to Janet Maslin, *New York Times*.
13. In this sense, *Twin Falls Idaho* can be seen as paving the way for the comic drama *Stuck on You* (2003), also a conjoined twin brother film about love and separation, but once that no longer needs to distance itself so emphatically from the horror genre and its patterns of representation and indeed barely alludes to motherhood.
14. The use of this technique is a convention of identical twin films (*Dead Ringers* being a prime example, with split screens showing Jeremy Irons confronting Jeremy Irons) but here it is *not* used for the twins (played by Mark and Michael Polish), but for other 'freaks.' Once again a convention is cited and transposed.

Chapter 5

1. The tradition inspired by Plautus's *Menaechmi* embraces not only Shakespeare's *A Comedy of Errors* but the musical comedies *The Boys from Syracuse* and *A Funny Thing Happened on the Way to the Forum*. Recent comic films on the theme of twins separated at birth and reunited include *Big Business*, *Twin Dragons*, and the multiple film versions of Erich Kästner's tale *Das doppelte Lottchen* (including *The Parent Trap*).
2. Stewart's interviews with parents of twins show just how widespread this experience is (2003: 125).
3. In Robert Musil's *Man without Qualities*, the fantasy is that of narcissistic union in an incestuous relation between Ulrich and his sister Agathe: 'It goes back a very long way, this desire for a Doppelgänger of the opposite sex, this craving for the love of a being that will be entirely the same as oneself and yet another, distinct from oneself' (Musil, 1995, Vol. 2: 982). Hillel Schwartz points to a further narrative use of mixed sex twins, noting

the frequency with which virtually identical boy/girl twins have appeared in children's literature, often being used to show that with the same upbringing, girls and boys are equally capable. He cites not only the Bobbsey Twins books by Laura Lee Hope, but also a series by Lucy Fitch Perkins dating from 1911–14 (Schwartz, 1996: 29–30). A parallel purpose can be found in a recent New Zealand film, Niki Caro's *Whalerider* (2002), in which the use of mixed sex twins provides the opportunity for a feminist intervention in Maori tradition: a girl takes her dead twin brother's place in the hierarchy of the clan.

4. Cf. Levitan and Montagu (1977), cited Haynes (1995: 102).
5. The hypothesis of oocytic twins (in which a single ovum splits and is fertilised by two separate sperm) is also discussed by Gedda (1961), Bulmer (1970: 8–18), MacGillivray *et al.* (1975), and Farber (1981: 9). The degree of genetic similarity of such twins would depend on the timing of splitting of the female cell: Bulmer distinguishes between (in order of increasing genetic similarity) primary oocytary, secondary oocytary, or uniovular dispermatic possibilities of oocytic twin fertilisation (1970: 9–12).
6. Cf. 'in certain rare instances, singletons are discovered years after birth to carry cells that have been incorporated into their bodies from a DZ twin who died prenatally. Such cases are known as *chimeras*' (Farber, 1981: 7).
7. Pam *et al.* (1996) offer a highly critical analysis of the 'equal environments assumption' at the basis of many influential twin studies purporting to distinguish hereditary and social factors.
8. Researching the extent to which these similarities can be taken as proof that such behaviour is genetically determined is clouded by logistical difficulties in data collection, a point highlighted by Wendy Doniger in 'What did they name the dog?' (1998). As Bouchard himself admits:
   [T]he probability that two people have the same name can't be validated against some random action. What you need is a population of couples the same age as the twin couples with their kids, and then you'd need to know the frequencies of all these names. Think about how much work you'd have to do to gather that kind of information – but then you'd have to do it for everything! About the car they owned! About the beach they went to! What they named their dog! You'd have to collect that data from every pair. And then, what would it tell you? (quoted Wright, 1997: 50)
   In a thorough study of the existing research on monozygotic twins reared apart, Farber concluded in 1981 that it was flawed by blatant bias in the data collection: lack of random sampling, tautological determination of zygosity, over-representation of families of low socio-economic status, variation in the degree of separation, and in the awareness of twinship (15–21). Many of these design flaws persist in recent studies. For example, when zygosity is determined by an assessment of similarity (rather than DNA), monozygotic twins who differ significantly from each other are excluded from MZ statistics, biasing the sample (cf. Stewart, 2003: 46).
9. While Kinsey's 1948 seven-group continuum is considerably more refined than the het/homo binary, it is worth noting that it still lacks the capacity for nuance of Hirschfeld's 1896 bi-dimensional scale, which allowed for twenty permutations (cf. LeVay, 1996: 22, 47).

10. Wendy Doniger defines the bedtrick as a case of 'going to bed with some-one whom you mistake for someone else' (2000: xiii).
11. In fact, it reflects behavioural research findings far more than it reflects the discourses of gay culture: sex with brothers regularly appears on Internet discussion sites in narratives about first sexual experiences and is a common pornographic trope. Photographic volumes *The Brewer Twins: Double Take* (1998) and Steven Underhill's *Twins* (1999) are examples of gay erotica featuring twins. My thanks to Mark McLelland for alerting me to this point.
12. The recognition scene in *Drag Queen* can be contrasted with that of John Irving's *A Son of the Circus* (1994), which follows a more usual pattern: when the identical twin brothers, separated at birth, finally meet towards the conclusion of this lengthy novel, each recognises his gayness in the other. This lengthy novel works through (and displaces) a number of recur-rent twin motifs – the twinning of cultures (Canada/India, Hindi/Western), the twinning of life and art, circus freaks – and even dwells on the identical male/female pair in the character of the transsexual serial killer.
13. David Halperin outlines the definitional problems and the uses and abuses of the label queer (1995: 61–7), while Annemarie Jagose explores in detail the shifting identifications associated with the term, its lack of definitional limits, and its political consequences and contestations (1996).
14. The idea that sexuality and sexual behaviour reveal the truth of the self is analysed by Foucault (1976, Vol. 1: 101–5).
15. The interpenetration of these discourses is not uncommon, as Jagose points out: 'Combinations of the two positions [essentialist and constructionist] are often held simultaneously by both homophobic and anti-homophobic groups' (1996: 9).
16. Cf. Terence Cave on signs and tokens of recognition: 'the birthmark, the scar, the casket, the handbag – all those local and accidental details on which recognition seems to depend' (1988: 2).
17. A similar point is made in Jennie Livingston's documentary film *Paris is Burning*, which demonstrates that the seeming naturalness of normative identities is not a given but something to be accomplished. Competitors at drag balls act out straight identities such as 'businessman' and explain that 'the idea of realness is to look as much as possible like your straight counterpart,' 'to be able to blend, that's what realness is.' As Butler explains, '"naturalness" [is] constituted through discursively constrained performat-ive acts' (1990: viii).

Chapter 6

1. SBS (Australian Special Broadcasting Services) television news, 14 August 1997, 6.30 pm AEST.
2. When stories of twin rulers surface in modern times, these too invariably conclude with the elimination of one twin. In these tales, however – and to date there are nine film and television versions of Alexandre Dumas's novel *The Man in the Iron Mask* – the twins are identical. Typically a just king and a despot, they no longer represent the nation but personal qualities, good and evil. Individual rather than social identity is in question.

3. Marie Vautier (1986, 1991) details the historical parallels and Gary Smith (1995) analyses the ideological concerns of the novel. It is perhaps overdetermined that a bilingual country continually obliged to distinguish itself from its powerful neighbour should be represented in terms of twinship of one kind or another. In fact, all three of the scenarios sketched in this chapter have been used to symbolise Canadian identities: Saul's socio-political analysis and Godbout's novel invoke conjoined twins; Sylvie Gagnon's *La Bibliothécaire et l'Américain* (2002) uses twins raised apart to figure Quebec/U.S.A. relations and identities (interestingly the twins are of mixed sex, highly rare in allegories of national identity, but explained through the unequal power relations between the two countries); and the film *The Third Walker* features a changeling twin in its tale of francophone and anglophone brothers.

4. Interesting for the purposes of this chapter is the revelation that when they are reunited in their forties, Jack is astounded by their absolute resemblance (Oskar was 'wearing my face') while Oskar is shocked by their difference (Jack seemed an old man, twenty years older than himself). Sameness and difference are apparently in the eye of the beholder. The conflicting interpretations echo the ambiguity in Humbert's twin novel discussed below.

5. If the twins' underlying sameness is here valorised as the precondition of peace and understanding, we saw in Chapter 2 that sameness posed a threat to the twins' very survival. The crucial difference is that between stories of cohabiting twins (stifled by sameness) and, here, separated twins (united by similarities).

6. The theme of parallel lives is widely exploited in the literature of the double. Characters encounter their alter egos and see the life they could have lived if different choices had been made. The contrast sometimes coincides with a difference in nationality, for example in Henry James's 'The jolly corner' (first published 1908), in which, after leading a hedonistic adult life in Europe, the middle-aged protagonist confronts the American businessman he would have become had he stayed in New York. Zizek (2001) sees the exploration of alternative lives as an important theme in Kieslowski's films, especially *La Double Vie de Véronique* (1991), in which French Véronique and Polish Weronika are not twins but – like their countries of origin – elusive doubles of one another.

7. The film is, however, as much concerned with exposing the split image of womanhood discussed in Chapter 3 as it is with national or political divisions. See Imre's (2003) discussion of the feminist critique doubling the national allegory.

8. Stewart's research demonstrates the Anglo-American tendency to associate twinship with notions of identical appearance and behaviour (2003: 119–25, 157–60).

9. All quotations from Humbert's novel are my own translations.

10. Michael Walling describes the ethnic composition of Mauritius and its consequences for cultural identity:

> There is no indigenous population: the African or Creole group are the descendants of slaves from Madagascar and Mozambique, the Indians of indentured labourers imported after the abolition of slavery. More recent arrivals include Chinese traders and Filipino migrant workers. There is also a numerically small but economically and politically powerful group of

Franco-Mauritians, the white descendants of the original colonisers. The island is very small–about 1,860 square kilometres – but has a population close to 1.2 million. This makes it one of the most densely crowded and culturally diverse spaces on the planet. In such an environment, the emergence of a national identity is fraught with problems. People tend to define themselves in opposition to other Mauritians (and hence through communal politics), rather than through identification with them. The one unifying factor is the common Creole language. (Walling, 2002)

11. The authoritative French dictionary *Le Petit Robert* demonstrates the paradox quite explicitly, defining *identité* as both 'caractère de deux objets de pensée identiques' (quality of two identical objects of thought) and 'caractère de ce qui est un' (quality of oneness).

12. Here I extrapolate to the context of another island nation of mixed heritage – my own. In 1996, a political party calling itself 'One Nation' was formed in Australia, attracting support for its anti-immigration, anti-multicultural-ism platform. The ideal oneness of the nation was evidently to be achieved through the uniformity of its citizens.

13. From this potted summary it should be clear that – true to its cover promise – *A l'autre bout de moi* is indeed a classic twin tale, reproducing many of the narrative elements discussed in Chapter 2. In particular, it is worth noting the parallels between the 'solution' to Anne's dilemma and the conclusion of Michel Tournier's *Les météores* (1975), in which Jean disappears and Paul synthesises his lost brother into his own existence. It appears that in the imagination of twinship, it is only when one twin disappears that the two can really become one.

14. Here I am indebted to the work of Ross Chambers in *Room for Maneuver: Reading (the) Oppositional (in) Narrative* (1991) on resisting recruitment by the narration.

15. An island ... or an egg (see Chapter 2).

16. The article quoted here, 'The inexpressible child,' was first published in 1988.

17. I use the masculine pronoun advisedly in referring to Lacan's scenario.

18. This is in marked contrast, not only to Lacan's theory of the mirror stage, but also to traditional stories such as *Die Frau ohne Shatten*, or the myth of the vampire invisible in the mirror. As Clément Rosset points out in *Le réel et son double*, the shadow customarily represents external evidence of tangible existence in these stories (1976: 112–13).

19. The grammatical impossibility of the French – a singular subject 'I' with a first-person plural conjugated verb – is difficult to reproduce in translation.

20. The sudden Oedipal recuperation of the story does not resolve the complex-ities of the relation between the sisters sufficiently to be driving the narrat-ive in the way Anne suggests. Indeed it provides further evidence of Anne's unreliability as interpretor of her story.

Chapter 7

1. Although Herdman does not cite Nabokov's novel specifically, he would appear to concur with these assessments, for he writes: 'When a phantom

double is clearly ascribed by the author to mental delusion and functions as nothing more than a symptom of madness, then the device of the double is in a state of decadence' (1991: 50).2.

2. For Slethaug, Nabokov 'leads his readers to understand that resemblances and signifying associations are not inherent in the objects themselves but lie in the perceptions, deliberate and intentional misconceptions, metaphorical linkings, and acts of the viewer' (1993: 189).

3. Penelope Farmer devotes a chapter of her anthology *Two or The Book of Twins and Doubles* to the trope of the author as double (1996: 447–70).

4. Miller notes Amis's admiration for Nabokov's *Despair* (1985: 414–15).

5. Page numbers refer to the published shooting script of the film (Kaufman and Kaufman, 2002).

6. In an interview with Rob Feld, Kaufman explains that the film reflects fairly accurately his 'false starts' and the confusion he experienced in trying to adapt the book for the screen (Feld, 2002: 123).

7. For example, postings to http://us.imdb.com/title/tt0268126/board/ under the threads 'Is Donald real?' (28 May–24 July, 2003) and 'Is Charlie a schizo?' (5–8 July, 2003).

8. Contributions to http://us.imdb.com/title/tt0268126/board/ by 'wompa1,' (31 May and 2 June 2003).

9. Kaufman reveals his anxiety about repetition in the interview with Feld: 'I hate it when I repeat myself' (Feld, 2002: 120).

10 In a further connection between the texts, we may note the popularity of King's non-fiction volume, *On Writing* (2000), offering budding writers the kind of advice that Charlie sees as 'dangerous.'

Bibliography

Amis, Martin (1978) *Success*, London: Jonathan Cape.
—— (1984) *Money: A Suicide Note*, London: Jonathon Cape.
Auster, Paul (1990 [1985–86]) *The New York Trilogy: City of Glass; Ghosts; the Locked Room*, New York: Penguin.
Badley, Linda (1995) *Film, Horror, and the Body Fantastic*, Westport, Conn.: Greenwood Press.
Bailey, J. Michael and Pillard, Richard C. (1991) 'A genetic study of male sexual orientation,' *Archives of General Psychiatry*, 48 (12), 1089–96.
Bailey, J. Michael, Pillard, Richard C., Neale, M. C. and Agyei, Y. (1993) 'Heritable factors influence sexual orientation in women,' *Archives of General Psychiatry*, 50 (3), 217–23.
Barth, John (1968) 'Petition,' *Lost in the Funhouse*, Garden City, N.Y.: Doubleday, 58–71.
—— (1982) *Sabbatical: A Romance*, New York: G. P. Putnam's Sons.
Bersani, Leo (1995) *Homos*, Cambridge, Mass.; London: Harvard University Press.
Bille, S. Corinna (1974) 'Le noeud,' *La Demoiselle sauvage*, Lausanne: Bertil Galland, 61–71.
Blum, Joanne (1988) *Transcending Gender: The Male/Female Double in Women's Fiction*, Ann Arbor; London: UMI Research Press.
Boehm, Beth A. (1994) '*Wise Children*: Angela Carter's swan song,' *The Review of Contemporary Fiction*, 14 (3), 84–9.
Boolell, Shakuntala (1997) 'Littérature mauricienne: littérature entre-deux,' unpublished paper.
Bowering, Marilyn (1998) *Visible Worlds*, London: Flamingo.
Brewer, Keith, West, Paul, Losser, Jason, Brewer, Derek S. and West, Cameron (1998) *The Brewer Twins: Double Take*, New York: Universe Books.
Bristow, Joseph (1992) *Sexual Sameness: Textual Differences in Lesbian and Gay Writing*, London; New York: Routledge.
Brown, Sandra (2000) *The Switch*, New York: Warner Books.
Bryan, Elizabeth M. (1992) *Twins and Higher Multiple Births: A Guide to their Nature and Nurture*, London: Edward Arnold.
Bullough, Vern L. (1973) 'Medieval medical and scientific views of women,' *Viator, Medieval and Renaissance Studies*, 4, 485–501.
Bulmer, M. G. (1970) *The Biology of Twinning in Man*, Oxford: Clarendon Press.
Butler, Judith (1990) *Gender Trouble: Feminism and the Subversion of Identity*, New York; London: Routledge.
—— (1993) *Bodies That Matter*, New York; London: Routledge.
Byne, William and Parsons, Bruce (1993) 'Human sexual orientation: the biologic theories reappraised,' *Archives of General Psychiatry*, 50, 228–39.
Carter, Angela (1991) *Wise Children*, London: Chatto & Windus.
Cave, Terence (1988) *Recognitions: A Study in Poetics*, Oxford: Clarendon Press.
Chambers, Ross (1984) *Story and Situation*, Minneapolis: University of Minnesota Press.

—— (1991) *Room for Maneuver: Reading (the) Oppositional (in) Narrative*, Chicago; London: University of Chicago Press.

Chatwin, Bruce (1982) *On the Black Hill*, London: Jonathan Cape.

Clapp, Susannah (1997) *With Chatwin: Portrait of a Writer*, London: Jonathan Cape.

Coates, Paul (1988) *The Double and the Other: Identity as Ideology in Post-Romantic Fiction*, London: Macmillan.

Cocteau, Jean (1970 [1925]) *Les Enfants terribles*, Paris: Grasset.

Cohen, Jeffrey Jerome (1996) 'Monster culture (seven theses),' In Cohen, Jeffrey Jerome *Monster Theory: Reading Culture*, Minneapolis; London: University of Minnesota Press, 3–25.

Colapinto, John (2000) *As Nature Made Him: The Boy Who Was Raised as a Girl*, New York: Harper Collins.

Cornwell, Patricia (1995) *From Potter's Field*, London: Little, Brown and Company.

Corrick, Martin (2002 [1997]) *The Navigation Log*, London: Scribner.

Courtenay, Bryce (1995) *Tommo and Hawk*, Harmondsworth, Mddx: Penguin.

Creed, Barbara (1990) 'Phallic panic: male hysteria and *Dead Ringers*,' *Screen*, 31 (2), 125–47.

—— (1993) *The Monstrous-Feminine: Film, Feminism, Psychoanalysis*, London; New York: Routledge.

Davis, Colin (1988) *Michel Tournier: Philosophy and Fiction*, Oxford: Clarendon Press.

Day, Aidan (1998) *Angela Carter: The Rational Glass*, Manchester, UK; New York: Manchester University Press.

de Loo, Tessa (2000 [1993]) *The Twins*, New York: Soho Press.

de Nooy, Juliana (1988) 'Double jeopardy: a reading of Kristeva's 'Le texte clos',' *Southern Review*, 21 (2), 150–68.

—— (1991a) 'The double scission: Dällenbach, Dolezel and Derrida on doubles,' *Style*, 25 (1), 19–27.

—— (1991b) 'Source de l'image/image de la source: les métamorphoses de Narcisse,' *Psychanalyse à l'université*, 16 (61), 57–67.

—— (1998) *Derrida, Kristeva, and the Dividing Line*, New York; London: Garland.

Derrida, Jacques (1982 [1972]) *Margins of Philosophy*, Chicago: University of Chicago Press.

—— (1986 [1974]) *Glas*, Lincoln: University of Nebraska Press.

Descombes, Vincent (1979) *Le Même et l'autre: quarante-cinq ans de philosophie francaise*, Paris: Minuit.

—— (1980) *Modern French Philosophy*, Cambridge; New York: Cambridge University Press.

Diamond, Milton and Sigmundson, H. Keith (1997) 'Sex reassignment at birth: a long term review and clinical implications,' *Archives of Pediatrics and Adolescent Medicine*, 151, 298–304.

Doane, Mary Ann (1984) 'The woman's film: possession and address,' In Doane, Mary Ann, Mellencamp, Patricia and Williams, Linda *Re-Vision: Essays in Feminist Film Criticism*, Frederick, Md: American Films Institute and University Publications of America, 67–82.

—— (1987) *The Desire to Desire: The Woman's Film of the 1940s*, Bloomington; Indianapolis: Indiana University Press.

Dolezel, Lubomír (1985) 'Le Triangle du double,' *Poétique*, 64, 463–72.
Dolto, Françoise and Nasio, Juan David (1987) *L'Enfant du miroir*, Paris: Rivages.
Doniger, Wendy (1998) 'What did they name the dog?' *London Review of Books*, 20 (6), http://www.lrb.co.uk/v20n06/doni2006.htm.
—— (2000) *The Bedtrick: Tales of Sex and Masquerade*, Chicago; London: University of Chicago Press.
Eagleton, Mary (2000) 'Genre and gender,' In Duff, David *Modern Genre Theory*, Harlow, England; New York: Longman, 250–62.
Eckert, E. D., Bouchard, T. J., Bohlen, J. and Heston, L. L. (1990 [1985]) 'Homosexuality in monozygotic twins reared apart,' In Puterbaugh, Geoff *Twins and Homosexuality: A Casebook*, New York: Garland, 123–34.
Eco, Umberto (1985) *Reflections on 'The Name of the Rose,'* London: Secker & Warburg.
Ellis, Havelock (1915) *Sexual Inversion, Studies in the Psychology of Sex*, Vol. 2, Philadelphia: F. A. Davis.
—— (1928) 'Eonism and Other Supplementary Studies,' *Studies in the Psychology of Sex*, Vol. 7, Philadelphia: F. A. Davis, 347–75.
Elsaesser, Thomas (1989) 'Social mobility and the fantastic: German silent cinema,' In Donald, James *Fantasy and the Cinema*, London: British Film Institute, 23–38.
Farber, Susan L. (1981) *Identical Twins Reared Apart: A Reanalysis*, New York: Basic Books.
Farmer, Penelope (1996) *Two or The Book of Twins and Doubles: An Autobiographical Anthology*, London: Virago.
Fausto-Sterling, Anne (1993) 'The five sexes: why male and female are not enough,' *The Sciences*, (March/April), 20–5.
Feld, Rob (2002) 'Q&A with Charlie Kaufman and Spike Jonze,' *Adaptation: The Shooting Script*, New York: Newmarket Press, 115–30.
Fiedler, Leslie (1981) *Freaks: Myths and Images of the Secret Self*, Harmondsworth, Mddx: Penguin.
Field, Andrew (1967) *Nabokov, His Life in Art: A Critical Narrative*, Boston: Little, Brown.
Fischer, Lucy (1989) *Shot and Countershot: Film Tradition and Women's Cinema*, Princeton, N.J.: Princeton University Press.
—— (1990) 'The desire to desire: *Desperately Seeking Susan*,' In Lehman, Peter *Close Viewings: An Anthology of New Film Criticism*, Tallahassee: Florida State University Press, 200–14.
—— (1996) *Cinematernity: Film, Motherhood, Genre*, Princeton, N.J.: Princeton University Press.
Foucault, Michel (1976) *L'Histoire de la sexualité*, Paris: Gallimard.
Frank, Marcie (1991) 'The camera and the speculum: David Cronenberg's *Dead Ringers*,' *PMLA*, 106 (3), 459–70.
Freadman, Anne (1988) 'Untitled: (on genre),' *Cultural Studies*, 2 (1), 67–99.
—— (1997) 'Reflexions on genre and gender: the case of *La Princesse de Clèves*,' *Australian Feminist Studies*, 12 (26), 305–20.
—— (2001) 'Hair – and how to do it,' In Nelson, Brian, Freadman, Anne and Anderson, Philip *Telling Performances: Essays on Gender, Narrative and Performance*, Newark: University of Delaware Press, 185–236.

Freadman, Anne and Macdonald, Amanda (1992) *What is this Thing called 'Genre'?: Four Essays in the Semiotics of Genre*, Mt Nebo, Qld: Boombana Publications.

Freud, Sigmund (1953–74) *The Standard Edition of the Complete Psychological Works of Sigmund Freud*, London: The Hogarth Press.

Gagnon, Sylvie (2002) *La Bibliothécaire et l'Américain*, Montréal: Les Intouchables.

Garber, Marjorie (1992) *Vested Interests: Cross-Dressing and Cultural Anxiety*, New York: Routledge.

Gedda, Luigi (1961) *Twins in History and Science*, Springfield, Ill.: Charles C. Thomas.

Genet, Jean (1953 [1947]) *Querelle de Brest, Oeuvres complètes*, Vol. 3, Paris: Gallimard, 171–350.

Gilbert, Scott F. (1996) 'Types of Conjoined Twins,' In *Zygote* [online]. Available at <http://zygote.swarthmore.edu/cleave4a.html> [Accessed 6 September 2004].

Girard, René (1965 [1961]) *Deceit, Desire and the Novel*, Baltimore: Johns Hopkins University Press.

—— (1977 [1972]) *Violence and the Sacred*, Baltimore; London: Johns Hopkins University Press.

—— (1981) 'Comedies of errors: Plautus, Shakespeare, Molière,' In Konigsberg, Ira *American Criticism in the Poststructuralist Age*, Ann Arbor: University of Michigan, 66–86.

Godbout, Jacques (1981) *Les Têtes à Papineau*, Paris: Seuil.

Grosz, Peter (1996) *Adeline, Adelune et le feu des saisons*, Gossau Zürich: Editions Nord-Sud.

Guerard, Albert J. (1967) 'Concepts of the double', In Guerard, Albert J. *Stories of the Double*, News York: J. P. Lippincott, 1–14.

Halberstam, Judith (1995) *Skin Shows: Gothic Horror and the Technology of Monsters*, Durham; London: Duke University Press.

Hall, Radclyffe (1982 [1928]) *The Well of Loneliness*, London: Virago.

Hallam, Clifford (1982) 'The double as incomplete self: toward a definition of doppelgänger,' In Crook, Eugene J. *Fearful Symmetry: Double and Doubling in Literature and Film*, Tallahassee: University Presses of Florida, 1–31.

Halperin, David M. (1995) *Saint Foucault: Towards a Gay Hagiography*, New York; Oxford: Oxford University Press.

Hardin, Michael (1994) 'The other other: self-definition outside patriarchal institutions in Angela Carter's *Wise Children*,' *The Review of Contemporary Fiction*, 14 (3), 77–83.

Harris, J. Rendel (1903) *The Dioscuri in the Christian Legend*, Cambridge: Cambridge University Press.

—— (1906) *The Cult of the Heavenly Twins*, Cambridge: Cambridge University Press.

Haynes, James D. (1995) 'A critique of the possibility of genetic inheritance of homosexual orientation,' *Journal of Homosexuality*, 28 (1–2), 91–113.

Herdman, John (1991) *The Double in Nineteenth-Century Fiction*, New York: St. Martin's Press.

Herrnstein-Smith, Barbara (1981) 'Narrative versions, narrative themes,' In Konigsberg, Ira *American Criticism in the Poststructuralist Age*, Ann Arbor: University of Michigan, 162–85.

Heston, L. L. and Shields, James (1990 [1968]) 'Homosexuality in twins: a family study and a registry study,' In Puterbaugh, Geoff *Twins and Homosexuality: A Casebook*, New York: Garland, 45–65.

Humbert, Marie-Thérèse (1979) *A l'autre bout de moi*, Paris: Stock.

Humm, Maggie (1997) *Feminism and Film*, Edinburgh: Edinburgh University Press.

Imre, Aniko (2003) 'Twin pleasures of feminism: *Orlando* meets *My Twentieth Century*,' *Camera Obscura*, 54, 177–211.

Indyk, Ivor (2003) 'A paler shade of White,' *Sydney Morning Herald*, Sydney, 21 June. Available at <http://www.smh.com.au/articles/2003/06/20/1055828480900.html> [Accessed 6 September 2004].

Irving, John (1994) *A Son of the Circus*, New York: Random House.

Irwin, John T. (1975) *Doubling and Incest, Repetition and Revenge: A Speculative Reading of Faulkner*, Baltimore; London: Johns Hopkins University Press.

Jagose, Annamarie (1996) *Queer Theory*, Melbourne: Melbourne University Press.

James, Henry (1991 [1908]) *The Jolly Corner and Other Tales*, Harmondsworth, Mddx: Penguin.

Kallmann, F. J. (1952) 'Comparative twin study on the genetic aspects of male homosexuality,' *Journal of Nervous and Mental Disease*, 115, 283–98.

Kästner, Erich (1949) *Das doppelte Lottchen*, Berlin: Verlag Cecilie Dressler; Zürich: Atrium Verlag.

Katz, Jonathan Ned (1996) *The Invention of Heterosexuality*, New York: Plume.

Kaufman, Charlie and Kaufman, Donald (2002) *Adaptation: The Shooting Script*, New York: Newmarket Press.

Kendler, K. S., Thornton, L. M., Gilman, S. E. and Kessler, R. C. (2000) 'Sexual orientation in a U. S. national sample of twin and nontwin sibling pairs,' *American Journal of Psychiatry*, 157 (11), 1843–6.

Keppler, C. F. (1972) *The Literature of the Second Self*, Tucson, Arizona: University of Arizona Press.

Kessler, Suzanne J. (1998) *Lessons from the Intersexed*, New Brunswick, N.J.: Rutgers University Press.

King, M. and McDonald, E. (1992) 'Homosexuals who are twins: a study of 46 probands,' *British Journal of Psychiatry*, 160, 407–9.

King, Stephen (2000) *On Writing: A Memoir of the Craft*, London: Hodder & Stoughton.

Kinsey, A. C., Pomeroy, W. and Martin, C. (1948) *Sexual Behavior in the Human Male*, Philadelphia, PA: Saunders.

Kirk, K. M., Bailey, J. M., Dunne, M. P. and Martin, N. G. (2000) 'Measurement models for sexual orientation in a community twin sample,' *Behavior Genetics*, 30 (4), 345–56.

Kristeva, Julia (1982 [1980]) *Powers of Horror*, New York: Columbia University Press.

—— (1984 [1974]) *Revolution in Poetic Language*, New York: Columbia University Press.

—— (1987 [1983]) *Tales of Love*, New York: Columbia University Press.

—— (1995 [1993]) *New Maladies of the Soul*, New York: Columbia University Press.

Kristof, Agota (1997 [1986–91]) *The Notebook, The Proof, The Third Lie*, New York: Grove Press.

Lacan, Jacques (1977 [1949]) 'The mirror stage as formative of the function of the I,' *Ecrits: A Selection*, London: Tavistock, 93–100.

La Piana, Siobhan (1990) 'Homosociality and the Postmodern Twin,' *Constructions*, 15–33.

Laurence, Margaret (1966) *A Jest of God*, London: Macmillan.

Lawson, Valerie (2003) 'Patrick White's "mandala" dies at 91,' *Sydney Morning Herald*, Sydney, 20 November.

Leonard, Marjorie R. (1961) 'Problems in identification and ego development in twins,' *Psychoanalytic Study of the Child*, 16, 300–20.

LeVay, Simon (1996) *Queer Science: The Use and Abuse of Research into Homosexuality*, Cambridge, Mass.: MIT Press.

Levitan, M. and Montagu, A. (1977) *Textbook of Human Genetics*, New York: Oxford University Press.

McConaghy, N. and Blaszczynski, A (1990 [1980]) 'A pair of monozygotic twins discordant for homosexuality: sex-dimorphic behavior and penile volume responses,' In Puterbaugh, Geoff *Twins and Homosexuality: A Casebook*, New York: Garland, 79–87.

MacGillivray, I., Nylander, P. P. S. and Corney, G. (1975) *Human Multiple Reproduction*, Philadelphia: W. B. Saunders.

McKee, Robert (2002) 'Critical commentary,' *Adaptation: The Shooting Script*, New York: Newmarket Press, 131–5.

Maclean, Mairi (2003) *Michel Tournier: Exploring Human Relations*, Bristol: Bristol Academic Press.

Maney, Mabel (2001) *Kiss the Girls and Make Them Spy: An Original Jane Bond Parody*, New York: Harper Collins.

Marr, David (1991) *Patrick White: A Life*, Sydney: Random House.

Maslin, Janet (1999) 'Film festival review: it's not the usual *ménage à trois*,' *New York Times*, New York, 9 April.

Miller, Karl (1985) *Doubles: Studies in Literary History*, Oxford: Oxford University Press.

Monette, Madeleine (1988 [1980]) *Le Double Suspect*, Montréal: Quinze.

—— (2000) *Doubly Suspect*, Toronto: Guernica.

Money, John and Ehrhardt, Anke A. (1972) *Man and Woman, Boy and Girl: The Differentiation and Dimorphism of Gender Identity from Conception to Maturity*, Baltimore: Johns Hopkins University Press.

Montgomery, Bruce and Walker, Jamie (1996) 'Scrutiny for twins' death,' *Australian*, Sydney, 29 May.

Musil, Robert (1995 [1930–43]) *The Man Without Qualities*, New York: Knopf.

Nabokov, Vladimir (1989 [1965]) *Despair: A Novel*, New York: Vintage Books.

Noël, Francine (1990) *Babel, prise deux: ou Nous avons tous découvert l'Amérique*, Montréal: VLB.

'Oh, brother!' (anonymous) (1997) *Courier Mail*, Brisbane, 3 July, 22.

Orlean, Susan (1998) *The Orchid Thief*, New York: Random House.

—— (2002) 'Foreword,' *Adaptation: The Shooting Script*, New York: Newmarket Press, vii–ix.

Pam, Alvin, Kemker, Susan S., Ross, Colin A. and Golden, R. (1996) 'The "equal environments assumption" in MZ-DZ twin comparisons: an untenable premise of psychiatric genetics?' *Acta Geneticae Medicae et Gemellologiae*, 45 (3), 349–60.

Peach, Linden (1998) *Angela Carter*, Houndmills, Basingstoke: Macmillan Press.

Perrot, Jean (1976) *Mythe et littérature sous le signe des jumeaux*, Paris: Presses Universitaires de France.

Pingree, Allison (1996) 'America's 'United Siamese Brothers': Chang and Eng and nineteenth-century ideologies of democracy and domesticity,' In Cohen, Jeffrey Jerome *Monster Theory*, Minneapolis; London: University of Minnesota Press, 92–114.

Poe, Edgar Allan (1965 [1840]) 'William Wilson,' In Harrison, James A. *The complete works of Edgar Allan Poe*, Vol. 3, New York: AMS Press, 299–325.

—— (1965 [1845]) 'The fall of the House of Usher,' In Harrison, James A. *The complete works of Edgar Allan Poe*, Vol. 3, New York: AMS Press, 273–97.

Prone, Terry (1999 [1996]) *Racing the Moon*, London: Coronet.

Puterbaugh, Geoff (1990) *Twins and Homosexuality: A Casebook*, New York: Garland.

Rank, Otto (1914) 'Der Doppelgänger,' *Imago*, 3 (2), 97–164.

—— (1971 [1925]) *The Double: A Psychoanalytic Study*, Chapel Hill: University of North Carolina Press.

—— (1973 [1932]) *Don Juan et le double*, Paris: Payot.

Raoul, Valérie (1996) 'Cette autre-moi: hantise du double disparu dans le journal fictif féminin, de Conan à Monette et Noël,' *Voix et images*, 22 (1), 38–54.

Redonnet, Marie (1986) *Doublures*, Paris: P.O.L.

—— (1988) *Tir & Lir*, Paris: Minuit.

—— (1990) *Silsie*, Paris: Gallimard, coll. NRF.

Roberts, Glenys (2003) 'Joined in misery to the bitter end,' *Sunday Mail*, Brisbane, 27 April, 14.

Rockwell, Paul Vincent (1995) *Rewriting Resemblance in Medieval French Romance: Ceci n'est pas un graal*, New York; London: Garland.

Rodi, Robert (1995) *Drag Queen*, New York: Dutton.

Rogers, Robert (1970) *A Psychoanalytic Study of The Double in Literature*, Detroit: Wayne State University Press.

Rosello, Mireille (1990) *L'In-différence chez Michel Tournier*, Paris: Jose Corti.

—— (1998) *Declining the Stereotype*, Hanover, NH; London: University Press of New England.

Rossellini, Isabella (1997) *Some of Me*, New York: Random House.

Rosset, Clément (1976) *Le Réel et son double*, Paris: Gallimard.

Rossner, Judith (1977) *Attachments*, New York; London: Simon & Schuster.

Roy, Arundhati (1997) *The God of Small Things*, London: Harper Collins.

Rubin, Gayle (1975) 'The traffic in women: notes toward a political economy of sex,' In Reiter, Rayna *Toward an Anthropology of Women*, New York: Monthly Review Press, 157–210.

Rushdie, Salman (1981) *Midnight's Children*, London: Jonathan Cape.

Russell, Mark (1996) 'The amazing double life of Tweedledum and Tweedledee,' *Courier Mail*, Brisbane, 1 June.

Russell, David J. (1998) 'Monster roundup: reintegrating the horror genre,' In Browne, Nick *Refiguring American Film Genres: Theory and History*, Berkeley: University of California Press, 233–54.

Sanders, Craig (2003) 'Conjoined Twins,' In *Twinstuff* [online]. Available at <http://www.twinstuff.com/conjoined.htm> [Accessed 6 September 2004].

Saul, John Ralston (1997) *Reflections of a Siamese Twin: Canada at the End of the Twentieth Century*, Toronto: Penguin.

Schwartz, Hillel (1996) *The Culture of the Copy: Striking Likenesses, Unreasonable Facsimiles*, New York: Zone Books.

Sedgwick, Eve Kosofsky (1985) *Between Men. English Literature and Male Homosocial Desire*, New York: Columbia University Press.

—— (1990) *Epistemology of the Closet*, Berkeley: University of California Press.

Serres, Michel (1982 [1980]) *The Parasite*, Baltimore: Johns Hopkins University Press.

Showalter, Elaine (1992) *Sexual Anarchy: Gender and Culture at the fin de siècle*, London: Virago.

Slethaug, Gordon E. (1993) *The Play of the Double in Postmodern American Fiction*, Carbondale, Edwardsville: Southern Illinois University Press.

Smith, Gary (1995) 'A la marge de l'américanité: l'idéologie culturelle des Têtes à Papineau de Jacques Godbout,' In Baider, Fabienne, Friesen, Erika and Watanabe, Anthony M. *La Marge* (conference), University of Toronto, 20–21 May, 52–60 [online]. Available at <http://www.chass.utoronto.ca/french/SESDEF/marge/smith_source.htm> [Accessed 6 September 2004].

Smith, Rosamond (Joyce Carol Oates) (1987) *Lives of the Twins*, New York: Simon and Schuster.

—— (1988) *Kindred Passions*, London: Collins.

Spivak, Gayatri Chakravorty (1987) *In Other Worlds: Essays in Cultural Politics*, London: Routledge.

Steel, Danielle (1998) *Mirror Image*, London: Bantam Press.

Stevenson, Robert Louis (1979 [1886]) *The Strange Case of Dr Jekyll and Mr Hyde, and other stories*, Harmondsworth, Mddx; New York: Penguin Books.

Stewart, Elizabeth A. (2003) *Exploring Twins: Towards a Social Analysis of Twinship*, Basingstoke: Palgrave Macmillan.

Strauss, Darin (2001) *Chang and Eng: A Novel*, London: Allison & Busby.

Stuart, Dabney (1995) 'Le roman comme plaisanterie,' In Troubetzkoy, Wladimir *La Figure du double*, Paris: Didier Erudition, 189–99.

Thompson, Alice (1996) *Justine*, Edinburgh: Canongate Books.

Thompson, Charles J. S. (1968 [1930]) *The Mystery and Lore of Monsters*, New Hyde Park, N.Y.: University Books.

Tournier, Michel (1975) *Les Météores*, Paris: Gallimard, coll. Folio.

—— (1977) *Le Vent Paraclet*, Paris: Gallimard, coll. Folio.

—— (1981) *Gemini*, Garden City, NY: Doubleday.

Troubetzkoy, Wladimir (1995) *La Figure du double*, Paris: Didier Erudition.

—— (1996) *L'Ombre et la différence: le double en Europe*, Paris: Presses Universitaires de France.

Tupper, Martin Farquhar (1849) *The Twins: A Tale of Concealment*, London: Virtue & Co.

Twain, Mark (1899 [1894]) *Pudd'nhead Wilson and Those Extraordinary Twins*, New York; London: Harper.

—— (1921 [1882]) *The Prince and the Pauper: a Tale for Young People of All Ages*, New York: P. F. Collier.

Tymms, Ralph V. (1949) *Doubles in Literary Psychology*, Cambridge: Cambridge University Press.

Underhill, Steven and Gmunder, Bruno (1999) *Steven Underhill's Twins*, Berlin: Bruno Gmunder Verlag.

Vautier, Marie (1986) 'Fiction, historiography and myth,' *Canadian Literature*, 110, 61–78.

—— (1991) 'Le mythe postmoderne dans quelques romans historiographiques québécois,' *Québec Studies*, 12, 49–57.

Wallace, Marjorie (1986) *The Silent Twins*, Harmondsworth, Mddx: Penguin.

Walling, Michael (2002) 'Inter-cultural tempests: India, Mauritius and London,' In *Peripheral Centres, Central Peripheries: Anglophone India and its Diasporas* (conference), Saarbrücken, 29–31 August [online]. Available at <http://www.bordercrossings.org.uk/tempests.html> [Accessed 6 September 2004].

Waterston, Elizabeth (1990) 'Double is trouble: twins in *A Jest of God*,' In Nicholson, Colin *Critical Approaches to the Fiction of Margaret Laurence*, Vancouver: University of British Columbia Press.

Webb, Kate (1994) 'Seriously funny: *Wise Children*,' In Sage, Lorna *Flesh and the Mirror: Essays on the Art of Angela Carter*, London: Virago Press, 279–307.

Whitam, Frederick L., Diamond, Milton and Martin, James (1993) 'Homosexual orientation in twins: a report on 61 pairs and three triplet sets,' *Archives of Sexual Behavior*, 22 (3), 187–206.

White, Patrick (1982) *Flaws in the Glass: A Self-Portrait*, New York: Viking Press.

—— (1966) *The Solid Mandala*, London: Northumberland Press.

Williams, Linda (1984) 'When the woman looks,' In Williams, Linda, Doane, Mary Ann and Mellencamp, Patricia *Re-Visions: Essays in Feminist Film Criticism*, Frederick, Md.: University Publications of America, 83–99.

Wolfenstein, Martha and Leites, Nathan (1950) *Movies: A Psychological Study*, Glencoe, Illinois: The Free Press.

Wright, Lawrence (1997) *Twins: Genes, Environment and the Mystery of Identity*, London: Weidenfeld & Nicolson.

Zazzo, René (1960) *Les Jumeaux: le couple et la personne*, Paris: Presses Universitaires de France.

—— (1984) *Le Paradoxe des jumeaux: précédé d'un dialogue avec Michel Tournier*, Paris: Editions Stock/Laurence Pernoud.

Zizek, Slavoj (2001) 'Chance and repetition in Kieslowski's films,' *Paragraph*, 24 (2), 23–39.

Filmography

Adaptation (2002) dir. Spike Jonze.
The Bad Sister (1983) dir. Laura Mulvey and Peter Wollen.
Basket Case 1 (1981) dir. Frank Henenlotter.
Basket Case 2 (1990) dir. Frank Henenlotter.
Being John Malkovich (1999) dir. Spike Jonze.
Big Business (1988) dir. Jim Abrahams.
The Boys from Syracuse (1940) dir. A. Edward Sutherland.
Cet obscur objet du désir (1977) dir. Luis Buñuel.
Charlie and Louise (1994) dir. Joseph Vilsmaier.
Cobra Woman (1944) dir. Robert Siodmak.
The Dark Half (1993) dir. George A. Romero.
Dark Mirror (1984) dir. Richard Lang.
The Dark Mirror (1946) dir. Robert Siodmak.
Dead Ringer (1964) dir. Paul Henreid.
Dead Ringers (1988) dir. David Cronenberg.
Despair (1978) dir. Rainer Werner Fassbinder.
Desperately Seeking Susan (1985) dir. Susan Seidelman.
Dominick and Eugene (1988) dir. Robert M. Young.
Doppelganger: The Evil Within (1992) dir. Avi Nesher.
Das doppelte Lottchen (1950) dir. Josef von Báky.
Double Edge (1992) dir. Stephen Stafford.
Double Impact (1991) dir. Sheldon Lettich.
La Double Vie de Véronique (1991) dir. Krzysztof Kieslowski.
Double Vision (1992) dir. Richard Knights.
Les Enfants terribles (1949) dir. Jean-Pierre Melville.
Equinox (1992) dir. Alan Rudolph.
Fight Club (1999) dir. David Fincher.
A Funny Thing Happened on the Way to the Forum (1966) dir. Richard Lester.
The Guilty (1947) dir. John Reinhardt.
It Takes Two (1995) dir. Andy Tennant.
Jack's Back (1987) dir. Rowdy Herrington.
Joined: The Siamese Twins (1989) dir. Paul Norman.
Keeping the Faith (2000) dir. Edward Norton.
Killer in the Mirror (1986) dir. Frank De Felitta.
A Kiss Before Dying (1991) dir. James Dearden.
The Krays (1990) dir. Peter Medak.
Lies of the Twins (1991) dir. Tim Hunter.
The Lookalike (1990) dir. Gary Nelson.
Maximum Risk (1996) dir. Ringo Lam.
Mirror Images I (1991) dir. Gregory Hippolyte.
Mirror Images II (1993) dir. Gregory Hippolyte.
My Twentieth Century [Az én XX. századom] (1988) dir. Ildikó Enyedi.
On the Black Hill (1988) dir. Andrew Grieve.

Oskar and Jack (1997) dir. Frauke Sandig.
The Parent Trap (1998) dir. Nancy Meyers.
The Parent Trap (1961) dir. David Swift.
Paris is Burning (1990) dir. Jennie Livingston.
The Prince of Tides (1991) dir. Barbra Streisand.
Querelle (1982) dir. Rainer Werner Fassbinder.
Raising Cain (1992) dir. Brian De Palma.
The Silent Twins (1985) dir. John Amiel.
Silent Twins: Without My Shadow (1994) dir. Olivia Lichtenstein.
The Simpsons: The thing and I, Treehouse of horror VII (1996) dir. Mike B. Anderson, Season 8, 4F02.
Single White Female (1992) dir. Barbet Schroeder.
Sisters (1973) dir. Brian De Palma.
Sisters or The Balance of Happiness (1979) dir. Margarethe von Trotta.
Steal Big Steal Little (1995) dir. Andrew Davis.
A Stolen Life (1946) dir. Curtis Bernhardt.
A Stolen Life (1939) dir. Paul Czinner.
Stuck On You (2003) dir. Bobby Farrelly and Peter Farrelly.
Take Two (1987) dir. Peter Rowe.
Thicker Than Water (1993) dir. Marc Evans.
The Third Walker (1978) dir. Teri McLuhan.
This World Then the Fireworks (1996) dir. Michael Oblowitz.
Twin Dragons (1992) dir. Ringo Lam and Hark Tsui.
Twin Falls Idaho (1999) dir. Michael Polish.
Twin Sisters (1992) dir. Tom Berry.
Twin Sisters [De Tweeling] (2002) dir. Ben Sombogaart.
Twins (1988) dir. Ivan Reitman.
Twins in Black and White (1998) dir. Dagmar Charlton.
Twins of Evil (1971) dir. John Hough.
Whalerider (2002) dir. Niki Caro.
The X-Files: Humbug (1995) dir. Kim Manners, Season 2, Episode 44, Production n° 2x20.
A Zed and Two Noughts (1985) dir. Peter Greenaway.

Index